Ravished by a Viking

Ravished by a Viking

Delilah Devlin

HEAT | NEW YORK

THE BERKLEY PUBLISHING GROUP
Published by the Penguin Group
Penguin Group (USA) Inc.
375 Hudson Street, New York, New York 10014, USA
Penguin Group (Canada), 90 Eglinton Avenue East, Suite 700, Toronto, Ontario M4P 2Y3, Canada
(a division of Pearson Penguin Canada Inc.)
Penguin Books Ltd., 80 Strand, London WC2R 0RL, England
Penguin Group Ireland, 25 St. Stephen's Green, Dublin 2, Ireland (a division of Penguin Books Ltd.)
Penguin Group (Australia), 250 Camberwell Road, Camberwell, Victoria 3124, Australia
(a division of Pearson Australia Group Pty. Ltd.)
Penguin Books India Pvt. Ltd., 11 Community Centre, Panchsheel Park, New Delhi—110 017, India
Penguin Group (NZ), 67 Apollo Drive, Rosedale, North Shore 0632, New Zealand
(a division of Pearson New Zealand Ltd.)
Penguin Books (South Africa) (Pty.) Ltd., 24 Sturdee Avenue, Rosebank, Johannesburg 2196,
South Africa

Penguin Books Ltd., Registered Offices: 80 Strand, London WC2R 0RL, England

This book is an original publication of The Berkley Publishing Group.

PRINTING HISTORY
Heat trade paperback edition / January 2011

Library of Congress Cataloging-in-Publication Data

Devlin, Delilah.
Ravished by a Viking / Delilah Devlin.—Heat trade pbk. ed.
p. cm.
ISBN 978-0-425-23961-2
1. Vikings—Fiction. I. Title.
PS3604.E88645R38 2010
813'.6—dc22

2010023005

PRINTED IN THE UNITED STATES OF AMERICA

10 9 8 7 6 5 4 3 2 1

Dagr and the Utlending

*I*n the dusk of the final age of man, the bravest of warriors fought a
fierce battle, joining all the peoples of the northern lands to battle
a common foe, sure that the war they waged was Ragnarok—the end
of times for all Norsemen. For the gods had come to Midgard, Earth,
setting challenges for the warriors and plucking the fiercest, the strongest, and the most prolific breeders to abide with them in the new world
where the "Regeneration" would occur. As the fires of the great war died
to smoldering embers, the Chosen followed the gods onto the Bifrost,
the shimmering bridge leading from Midgard to Asgard, where the
gods reside, carrying their worldly goods and bringing their women and
their animals to settle the golden world they'd been promised.

But the dreams of a land of endless harvests, green pastures rich
enough to sustain them through the ages, gold vessels to sup from, and
jewels to adorn their women, proved false. The gods sought to trap the
warriors in endless labors, forcing them to burrow under icebound
plains in search of "pure light." Abandoned on their frozen world, the

warriors rebelled against their slavery and returned to old habits and old ways, building fortresses of rock and ice. They chased away the gods, but soon they battled one another, raiding to survive, stealing food and women to sustain their endless appetites.

Until the day the gods returned . . .

—New Icelandic Chronicles

Prologue

Eirik *Ulfhednar* glared into his opponent's reddened face and adjusted his hand, just a slight movement to improve his grip, and then bore down with all his might. The muscles of his forearm and biceps burned. A spike of adrenaline seared his blood.

Harald, who had boasted his prowess over drinks, didn't seem so confident he'd win this contest now. His lips pulled away from his teeth in a feral snarl, but his bushy red brows rose, betraying his surprise that the man in front of him—so much younger and more privileged than he—hadn't already crumpled.

A smile eased up the corners of Eirik's mouth, and he narrowed his eyes. He would prove he was every inch his brother's equal and deserving of respect from the crew at the mining camp. Respect that they'd denied him since his arrival that afternoon.

However, respect had to be earned from these fierce, rough men. An accident of birth didn't grant an *Ulfhednar*, a Wolfskin, any special favors inside this clan. Further, Eirik's status wasn't helped by the fact that the last time he'd visited the camp, he'd been a gangly teen with blemishes on his face, tagging behind his elder brother.

But Eirik wasn't a boy anymore. This challenge was a good place to prove it.

Without a hint to warn his opponent, Eirik opened his jaws and yawned, then squeezed harder around Harald's huge fist and slammed it into the table.

The crowd surrounding them roared. Large, meaty hands slapped his shoulders in congratulations. Eirik gave Harald a chagrined smile and stood to reach over the table and offer his hand.

Harald shook his head, scowling, looking none too happy to have been bested, but he gripped Eirik's wrist. "You won fair. Only other man who ever bested me was your brother."

Prideful pleasure warmed Eirik, and he wondered why he'd been so resistant to return to this rough camp. He'd thought he wouldn't enjoy it. That the journey itself would bring back hurtful memories of his father. However, his brother had been right about his needing to learn more about his heritage than just the art of battling like a Norseman. His brother was right about most things, and it was time for Eirik to accept that fact.

He let the crowd draw him toward the sleeping quarters of the mining camp's longhouse. Blue-gray light gleamed through the curved ice-block walls and ceiling where "windows" had been cut in the animal-skin lining. Although it was nearing time to sleep, daylight rarely waned in this region of New Iceland.

The smells of roasted animal and a pot of savory stew permeated the longhouse since no vents were cut to allow them to escape. A chimney had no place in the ancient structure, built in the time their ancestors had first arrived on this cold planet.

"Tell us of your journey," Harald said, taking up one of the stools set around the crude fire pit. Chunks of the precious ore the miners cut from the earth deep beneath the icy crust lay nestled in the bottom of the pit, emitting an eerie glow and warmth that tempered the cool, wet chill lingering in the air.

With the melodic sound of water dripping from the walls nearest the pit and the earthy smells of the men around him, Eirik relaxed, ready to spin a tale worthy of the brother to their clan-lord, for he'd traveled to this frigid outpost without the comfort and safety of a tracked snow-eater by land. He'd come the more direct route, by ice-skiff, over the frozen waters. A feat made even bolder by the fact his father had been lost, no trace ever found, during a similar trek to this mine, which lay farthest from the Wolfskins' seat of power.

"It was a harrowing journey," Eirik began, pausing as a beaker of mead was handed to him.

"Did you see serpents?" one of the men asked, a hint of awe in his voice. Few dared travel the open, frozen sea. They fished near the shores, but rarely ventured over deeper water because of the monsters lurking there.

Eirik nodded and leaned forward. "A pod of the beasts trailed after me from Skuldelev all the way here. Streaks of blue, green, and bright flame shot past me, gliding close beneath the surface of the ice. They circled, closing tighter and tighter. But I let out my sails and skimmed past their death spiral."

"Did any of them break the surface?" Harald asked. "Did you see their horned heads?"

"I never looked back." A lesson he'd learned from his brother when he'd first taught Eirik to sail.

If you look back, little brother, you risk losing your nerve. Always, always keep your eyes on your destination.

"But the winds favored me. The bastards pounded the ice behind me with their huge heads." He gave the men a sly smile, relishing the attention. "The breaks only added a little lift to speed me along."

Soft laughter surrounded him. Outracing the monsters who ruled the seas wasn't a sport. The consequences of one mistake could end in an agonizing death—dragged beneath the ice to an underwater berg-cave to be ripped apart and devoured by the pod.

Which was why so few dared. However, Eirik had a long tradition to uphold. The lords of the Wolfskins were fearless; neither the cold nor formidable odds could conquer them. Hence his mode of travel and the bearskin cloak sitting on his shoulders. Even the miners wore the Outlanders' deep-space clothing, which insulated better against the freezing temperatures. Eirik wore garments crafted in the old ways by the women of his clan. Boiled wool undergear and a thicker wool shirt; bearskin chaps tied around his wool trousers. Thick boots made of several layers of cowhide encased his feet.

Yes, his toes were cold, but he could still feel them. If he'd taken a spill in the skiff and damaged the hull or steering skimmers, he'd have frozen to death if the ice dragons hadn't killed him first. But Eirik would never think to complain about the harsh strictures his brother and he lived by. Their lack of comforts was only a small part of what they sacrificed to make themselves worthy to lead their clan.

Harald lifted his chin to the men around him, then bent toward Eirik. "You'll be wanting to see what we found." Gone was the blustery, overloud voice. Even his expression changed, shifting from brusque savage to sharp-eyed warrior.

The miners standing nearest turned to face outward to ensure none of the Outlanders in the longhouse came close enough to overhear their conversation.

"My brother wants this kept secret," Eirik whispered. "Until we're sure."

Harald nodded. "Not a word. And our production hasn't suffered in spite of the extra work. No one will suspect anything is amiss. The shipping containers are already stacked high in the main cavern in preparation for the next delivery."

"Does the artifact appear damaged in any way?"

"What we've uncovered thus far is intact. We're working with picks and shovels rather than large drills. When we get close to parts of the mechanism, we use our chisels."

"Good." Relieved, Eirik gave Harald a smile. "My brother will come when it's fully excavated. For now, we pretend I'm here to inspect the mine."

Harald nodded, and in an instant his expression changed from keen intelligence back to affable companion. "We'll talk more tomorrow. Below."

Eirik understood. The less said here, the less chance of discovery. If what the miners had found beneath the ice pack was what Eirik and his brother thought, the Icelanders had a new weapon in their arsenal that would ensure their hard-won freedom. "Tomorrow is soon enough to see the mine," he said, raising his voice for the benefit of anyone trying to overhear. "Is there a pallet for me?"

"A pallet in a private nook." Harald winked. "And a woman to warm you while your clothing dries above the fire."

Low, masculine laughter erupted around the circle as men raised their cups and shared sly glances.

Eirik grimaced. "I've frost coating my balls." He drained his drink. The honey mead, made from the honey of the bees in Hel's meadow, slid down his throat, warming his belly.

"I bet you do. But we have the cure." Harald smiled and clapped his shoulder hard, and then shoved off his stool to lead Eirik away from the fire and toward a row of sectioned-off sleeping berths. He pulled back a heavy curtain from one.

Inside, a shelflike bed stretched across the back wall draped in gray wolf and brown bear skin. A small fire pit glowed in the center of the small cubby.

A woman knelt on the floor beside it, nude but for a soft, woven blanket clutched around her shoulders. Dark, sloe eyes lifted slowly and widened as Eirik entered.

Never looking back, Eirik reached behind him and snapped the curtain closed, leaving Harald laughing outside. Then he stepped closer, reached for the edge of the blanket, and inched it away to reveal the figure of the woman who sat still, chin down, her small catlike features glowing gold in the pure light.

She was a dark beauty, with long black hair and creamy brown skin. Perfect, if a little too petite. Still, she was a sex-thrall, so identified by the stamped metal cuff encircling one wrist, one of the women contracted to service the men because no Icelandic woman would demean herself to act the whore. His size shouldn't prove a problem.

His blood heated as he stared at her small, round breasts with their brown nipples. A hint of her sex, tucked between her thighs, was smooth and gleaming in the warm light. He noted her slender curves, her supple legs. She'd do nicely.

"Undress me. My fingers are numb," he growled, enjoying her quiver of fear. Best to let her know now that he wasn't a soft man.

Color infused her dusky cheeks, but she rose without hesitation and drew away his clothing, one item at a time.

Her spicy scent and lingering touches warmed him more than the radiant heat rising from the stones.

When he was naked and seated on the edge of the pallet, she dipped the blanket into the pit to warm the fibers, then rubbed his body with it, chafing away the cold, igniting a languorous heat that stirred his blood.

He breathed deeply, keeping his gaze averted, pretending to be unmoved although his cock was thickening and pulsing to the thrum of his heartbeat. Like a lynx, he waited until she circled to his front. Then he pounced, grabbing her hips and lifting her off the ground.

She gave a startled gasp, but opened her legs and straddled him, nestling her knees beside his hips on the mattress and bracing her hands against his shoulders. Her gaze locked with his as she slowly lowered herself onto his cock.

Slick heat surrounded him, obliterating the last vestige of the numbing cold that had slowed his body and his thoughts. "What is your name?" he murmured, his lips hovering over hers.

"Fatin," she whispered, meeting his gaze.

"You please me. I'll see you're well compensated."

She bit her lower lip and her glance fell away.

With a callused finger, he nudged her face and she tilted it, meeting his kiss, her eyes never closing.

She seemed young for her profession, and he wondered if he might be among her first lovers. The thought made him gentle his kiss, and he suckled at her lush lower lip, enticing rather than forcing her cooperation.

Her sweet breath seeped into his mouth, the sigh edged with a delicate moan that increased the tension in his body. He pushed back the rich fall of her hair, cupped her head in one large palm, and tipped her face to drink from her lips.

She panted and shivered as she rose and fell upon his lap. Eirik growled deep inside his chest, and she gave him a little half-smile, then shook back her hair.

He gripped her hips hard, with both hands, urging her to rise and fall faster. Her eyelids drooped and moans trailed from her lips, one after another like chanting.

He could tell she enjoyed herself. Could feel the faint ripples building along her silky, inner walls. "How you please me, darkling," he breathed, willing himself to stave off his pleasure just a little while longer because he didn't want to lose the warm haven caressing his cock.

But something changed in her expression as he dragged her off his shaft and lowered her again. A crease deepened between her brows. Those brown doe eyes glittered. "You're mine, Viking," she whispered.

Eirik didn't have time to wonder what she meant. A sting pricked his neck, and his legs trembled. He fell to the floor on his knees, still clutching the girl close, his muscles locking as though frozen. "What . . . ?"

"Sleep," she whispered, excitement tightening her voice. "You'll feel no pain."

But it wasn't entirely true. His body felt heavy, leaden for a second, unresponsive to his will, and then it exploded in a burst of white heat, fragmenting and spilling away.

A silent scream echoed in his mind before Eirik, heir apparent to the Wolfskin clan, slipped into oblivion.

One

The great hall of the *Berserkir* king's keep was filled to capacity with the clan's warriors. Light cast from the iron chandeliers high above the black marble floors gleamed on the muted metal-fiber composite of their armor and the steel nozzles of the laser-spears they held.

Birget stood among the *Valkyrja* contingent, which formed a half circle around King Sigmund's throne. As his personal guard, they were the only females allowed inside the hall on this night. True to the traditional nature of the tiny band, they wore hammered metal breastplates over their modern black uniforms, the gold outer plate embossed with the figure of Freya, their patron goddess, standing in her feline-drawn chariot. Because a truce had been called, their swords remained sheathed, their shields stayed locked inside the armory, and they'd left off their gold, conical helmets.

Word had come that Dagr, clan-lord to the Wolfskins, had been spotted offshore, his plain, unadorned skiff sailing between the frozen peaks of Hymir's Sea until he'd skidded onto the rocky beach beneath the fortress walls.

Soldiers had been dispersed to keep watch along the shore to find the rest of his *floti*, but strangely, none was spotted. He'd come alone.

"Has he gone daft? Or does he believe his own legends?" her sister Ilse asked, clutching her pike.

Dagr, the leader of the Wolfskin clan, struck awe in the hearts of all *Berserkirs*. His many fierce battles with their army had grown his stature to epic proportions, some even saying that Thor himself had bestowed his blessing on the sword of the great warrior king.

"Quiet, daughters," Sigmund said. "Whatever brings him here alone cannot bode well for the rest of us."

"We should capture him," Birget muttered, unimpressed with the *Ulfhednar* warrior's reputation. Dagr was a man like any other—complete with faults. "If he is stupid enough to enter this hall alone," she groused, "we should enjoy the spectacle."

Her father shot her a reproving look. "He comes under a flag of truce," he said for her ears only. "We won't dishonor our promise to leave him unmolested upon his arrival. We will listen to what he has to say—before we decide whether to detain him." He gave her a little waggle of his eyebrows.

Birget suppressed a smile and straightened.

The large metal doors at the entrance of the keep creaked open. Bearshirt soldiers marched into the hall, the contingent surrounding the enemy king. When they parted in front of the dais upon which Sigmund's throne sat, a tall black-haired warrior strode fearlessly from their center.

Birget's breath caught, her incredulity forgotten. If her future husband was cut from the same cloth, she was doomed.

Dagr, the Black Wolf, stood taller than most of the *Berserkir* warriors around him. His thickly muscled body radiated strength the way the "pure light" did heat, blaring potent masculinity and power.

His features were harsh and colder than the gray stones cut from Odin's Mountain peaks to build this fortress. Black brows sheltered deep-set, piercing blue eyes. The sharp-bladed nose, chiseled cheekbones, and square jaw reflected granite will.

Rustling sounded as the warriors inside the hall tensed, and Birget understood their anxiety. Yes, he might stand alone, but who would want to be the first to draw a weapon against such a man? He looked and dressed like a savage, like the legendary warriors from their shared past.

A black wolf's head sat atop his long dark hair, the eyes of the dead beast seeming to glitter with menace. Bearskin cloaked his massive shoulders. A silver metal breastplate spanned his broad chest. His thick, muscular legs were encased in leather and fur, as were his boots.

His only weapons were the large, double-headed ax that peeked above his head from where it rested between wide shoulders, the famed sword that hung at one side of his hips, and a long, thick-bladed knife sheathed at the other. Primitive weapons, but no one now staring at him doubted he'd be deadly in a fight.

Fury emanated from every inch of his taut frame.

"Lord Dagr," her father intoned, lowering his chin in a decidedly undeferential manner.

Birget wondered how her father managed to sound so confident when her whole body was strung tighter than a bow.

"My brother," Dagr ground out in a deep, raspy baritone. "Is he with you?"

Her father's breath drew in slowly, and then his gaze sharpened on Dagr for a moment before he spoke. "We haven't had the pleasure, even after the announcement of his coming marriage to my daughter. A slight I have not forgiven."

Dagr's features stilled.

If not for the curling fists at his sides, Birget might have thought his anger cooled a fraction of a degree.

"What is your mission here today, Dagr?"

Birget started at the slight note of compassion in her father's voice. These two men were sworn enemies, and yet her father didn't gloat over the missing heir.

"If you are not responsible, then what I have to tell you must be said in private."

Sigmund's gaze raked the stoic warrior. Then he pushed up from his seat and turned, signaling to his guard. "I will only bring my most trusted."

Dagr's jaw ground audibly, but he nodded. "Quickly, then."

Sigmund signaled the *Valkyrja*, who followed the two great *jarls* of New Iceland a step behind.

Ilse dug an elbow into Birget's side and lifted her chin toward the tall, broad frame of the Wolfskin. Her lips pursed around a silent whistle.

Birget gave her a hard glare. Now wasn't the time to ogle the legendary warrior. There'd be plenty of opportunity later—after he'd been tossed into a dungeon cell.

They strode from the hall, down a long corridor, toward Sigmund's private chambers, and halted in front of the oaken door.

Rather than wait for a servant to open it, Dagr slammed both palms against the thick wood and shoved.

Ilse's brows rose. "He's in a snit," she whispered.

Birget shook her head, irritated with her sister. Only Ilse would find the Black Wolf's ill humor funny. Five female guards were all that stood between the angry man and her father.

Not that she didn't think they were up to the task. No one trained harder than the Valkyries. Where brawn was prized among the men, the women's dexterity and speed won many contests.

Still, eyeing the giant's muscular form, she felt her first misgivings and vowed to stay close to her father.

"Have a seat, Dagr," Sigmund said before sitting in an armchair set beside the brazier steeped with ore in the center of the room.

A muscle along the edge of Dagr's jaw flexed, and he reached behind him for the ax.

Every Valkyrie rushed forward, drawing her sword and pointing the tip toward Dagr's throat.

Ice-shard eyes gave a chilling stare, but he continued to slowly draw up the weapon, then lowered the heavy blade to the floor with a clank. "I would sit."

His words were soft, but the deep, stony tone did little to still the hammering of Birget's heart.

A dark brow arched, and his gaze slammed into hers.

Birget took a deep breath and forced anger into her voice. "Lower your swords."

The women pulled back, but Birget kept her blade aimed at his throat and continued to meet his stare, an instinct she immediately regretted. She'd never felt so drawn by a gaze—as though her soul had been captured and weighed to determine its worth.

Without blinking, he murmured, "You're my brother's betrothed?"

She gave him a curt nod, quelling the urge to snarl.

"She's strong, well built," Sigmund said. "I did tell you that."

Birget didn't have to look to know her father's eyes snapped with humor.

"My sister has courage," Dagr said, his voice uninflected.

"More than most men," her father murmured.

"But she's not very bright."

Birget gave him her own flinty stare but bit her tongue to catch the scathing retort he deserved. Instead, she'd show the savage discipline worthy of her position. She schooled her face into an impassive mask and lowered her weapon. Then with one last warning glance she stepped behind her father's chair.

"What brings you here, Dagr?"

Dagr's glance swept to her father as though she was of no consequence. His rigid mask didn't slip. "Eirik's been abducted."

"Is it pirates seeking ransom?"

"He was spirited away from inside one of the mining camp's barracks." Dagr's dark brows lowered. "Gone in a flash of light."

"And you thought it might have been me?" Sigmund's voice rose, and he leaned forward. "We don't have that kind of technology."

"You've been the lead negotiator for all the kingdoms with the Outlanders. You've met with them alone." Dagr smacked the chair arm, causing them all to jump. "You could have traded ore for a transporter. Under the table."

Her father's face reddened. "The Consortium set embargoes against that sort of machine centuries ago. You know that. We can only trade for drills and equipment to aid the mining, and for building materials and foodstuffs." Sigmund sat back and sniffed. "Besides, I would not betray our treaty for such a scurrilous use. You would have been contacted immediately to arrange a suitable ransom."

Dagr gripped his armrests so hard Birget expected the sturdy wood to snap.

Within seconds, the great warrior loosened his grip, slumping in his chair. "I had hoped it was you."

"So that you would have a reason to war with us again?" Sigmund asked, a hint of wry humor in his voice.

Dagr's lips curled into a snarl. "Warring with cousins is much more enjoyable than fighting cowards who can swoop in and out at will."

"Enjoyable?" Her father snorted and waved his hand. "But I do understand your meaning. We have a long history of warfare, interrupted by brief moments of harmony when marriage or games bring our clans together—our interactions always contained within the bounds of our codes of honor. I had hoped for a lull in our warring so that I could secure my clan's future. And yet, this marriage I proposed wasn't to your liking."

Dagr's gaze lifted to Birget again, spearing her with an unspoken challenge. "It's not that your daughter isn't suitable."

"Is it because she will be a *Berserkir* among Wolfskins? Do you fear she will wreak havoc within your keep?"

"Once your daughter takes a Wolfskin husband, she ceases to be *Berserkir*."

Birget's body tightened with fury. Never would she subjugate her will or her heritage to wolves!

"Sigmund," Dagr continued, his gaze narrowing in challenge. "We've raided each other for centuries for women and plunder. This woman will be like any other . . . easily conquered."

The swift intake of breath she couldn't stop didn't go unnoticed. Her father's head turned slightly toward the sound.

Dagr's cold gaze met hers and she would have sworn he smiled, except his lips remained pressed into a firm straight line. "I simply find myself restless. A lull in our battles will make my men and myself lazy."

"I have no fears that you will grow fat, Dagr." Her father cleared his throat, drawing the *Ulfhednar* king's gaze again. "If what you believe about your brother is true—that others have kidnapped him—it explains much. We've experienced more disappearances than usual. Too many to put down to ice-madness. And all men in their prime."

"There can be only two reasons for the Outlanders' return." A muscle flexed along the edge of Dagr's square jaw. "They either wish to ransom the men back to force us to lower the price of our ore, or they may be preparing another invasion to conquer us and return us to slavery."

"But it's been so long," Sigmund replied. "Surely they've given up wanting to subjugate us again."

Dagr grunted, apparently unimpressed with the argument. "They say that they stay in orbit to protect the shipments, but we both know their true intent is to intimidate us. Would you surrender so much wealth and power?"

"If they intend another attack, why take our men one at a time?"

Birget nodded. Exactly what she'd been thinking. Dagr might be a fearsome fighter, but his intellect lacked. Her father, although twenty years Dagr's senior, was still feared for his physical prowess, but he had long ago embraced the value of logic.

Dagr's expression hardened again. "They've learned they cannot defeat us from the sky. They must occupy the ground they seize. To succeed, they need stronger warriors to oppose us in battle."

"Do you think they plan to breed stronger warriors from ours?" Sigmund scoffed. "But that could take decades."

"Only months," Dagr said, leaning forward in his chair. "One of the Outlanders who sought refuge with us has seen what they work on in their laboratories. They can take a child after birth and force speedy growth."

Birget barely suppressed a snort at the ridiculous idea.

The *Berserkir* king's fingers drummed on the arm of his chair. "Neither scenario bodes well for either clan. You've come under a flag of truce to seek an audience. What is your request?"

"To defeat them, we must combine our forces. Once I put my plan into motion, I need you to spread your army to provide protection for the mines bordering your lands."

"You would trust me not to take them?" her father said with sly humor in his voice. "The temptation might be more than I can resist."

Dagr's cold blue eyes narrowed. "I would ask for a hostage. Someone I swear I will put to the dagger if you fail me." His glance speared Birget. "She will do."

"You want my daughter? But you've already said that upon marriage she will cease to be a Bearshirt." Sigmund waved his hand. "Why would I care, then?"

"Because she is not yet wed. And because you love her."

"I have affection and respect for my *Valkyrja* captain. But you know as well as I do that warriors don't love. Deep emotion makes us vulnerable. There is no one I would not sacrifice for my people."

"And I think you lie," Dagr said slowly, his gaze narrowing as he studied the other king's face. "Why else would you insist that Birget wed here? You refused to allow her to travel to Skuldelev. Did you fear we would not make her ours after all and use her against you?"

"You are an honorable man, Dagr. My daughter was the one who insisted the wedding take place here. She is the one who feared you only bargained to get your hands on one of the ruling family for foul purpose."

Dagr's head canted slightly, and if possible, his stare intensified. "And yet, you are a king and a man, and you did not insist that a female in your household obey."

Sigmund sighed and nodded his head. "My daughter will be your hostage. I will do nothing to cause her harm."

Birget's throat tightened. Not once in her life had she heard her father say he loved her, and yet he'd conceded it here and now. She'd known he was proud of her but she had thought, like all Viking women did, that their men were too hardened to ever love.

"How do you plan to battle a foe that lives in the sky?" her father asked.

This time, Dagr's smile wasn't a ghost lurking in his eyes; it spread across his face, making him handsome, and every one of the *Valkyrja* drew in a deep breath.

"By joining them there."

*E*irik *awoke to the sounds of women's voices engaged in a bitter argument. He opened his mouth to tell them to shut up, but his tongue stuck to the roof. He swallowed hard and groaned. Everywhere, his muscles ached as though he hadn't moved them in days, and he was cold. He lay on his side on a chilly metal floor.*

And then he remembered. Fatin whispering, "You're mine" . . . the prick of a needle . . . the searing pain as he'd shredded into molecules . . .

His heart, sluggish when he'd awoken, pounded heavier, faster inside his chest. He bit back a moan and stretched his legs beneath the scratchy blanket covering his nude body.

The women were near him, speaking in low whispers.

He cracked his eyelids open to peek at them through the bars of a cage.

Nearest to him stood Fatin, but she didn't look as innocent as she had, kneeling beside the fire pit. Her beautiful black hair was pulled away from her face and hung in a long braid down the center of her back. Her face was stark, sharply angled, hard. She was dressed in black leather boots and close-fitting olive trousers, a figure-hugging brown jacket with fur cuffs and collar.

He remembered every sweet curve her clothing hid, the wet heat of her tight little pussy, and he hardened, even though he knew the bitch was responsible for his current miserable condition.

Fatin faced another woman dressed in tight-fitting black trousers with gold braids running down the outer sides of her legs—like a Consortium officer's uniform. A hip-length jacket, also black, with gold epaulets worn at the shoulders, confirmed his first thought. She was lovely—dark eyes, shiny, chin-length hair, bronze skin—and she was furious.

"This is unacceptable," she ground out. "You'll return them to the surface. This isn't a pirate ship. We don't kidnap humans."

Fatin stepped closer and sneered down her nose. "Your orders were to allow us the freedom of your cargo hold and your transporter facility—and secrecy. You shouldn't be here."

"I ferry ore from the planet to the refineries. I don't transport human cargo." Her arm flung toward the cage. "Are they criminals?"

Fatin smirked. "They are wanted. And that's all you need to know."

The officer raked a hand through her shiny hair. "It ends today. I want you and your cargo off my ship."

"We aren't finished."

"Believe me, you are. By eighteen hundred hours, you'd better be gone or I'll send every one of your asses back to the surface." The Consortium officer turned on her heel. Her glance fell to Eirik.

He read regret in her expression, but she firmed her chin and walked away.

"I see you're awake," Fatin said, stepping closer to his cage, her hungry gaze sweeping his body.

"Why?" he croaked.

She smiled, a mere stretching of her lips. "You have something the Consortium wants. And you were too tempting a prize to leave behind." She leaned closer and blew him a kiss. "When the drug has worn off, I'll be back."

Eirik growled, but the sound was more of a weak gurgle. He got his hands beneath him and pushed up from the cold floor. That was when he saw the row of cages that stretched the length of the brightly lit room— a ship's cargo hold, he surmised. Every cage held a man—everyone was large, shaggy-haired, and for the most part dressed like Vikings.

What Hel had he landed in?

Two

The uneven scrape that caught the ice boat's skimmers was Dagr's only clue they'd reached the edge of the rugged half-moon beach below the mining camp. In the last hour of the journey, a swift wind had kicked up blinding snow. He'd navigated using the onboard instruments rather than the sun's position or the looming snow-covered mountain range that on a clear day could be seen for hundreds of leagues.

Dagr gritted his teeth. His back ached from the unnatural position he'd had to assume, standing in the steering harness with the warrior-woman plastered to his back.

Still, the discomfort had been worth it to hear Birget's soft gasps when the serpents caught the sound of the skiff racing across the ice and circled beneath the boat's small hull.

Her arms had tightened like iron bands around his neck and her thighs had climbed to cling to his waist. When he'd finally shaken off the beasts with a series of jagged tacks, she'd lowered her legs instantly and kept a respectable distance ever since—if cloaking his backside against the elements wasn't intimate enough.

From the first moment he'd seen her, Dagr had admired her grit. He'd swept her with an assessing glance when he'd realized who she was and had tightened against an unexpected attraction. She was promised to Eirik, and he had no desire to take a Bearshirt woman for his own wife. He already supported two females in his household—self-sufficient women who understood their place and didn't require too much of his attention. The heat stirring in his loins would be remedied quite nicely once he returned to Tora and Astrid's warm embraces.

As clan-lord, his days were full. Adding another woman to his household would provide an unnecessary distraction.

Eirik, the stupid bastard, had assumed his bride would be broad and mannish, and had complained she'd have a mustache thicker than he could grow because he'd heard she was *Valkyrja*. While a couple of the female guards did indeed have shoulders a miner would envy, Sigmund's two daughters were handsome women, tall and slender with long blond hair and eyes the same color as the leafy greens Tora coaxed from the gardens flourishing beneath the permafrost.

Eirik, if he ever returned, would have no complaints concerning the appearance of his mate. Although, knowing his brother, the woman's stubborn belief that she was a warrior's equal would cause them conflict. Neither Eirik nor Dagr would stand for any member of the fairer sex putting herself at risk. No woman of the *Ulfhednar* clan had ever raised a sword to defend herself. There had never been a need.

He pushed aside thoughts of his brother. In the first hours after Eirik's abduction, Dagr had driven himself mad thinking of the torture his brother must be enduring while he'd made the solitary trip to the *Berserkir* keep. Having company, even this surly woman, did much to keep his mind focused on the here and now.

The skiff bumped to a halt on the shore. Harald, the camp overseer, strode through the swirling snow to pull the prow forward, catching the rope Dagr sailed his way and tying it to an iron spike stuck into the frozen ground for just that purpose.

When Harald's hand closed around Dagr's wrist to help him from the boat, there was worry in his eyes.

Dagr knew well the man's emotion—one he currently shared. "You could not have known, Harald. Have no fears that I'm here for reprisal. I only want to hear firsthand what you know and to see what you've uncovered."

Harald's gaze slid away. "I am ashamed that such a breach occurred beneath my nose, milord."

"The breach wasn't one you could have prevented. Did you question the other Outlanders in your service about the woman?"

Harald nodded. "None knew the girl. She arrived with the last supply shipment and kept to herself. Yet she was eager enough when she learned Eirik would be in need of 'comfort.'"

Frustrated, Dagr blew out a deep breath. "Let's continue our conversation inside in warmth."

Harald's eyebrows rose. No doubt, he wondered at Dagr's admission of the foul weather until his gaze drifted beyond his clan-lord's shoulder.

Dagr turned toward Birget and jerked his head. "Sigmund's daughter," he said, keeping his introduction purposely short and rude.

"Your brother's betrothed?" Harald asked, his eyes rounding in surprise.

"My hostage." Dagr suppressed a smile at the stubborn tilt of the woman's chin. "I would see her safe from the elements."

"I'm not cold," Birget bit out through stiff lips.

Indeed, likely she wasn't, even if her breaths fogged the brisk air. Besides the black, deep-space skin-suit and uniform trousers, she wore a long, fur-lined woolen cloak that covered her from her head to just below her knees.

"A Wolfskin sees to *every* woman's comfort." Her darkening glare amused him, but he didn't let her see it. He stepped toward her. She extended a gloved hand for him to help her down, but he reached inside her cloak and grasped her waist, ignoring her gasp as he set her on the ground beside him.

Then, without another word, he turned his back and followed Harald to the entrance of the long tunnel cut into the hill that led to the mining camp compound.

"Have you made progress since your last transmission?" Dagr asked, tugging off his gloves.

Harald's gaze shot to the girl as he held open the thick metal door and stood aside while Dagr and Birget entered.

"Our little Valkyrie will be *Ulfhednar* soon enough," Dagr assured him. "She will never be returned to her father. Besides, our artifact's existence will benefit both our peoples."

"But it will most benefit the ones who control it," Harald grumbled, "which makes it a valuable prize, milord."

"Relax, Harald," Dagr said, clapping the stout man's shoulder. "She'll never get the chance to betray us." He fought the urge to glance behind him to gauge her reaction. He didn't know why he enjoyed baiting her so much. Perhaps it was only an urge for revenge because she'd dared to raise a sword against him.

"Where to first, milord?" Harald asked.

"Since I would make Skuldelev before nightfall, straight to the site."

* * *

Birget had accompanied her father on visits to their own mines, but the contrast between her people's modern facilities and this crude camp couldn't have been more surprising. The wolves' mines were the most productive, their ore the best quality, and yet their miners lived in ancient structures, bereft of even basic amenities.

Still, the men they passed heading from the mine appeared healthy and well fed, and all shouted out happy greetings.

The trio bypassed the entrance to the miner's barracks and climbed down steps cut into the mine's rock walls toward a large, brightly lit cavern. With a quick glance, she surveyed the area. Played-out veins of ore radiated warmth and light. Shirtless men operated rock-movers, the large mouths of the motorized beasts emptying into carts along a metal track. Here the technology was much the same as in her father's mines. Apparently, they didn't stint the workers what they needed to accomplish their tasks.

"It's down this tunnel," Harald said, leading the way past armed guards at the entrance of a long passage whose sides were waist-high rock but solid ice above. Artificial lights were strung along the ceiling. If ore had been exposed here, the roof would have melted, filling the tunnel.

The passage led into a dark ice cavern. Ice shavings were piled against one side. Even though she thought it seemed an odd place to dig, her attention was caught by a structure sitting on the exposed bedrock. The face of a tall pointed arc was still trapped in ice, but the center had been cleared.

Men worked with mallets and chisels, carefully shaving away the ice to reveal more of the structure's mysteries.

Something about the shape, about the carvings surrounding the sides of the hollowed-out object, stirred a memory.

"She's a beauty," Harald said, his gaze clinging to the object. "Cyrus has already deciphered most of the markings. They are instructions."

Dagr's intent stare skimmed the symbols on the arch, then rested on the base, which stretched three arm spans wide. "Does he know if it still works?"

"He found a hidden recess in the base, with a level drawn to indicate how much ground ore is needed to power her—and a control panel. We've done some preliminary tests, but he's days away from learning all its secrets."

Dagr tensed and turned. "Harald, we haven't days. And I need him to discover only one secret. I will cross tomorrow."

Harald's shaggy eyebrows shot up. "I'll tell him. He'll not sleep tonight."

"Tell him that he must also train another in its use, because he's accompanying our contingent."

The overseer gave Dagr a curt nod and headed toward a corner of the cavern where a large table sat, covered in scrolls. An Outlander, his close-cropped hair, lean, muscular build, and olive-tinted skin setting him apart from the burly, long-haired Vikings, straightened as Dagr gave him a nod.

"You will cross?" she said, and her gaze shot to the alien structure. Could it be? *It was.* Her jaw dropped as she swung back to the clan-lord.

Dagr gave her a sideways glance. His stare sharpened, blue eyes studying her expression. "Yes, the Bifrost. Or at least half of the bridge our ancestors were tricked into crossing."

Her heart beat faster. How could Dagr remain so calm? He'd found proof of the legend. That alone was news worth touting far and wide. "You're sure that's what this is? It wasn't just a story?"

"It is the end of the bridge. And it is fully functional."

"Can it return our people to Midgard?"

"Do you even think it still exists?" he asked, one eyebrow rising. "We could cross into empty space or to an uninhabitable world without the means to return. No, I have another purpose in mind."

His expression grew shuttered, telling her that was all he would say for now, and she gritted her teeth. How could she get word to her father? The mine overseer was right. Whoever possessed access to the artifact controlled the fate of all New Iceland. "What will you use it for?"

He shook his head, his gaze flicking to the structure. "You have no need to know. We leave for Skuldelev now."

Undeterred by his abrupt refusal to answer her question, she tried again. "But you're returning here tomorrow. Why bother to leave at all?"

He turned with hands braced on hips. His smile was grim and thin-lipped. "I must give you into your keepers' hands. Otherwise, I wouldn't. Your presence is an inconvenience."

She was an inconvenience? Birget gritted her teeth. "But you needn't escort me. Send me along with one of your men. Or better yet, let me stay. I won't get in the way."

"I have promised to keep you safe so long as your father holds to his end of the bargain. I will deliver you to my household guard myself."

She opened her mouth to argue.

But he shook his head. "Harald," he said, holding her mutinous stare. "Cyrus has until morning."

"Yes, milord. All will be ready."

The journey to Skuldelev passed in silence. Strapped into the back seat of a small, two-man snow-eater, she watched the endless drifts of white, stirred only by the shifting winds and blowing toward the frozen sea that bordered the lowlands they crossed. In the distance, the jagged peaks of the Keel Mountains sawed into the face of Sunni, the sun goddess, stretching the shadows of night to cloak the mountains and the city fortress of Skuldelev at its base.

Birget straightened to peer over Dagr's shoulder at the city few Bearshirts had ever willingly entered. Where her own fortress stood as evidence of strength and precision, the keep rising several stories high, Skuldelev stretched like a lazy dragon resting across the top of the foothills. The fortress wall hugged the contours, turrets spiking like ridges on the beast's back. Even the great, gated entrance gave the appearance of a dragon's large, crenellated head with its mouth gaping.

A shiver rippled down her spine. The day's happenings had passed in a whirlwind, and only now did it strike her that this might be her home for the rest of her life—this foreign, craggy, monstrous castle where men as rugged and unforgiving of weakness as their clan-lord lived.

Birget had no fear of death. She did, however, fear showing weakness. Not once in her life had she quivered at the sight of a man, but Dagr made her knees weak. The cause wasn't one she wished to explore. From his reputation, she knew him to be cruel, relentless, and merciless—qualities she normally admired. But she also knew he loved his brother, honored his promises, and cared for the welfare of his people. That she was the enemy's daughter meant little to him other than the fact that she served as a valuable pawn.

No, she didn't really fear for her life, but she felt as though the ground beneath her feet had somehow shifted. She no longer knew her place in the harsh world he delivered her to.

Dagr turned the wheel of the vehicle and it cut through gravel and ice, coming to a halt in a wide-open lot where more of the tracked vehicles were parked. "This will be your new home,

Princess," he said, not bothering to look over his shoulder to see if she followed him out of the vehicle's door.

They climbed the snow-packed trail to the iron gate, which creaked slowly upward. More *Ulfhednar* warriors rushed forward, forming a phalanx around their leader as he traipsed through the compound toward the keep.

Ignored, Birget trudged behind them, her misgivings turning into irritation. Were they all this rude? She was a princess, which held certain rights. Never had she been so demeaned.

The keep's great metal doors slowly opened, and they stepped inside. Birget stared at the rough-hewn stone that served as the flooring, at the equally unpolished rock walls. No carpets warmed the floor, but rich tapestries hung on the walls to tell the glorious, bloody past of the clan.

At the far side of the hall, the largest of the tapestries told the ancient tale of the ancestors' journey to this cold world. The Bifrost, which she'd only just discovered was real, was featured at the center, a blinding rainbow leading from the grass- and lichen-covered fjords of Midgard to the perpetually snow-covered plains of New Iceland. The small figures of the original settlers were shown as they stepped off the bridge, and the many animals they'd brought along to populate their new world spilled from their wooden cages.

Those first settlers had believed they'd been dropped into Niflheim, the cold realm of Hel, goddess of the Underworld. But it hadn't taken long for them to realize they'd been tricked into serving as slaves to an alien culture in an inhospitable world they were uniquely suited to survive.

"Are you coming?" Dagr asked, his voice tinged with impatience.

Birget shook back her hair and lifted her chin, aiming her glance upward to meet his cold gaze. "Are you talking to me? Because I thought you'd forgotten my existence."

His lips twitched, but he extended his arm, urging her to precede him into the great hall to the right of the entryway.

She blinked as she entered. In the foyer, all comfort had been scrubbed clean, but here warmth and pale, sunny colors filled the room, and she instantly understood the reason. This was the women's realm.

Female servants bustled, rubbing beeswax into oak tables, and scouring the smooth stone floor with woolen mops while children played with wool-hair dolls in a far corner. Food was carried in on large platters, and bread trenchers set on long planked tables. The smell of roasted meat and onions permeated the air and her stomach growled. Heat spilled from grates set in the floor, chasing away the chill and allowing the women to wear single-layer, long-sleeved gowns cut from thin twill, much as the servant women in her own home wore.

Dagr led her to a dais at the end of the hall where the lord's table rested. Two women waited at the top of the stairs with their hands folded in front of them, smiles wreathing their faces at his approach.

When he leapt up the steps, Dagr held out his arms and they rushed forward, pausing to curtsy, before lifting their faces to receive a kiss on their smiling mouths.

"We feared you'd be delayed," the taller one said. A long golden braid was wound into a coronet atop her head. Her sleeveless overgown was made of fine red wool; the pale, long-sleeved shift underneath was thin enough to show all her feminine parts, had it not been for the gold belt that kept the overgown in place. A thick gold band, almost like a thrall's cuff, encircled one wrist and was engraved with the shape of a running wolf.

Birget stiffened. So she was one of Dagr's concubines. Birget gave the woman's features a more thorough inspection but was unimpressed by her round cheeks and bright blue eyes. She wasn't a beauty, only a healthy, sturdy woman like so many of their breed.

The other woman was shorter, her figure more rounded. Her hair was a nondescript brown, which she wore down with a gold circlet to keep it off her face. Her clothing was brown and gold, the undergown made of a more conservative fabric than the first concubine's. This one was older than Dagr, and Birget wondered what he saw in her. She was past childbearing age, or should have been. But her soft smile as she greeted Dagr held a hint of what must attract him. Happiness glowed in her pink cheeks.

Uncomfortable, and again ignored, Birget shifted restlessly beside him.

His gaze dropped to his side. "These are Astrid and Tora. You will reside with them in my quarters until I return."

The blonde's eyes widened. "But she's *Valkyrja*, Dagr. Are you certain she shouldn't be housed in the barracks?"

Birget snorted. At least the woman realized the threat she posed.

Dagr rested a hand on the fair-haired woman's shoulder. "Astrid, she's my brother's betrothed. She belongs in my care."

Astrid lifted a brow and gave Birget another sweeping glance. "I'll find clothing more suitable for a woman in our king's household."

Birget bristled, recognizing the subtle challenge the other woman had thrown down. "I prefer what I'm wearing."

One fine blond brow arched. "But it will soon reek if you don't change."

Dagr's snort drew both their glances, and the corners of his lips curved. The smile did not reach his eyes. "You will give these ladies no trouble while I'm gone, Princess."

"And who will be here to ensure my cooperation?"

Dagr lifted a hand, waving a tall, older warrior closer. "This is Odvarr, a member of *my* personal guard. I am not a soft old man who humors his womenfolk. Should you prove difficult, Odvarr has my permission to administer a woman's proper punishment."

Both Astrid and Tora pressed their lips together to hold back their smiles.

Birget gave Dagr a fierce scowl, knowing full well what a Viking considered "proper." However, her bottom hadn't been spanked since she was a child. She turned to aim a daggerlike glare at the guardsman.

Odvarr's dark, shaggy brows rose. His beefy hands rested on his well-muscled hips.

"He's not a lazy bear," Dagr whispered, bending toward her ear. "He won't let you win."

"Do you really think I cannot take him?" she replied angrily. To ignore her was one thing; to impugn her fighting skills was quite another.

Dagr grunted and straightened. "It would almost be worthwhile to watch a contest between you two. Sadly, my ears wouldn't take the shrieking when you lose."

Her mouth fell open. He had no respect for her skills or her heritage. If she allowed him to leave her among these people, she'd never prove her worth.

Birget stiffened her back and wiped all emotion from her face. Let him think she'd resigned herself to her fate. The bastard would learn soon enough she wasn't to be dismissed.

Aye, she'd show him the deadly sharpness of a bear's claws.

Three

After dinner, Dagr stood watching as Tora led the *Valkyrja* from his chambers to find a bath and suitable clothing. The woman hadn't said a word throughout their meal, which should have been a relief. She'd been equally silent when he'd brought her here to share a drink. He'd wanted to welcome her, but she'd remained stubborn. Dagr didn't trust the surly pout of her mouth.

"That one's going to be a handful," Astrid murmured as the door closed. Her arms encircled his waist from behind, and her palms drifted downward to cup his swelling sex.

"She's a woman," he said, gripping her hands and slipping them inside his trousers to enjoy the greedy grasp of her long fingers. "She will learn her place."

"I don't think Birget understands how fortunate she is to be marrying with men such as you or your brother." Her fingers stroked the length of him, squeezing and tugging until his cock thickened.

Dagr let his eyelids drift half-closed, finally beginning to relax

after a long day filled with worries over his brother and the preparations for the next day's journey. This was what he needed from
a woman. All he needed. "I'm afraid Birget would disagree. She is
fierce. She could be dangerous. Don't underestimate her."

"Odvarr will never be far."

Blood beating in a sensual thrum, he pulled her hands free and
drew her slowly around his body.

As she stepped in front of him, Astrid's pink mouth stretched
into a sly smile. Her eyes sparkled with humor. "She interests you."

Dagr arched an eyebrow. "She's my brother's woman. And while
clan law grants me the right to have her first, I will not take her.
She's not the sort of woman I want." His hands reached down and
clasped her buttocks, bringing her belly against his wakening cock.

Astrid grinned. "Am I more to your liking, milord?" she asked,
growing breathless.

Keeping his expression shuttered, he waited for her gaze to meet
his. "You serve my needs," he said, his words measured.

Astrid's smile faltered, but only for a moment. She drew in a
deep breath and pressed her body closer. "I'm glad I have you to
myself."

Dagr knew he had hurt her, but he'd never lied to her or Tora
about his wants and expectations. He lifted his hands and dug his
fingers into her scalp to tilt back her head and kiss her full mouth.

Astrid responded eagerly.

She was the widow of his best friend, killed in a "friendly" skir-
mish with Birget's clan. When Bren died five years previous, Dagr
had done his duty by offering Astrid a place in his household and
hadn't regretted it. She'd proven loyal and a good helpmate. Her
skills with herbs and healing complemented Tora's green thumb.
Together, they ministered to the ill and injured.

He rubbed his lips in circles over hers, thrust his tongue into her mouth, and widened his stance. Actions meant to evoke the desired response and kill any further conversation.

Her body ground closer. Her ripe, womanly scent surrounded him, pulled him deeper into arousal. Dagr walked Astrid backward toward his bed and the *Berserkir* girl faded from his mind.

They fell amid the covers and pillows, both struggling with their own clothing until they lay together panting and nude.

Astrid's body never failed to please him. Long limbs, round breasts, full hips. He enjoyed her sturdy frame and lush curves. With this one, he needn't be gentle.

Dagr pushed a knee between her legs to ease them apart, then settled over her, his cock nudging her moist folds.

Astrid groaned and slipped a hand between them. She wrapped her fingers around his shaft and pumped once before feeding his cock into her body.

Braced on one elbow, Dagr skimmed a hand over a rounded breast, pausing to scrape a rough thumb over a sharpening nipple, before gliding down her taut middle to her hip.

Astrid strained upward to kiss him, then smiled against his mouth and let her head fall to the pillow. She lifted her hips. When he cupped her bottom, she began to undulate, dragging her slick channel up and down his shaft.

Blood pumping, muscles straining, Dagr sank his face against her shoulder and gripped her ass in his palms, grinding his cock deep inside her.

"I would please you," she whispered.

"You do, *elskling*." He drew back and thrust harder, watching her face for the familiar signs that she neared her peak.

Her cheeks flushed a creamy rose; her eyelids dipped; her gaze blurred. Moist and lush, her mouth parted, softening around shallow gasps.

Sex play was a particular skill he possessed. He'd competed as a younger man in bedsport, often with company, learning his way around a woman's body. Astrid, an experienced woman even before she took Bren as husband, had added to his expertise, bestowing acts guaranteed to satisfy the lustiest appetite.

These days, she didn't pout so much over the fact she'd lost stature as the only woman in his household or that he enjoyed the occasional dalliance with an unencumbered woman. Still, she defied him in subtle ways, ensuring his continued interest.

Her eyelids lifted, her blue gaze issued a feminine challenge, and then she squeezed her inner muscles, caressing his cock.

Caught by her sensual play, he slowed his thrusts and closed his eyes, his jaw clenching. His balls hardened and drew closer to his groin. "Witch!"

She laughed, a throaty sound that tightened his groin further.

Dagr pulled free, crawled from between her legs, and turned her roughly with his hands while she giggled like a younger girl and came up on her hands and knees in front of him.

Astrid tossed back her long hair and turned her head to give him a wicked grin, her blue eyes flashing.

With a quick move, he slapped her bottom, then fisted her hair and tugged. A soft gasp escaped her lips, and she arched her back, lifting her ass in invitation.

He gripped his shaft and placed the blunt crown at her entrance and again slammed forward, her soft, plush mounds cushioning him and jiggling with the forceful strokes.

All playfulness drained from him, and he hammered her pussy, ignoring her groans and pleas for him to end it. Then the tension in his balls cramped. Muscles burning, he shouted and pounded faster. At the first hot, slick wash of her pleasure, he unleashed his own, his seed pumping deep.

When he slowed, she dropped her chest to the bed, her face turning to the side. A smile stretched her mouth. "I'm a lucky woman."

"As I am a very lucky man," he growled, collapsing atop her to nuzzle into the corner of her neck, her rose and sage scent tickling his nose.

They lay like that, still connected, until the door closed quietly. He opened his eyes to find Tora striding into the room, her soft, full curves swaying as she neared the bed.

Dagr rolled off Astrid and lifted an arm, inviting Tora to settle on the mattress beside him. "Is our little hostage resting now?"

She wrinkled her blunt nose and grinned. "I doubt it. She allowed me to bathe her, but she's planning something."

Dagr cupped her ample breast through her shift. "Odvarr stands at her door?"

Her soft smile widened. "Odvarr hopes she will try to escape. She insulted his manhood all the while he hovered over me."

Dagr kissed her soft cheek. "You should accept Odvarr's suit. He would be a good husband to you."

Tora blushed. "Perhaps I will. But only when I know you're happy, milord."

Dagr grunted. Tora worried over everyone's *happiness*. Didn't she know a man needed only a full belly and a warm woman beside him to make him content? "You think I'm not happy?"

Tora traced the edge of his jaw with a finger, while her clear blue gaze sought his. "You have yet to accept a woman as your wife. When you succumb, I will be satisfied."

Dagr snorted. "What need have I of a wife? Eirik is my heir," he said stubbornly. His chest tightened. His brother would be found.

"A wife would see to your heart's needs, milord," she whispered.

Dagr plucked the circlet from the top of her head, then pushed a lock of her brown hair behind her ear. "You will never understand the mind of a warrior."

Always so pliable, this time Tora arched a brow and drew back her head. "I was married to one. And he did come to love me. So I know you only posture." She sighed, and then rose from the bed, drawing off her clothes and hanging them on the hooks beside the door.

Always methodical, always so feminine in the way she saw to his comforts and the tidiness of his rooms, she glided around the chamber, covering the pots of ore to douse the light, leaving only one so that he could enjoy the sight of the two women as they all made love.

Tora had come to him as Astrid had. As a widow.

At first, her grief had kept her from his bed. Then Astrid's possessiveness had left Tora reticent about admitting her desire for him. When at last she'd gathered her courage and approached him, he'd cautioned Astrid to accept her or find another's bed to warm. Over time, the women had come to an understanding and forged a strong friendship. All without bothering him again over the details.

When Tora returned to the bed, she glanced at Astrid, who lay on her side, a thigh draped over Dagr. "'Tis our lord's last night here. Shall we show him how much we shall miss him?"

Dagr lifted his brows, any fatigue he'd felt fading at the sparkle of mischief in his concubines' eyes. What need had he of a wife when he had two lovely, intelligent women so intent on giving him pleasure?

Astrid laughed, a sultry sound that rasped along his spine.

Tora sank onto the bed beside him, smiling, her sweet floral scent and plump curves snuggling close.

Astrid came to her knees and bent over him, trailing her long hair down his belly as she lapped at the edges of the large tattoo that wrapped around one side of his torso.

Tora pressed light, wet kisses against his cheeks and mouth, then set her head on her hand and traced a finger around the curve of his shoulder, gliding down to the gold ring banding his upper arm. Her finger skimmed the wolf's head etched into the metal.

Calm left her expression as her cheeks filled with hectic color. Her eyes danced with pleasure. "Have I told you how handsome you are?"

As always, one woman challenged his mind for attention while the other began to tease his body. Astrid's mouth was gobbling up his softened shaft, making lusty noises as she consumed him. "I'd rather have you extol my prowess in the lists or this bed," he growled.

"Such a man, you are," Tora said, shaking her head.

Astrid backed off his cock and licked around the crown.

He dragged in a deep breath and forced his attention back to the woman beside him whose keen eyes gleamed with humor. "You say that as though it were a flaw," he muttered.

"If you have a flaw, milord, it's your stubborn belief that a woman serves only two purposes."

"I'm not ignorant of everything you and Astrid do for this clan," he said, grasping her hand and bringing it to his mouth to kiss.

Her gaze softened. "We serve you with glad hearts."

Astrid's tongue stroked his shaft in long glides, and his body tightened; his balls cramped. He cleared his throat. "A heart beats to push blood throughout a body. How can it be glad?"

This time Tora's sigh was filled with exasperation. "One day, you will find another purpose for that cold, withered thing inside your chest."

Dagr kissed her hand again. "Don't be angry, Tora. I would have our last night be a pleasant memory. I don't know how long I will be gone."

Contrition lowered the corners of her lips. "And I'm not serving your needs."

"But I know that you will," he said. "You are ever diligent."

Glancing from beneath her lashes, she laughed. "'Diligent' is a pale word for the pleasure we will give you."

"Prove your words, woman."

Laughing still, she leaned over him, her mouth following Astrid's trail down his taut belly.

Dagr placed his hands on their heads and closed his eyes, not caring whose lips and tongue stroked him. A full belly, two warm and willing women . . . Morning would bring a new set of problems. For now, he'd enjoy all the pleasures a warrior of the Wolf clan deserved.

Ulfhednar warriors filled the ice cavern. Dagr nodded his approval at their appearance. Fur leggings and cloaks, ancient metal helmets and breastplates, round shields, short swords, and modified axes for close combat. More frightening were the masks of paint they'd used to demonize their faces and bodies. He hoped they wouldn't have to battle long, that their appearance served its purpose—to intimidate the Outlanders into a quick surrender.

"I've located the ship," Cyrus said, striding toward him, excitement reddening his dusky cheeks. "It hovers outside our orbit. I've estimated a likely entry point, somewhere with enough space to safely transfer your men. I'll do it in three relays. Since we only have one end of the portal, we won't be able to return if something goes wrong."

Dagr grunted. Despite Cyrus's unfortunate origins, Dagr trusted him. From the moment he'd been tossed out drunk from a supply ship four years previous, he'd thrived among the Vikings, using his vast knowledge of technologies denied this world to help them. "Cyrus, you'll be in the last wave. I'll need your expertise to pilot the ship."

Cyrus grinned. "Aye, aye, Captain."

Dagr raised a brow, but couldn't help returning the smile. Adrenaline spiked through his veins. At last, he had a battle worthy of his clan, and he could expend some of the restless energy that had consumed him since his brother had been taken.

They'd left the fortress before dawn, traveling by convoy, but not before they'd been offered a proper leave-taking by those remaining behind.

His people had filled the bailey of the keep to see off the warriors. Tora and Astrid stood silently on the stone steps, offering him their cheeks for a final kiss.

At the last moment, Tora had pulled something from her pocket—a black stone dangling at the end of a leather cord.

He halted her as she rose on tiptoe to slip it over his head. "I have no need of talismans."

"Humor me, milord," she said with a gentle smile. "'Tis only a gift from one who shall miss you."

Releasing her hand, he bent his head.

When it lay against his chest, she traced the bind-rune figure carved into the shiny, polished stone. "This character," she said, tracing the shallow indention, "is Raido bound with Teiwaz. Raido invokes Thor's blessings on your journey. The arrow is for your totem, the wolf. Teiwaz shall help you find justice. Do not remove it. I polished the rock and carved it by hand to keep you safe and help you find your destiny."

He didn't believe in magical amulets, didn't rely on omens or signs to chart his course. "I do not need your magic, Tora, just the strength of my sword and my will." Dagr gazed into her earnest face and then relented. "Thank you."

"Remember, do not remove it," she whispered. Then she stood aside to allow Astrid to offer her farewell.

"No gift?" he said, arching a brow.

Astrid's lips curved even though her gaze shimmered with gathering tears. "My gift was the ease I gave you last night, milord."

"And a fine gift it was," he said, gathering her closer. "Watch over the princess."

"She won't make a move without me knowing it."

The *Valkyrja* hadn't stirred from her bed. Which was just as well—he hadn't wanted another argument from the stubborn woman.

Banishing thoughts of her from his mind, he turned to face the crowd gathered inside the ice cavern.

Dagr gazed over the heads of his men and pulled his sword from its scabbard, ready to swear his men to their new cause. He lifted it high. "By the steel of my fathers' sword, I swear to battle to the death. Glory to Odin! Victory to the wolves!"

A cheer rang out, echoing around the frozen cavern, and he handed the sword next to Frakki, his second-in-command, then to Cyrus, who raised it high and repeated the oath. One by one, his warriors gave their promise, their eyes and features hardening, cheeks reddening with their zeal.

Then he counted off the first men who would invade the spaceship. He gave Cyrus a nod, watching as the Outlander depressed a symbol at the base of the portal.

Cyrus stood back, his eyes glittering, his breath catching until a vibration filled the cavern, causing the ice around them to crackle and snow to rain down on their heads from the ceiling. The arms of the arch lit up, every color of the rainbow emerging from the carvings along the arms, brightening until Dagr had to shield his eyes with a hand.

Cyrus clamped a hand on his shoulder. "It's ready, milord," he shouted. "Walk toward the center. You should find yourself in the ship's hold. You remember the map I drew?"

Dagr clenched his jaw and nodded, gripped his sword tightly in his fist, then stepped onto the platform and into the bright center of the portal. He didn't look behind him. His warriors wouldn't hesitate to follow.

Gritting his teeth, he raised his sword and stormed toward his destiny.

Birget's jaw sagged as the warriors disappeared one by one, blinking out as they passed through the brightly lit portal. Not that she hadn't witnessed teleportation before. The envoys who arrived to negotiate trade agreements beamed in and out. Shipments of containerized ore flickered and winked out as well.

But this was different—this was the Bifrost, a piece of her heritage. This glorious moment would be recorded in the clans' annals and retold for generations.

The men around her were silent, stoic, their expressions never betraying their fear, although if they felt like she did, they were trembling inside. Meeting a foe in battle was one thing, but walking calmly toward an uncertain fate was quite another. She hung back to avoid detection and to give herself a few more moments to contemplate her plan.

From the early-morning briefing Dagr's second-in-command, Frakki, had given aboard the multipassenger snow-eater, she knew they were going to commandeer a spacecraft, the Outlanders' ship hovering above New Iceland's atmosphere.

They'd used the crude radar Cyrus had assembled to detect the location of the ship, locked onto the target, and determined, according to everything the former cruiser captain remembered, the optimal point of entry.

Maps had been drawn of the route they would take to flood out of the ship's hold at the tail end of the central fuselage and capture the crew.

When Frakki had finished the briefing, he'd eyed every one of the warriors. "Dagr will understand if you choose not to accompany us. We will meet an uncertain fate. We have plenty of volunteers."

A younger warrior, a cousin to the king, clapped a fist against his shield. "That message is for me, isn't it? Does the Black Wolf think I'm not ready?"

Frakki gave him a smile that didn't quite reach his solemn eyes. "He would have you live to fight another battle, Grimvarr."

None of the warriors had backed down from the challenge. They all stood, awaiting their turn to enter the arms of the artifact.

A shiver worked its way down Birget's spine, and she ducked her head, afraid that at the last moment someone would recognize her.

In the early hours, she'd creaked open her door, and then stood to the side as Odvarr entered to investigate the noise. She'd shoved him inside, slammed the door closed, and took him in a series of moves the slow-moving giant couldn't counter.

A swipe of her foot to the backs of his knees had forced him to the floor. Then she'd slammed the heavy end of a wooden bedpost she'd worked free against the back of his hard head. She'd paused only a moment to ensure she hadn't killed him, then gathered his weapons and ran out the door. Stealthily, she'd combed the empty rooms around her, seeking weapons and clothing, disguising her form in bulky fur and wool, painting her face blue and black to mask her features.

When she strode boldly out of the keep and into the courtyard, she'd stood tall, slipping among the warriors gathered to march out the gate to the transport vehicles waiting at the bottom of the hill. No one had looked twice. She'd ridden a high, elated by her success, until she sat among the warriors inside the vehicle that took them back to the mine and at last learned the Black Wolf's insane plan.

They'd hijack a ship, use it to take others, and, if necessary, make their way to the Outlanders' home world to storm the planet and find the missing men.

Dagr's plan was bold. Suicidal. And yet, out of all the men she knew, he was the only one who just might pull it off. Which was why she remained, awaiting her turn to step onto the rainbow bridge. With Freya's hammered breastplate worn under her furs, Birget would represent *her* clan and ensure their honor was upheld in this courageous battle.

That, or die fused to the inner wall of an alien ship.

The men in front of her stepped forward, and she sank her chin toward her chest lest anyone gaze upon her features at the last moment and thrust her back. The steps at the base of the platform were steep, but she didn't falter, didn't slow. The intense light blinded her, and she reached out to grab the cloak of the man in front of her, but she touched nothing but air.

Heat embraced her, searing her in a suffocating instant, and then she was stepping into a cool, airless space. Or so it seemed for a moment because the air was thin compared to the rich atmosphere of her own world. The light was different too, tinged green from the overhead lights, and the air was filled with the incessant low hum of machinery. Around her, warriors sucked in deep breaths before moving out in different directions, clearing the floor of the cargo bay to make room for the others coming behind them.

She'd already been assigned a route and followed the column of soldiers toward the far end of the open bay and the narrow metal ladder that led to the upper level of the ship. Their mission was to take the bridge—a second wave to follow Dagr's in case he met strong resistance.

She stuck an arm through the loop on the back of her shield, sheathed her sword, and started to climb.

Halfway up the rungs, an ear-shattering siren droned and overhead lights strobed.

"They know we're here," someone exclaimed, and then no one worried about stealth. The Vikings shouted and raced toward their destinations. "For the wolves!"

Birget's heart tripped, then thundered, trying to keep apace of her excited breaths. Fear didn't make her tremble. Her *Valkyrja* heart burst with pride, and her voice rose to join with the shouts that screamed throughout the vessel. Her fist beat her shield as she ran down the cramped corridor on the heels of another warrior. Battle sounds echoed from just ahead—swords thudded against bodies, clanged against the metal panels of the ship. Powerful explosions ripped through the air.

At last, they spilled onto the bridge where a fierce battle raged. The tight quarters held a dozen warriors fighting uniformed crewmen. The Vikings, though hampered by their huge size and the cramped confines, fought valiantly, repelling blasts of the crew members' stun guns with treated shields while thumping heads with their fists and the flats of their blades.

Orders had been given to minimize loss of life, where possible. So far, blood flowed from noses and gashes on foreheads. Fighting hand to hand, the Vikings were beating the crew back against brightly lit consoles, the skinny aisles allowing no room for retreat.

She spotted Dagr in the center of the fight, moving in a surprisingly graceful dance against a large, dark opponent, who drove a fist beneath Dagr's shield. The Outlander's face was tinged red, his teeth pulled back in a feral grimace. His zeal surprised Birget, because she'd thought of all Outlanders as lacking in passion and courage.

Keeping Dagr in her sight, she targeted another Outlander who lifted a stunner in his hand and took aim at the Wolfskin leader's back. She raised her sword and flew down the steps to plow into him, shoving him to the floor. Her helmet slipped, and then rolled away. Long hair spilled out and her opponent's eyes widened.

Before he had a chance to think he might best her, she drove her knee between his legs and slammed the pommel of her sword into his nose. Blood splattered her, but she grinned as his body slumped. She drove up to her feet, blood heating with primal passion, and scanned the immediate area for her next opponent.

The Black Wolf's daring plan appeared a stunning success. Who would have thought Outlanders would be so easy to conquer?

Four

Before the siren finished its first warning peal, Honora Turgay rolled to her feet from her bunk and slammed the comm switch on the wall with her palm. "Turk, tell me what's happening."

"Captain, we've been boarded by Vikings!"

"Pirates?" Her heart stuttered, then pounded hard against her chest. Norse pirates were a scourge on civilian vessels, but hadn't dared threaten Consortium ships. Her ship couldn't be the first. She could already hear the scornful whispers: *What more would you expect from the daughter of Ahn Turgay?*

"Not sure," Turk said, his voice tight with excitement. "They entered through the hold. No other ships appear in our quadrant."

"How many?" she bit out, pulling up her deep-space skin-suit and locking the tab at her neck.

"A dozen—no, two! More coming! They're huge!"

She ignored the edge of awe in his voice. "Keep them from the controls. I'm on my way." Touching the comm patch on her collar to activate it, she decided against the additional seconds needed to don the outer layers of her uniform, opting to add only her boots. Time was of the essence. She had to get to the deck.

She slipped a stunner from its wall-mounted holster, then eased open her cabin door and glanced up and down the small private corridor in the left wing of the ship, leading from the officers' quarters to the bridge.

Finding it empty, she hurried down the corridor to the end and up a narrow, ringed ladder to the hatch that opened directly onto the command deck.

"This can't be happening," she muttered under her breath. First the Viking cargo the bounty hunters had gathered, and now Vikings attacking her ship. Definitely not a coincidence.

A bad, bad feeling sat like a lump of the cook's oatmeal at the bottom of her stomach. *I am not my father. This moment will not define me.*

Even before she shoved the door upward, she could hear angry shouts and the dull clang of metal. What the fuck kind of weapons were the pirates using?

Honora gripped her stunner tighter, slammed open the small round door, and climbed quickly through the hatch. All around her a pitched battle raged, and no one noticed her. She crouched behind the metal railing dividing the captain's dais from the rest of the bridge, and edged toward her chair. If only she could get a message out to her command . . .

But then she got a good look at the invaders, and her stomach dropped to her toes.

What could the Consortium do against warriors like these? The men who'd dared invade a Consortium ship fought like maddened animals with primitive weapons—*and they wore animal skins!* They bared their teeth in feral smiles. Their shouts and grunts filled the air with an awful noise that had to rattle the composure of even her most seasoned fighters.

She spotted Baraq Ata, her head of security, battling a black-haired giant with blue stripes painted diagonally across his face. Staring at the giant, she couldn't hide her surprise, and her mouth dropped open. Turk hadn't been exaggerating. The man was enormous. And Baraq was losing, if the sweat running in rivulets down his face and the whites of his widening eyes were any indication.

More invading Norsemen pushed through the doorway from the direction of the hold. In that moment, Honora conceded they'd have to surrender sooner or later.

She sank nearer the floor and crawled on her hands and knees toward her chair while keeping an eye on the battle around her.

The pirates fought with their fists and swords—heavy weapons needful of strong arms and close contact that should have hampered the invaders.

Her officers' stunners were the latest technology—nonlethal but effective at dropping a man while preserving life and equipment as well as the ship's delicate hull. But the crude-looking shields the pirates employed deflected the *Proteus* crew's stun charges, bouncing them off their surfaces to crash with sharp pings against the walls. The shields must have been treated to repel the stuns. How had barbarians managed to get the know-how only Consortium labs possessed?

Still, all the technology in the galaxy wasn't effective in a close fight, especially not when every painted, hairy barbarian on the bridge fought with fevered determination.

She ducked behind the navigator's console and peeked around. Only the length of her body stood between her and her goal.

Honora's gaze caught on one warrior more slender than the

rest, clean-shaven, who took her first mate, Turk, to the ground, and then proceeded to pummel him to unconsciousness.

The warrior's beaten metal helmet tumbled to the floor, and a long blond braid spilled down the warrior's back. *A woman?*

The black-haired barbarian fighting Baraq caught sight of the woman, cursed, and crashed the pommel of his sword against Baraq's temple, which sent her lieutenant sliding limply to the floor. Then the barbarian glared daggers at the woman, who had already leapt to the aid of another Viking.

The giant roared.

The guttural sound caused Honora to jump.

"Frakki!" he shouted, catching the attention of the man battling beside him. "Protect her!"

The female barbarian glanced back to the leader. Her eyebrows lowered. Her blue-and-black-painted face settled into a fierce scowl.

Honora wondered at the woman's courage and sanity to face such a fearsome warrior with irritation rather than terror. A tremor ran through her body. Even the Viking's fairer sex was a force to be reckoned with.

The giant, blond-haired, and bearded Frakki moved toward the female, shoving her behind him, and then faced outward to block a blow from one of Honora's crewmen, a young ensign, who crumpled at his feet at the first clout from the warrior's ham fist. The woman behind Frakki appeared to chomp at the bit as every time she tried to push past him to enter the fray, he or another of the Vikings battling nearby stepped in to block her.

Honora held her breath, waiting for the right moment to make her move when the leader's back was turned. She considered shooting him, but knew that as soon as she did she'd lose any advantage because she'd be spotted. Right now, getting a message to high command was first priority.

She ducked her head and crept beside her console. Crouching next to the chair, she reached up and slid her hand into the grooves at the end of the armrest that fit every digit, and depressed the hollow beneath her forefinger to open a hailing frequency.

But a heavy hand closed around the back of her neck and jerked her away. She swung back her elbow, but it bounced off metal, jerky tingles running along her nerves. The man shook her until her teeth rattled before he dropped her. A foot stomped on the stunner, catching her fingers beneath it, and she slipped them free.

She fought her way to her feet, cradling her throbbing hand, and turned to face her attacker, ready to do battle if need be. No Consortium ship's captain had ever surrendered to a pirate.

Her gaze rose to a broad chest covered in beaten metal, up to shoulders cloaked in thick animal fur. Even before she looked higher, she knew whom she faced and her heart pounded.

So much fur, leather, and face paint would have looked ridiculous on another man, but made the barbarian look like a demon. Her gaze snagged again on his wide, thickly muscled shoulders.

Had to be all that fur.

Sucking in a deep breath, she shuttered her expression, drawing on her courage and her knowledge that however humiliating this defeat might be, the pirates wouldn't harm her or her crew. They were too valuable as hostages.

She met his hard-eyed gaze, staring into a face swept clean of all mercy. His features appeared cut from stone. His expression as sharp and lethal as the blade he held.

His glance swept down her body, his mouth crimping at the corners into a thin-lipped smile. When he speared her again with that ice-cold glare, she fought hard not to shiver. The thought of that hard, muscular frame cloaked in the trappings of a barbarian caused her to tremble—but this time not from fear. For the first time in her life, she felt dwarfed by a man. Supremely feminine. Not a reminder she needed at that precise moment. Completely inappropriate.

And still, she couldn't stop herself from imagining what he looked like nude, wondering if the fur hid a belly but seriously doubting it by the hard edge of the jaw clamping tight as he returned her stare. Arousal stirred deep in her belly. He'd be ripped—arms, abdomen, thighs. Gods, she loved a man with huge, muscled thighs and a hard ass—so perfectly honed to deliver deep, powerful thrusts . . . She gave herself a mental shake and tried to dart away.

His arm shot out, grabbing her arm and turning her quickly to bring her back against his taut chest and belly.

She lifted a foot and stomped on his toes, then dug an elbow into his side. His embrace tightened. "Barbarian!" she gasped, and wriggled against him, but to no avail. His arm settled beneath her breasts and squeezed until she could barely breathe. Which was helpful. Her unwise attraction waned at the thought of the bruises his fierce grip would leave.

Cold steel tapped her neck, and she strained away from the wicked knife he held.

"Cease fighting!" he bellowed, the sound blasting her eardrums.

One by one, the Vikings quieted and straightened, their gazes still on their opponents, but their weapons easing back. Her own crew heaved deep breaths, turning to face the man who held her trapped against his body.

"I will know who your captain is," he ground out in a rasping baritone.

Baraq's black gaze locked with hers, and she gave him a subtle shake of her head. His jaw tightened, but he glanced around to warn the others not to speak.

"Warriors are fools to have women among them," the giant

whispered against her ear. "It makes them weak. Makes them hesitate."

Although tempted, she didn't dare ask him why he'd brought a woman along with him. Maybe he didn't consider her female because she fought with all the skill and ferocity of any other Viking.

He shoved her forward and drew his sword, laid the blade against the side of her neck, and then swung back his arm.

Honora sucked in a deep breath.

"I will know who your captain is," he shouted, "or she will be the first to die."

Honora tipped back her head to glare at the odious man, her body growing calm as she breathed slowly, filling herself with rage to stave off a crippling fear. He meant it. He'd kill her. She saw it in his hard, blue gaze.

"So be it." He drew back his arm and sliced toward her neck.

"She's the captain!" two of her crew burst out.

The sword stopped an inch from her flesh, and Honora didn't blink. Wouldn't give him the satisfaction of showing him her fear—or her soul-deep relief that she'd lived past that moment.

A dark brow rose, and he swept her body again with a ruthless glare. "You will relinquish control of your ship."

She jutted out her chin, hoping that pretending she wasn't fearful for her life would lend her more courage. Maybe no one would notice that her knees were knocking together.

He slid his sword into its scabbard and fisted his hands on his hips. "I will have your hand on the controls," he said slowly, as though she were dim-witted. "You will then transfer command to my man."

She raised her chin higher, relieved she was finally getting pissed. "Make me."

He grunted. "Very well." His gaze cut toward one of his own men and he jerked his head.

The man he signaled grasped the collar of one of her crew and dragged him forward.

The Viking narrowed his gaze, not letting her look away. "Every time you refuse me your hand, one of your men will lose his. Don't doubt that I will be ruthless."

Shock at the barbarity of the threat shuddered through her. Her gaze wavered; her cheeks cooled as a sickening image of crewmen cradling bloody stumps flashed through her mind. "Taking this ship is a big mistake. You and every one of your men will be hunted down like dogs. You still have a chance to save yourselves—if you leave now."

His mouth firmed. "We are wolves, not dogs. Make your choice. Save your pride at the cost of your men's hands or transfer command to me."

She couldn't do it. Couldn't risk such grievous injuries for her pride's sake. Her crewmen weren't warriors; they were merchant marines.

She gave the barbarian a small, almost imperceptible nod, and stepped toward the captain's seat, settling into the cool leather. Then she slowly lifted her left hand to slide it over the controls. Light burst around the silhouette of her hand as the computer verified her identity.

The Viking came behind her. His large hands clasped her shoulders and squeezed until she winced. "No tricks. My man will know if you try anything."

She glanced up to see a Heliopolite, one of her own people, dressed in furs, his dark eyes glittering as he stared with ill-concealed excitement.

"I will know if you try to hail another ship," he said, his voice even, his face lowering to hers. "You know that I will."

Honora blinked, recognizing him beneath the paint. "Cyrus,"

she whispered, shock holding her still for a long moment. "You would ally yourself with these men?"

"What choice was I left with?"

She shook her head, knowing she couldn't fool him. They'd served as ensigns together on the same ship after graduating the academy before being promoted and separated. He'd been among the best of her class until his fall from grace.

He's a pirate now—just a pirate. All he wants is ransom. Cyrus knew as she did that her superiors would prefer to pay rather than see one of their precious ships damaged. She had no alternative but to concede.

Her middle finger tapped the release. "Speak your name," she said, her voice tight. "The ship is yours."

Cyrus's gaze lifted to his leader's. The tall Viking nodded, and Cyrus spoke, "Cyrus Tahir assumes command." He gripped her hand, lifting it from the control grid, and placed his own over the indentations. Light flared around the edges of his palm as the computer imprinted his whole hand and DNA into its database.

Then he grabbed her arm and pulled her from the chair. He seated himself, his jaw rippling with tension. "Lord Dagr," Cyrus said, turning toward his leader. "We have control of the ship's systems."

"I would send a message to those who still fight."

Cyrus nodded and pressed the universal comm switch. "Just speak."

The black-haired Viking's gaze settled on Honora.

Her breath hitched, and she acknowledged deep inside that she'd been beaten and was completely at the Viking's mercy. Her life had changed, veering on an uncharted course.

Satisfaction gleamed in the warrior's ice blue eyes as his stare bored into hers. Tension rippled along the edge of his jaw. "This is Dagr, clan-lord of the Wolfskins. We've taken your ship. I have your captain. Surrender your arms or die."

Honora stood beside the captain's chair while the Vikings seized her ship. Through force of will, she kept her back straight, her chin high, and her expression ruthlessly neutral.

Inside, acid gnawed at her stomach, making her nauseous. She clenched her hands together at the small of her back to hide the fact they trembled. Not from fear. Death would be easier to face.

She'd failed. And her blunder was far worse than the one committed by her father. An act that had hounded her all her career. While he'd had his command romanced from beneath him by a rival, his honor compromised beyond repair, she'd allowed her entire ship to be stolen by a primitive band of barbarians using only metal swords.

As the first captain of a Consortium ship to lose her command to pirates, she knew her career was ruined, her name destined to be listed among the commanders whose failures were a lesson to all—unless she could find a way to retake the *Proteus*.

But how? Close-quarters combat had failed to defeat the invaders. They were simply too powerful. The stunners, her crew's only onboard weapons and only worn by officers to stave off mutiny and protect crewmen traveling to hostile planets, had been seized and stuffed into the pirates' belts and pockets.

Superior intellect and cold, calculated cunning were now their only weapons. A conspiracy of silence had already begun.

Since their surrender, the crew had stayed off their communicator patches, knowing their use was the only advantage they still held. The touch-sensitive circles built into the collars of their uniforms looked like an adornment. And they were so new that Cyrus might not know their function.

However frustrating it was not to know what was happening throughout the ship, she took comfort in the fact every Heliopolite aboard the *Proteus* was ready to do their part. Even if their only strategy now was silence.

The Vikings had boarded an hour ago, but already, the changes were profound. The atmosphere felt thin and cold, likely because the atmospherics computer was struggling to compensate for the extra men. The noises, the creaking of the ship, the whir of the venting, even the chirps from the navigator's and security officer's panels seemed overloud.

No one tended them. No one poised around the deck knew how.

Most of the crew members who'd been on the command deck when the ship was attacked had already been led away. Only Turk, Baraq, and the shift engineer remained, all seated cross-legged on the ground. All sported bruises and split lips. Baraq looked the worst, his face misshapen from blows to his cheeks and lower jaw, blue and purple bruises mottling his skin. However, his pride never wilted. His hot glare followed the warrior who'd bested him.

Honora wished she could mirror his strength of will, draw on a belly-deep hatred and stay focused, but her mind and body were confused—out of sync with what was happening around her. All the while she cast around her head for a plan, a strategy to resolve this disaster, her body reacted to the presence of the Vikings on an unexpected level—and to their leader in an all-too-familiar way.

She found herself unaccountably aroused. Curious about his body and superior strength. It didn't seem to matter that he was a barbarian with a primitive brain. *Watyie!* she cursed the traitor residing inside her skin. Maybe she *was* just like her father—weak of flesh.

"Milord, the crew has surrendered," Cyrus said, glancing past her as he addressed the tall, silent man who stood at her back.

Did Cyrus gloat? Or did he feel a smidgeon of guilt? Once upon a time when they'd both been fresh from the academy, they'd dreamed of sharing a captaincy before they'd realized their partnership would be a never-ending war of wills.

"Any injuries?" the Viking asked from closer than she'd expected.

His words stirred her hair and caused the finer down on the back of her neck to rise. Her hands curled, nails digging into her palms.

"No injuries worth noting to your men, sir," Cyrus said.

A grunt sounded behind her, but she didn't turn, didn't want the leader of the pirates to see the defeat in her eyes—or question the glow heating her cheeks. The only injuries "worth noting" had been to her own crew and their pride. The raiders' victory had been decisive and humiliatingly swift.

Cyrus glanced at the panel before him. "The ship's surgeon has been identified and escorted to the makeshift brig in the ship's hold."

Another soft grunt. "Begin the search. We will need the woman's next in command to assist."

"Navigator!" Cyrus called out.

Turk, who sat on the first step of the dais cradling his head and using his shirt to wipe the blood from his nose, straightened and cast a glance at Honora.

Her lips curled in self-directed disgust. She wasn't his captain anymore. "Cooperate. This will soon be over." At least, she hoped that was true.

Turk uncrossed his legs and pushed up from the stair.

Dagr moved from behind her, his hip nudging her backside, reminding her of her unwanted attraction. "We'll scour the ship for the captives you are hiding." He tucked a finger beneath her chin and raised her face. "You could make this easier on yourself and your men by telling me where they are."

Shock caused her to rock on her heels—from the flare of heat that left her sweating because he touched her and from realization of what he sought. But she remained silent, wondering why the hell he cared about the savages who'd been plucked from the planet's surface.

Pirates weren't known to be sentimental and wouldn't care that their land-bound brethren had been spirited away. Perhaps they intended to ransom them back to the kingdoms below. The wealth of the planet's fiefdoms was immense—considerable enough to keep a Consortium ship in their planet's orbit at all times, ostensibly to protect the ore shipments leaving the planet, but in fact to remind the rulers that they were once slaves and would be again one day.

She held the pirate's icy gaze, fighting her growing alarm at the intensity of his expression.

When his thumb swept her bottom lip, she fought the inappropriate urge to lick it. *Balls!*

Captives, she reminded herself. *He searches for the captives.*

She dragged her gaze from the Viking's and slammed it into Baraq's. She read the quiet fury there. He'd argued bitterly for her to raise a complaint over the nature of their mission to this planet after she'd confided what she'd discovered in the ship's hold.

It was one thing to conduct an attack, he'd argued, but there was no honor to be found in kidnapping men. And for what purpose? She hadn't been willing to ask the high command why, believing they had reasons, that they kept the greater good in mind.

And her crew hadn't extracted the Norsemen. They'd only housed the bounty hunters, fed them food and ale. Given them access to the teleport. The *Proteus's* crew wasn't directly responsible.

A distinction this pirate would probably not allow, she was sure. Not that she would admit a thing. The longer she and her crew held out, the longer they stayed out of communication with the Consortium, the better the chance they could solve this problem themselves.

The rasp of his callused thumb scraped her lip again. Honora swallowed hard and glared.

"Perhaps you aren't so eager for us to quit your ship," he murmured.

Honora's breath hitched. She didn't dare breathe, didn't want to inhale the scent of him—sweat and male musk, yes, but the underlying freshness, an herbal scent she couldn't quite place, drew her. She swayed closer.

"Breathe," he whispered. "Or you'll faint."

She tugged her chin from atop his fingers and turned away her face. "I won't faint. I don't fear you."

"I know."

Her gaze shot to his. His eyelids dipped as he raked her body with an assessing glance.

Baraq's low growl pulled her back. He was the only one who understood what was happening. Being lovers in the past clued him in to her body's reactions to an aggressive male.

Dagr's hand fell away and he tipped his head to Turk, telling him to follow. Only when they disappeared down the corridor leading to the lifts did she drag in a deep breath.

Cyrus's low chuckle made her cheeks burn. "Good to know some things never change."

"And you've come so far?" she sneered.

"Careful, kitten," he said, his voice soft. "You wouldn't want Lord Dagr to return to punish you."

"I'm not afraid of him."

His head tilted as he studied her features. "No, I don't suppose you are."

"Tell me, Cyrus, since you seem to be the brains of this operation, do you really think this is going to end well?"

"The brains?" He chuckled. "Sweetheart, you've a thing or two to learn. Just a friendly warning—from an old friend—don't underestimate them."

Honora scoffed. "Don't count me out either."

Five

Dagr, his patience at an end, pushed the navigator against the wall of the last cabin they'd searched and gripped his throat. The smug little rodent had shown him every closet, every latrine and storage bin. "The men who were taken—where do you keep them?"

"I don't know what you're talking about," the slender man gasped. "We've been over every inch of this ship. You know they aren't here."

"But they were." He squeezed harder.

The navigator's face turned red, then purple. His lips pulled away from his teeth, but he didn't try to fight Dagr's hold. Wouldn't give him the battle he wanted. He likely knew Dagr was ready to strangle him.

"Dagr, you will kill him," Frakki said beside him, although there was no chiding in his tone. His oldest friend, Frakki didn't care whether he killed the little man or not, and left the choice to him.

Dagr growled. He'd hoped his mission would be simple. Board the ship. Free the men. Disable the ship and send it hurtling toward the Helio sun—the Consortium warned not to send another of their prized fleet to rape his world. But nothing had been simple and clear-cut since he'd stepped aboard this metal, star-jumping boat.

Dagr released the navigator's neck and turned on his heel as the man wheezed and slid to the floor.

Frakki kept a step behind him as he stomped away. "The men aren't here, milord."

An obvious statement, but Frakki was reminding him that they should think of next steps.

Dagr slammed his fist sideways against the metal wall, the sound ringing up and down the corridor. The impact vibrating through his arm and shoulder felt good. "Do you think he still lives?"

"I am sure of it, milord. Eirik's too valuable for them to slaughter."

Dagr tightened his jaw. "We will bring war on Helios if I find him harmed."

Frakki grunted. "However outnumbered we may be?"

"They cannot stand against our wrath." His fists clenched.

This time Frakki laughed. "They are a puny race. The battle didn't give our men a chance to even break a sweat."

"They are slender, barely muscled."

"Are you speaking of the female?"

Dagr shot a glare over his shoulder. He was, but didn't like the fact Frakki had noted his interest.

"Interesting where your mind traveled," Frakki drawled, his tone teasing. "Did Astrid not dull the edge of your sword?"

"My sword doesn't dull with use," he bit out.

Frakki laughed again. "I'll head to the brig and see how our prisoners are faring."

Frakki's footsteps veered away, and Dagr strode back through the narrow, suffocating corridors, up a ringed, metal ladder to the bridge, ready to unleash his anger and frustration—and he knew exactly whom to punish.

Her head snapped toward him the moment he stepped onto the deck. The ship captain's gaze swept his face, and her expression shifted from shuttered to wary in the space of a heartbeat. She knew he'd found nothing.

While frustration fueled the anger boiling inside him, the woman herself provided another source of consternation. Physical awareness itched along his skin. Her slender frame, so delicate in comparison to the women of his clan, gave him pause, made him subdue the violent tension in his body. Which infuriated him. He didn't want to show restraint toward any Outlander.

Her short, dark brown hair was smooth and shiny as any subterranean crow, feathering against her cheek whenever she sharply turned her head. And her golden brown eyes, tilting at the corners, gave away her wariness every time her glance rested on him.

Even in the midst of the fighting, he'd noticed her creeping toward the chair, her slim body crouched low, her bottom and even the outline of her pussy so perfectly revealed by the black skin-suit. He'd clipped the large warrior, sending him to the ground, and stalked toward the woman whose attention was so focused on the indentations on the chair's arm that she never noticed him behind her until he grabbed the back of her neck and shook.

As well, her courage when he'd swung his blade toward her neck had impressed him. Although her golden skin had drained of color, she hadn't flinched. That she'd betrayed attraction even while he'd threatened her existence only fueled his lust. Her amber gaze had raked him head to toe, her nostrils flaring in her small oval face, her pupils dilating. Her nipples had sprung, the areolas swollen and outlined. She'd been aroused, which had sent an unwanted spike of desire south to harden his cock.

He'd been irritated then, but was furious now for the distraction. If he hadn't been in such a hurry to put space between them, he might not have wasted time scouring the ship top to bottom.

Still, the search hadn't been a complete waste of time—it had taught him much about the crew and the workings of the ship, and the exacting nature of the woman in charge.

Dagr slowed his pace as he approached her now. He hardened his expression, flexed his fists and his arms.

The large, unusually skilled man whom he'd fought on the bridge stiffened and started to rise when he saw Dagr's direction, but his cousin Grimvarr clapped a hand on the man's shoulder to hold him down. "This is not your fight, Outlander."

When Dagr stood inches from the woman, he glared down his nose. "Where have the men been taken?" he asked, adding a razor edge of tension to his softly spoken words.

The deepening furrow on her forehead said she didn't like having to lift her gaze so high. But she didn't step back. "What men?"

Dagr gave a low growl and crowded closer to her body. "We can play this game, but you will not win. Save yourself unnecessary pain."

She arched a brow. "Will you beat me? Do you want an answer that pleases you or one that is closer to the truth?"

Blood pounded in his ears, and he tightened his fists, wishing she were male because he wanted to trade blows. But there were other ways to conquer. Ones that appealed more than they should.

The glint of stubbornness in her golden brown eyes decided him. When was the last time anyone had defied him?

"Before you interrogate her," Cyrus said, his tone dry, "you'll want the communicators removed from all the crew's uniforms."

Dagr's head whipped toward Cyrus. "Communicators?"

"I think the patches on their collars are radios. They don't wear utility belts anymore, so I wondered where they put them. Check the patches on their collars. They'll be set to allow the crew to talk among themselves and to the ship's systems, but they can be reprogrammed to access an external channel."

Dagr jerked his blade from its scabbard and held it in front of the woman's face. Her skin whitened, but again she didn't flinch. When he tucked his finger beneath her collar to drag it open, the pulse at the side of her throat leapt. He pressed his finger against the spot and noted the quickening of her heartbeat.

Her glare was withering, which amused him.

He glided the finger under her chin and raised it, then fisted the banded collar and carved out the small patch, taking more material than he needed, baring her throat and the top of her chest. Holding the fabric between his fingers, he dropped the collar on the floor and crushed the patch beneath his boot.

"Give the order," he said to Cyrus, not tearing his gaze from the woman.

Her cheeks were reddening, her body quivering. With anger now. *Good.* He ducked, shoved his shoulder into her belly, and lifted her off the ground.

"Khasi-bastard!" she said, her fists swinging at his head and kidneys.

"Cyrus! Check the computer. See whether another ship has docked here recently."

"Aye, Captain," Cyrus shouted after him, laughter in his voice. "I'll check the logs and the manifests while you're . . . busy."

The woman bucked hard, legs and arms flailing to escape, but he clamped an arm around her thighs and strode toward the maintenance lift at the side of the corridor.

"Your cabin," he bit out, nearly smiling because she wiggled harder than a black-headed eel. "Where is it?"

"Find it yourself, bastard!"

"Shall I take you against the wall, where anyone might see?" He didn't mean it, but he wanted her nervous. He'd dull the edge of authority from her stubborn chin. Didn't she know women were meant to be soft and yielding?

"That's right. Prove you're a *watyie* pirate. Rape me!"

When her toes slammed perilously close to his groin, he swatted her backside. "It will not be rape. We both know that."

The wriggling calmed, but only because she'd worked a hand beneath his wolf headdress and was pulling his hair. "I'll fight you."

He grimaced. Her grip was fierce, and his scalp stung. "You'll only make a show of it because you should, *elskling*."

The doors of the lift closed, and the conveyance slid downward. When the doors opened again, he stepped into a deserted corridor, narrower than the one that tracked along the spine of the bird-shaped ship. "Which way?" His hand rubbed her bottom, and she squirmed harder, trying to break his hold. "Make your choice. Will I take you here, where anyone might see us? Or in your room?" To prove his threat, he slid his hand between her legs and stroked her folds through the thin black skin.

Her body stiffened, and her gasp echoed in his ear. "Damn you. End of the hall."

The corridor was barely higher than the top his head, and he pushed forward, crouching slightly but not caring that her bottom hit the ceiling here and there.

Her hands clasped his hips to steady herself and he grunted, enjoying the fact she was already adjusting, adapting to his control although she likely thought she was only trying to avoid further injury.

He came to the last door, pressed down the latch, and pushed open the oval metal hatch. He ducked inside and halted, remembering it from his search. The room was barely larger than the many closets he'd seen. The bed was little more than a shelf and too short for his body. Her furnishings were sparse—just the bed and a small built-in cabinet beside it with a gooseneck lamp jutting from the wall.

There were no pictures, no art or even maps on her walls, which were no more than cabinet doors. Not a single note of color warmed the small, airless, gray room. No softness was betrayed whatsoever. And yet she was fully feminine. The curves surrounding his shoulder and digging into his back were proof.

He set her on her feet, ignoring her as she sputtered and slammed her fists against his chest as any woman would when furious with a mate.

Standing still, he waited while she regained control of herself. Her fists landed again, but froze on his chest, which rose and fell in shallow swells while hers billowed wildly. Her gaze flitted up, perhaps to gauge his expression and see whether she'd angered him.

She hadn't. He couldn't be more pleased with her womanly tantrum. It revealed passion, and the hardness of her blows proved her wiry strength. She might be slender, but she wasn't truly delicate. He could already imagine how tight her woman's passage would be, how it would squeeze deliciously around his cock. A small, tight fit like the tiny space where she slept.

Her furrowed brows remained set, shadowing her eyes, but her hands flattened on his chest. With her soft, shiny hair mussed and her mouth soft and pouting, she was lovelier, more tempting, than she should have been, dressed as she was in the ugly black skin-suit.

He waited, letting the thud of his heart tell her of his attraction, his muscles rippling as she curled her fingers and pulled her hands slowly away.

With slow steps, she backed up to the far wall, her eyes glittering with anger, but her body quivering with something else. Her intense arousal perfumed the thin, stale air of her cabin.

Remembering that he did have a purpose for bringing her here, alone, he hardened his expression. "Where are the men your people captured?"

"Not here. Obviously," she said, her features neutral. Her eyes, however, betrayed her. She blinked.

Dagr grunted, wondering why he enjoyed her defiance so much. He hoped she'd force him to take stronger action. "Why aren't they here?" he said just as evenly.

"Another transport arrived to take them away."

"I want the name of the ship."

Her jaw tightened. "I don't know it."

"I don't believe you."

"I don't care what you believe."

Annoyed now, he bit out, "You should. Your life and that of your crew depends upon my mercy."

"You and your men are criminals. The Consortium doesn't negotiate. They'd sooner destroy the whole ship than see you reap a profit from this . . . venture."

"So we are at an impasse . . ." he said softly.

"Looks like it."

Dagr shook his head, wondering at her mental state. She faced a foe who weighed easily twice her weight, and yet she wouldn't back down an inch. Perhaps she needed a little softening first. He dragged off his wolf headdress, toed off his soft leather boots.

"What are you doing?" she asked, a catch in her voice.

"What we both want."

"You just captured my ship, throttled my crew," she said, her voice rising. "You threatened to cut off my head, you barbarian. You think I want you?"

She did. He was sure of it. "Next time you decide to tell a man you don't desire him, dress in a few more layers." With deliberation, he dropped his gaze to her chest, to the nipples that spiked hard against the thin, oiled skin.

Her gaze followed, then jerked back. "You arrogant ass! I don't want you." Her chin jutted upward.

A gesture that was beginning to amuse him. He stepped toward her, crowding her against the wall she hugged, and stuck his hand between her legs, cupping her sex. "If you say it again, I will leave you here. And we will never know. This isn't punishment. It's not rape. We shed our clothes; we shed who we are." A shoulder lifted in an easy shrug. "When we are done, we resume the battle. I find I enjoy your resistance."

Her mouth opened around ragged breaths. "I won't be used. My surrender won't be held up for you to mock later."

"Lady Captain, we will use each other. Whatever passion we share remains between us." He held her stare, keeping his expression set, waiting for her to decide.

Without breaking with his gaze, she squeezed her thighs together, trapping his hand. "I'm not some pleasure thrall."

"Are you telling me this because you lack skill and fear I'll be disappointed?" he drawled.

"I couldn't care less whether you are disappointed," she spat out.

He leaned closer and trailed his lips across her forehead.

She jerked and turned away, her chest trembling around her quickening breaths.

"Why do you resist me? We can both seek our pleasure. You are as aroused as I am." He pressed his fingers harder against her sex.

Her head swung back. Stark longing mixed with rage were reflected in her amber gaze. "You are my enemy."

"Then treat this like another form of battle."

Her jaw tensed, her lips firming, but she rolled her hips, a slight, shallow movement that ground her pussy against his palm as moisture soaked through to wet it.

He held her there, giving free rein to his arousal. His heart beat like a skin drum, pulse quickening at his temples and his groin. He strummed his fingers over her clothed folds and moved in to trap her chest.

Her hands came up to push at his shoulders. "I fight because I should," she whispered.

Dagr gave a curt nod, then bent to cover her mouth, plunging into moist heat. She tasted exotic, smelled of musk and sweat, not too pungent, but tantalizing enough to capture his arousal, full-blown and surging to rut against her.

He clapped his hands on the wall on either side of her, afraid to touch her until he'd bridled his lust because he'd leave her skin bruised.

His lips rubbed hers, his tongue probed, waiting for her to reciprocate the exploratory penetration. When she moaned her surrender and thrust her tongue into his mouth, he gave a rumble of approval that vibrated his chest against hers.

He broke the kiss, clasped her hands, and slid them outward, pressing them against the wall to tell her to keep them there. Then he drew his knife again, stretched what remained of the top of her uniform, and inserted the blade, sharp edge outward, to slit it from her neck to low on her belly.

Her shaky exhale brushed against his neck.

When the edges parted, he stared at her nude breasts and abdomen. Her nipples were a rusty brown and large, the tips reddening as they elongated. Her belly quivered against the cold, blunt edge of the blade. He pulled the knife away and thrust it into the metal wall beside her head, then clutched both sides of her opened suit and ripped it the rest of the way off her.

When her arms were freed, she wrapped one over her breasts, and hid the dark thatch cloaking her pussy with an open palm.

Dagr let her have her false modesty. He stepped back and stripped off his tunic, trousers, and woolen socks, leaving on only his golden armbands and the black amulet.

He gripped his shaft and pumped his fist up and down once, deliberately drawing her attention there, giving her fair warning of his size and his intent.

Her eyes widened; her tongue wet her lips before she met his gaze again.

Now her whole body shivered, and Dagr understood. He too was filled with excitement and a strange sort of dread. As though the moment was somehow bigger, maybe destined. And he didn't want to feel the pull, wanted to keep this only about finding release inside a woman's body, any woman's body—but this slight, slender ship's captain wasn't like any woman he'd ever known before. She wasn't eager to sleep with the clan-lord. Didn't expect reward for her service to him. And she was equally appalled at her attraction. Her courage only enhanced her dark beauty.

How odd was it to travel into the heavens and find the one woman he might have kept for his own?

Honora leaned against the cool, smooth wall behind her because her knees weakened. Her pussy throbbed, the slow, deepening beat matching her heart's pulse for pulse.

The sight of him took away her breath, made her hot and wet.

There wasn't an inch of him that wasn't clad in thick ropes of muscle. His skin was pale. Sweat glistened on the swells, emphasizing their size, but he hardly needed the enhancement.

Everywhere she looked was massive and covered with dark hair and fine white lines, like threads and poorly stitched patches, crisscrossing his tall frame. So many scars. Gods, they turned her on.

A hint of a tat, wrapping around his narrow waist, had her wishing he'd do a slow turn so she could see it all, but then she'd have to drag her gaze from his Viking-sized cock.

The hand covering her pussy pressed against her pubic bone, trying to trap the sensations flooding her sex, making her swollen. A single glide of her thumb over her hardening clit might be enough to make her come.

Dagr took a step toward her, his expression dark and electrifying. "This first time," he growled, dropping his gaze to where his hand glided along his shaft, "will be fast."

"First?" she breathed. *Fuucck.*

At the end of one long pull, his thumb slid over the satiny, plush tip, smearing a drop of ejaculate.

She couldn't help it—she licked her lips.

"Remove your hand."

Honora wondered how'd she'd come to this. How she could even consider surrendering so quickly to the barbarian. It wasn't as though she were sex-starved. She turned to Baraq for sex when her needs clamored for relief.

Perhaps she was her father's daughter after all. This weakness of the flesh could be an inherited flaw—one unleashed by the excitement of battle and the melting heat of his glance. Maybe it was just curiosity about the power he wielded in his large frame. She'd never before encountered a man as large and intimidating as this pirate.

Or did her subconscious allow her to fold because deep down she truly feared him and hoped cooperation might earn her some lenience?

Her arguments dried up. She knew she was only fooling herself. Her attraction was inexplicable but so powerful she couldn't resist it.

"Remove your hand," he repeated, this time his voice grinding.

She was beyond pretending resistance to his commands. She dropped the hand between her legs that she'd used to shield herself from his view. Then she lowered the arm crossing her breasts and stood as naked as he did, waiting while his gaze swept her slowly, head to toe and back up.

What did he see? Was she too petite, too lacking in curves? Did he prefer creamy white to her own darkly tinted flesh?

Dagr closed in, reaching out with one hand. He touched her with only his fingers, sliding them between her folds to test her arousal. Silky, creamy heat coated his digits. She knew, because he used the moist tips to swirl gently over her clit.

The choice of the first place and how to touch her surprised her. She'd thought the savage marauder in this pirate would dig his hands into her flesh and force her quickly onto his cock. Not that she would have complained. Her pussy made succulent, smacking sounds as he continued to fondle the tiny, turgid knot.

"Wider," he whispered, sliding closer, one hand bracketing her shoulder, one side of his chest pressing against a soft, round breast as he leaned into her curves.

Blood sang through her veins. She parted her thighs tentatively, giving him just enough room to thrust his long middle finger inside her, while she looked away and tried to preserve a little of her tattered pride. He pressed the heel of his hand against her mons while he continued to swirl and tunnel inward.

All the while he probed, he watched her face. She felt his gaze move over her, his breaths gust against her cheek.

She tried valiantly not to let her excitement show, not to give him the satisfaction of knowing she was close to complete capitulation.

But her nostrils flared as her ripening scent surrounded them. Her eyelids dipped with the added pressure he applied to her clitoris as he stroked toward her core. With his other hand, he tweaked her clit, causing her to jerk her head toward him.

The corners of his mouth kicked up.

She wanted to look away again, but then he'd think her a coward. "Thought you said fast . . ." she muttered.

"I would see to your pleasure first."

She raised her chin. "Why do you care whether I come or not?"

"Because I would command you."

She glared, meeting his ice-hard gaze. "You think that if you make me come, I'll melt every time you crook a finger?"

"I think you will smolder quietly—until we are alone." His eyelids lowered to half-mast. "Then you will do my bidding—eagerly."

This time she nearly did swoon, or at least her knees wobbled. Moisture spilled from inside her.

As his fingers swirled in the fluid, he gave her a slow, predatory smile.

Heat crept across her cheeks, and she wished she had a little more self-control. She was making this too easy. "You think a lot of yourself," she ground out.

"I have experience."

Said so simply, she might have scoffed at another man, but she didn't doubt him. Not for a second. He'd be the best she'd ever had. "You think I don't have experience, or that I can't find partners who do?"

His eyes darkened. "I think you've never been completely at a man's mercy. That you've never been taken."

No doubt her short, sharp inhalation told him everything. Her body only echoed the response. Her nipples contracted, the tiny buds hardening like pebbles.

Oh, yeah, he knew. His gaze dropped to her chest. "I want to suckle them while you ride me."

Her throat closed. "You're too tall," she choked out.

"Interesting. You didn't say that you're too short."

"Because I'm not."

Leaning away, he pulled his wet finger from her sex and circled one nipple, then the other. Then he gripped her waist and slid her up the wall until her breasts were even with his face.

Honora flattened her hands against the wall and swallowed hard, trying to wet a dry mouth. Her belly quivered and jumped as she waited for his next move.

Dagr held her gaze for a long moment, the tension sharpening his cheeks and jaw making him more attractive and frightening. She knew she should be worried about the fact she found that so compelling, but she couldn't think because he was closing in on her chest . . .

He latched on to a nipple, growling against her skin, tasting her and letting loose the ravager, the conqueror she wanted.

Her hands clutched his hair, raking wildly through the thickness as she writhed.

Perhaps encouraged by her bucking, he sucked her hard, pulled her nipple between his teeth, wagging his head to root and suction, until she wrapped her legs around his muscled torso and hugged him closer.

Her breaths were ragged little sobs and quickening. Her heels dug into his back.

He released the nipple, laved it once with the flat of his tongue, then sucked its twin into his mouth, torturing it until her skin prickled with gooseflesh and her pussy spasmed. A long, thin moan slid between her lips.

When at last he let go and lowered her, he did it so slowly she groaned. He was letting her feel the strength in his hands, waiting while her palms smoothed compulsively along his rippling biceps.

He gave her time to acknowledge his power. She responded by gifting him with her surrender. With a long exhalation, she let her head fall back against the wall, let her eyelids drift dreamily down. Her lips parted, inviting his kiss.

He scooped up her lips and rubbed over them. His cock found her slick entrance, prodded once to find the center, and then he gripped her ass and guided her down his shaft, groaning as her tight, moist heat surrounded him.

He gritted his teeth as he buried his cock inside her. "You are every bit as small as I imagined."

And already coming apart. She moaned and ground her hips against his. Delicate convulsions rippled up and down her channel, caressing his shaft.

He changed the angle of his thrusts and slammed into her again.

Breath hissed between her teeth, and she would have hid her face against his shoulder, but he prevented it, bending to press his forehead against hers.

"Did I hurt you?" he growled, not slowing his motions.

She shook her head.

"Don't lie to me. Not while we share sex."

"Not lying," she bit out. "Just . . . *fuck* . . . it's good."

He smiled and kissed her hard, then crowded her against the bulkhead, holding her there. He began to dip and surge upward, fucking her hard, grinding at the end of every thrust, the powerful motions sliding her up and down the wall.

It was no gentle taking, a battle of another sort. She clawed at his shoulders and scissored her legs behind him to bounce her pussy on his cock and increase the friction.

Dagr leaned into her, his hands slapping the wall on either side of her, his hips the only thing pinning her there as he thrust deeper.

Honora's whole body fought and clawed, her skin stretching around tightening muscles, sweat sprouting on her face and belly. Liquid pleasure rushed from inside her, hot and melting, easing him deeper while her pussy clasped him hard.

She wrapped her arms around his shoulders and tilted back her head to let the moans, one after another, rip from her throat.

Clinging to the savage, she came hard, trusting him to see her through the darkness closing around her.

Six

D agr couldn't remember the last time watching another's climax filled him with so much prideful satisfaction.

The woman vibrated as she came apart. Her head thumped softly against the wall as she arched. Her hips slammed harder to take him as deep as she could. She groaned, the sound stretching into a painful wail. Her amber eyes stared sightlessly while deep, rhythmic shudders quivered through her core. He felt the flutter of those sensual convulsions all along his shaft, milking him, drowning him in silky, slick heat.

Then her eyes closed, and her body slackened beneath him, a deep sigh escaping her lips. She fainted—leaving him bemused and so aroused his cock felt harder than the tempered steel of his fathers' sword.

Dagr shook off the sweat dripping down the end of his nose, and stared at her blurred mouth. With the half-moons of her lids closed and a bruised blue, she looked so small and vulnerable that he felt a pang of guilt.

Until he reminded himself she was anything but a woman in need of protection, even from a warrior like himself. She was a Consortium ship's captain, had aided in the kidnapping of his brother, and would do her best in the coming days to defeat him, perhaps even to kill him.

Which left his conscience free to enjoy their little interlude, even if it had started out as punishment for her stubborn resistance.

She moaned softly, and her legs tightened restlessly around his waist. Before she came back to herself, he cupped the back of her head and gripped her bottom to hold her pressed against his body, and knelt to deliver her to the floor, never breaking their connection.

He smoothed back the hair sticking to her cheeks, and tucked it behind her ears. She stirred and cuddled her cheek against his palm.

While her breaths deepened and her eyes regained focus, he waited.

Her amber eyes blinked dreamily, then focused on his hovering face. Her expression reflected frozen dismay.

Dagr smiled grimly and stroked into her, a coarse reminder that he was still there, still hard and poised to do so much more.

She swallowed and looked down at her hands, biting into his shoulders. She eased her grip. "You didn't come."

"I said I'd see to your pleasure."

"Was that pleasure?" she whispered, sounding doubtful.

Had he hurt her after all? "You will tell me."

"I feel anything but happy." She blinked at a sudden wash of tears. "You captured my ship and now I'm pinned beneath you."

"Don't you dare to call this rape," he said hoarsely.

She shook her head, her lips curving downward. "That's the most appalling part. I wanted this."

Dagr bent and kissed her mouth, forcing himself to be gentle and coax her into compliance when what he wanted to do was devour her and finish this. His cock was hard, his balls aching, but she trembled beneath him, and he wanted more than just her consent. He wanted her to acknowledge that something had happened between them, that he'd marked her, made her his.

Which didn't make any sense at all.

When he drew back, her gaze locked with his. "When we're alone," she whispered, "will it be like this? Will you take command of me?"

Dagr liked that she already accepted they would do this again. With his body beginning to shake, he couldn't be anything but blunt. "When we are alone, you are mine."

"Not exactly what I asked."

"Did I hurt you?"

"How do I answer that?" Her lips trembled. "I'm . . . devastated."

He canted his head, aligning their mouths better for the deeper kiss he placed on her mouth. He stroked into her mouth at the same time as he tunneled into her body—one quick, hard thrust—then he lifted his head. "You think I am unscathed?"

She blinked; then her eyelids dropped as she scanned his expression. "Don't mock me."

"Never." A tight smile stretched his mouth. "I am pleased with you, Lady Captain."

Her gaze slowly swept his face. "You're handsome when you smile, even under all that blue paint. Makes me wonder what it would be like to see that smile while we're vertical."

A snort of laughter surprised him, and she gave him a small grin, but it quickly faded. "You didn't come."

"You're repeating yourself. Are you afraid you don't measure up to Viking women?"

She separated a lock of his hair and wrapped it slowly around her finger, staring at it, avoiding his gaze. "Do I? Measure up?"

"I had to hold back for fear I'd harm you," he said truthfully.

A frown sank a furrow between her brows. "You shouldn't have. I'm not fragile."

"You lost consciousness," he drawled.

Pink tinted her bronze cheeks, and her mouth pouted. "Only because the pleasure was more than I expected. Next time, I'll be prepared and much less impressed."

Dagr shook his head. He'd let her think she could control her response. She was his perfect complement. Only because he was truly more experienced had he been able to leash his own explosive reactions.

He pushed off the floor, lifting his chest from hers, but tilting his hips so his cock crowded deeper through her soft, hot channel. He wanted to go slowly, to hide the fact he was holding on by a thread, but his blood pounded against both temples and in his groin. His cock stirred inside her, quickening, swelling impossibly larger.

Air hissed between her teeth, but she didn't wince, her mouth opened around a low, guttural moan of pleasure.

The sound spurred him on. He flexed his buttocks and thighs and stroked inside her—long hard thrusts that rammed through her tender tissues.

She moaned and hissed, her hips popping counter to his motions. He drove faster, hammering her soft, yielding flesh, the force of his thrusts scooting her across the floor until she set her hands against the wall and held firm.

Shoving his arms beneath her knees, he lifted her ass from the floor, and pulled up her hips to control her motions, digging deep for control to calm the wildness surging through his veins. He wanted more than release. He wanted her to come again, to surrender completely.

He stopped moving and dragged in deep breaths, staring down at her while she rolled her head side to side. "Dagr, dammit, move now . . ."

He thumbed her clitoris, feeling it harden beneath the scrape of his callused pad. Her thighs opened wider; her hips tilted. Her clit stretched past the thin hood and he plucked it, squeezing to torture the rigid knot.

"I've already come," she panted, then averted her face. "You don't have to wait."

"I'm far from finished with you. And you will come for me again."

She shook her head. "I don't. I've never . . ."

"You will." He wet his fingertips and slid them over her the top of her folds again.

But she gritted her teeth and glared.

Dagr lowered her butt to the floor, then scooted quickly down her body, hunching over it because there wasn't room to stretch his legs behind him. He slid an arm around her thigh, bringing his hand over her belly to spread her folds and expose her clit. Then he dipped two fingers into her pussy, gathering her moisture, and trailed his fingertips downward to rub her second entrance.

Her body jerked. "No!"

At her strident tone, Dagr gave her a glare.

Her eyebrows shot up. "What? I can't complain if you do something I don't like?"

"You've never been taken here before?" he asked, pressing against her entrance and enjoying the way she squirmed and her cheeks reddened.

"I've never submitted to it. It's not comfortable."

He wondered at her choice of words. His finger stopped moving but didn't leave her asshole. Perhaps she needed a moment to get past the embarrassment. He lowered his face and licked at the creamy, silky fluid clinging to her folds. The tang of her arousal coated his tongue, feeding the fire building in his loins.

Her fingers dug into his scalp and pulled his hair. "I thought you wanted to conquer me. Eating a woman out is the most submissive thing a man can do."

He snorted and gave her another pointed glare but didn't pause in the lavish attention he gave her pussy. Didn't she know that supping from a woman's sex was the surest way to enslave her?

Tunneling with his tongue, he rimmed her entrance, then licked upward, centering his attention on her clitoris. He latched both lips around it and sucked it gently, testing her tolerance. When her hips trembled but didn't jerk, he sucked harder and circled her tiny furled hole again.

She blew out a breath, but didn't complain this time. Her thighs widened; her belly danced with excited quivers and flexes. He released her clit and feathered it, touching it over and over while he rubbed her back entrance until her hips rocked up and down and her moans trailed one after another.

Unable to wait a moment longer, Dagr kissed an inner thigh and straightened, kneeling between her legs. He held himself still while he waited for her to recover herself, for her to notice the hand he held out in her direction.

The lady captain rolled her head, then focused her gaze on him, a look of stark longing in her eyes.

How she pleased him. Even while they should be enemies, should be at each other's throats, she forsook her pride and held back nothing.

He curled his fingers, beckoning her.

She swallowed and sat up, then crawled over to him, meeting his gaze before straddling his lap. She rose high, waited while he fit his cock to her entrance, and then slowly lowered herself, not stopping until her pussy nestled against his groin. Her lips trembled, and she pressed them together.

Again, he held still, waiting for her to decide whether her pride was more important than her need. He gripped her bottom hard, digging his fingers into her soft flesh, not urging movement, but letting her know he was ready and barely leashed.

"What is it you want? Me begging?" she asked, scowling although her voice held a tremor. "You can have me any way you want. I'm your hostage. Haven't you ever pulled rank, used your superior strength to get what you want?"

"Have you 'pulled rank'?"

Eyes wide, she flushed, and he wondered about that, remembering the warrior on the deck and how he'd wanted to come to her rescue. "I have never pressured a woman using my station. They come to me—eagerly."

"Because you're the big bad pirate?"

He snorted, not bothering to correct her mistake. "Perhaps they come to me because they know I will make them scream."

She stayed planted on his cock, outwardly calm. However, her pussy clasped around him, giving him wet, rhythmic caresses.

"I hate that I want you," she whispered, leaning close enough the berry tips of her breasts scraped his chest. Her eyes closed for a brief second; heat flared on her cheeks. "You want me to beg."

"That would please me, but I will be satisfied if you only ask me very nicely for what you want."

After a deep sigh, she leaned her face on the top of his shoulder. "My legs are shivering. I want to fuck you, but I don't think I have the strength."

He petted her, smoothing a palm over her back. He didn't have hours to spend with her, probably had only minutes before someone sought him out. After the breakneck pace of the day's events, the quiet moment soothed ravaged nerves. "What is your name?" he whispered.

A short, muffled laugh gusted against his skin. "Honora."

"Honora," he repeated. It suited her. Soft sounding, but with an underlying strength. "Have you recovered?"

She tilted back her head, her amber gaze level with his, and nodded. He gripped her ass more firmly, giving her a gentle nudge of encouragement, and then she rocked tentatively forward, pulling on his length.

Dagr cursed beneath his breath, gritted his teeth, wanting to hold out a little bit longer to enjoy the feel of her moist caresses, but there was no stopping him now.

Honora moaned, her body too sensitized for her to pretend any longer that she held even a smidgeon of control over herself. Everywhere their bodies touched, her skin burned. His large cock stretched her deliciously, offering its own odd comfort.

Dagr's hand cupped the back of her head, his fingers pulling her hair to tilt her head. "They will come for me soon," he said, his voice tight.

"I know," she gasped. "I'm not ready to face it. Not just yet."

"Then don't. Pretend there is only this." Then both his hands gripped her bottom hard and moved her, lifting her up and down his shaft.

Her pussy was hot, already a little raw. She'd thought Dagr had brought her all the pleasure her body could bear, but again, fluid washed down her channel, spilling over his cock, easing his strokes as he shoved deep, then eased away.

"I don't believe this," she whispered, closing her eyes because she didn't want to give him more proof that she was his, here inside her own room. They might have only these stolen moments, but her idea of pleasure with a man was forever changed. All because she'd wanted to be controlled, needed a man to master her body, and he'd provided her the proof.

He'd given her that, along with hints of tenderness when her emotions spilled over, rough handling when her body craved it— empathy a man shouldn't possess. This pirate knew more about what she craved than she did. And she wanted more.

Honora pumped up and down, aided by his large hands cupping her butt, moving faster, grinding harder. She'd pay tomorrow for the effort, but gods, the tension was there again, curling tightly around her womb, building until she moved desperately against him, gliding now in the sweat slicking both their bodies.

His expression lost its shuttered stoicism. His jaw tightened, flexed. His cold blue gaze, always so intense, lost focus and his mouth opened around heavy, gusting breaths.

She rode him, pounding against his groin, her hands grasping, kneading, then clutching his hair to bring his face against her neck as she came apart again, shattering like glass. She cried out, then groaned as his arms wrapped around her back and he thundered upward, spearing her deeply and erupting, his seed coming in hot spurts to bathe her inner walls.

They slowed their opposing motions. She did so reluctantly because the convulsions rippling up and down her channel pleasurably faded away.

His hand cupped her head again and she leaned into it, giving him the weight because she felt so boneless it might have lolled on her shoulders like child's rag doll. Again, the comfort she derived from his touch, from the way his body crowded hers, inside and out, surprised her.

"This space, your room, isn't adequate," he growled, gliding his mouth across the top of one shoulder. "Find another."

She opened her eyes, startled by the implication. "Will you be here long enough for it to matter?"

"Since I didn't find what I was seeking, yes."

"The captives," she said, reality sharpening the edges of her consciousness again. She pushed at his chest, wanting him to relax his embrace so she could rise, but he continued to hold her tightly.

A deep breath eased from his chest, and then he slowly raised his face. His features were set in granite again. "I must know where they've gone."

Disappointment tasted bitter in her mouth. She'd known this was an interlude. She meant nothing to him. He was a pirate, a marauder. And she'd fucked him. *Stupid, stupid.*

"If I tell you where they've gone, will you leave my ship?"

Eyes flashing, he shook his head. "*When* you tell me, we will follow them."

"But you can't. My command will know something's up as soon as we leave this planet's orbit."

"Cyrus says the ship can be cloaked to prevent detection."

"If we disappear, we'll get the same result. They'll dispatch another ship to find us. And if they get close enough, cloaking won't help. They'll be able to detect the particle waves emitted by the ship's engines."

"Then we will capture them as well."

Honora let out an exasperated breath. "Why are these men so important to you?"

"Where are they?" he asked, his voice dead even.

How odd it was, she thought, that their bodies weren't yet separated, hadn't even cooled, and here they were at odds again. Honora knew he wouldn't relent. She sighed. "Another transport, privately owned, came yesterday. They were all removed to the other ship."

A muscle flexed along the edge of his jaw. "What is the name of the ship?"

"I told you. I don't know."

His glare said he didn't believe her this time either.

She gritted her teeth and tried to slide free of his cock, but his fingers bit into her hips, pinning her there. Honora trembled, unable to match his stare, not with her body still wet, and still stretched so deliciously. "I don't know. I swear it. Part of my instructions were to turn a blind eye to their mission. No contact. They ate their meals at specified times so that my crew didn't intermingle. The cargo bay was off-limits during their stay."

"You never poked your nose inside?"

She cringed, because she had. And the sight of all those cages filled with men had disturbed her. "Once."

Perhaps he read the regret in her expression, knew she hadn't been as callous as she should have been. His fingers eased a fraction. "Where are they headed?"

The man was as persistent as a migraine. She hedged again, deciding to parlay for more information from him. "You're very interested in this cargo. Why?"

"Not your concern. You're very good at minding your own business. Worry instead about answering my questions."

"I did that once before, and it ended in disaster. Make me understand," she said, smoothing her hand over his chest. "Why do you want them? Is it for ransom?"

Dagr's lips pulled away from his teeth in a fearsome snarl. His hands slid up and curved around her upper arms, tightening hard enough to bruise. "I couldn't care less about any riches *your cargo* might bring me. One of the kidnapped men is my brother."

Honora froze, dawning horror cramping her stomach. Kin. There'd be no bargaining with him.

"You will tell me where he's been taken—that, or I'll begin to kill your men."

She read the deadly intent in his eyes. "They're being taken to my home world," she whispered. "Helios."

His face appeared cut from stone—no expression at all unless you counted the ripple of muscle that slid along the edge of his jaw. He lifted her slowly off his lap, his cock sliding from her body—the connection, the warmth, severed. She stood on shaky on legs.

"Dress."

"I need to clean up."

"Do it quickly."

She opened the small cupboard that hid the sink and ran warm water, splashing her face and wetting a cloth to clean between her legs. She wet another cloth and handed it to Dagr. "For your face."

Dagr grunted but rubbed the paint from his skin, turned the fabric, and washed his cock while she tried to catch her breath after her first glimpse of his face free of the distorting blue lines. Arousal stirred anew. Gods, he was handsome. All sharp, masculine edges and brooding eyes.

A knock sounded at her door and it swung open. The one called Frakki glanced at her naked body, but showed no surprise. His glance darted to Dagr. "Cyrus has a party ready to begin bringing aboard the ore."

Dagr pulled on his clothing. "Tell him I will be up in a moment. I'll accompany the team. And get the crew in the hold ready."

Frakki nodded and closed the door.

"What is he talking about?" Honora asked, removing uniform

trousers and a jacket from a cupboard over her bed as well as a second skin-suit to wear beneath it for insulation.

At his frown, she blew out an irritated breath and placed the collar of the skin-suit on the floor, then stomped on it to crush the microphone. "Satisfied?"

He nodded, pulled his weapons belt around his lean hips, and buckled it. Then, with hands fisted at his sides, he drew a deep breath. "The air is thin. How do you breathe?"

By the hardness of his expression, he didn't expect an answer; he just wanted to complain. And she didn't dare tell him that the atmosphere was thinning because too many people were aboard the ship. The bastard might start pitching crewmen out the waste disposal unit.

She tried again to engage him in conversation. "You're leaving the ship?"

"You're coming along. Make sure you dress warmly."

A gasp she couldn't stifle escaped. "You're taking me to the surface? But it's an iceberg!"

"Finish. Without talking." He crossed his arms over his chest while she stepped into the suit and pulled it up to slip her arms inside. Once she'd closed the collar, he flung open the door. She grabbed the rest of her clothing and stepped out, hurrying to the ladder and not looking to see whether he followed because she heard his stomping footsteps behind her. She climbed up the rungs, conscious of him beneath her every step of the way.

She wished she'd had time to thoroughly bathe, but she was anxious to see what was happening now and whether the activity of moving cargo from the planet to the ship might give her a chance to get a message out to the high command. And what did he mean about getting the crew ready?

Outside the bridge, she finished pulling on her trousers and boots. When she entered, all heads turned her way and it took every ounce of her composure to keep from blushing. Everyone knew what had passed between her and the Viking pirate since she hadn't come back bloody and bruised.

Turk was seated now in the navigator's chair. Baraq was still planted on the floor with a guard hovering over him. The female Viking sat slumped in the science officer's seat, frowning at the multicolored warning lights.

Cyrus swiveled the captain's chair around. He watched her as she approached, a brooding discontent in his expression. "Are you all right?" he asked quietly.

She stiffened. "What do you care?"

"I wouldn't want to see you hurt, Honora."

She snorted and shook her head, letting him see her pain. "What you and your new friends have done," she whispered harshly, "has damaged me irrevocably. I'm ruined."

He glanced away, his jaw hardening. "If it's any consolation, there was no way I could have known you'd be the captain of this ship."

Honora curled her hands at her sides. His regrets didn't change a thing. Her ship was still being held hostage. Her career as a ship's captain was over.

Dagr walked up beside her, his gaze going from her to Cyrus. He raised a thick, dark brow.

"We know each other," Cyrus said. "From the academy. It's awkward."

"You'd do well to remember she is no longer your friend."

Dagr could have been warning the other man to remember the mission, but the possessive glare he gave her said something else. She was off-limits.

Cyrus narrowed his eyes, then cleared his throat, getting

immediately back to business. "We can't warn the men on the surface that you're coming without worrying about our transmission being intercepted."

Dagr exhaled. "If you can put us on the beach . . ."

Cyrus nodded. "Who do you want accompanying you?"

"She goes," Dagr said, his gaze landing on Honora. "Birget, too. I'm sending her back."

"Frigg!"

Honora heard the low curse and turned to the woman who'd fought alongside the Vikings.

Dagr aimed a deadly glare the woman's way. "Harald will see you safely to the keep."

The woman's mouth curled into a snarl. "If Odvarr couldn't keep me, why do you think another old man will?"

Cyrus chuckled softly and turned back to Dagr. "You'll need another to wheel the cart. You'll be too busy corralling women to use your own muscle."

Dagr grimaced.

Cyrus's grin stretched. "I'd come just to watch, but I'm a little busy here."

Dagr glanced around the deck, his gaze landing on Baraq, who stiffened. "You. And Frakki. I need you in the hold."

Frakki jerked his head in a sharp nod, then shoved Baraq's shoulder to hurry him to his feet.

Cyrus held out his hand, palm up. A small black locator clip lay in the center. "Dagr, attach this to your clothing. It has a timer. In one hour, wherever you are, we will retrieve you and whoever stands close by."

Dagr accepted the clip and attached it to the edge of his fur vest.

Honora thought fast. Everything was moving too quickly. Now was the time to act if she had any chance at all of turning this around. She sucked in a deep breath. "Dagr, I'll need my cold-weather gear. My coat's in my cabin."

Dagr gave her a hard stare. "Get it, but be quick. Meet us in the hold."

She nodded and gave Baraq a quick warning glance as she passed him.

Baraq's chest rose, but otherwise he didn't give away that he knew she was up to something.

As she left the bridge, Honora's heart raced. It might not be the smartest plan, but it was the only recourse she had left. She just hoped her crew could take advantage of her ploy before the Vikings adapted.

She couldn't underestimate them. They might seem primitive and savage, but they had managed to board a starship and take it without any damage to the craft or loss of life—something she wasn't sure the best-trained starfighters could manage.

Seven

Once she was out of sight of the bridge, Honora picked up her feet and ran. She headed in the direction of the lift in case anyone looked, but when the doors slid open, she ducked down the right wing of the ship, moving as fast as she could to get to the atmospherics room.

Luck was with her. She passed no one. The closet was locked, and she slapped her palm against the identifier, thankful it still answered to her DNA code. A soft snick and she opened the door and slipped inside, closing it behind her.

The room was filled floor to ceiling with the computer components responsible for maintenance of all the life-support systems aboard the ship. The component she wanted was at the bottom. The green, glowing safety switch was located behind a panel that she had to squeeze deep inside to reach.

With her hips wedged in the panel door, she reached, stretching her arm, her fingers tipping the toggle the first time, but the switch clicked back in place. Holding her breath, she reached again, not letting herself think twice about her plan or the consequences if she failed. This ploy would give her and her crew their only advantage against the Vikings' superior brute force.

She couldn't let her crew be moved from the ship. If that happened, there'd be no one left to help her retake the *Proteus*. No matter how tempting the Viking leader made her captivity, she wasn't ready to concede defeat.

Dagr was a dizzying temptation wrapped in fur and leather, but she knew she was merely a diversion. That fucking her gave him a way to ease the edge of his frustration over his failure to locate his brother. Sooner or later, the satisfaction he gained from forcing his enemy to submit would wane. She didn't want to consider what that might mean. Whether he'd still be as cautious about causing harm to her and her crew, or turn savage when he failed in his quest.

She reached again and a fingertip touched the toggle switch. With a quick prayer that her crew would indeed take advantage of her scheme, she flicked it down. Wiggling backward, she grinned, wishing she could see the look on Dagr's face when he realized what she'd done.

Dagr stood beside Cyrus in front of the transporter console that overlooked the open cargo bay. Below, his men had the prisoners lining up in two columns for them to funnel through a portal after the ore was transferred to the ship. He'd taken the precaution of having the prisoners dress in heavy clothing. A myriad of expressions played on the faces of the prisoners from worry to anger, and some displayed curiosity. They'd already been warned they were being sent to the surface where few Outlanders with any status had ever been. They would have none and would be quickly put to work or spend their time on New Iceland learning how cold a dungeon could get.

Cyrus turned to him. "She's taking too long."

Dagr crossed his arms over his chest, feeling tension tighten his body. "And that worries you?" It worried him too. Honora was a clever woman, but he'd given her just enough rope to hang herself. If she proved unworthy of his trust, he'd have to enforce stricter rules for her captivity.

"She knows this ship inside out," Cyrus said, turning to a screen and searching through security video feeds to find her. However, all the corridors were empty.

"What can she do? Have you considered all possibilities?" Dagr asked, staring at the screen, willing her to appear. "Is there some way she could retake the sh—"

Lights flickered overhead, then continued their static hum.

Cyrus froze and glanced out the window to the open bay, a small, tight smile tugging at his mouth. "Even she wouldn't dare try that . . ."

"What?"

That incessant hum that had become part of the background noise aboard the ship quieted.

"Clever bitch," Cyrus muttered admiringly. "Better grab hold of something."

He said it so calmly that Dagr didn't move for a second. Or at least he didn't *make* a move. The room seemed to tilt, and suddenly, his feet weren't planted quite so firmly on the floor.

Cyrus whooped, gripping the edge of the console.

Dagr floated upward, and he stuck his arm out to catch hold of the doorframe, but the sharp movement propelled him feet-first toward the ceiling. "What has she done?" he shouted, irritation sharpening his tone.

"She's turned off gravity. You won't be able to do battle as you're accustomed to, milord. You won't be able to crack any heads, other than your own if you don't adapt quickly."

Dagr flailed and pushed against the ceiling, turning to get his feet beneath him, but again the movement was too large and he careened against another wall. "Bloody Frigg!"

"Make gentle shoves in the direction you want to go," Cyrus said, calmly, his hand still curved around the console. "No big movements, milord. Oh, boy, take a look at the cargo bay." Cyrus pointed toward the window.

From upside down, Dagr watched as laughing prisoners floated away from his men's frantic grabs.

"Small movements," Cyrus reminded him. "You'd better get out there. I'm heading to the atmospherics closet to turn it on again."

Dagr grabbed for the edge of the doorframe and glanced back at Cyrus. "What does she hope to achieve?"

Cyrus shrugged, floating calmly away. "I don't know. Confusion. If she can keep your men floating on the ceiling, her crew might be able to make their way back to the deck, barricade it, and take back control of the ship. That's my guess, anyway."

If she'd wanted to cause confusion, her plan was working rather well. Dagr pulled himself under the top of the doorframe and floated into the large cargo bay. "Small movements, wolves! Gather the prisoners!"

It didn't escape him, the laughter from Honora's crew as they floated just beyond the grasp of their captors, using their feet to shove the Vikings in the opposite direction every time they drew close.

"Two on one!" he shouted, feeling foolish and clumsy, anger making his face hot. He grabbed Frakki's shoulder and pushed him toward one captive heading to the upper walkway. Had any of them made their way to the command deck?

Propelled by Dagr's shove, Frakki flew, arms outstretched. He wrapped them around the legs of the man he caught. "Now what, milord?"

What indeed? Dagr grimaced, watching from the opposite side of the bay from where he'd propelled himself. "Men, pull your way down the wall to the floor," he shouted. "Cyrus is going to fix this problem and you will not want to be high up when it's righted."

All around him his men fought, blows swinging wide, or worse, connecting impotently and pushing their opponents out of reach. Dagr shook his head, never having felt so helpless or that his size and strength were a handicap. The woman was too clever for her own good.

Dagr spotted another of the crewmen, drifting toward the front of the bay and the bridge. He pushed away from the wall, stretching one arm in front of him and holding the other against his body to shoot like a slow-moving arrow toward the crewman. He caught up to the man, opened his arms, and clamped them around him. Then he used his feet pressed against the railing to propel them both toward the floor.

The lights flickered. A whine and a hum, weight pulled everyone slamming toward the floor, but the hum cut out again, and they were saved from injury at the last possible moment.

"Forget the prisoners! Get to the floor," Dagr shouted, poking his fingers through the holes in the metal flooring to anchor himself while holding the thrashing crewman against his side.

The lights flickered again, and the hum resumed. The Vikings dropped, but thankfully not far, their prisoners landing beneath them, the breath knocked from their chests.

Laughter sounded from the upper deck and Dagr crawled to his knees and looked up to find Cyrus, holding Honora close to his chest. Cyrus hung on to the rail, bent double, his shoulders shaking.

The thunderous scowl on Honora's face caused Dagr to bark with laughter, and soon the Vikings roared, their captives looking sheepish and joining them.

Dagr pushed to his feet. "Frakki, gather the prisoners." He strode toward the ladder, taking every other rung, then climbed over the edge of the platform and stalked toward Honora, whose eyes widened as he approached.

Cyrus dropped his arm from around Honora, and she retreated a step, before stiffening her back.

Dagr reached out, grabbed her waist, and slammed his mouth on top of hers. The kiss he forced on her was brutal and hot.

Cheers erupted below and Dagr broke the kiss to stare down at her as she swayed, clutching his arms and gasping for air.

When she straightened, she slammed her palms against his chest and shoved.

He let her go, enjoying the stubborn pride she displayed in her proud posture and the defiant tilt of her chin.

Eyeing him warily, she said, "Why aren't you angry?"

"Is that what you want? Do you want to fight me?"

"I want you off my ship."

"That isn't going to happen. Not until I get what I came for."

She slammed a closed fist against his chest and raised the other to clip his chin.

He caught it midswing.

"You can't win," she said, gritting her teeth and trying to pull away her hand. "You may have this ship, for now, but you can't win against the rest of my fleet."

His hand squeezed around her fist and shoved it down his body, cupping it against his groin. "You can't make me angry enough to forget that you're a woman. I wouldn't have been angry with you even had your plan succeeded. You did what you thought you must.

And you proved yourself clever. I admire that. The fact my men enjoyed the exercise . . ." He grinned at the fierce scowl that drew her brows together.

He turned her with his hands and gave her a gentle shove toward the ladder. "Get below," he said, slapping her bottom, knowing the playful action would infuriate her, but he couldn't resist getting another rise out of her. "You're still coming with me."

Honora sucked in a sharp breath the moment the transporter released her. Air so cold it froze inside her chest kept her gasping.

Dagr reached for the hood of the cloak he'd tossed over her before they'd stepped through the portal and pulled it forward, cutting the chill wind slicing at her cheeks. A finger tucked beneath her chin, raising her face.

He bent close. "Keep the hood pulled around you. We will be inside in a moment."

She shivered and shoved her hands beneath her armpits as she gazed around at the others. The female Viking gave her a smirk and turned her uncovered head to follow Dagr's movements as he traipsed up a barely discernible path denting a snowbank toward a door cut into a frozen hillside.

Behind her stretched a vast frozen ocean, wind scurrying hardened snow across the surface, making whispery sounds. In front of her was only this lonely gray doorway cut into a hill of pure white. What sort of world was this? How did humans live here?

Baraq strode up beside her and touched her elbow. "Captain, are you all right?" he asked quietly.

The second man to ask her that question, and she still wasn't comfortable with the answer. "I'm fine. He didn't beat me for turning off the gravity. He thought it was a fine joke," she muttered.

"I meant what passed before."

She ducked her head, not wanting him to see the color rising on her cheeks. "He did nothing I didn't want."

Baraq's expression didn't change, but she sensed his disapproval. His breath released in a sharp exhale.

Frakki gave Baraq a rough shove from behind. "Quit talking. Do not fall behind. I would hate to lose you in a snowdrift. You would freeze solid in minutes." And he appeared to find that possibility amusing because he grinned.

Baraq growled but plodded forward.

Frakki turned his attention to her and raised a brow, then motioned her ahead of him. "I cannot lose you. Orders."

There were no discernible steps leading up to the door. Only the hollows left by the footsteps of everyone she followed. Her feet sank through the crisp top of the snow, into a softer layer that held her. She struggled to move faster.

Once inside the door, the bitter bite of the wind behind them, Honora pushed back the hood of her cloak and looked around. She'd never been in a mining colony, never stepped foot on such a primitive world. With too much to take in, she missed the first friendly greetings thrown Dagr's way before she realized the miners knew him well.

When she heard the first "milord," the title reverberated inside her mind.

"Clan-lord," he'd called himself. "Lord Dagr," Cyrus had called him. His true rank, not just the pretention or ambition of a pirate.

Her stomach clenched, and she felt suddenly nauseous and clammy.

He wasn't a pirate at all. Which meant the bounty hunters she'd sheltered had taken a member of one of the ruling houses of the planet, a violation of Consortium planetary law.

She wondered why he'd taken care not to cause mortal harm to her crew, because she didn't know a ruling house of any other planet that wouldn't have demanded blood for such a crime.

Her gaze sought him, and she found him staring back at her, his ice-blue gaze pinning her in place. "You know now why I will not be stopped."

Honora closed her eyes, wrapping her arms around her middle. Her life was forfeit and that of all her crew unless they found this noble's brother. The simple fact was that Dagr hadn't harmed any of them because he needed her ship and some of her crew's help to operate it. He'd known that at some point she would acknowledge the fact she had no choice but to help him in his impossible quest.

Her fate beyond his plot to find his brother was even more uncertain. She'd aided and abetted an illegal action. She'd committed a felony that carried a sentence of death.

Either way she sliced it, her life as she'd known it was over.

Honora and her crew stood in the center of a large, heated cavern where pallets of containerized ore were stored, ready for shipment. All around her, bare-chested giants driving heavy machinery stacked boxes in floor-to-ceiling rows, took inventory with handheld devices, and sealed the lids of the containers designed to stabilize the ore without allowing it to deplete its stored energy. Similar containers, although smaller, were stored in her own ship. One large box, like the ones being moved now to a manual dolly, would power a fleet of ships for a year.

Baraq sidled up next to her. "Did you know?"

"Did I know what?" she asked dully.

"That the bounty hunters took a prince?" he hissed.

Affronted, she snarled, "Of course not. I don't even know whether they're aware that they did. All I knew was the Consortium wanted Vikings." She gave him a sideways glare. "And don't you dare say I told you so."

"You knew it wasn't an honorable cause. You should have filed a request of refusal for the mission."

Honora stiffened and looked away, sorry she'd ever told him what she'd seen inside the cargo bay. "I've never refused an order."

"And look what it got you." He slipped a hand around her arm and forced her around to look at him. "Have you considered that's why they gave you this task? Because you wouldn't question it?"

She wrestled her arm free. "You overstep yourself, Baraq."

"Yeah, I'm your goon, your security chief." He leaned his head close. "And I fuck you occasionally, but you never really hear or see me, do you?"

Heat swept her cheeks. She cast her gaze toward Dagr, who once again was staring back from too far away to know what precisely was being said, thank the stars. A frown darkened his expression as he glanced from her to Baraq.

Taking heed of Dagr's silent warning, Baraq dropped his hand away. "He seems an honorable man," he said quietly, "but it doesn't mean that every one of us isn't expendable. And I wouldn't blame him."

"I wouldn't either," she murmured.

"You!" Dagr gestured to Baraq. "The hand truck is yours. When the portal opens, you will pull it through and take it into the hold."

The hand truck he gestured toward held two large containers of ore. Dagr's steady gaze dared Baraq to say he couldn't manage the feat.

"Why so much?" Honora asked while Baraq fisted his hands and strode toward the wheeled sled.

Dagr didn't acknowledge her with a glance or word. A large redheaded Viking had motioned to him, then strode to Dagr and grasped his forearm, leaning in to whisper in his ear.

Dagr's brows pressed together in a furious scowl, and he nodded. He eyed the locator clip attached to his fur vest. "We still have thirty minutes before Cyrus retrieves us." He stomped away.

Honora gave Baraq a quick glance before following, curious about what had annoyed Dagr now.

He left the cavern and strode through a long ice-block corridor that opened into a barracks of sorts, one dug out of ice and lined with skins. *Gods, they are a primitive bunch.*

A group of Vikings, all dressed in thick, deep-space gear but wearing animal-fur hats atop their long hair, was gathered around a bleacher of stairs that led down toward a large fire pit. At the bottom step sat the female warrior, her arms crossed over her chest and her expression as angry and deadly as any Dagr had ever leveled at Honora.

"Why isn't she strapped inside a snow-eater and on her way back to Skuldelev?" Dagr asked the men circled around the female.

"She disabled it," the older, redheaded man said, making a face. "She had to have done it when she said she needed to use the privy. I watched for her, I swear, but never saw her come around the front of the vehicle."

Dagr ground his teeth. "Get another."

The redhead blushed. "All three engines have been tampered with, milord."

Dagr's fists bunched at his sides. "Woman!" he bit out, staring at the smirk growing on the female warrior's face. "It doesn't matter how many times you sabotage the vehicles. You are not returning to the ship. I would have you safe and out of trouble."

She pushed off the bench and faced Dagr, hands braced on her hips. "But you won't be here to keep watch over me. Do you really think any of these men can keep me imprisoned?"

Dagr glared down his nose. "I could have you tossed into the dungeon."

The woman snorted, her lip curled higher. "You don't think I couldn't find a way out, couldn't prey on one of your men, lull him into thinking I am harmless and then escaping?"

"To what object?" Dagr asked, raking a hand through his hair and seeming at the end of his patience.

"You have something here worth stealing. *Worth warring over.* If you do not take me with you, I will tell my father about your machine."

Dagr's teeth ground again and a pulse ticked beside one eye.

Honora watched wide-eyed as the woman stood toe-to-toe with the Viking king and didn't flinch once.

Baraq blew a silent whistle beside her.

At the sound, Honora turned to find his gaze glued to the warrior-woman.

"Princess, we haven't time for this," Dagr growled.

Honora raised her brows at her address. Another noble. Fuck.

"'Tis the truth, we don't," the princess said.

The two Viking nobles stood nose to nose, their backs unbowing and their faces rigid with determination. Honora felt a twinge of jealousy for the other woman's courage and for the fact Dagr seemed impressed as well.

His scowl cleared. His gaze swept the woman from head to foot before he grunted in disgust. "You'll return to the ship."

The warrior-woman smiled.

Dagr shook his head, his jaw tightening again. His furious gaze left the blonde, and then landed on Honora. "You will come with me, *now*."

Honora jerked at the intent in his voice, then gave Baraq a quick, worried glance.

"Careful," he whispered.

She followed Dagr as he stomped through the sleeping quarters of the barracks, noting the sparse, primitive conditions. Stone floors, ice-block walls and ceilings, animal skins lining the walls, except for the occasional square cut to allow natural light to beam through the ice walls.

Dagr stopped abruptly beside a small, curtained sleeping room and pushed her inside. He flipped the curtain closed, then turned slowly toward her, his dark brows lowered into a fierce, frightening scowl. "Strip."

Honora's eyes widened. "It's damp and cold in here."

Dagr kicked the cover from the fire pit at the center of the room and warm light blazed from the bottom. He took a step closer. "Now."

She backed away, but there wasn't anywhere to go except backward to the narrow shelf-bed.

He opened his belt and shoved down his trousers, freeing his cock, which was already hard and thick.

"Anyone walking by will know what we do," she whispered, staring at his erection.

"They already know. Are you worried your guardian will know?"

Footsteps passed the curtain, drawing her gaze. "Are you talking about Baraq—" She closed her mouth. Just the mention of her security chief caused Dagr's jaw to flex. "We haven't time for this," she said, trying another tack.

"We have just enough time for me. Whether you find your pleasure depends on how much longer you argue."

She should have been furious, should have cringed against the thought of fucking in such a crude place with men walking past them just feet away.

Instead, the sensual heat that hadn't cooled since he'd taken her earlier flared brighter. The fierce intensity of his glare was really all it took. Nothing about Dagr was soft or easy. Nothing done in halves. He fucked the same way he fought—with every fiber of his will and body.

She removed her jacket and opened her trousers, then unzipped the skin-suit and pushed it down until the clothing pooled over the tops of her boots.

"That's good enough," he said. "Bend over the bed."

She knelt, breathing hard, her upper body bared but unable to spread her legs very far apart. Cool air hit her pussy and she gasped.

Behind her, fingers found her opening, dipped inside, then retreated. His hot cock prodded her and pushed inward, crowding through her raw, inner tissues and causing her to hiss between her teeth.

Dagr's fingers bit into her hips, but he held still. "I shouldn't care that I cause you pain," he said, his voice so tense it shook.

"Do you care?" she gasped, rolling her face into a clean but scratchy blanket. Even though he'd hurt her, her pussy released a flood of arousal, seeping around his cock to ease his way.

He didn't answer, but a few moments later, he began moving slowly in and out, his cock gliding in silky, moist heat. His hands continued to hold her hips in a merciless grip.

Her breaths deepened; her sex melted all around his cock. She didn't want to give him any response at all, but she was too aware of who held her, too excited because everything she'd learned about the man only increased her interest.

Already her body recognized his rule and surrendered, moistening her channel in honeyed welcome, rippling inside to caress his length and pull him deeper.

"How does it feel," he said, his voice hoarse, "to know I fuck you in the place where your whore fucked my brother?"

She froze, dread cramping her belly. "What?"

"Your Outlander whore waited for him here," he said, slamming deep. "She waited until he was naked and deep in her thrall. Then you transported them to your ship." He slammed again, grunting with the effort and so deep he touched her cervix.

Honora hissed again, fisting the covers. "I never saw the prisoners arrive. My crew didn't operate the transporter. Uh!" She sank her face into the bedding, biting her tongue because each stroke increased the friction building in her core. "My orders were to allow them secrecy," she said breathlessly. "I didn't know how the retrievals were accomplished."

Dagr's hands readjusted, cupping her ass and squeezing harder; then he hammered her again and again. "It was accomplished like this . . . engaged in sex . . . my brother too stupid with desire to care whether the sex-thrall acted oddly."

He slowed his thrusts and lay over her back to whisper in her ear. "Do you think she even let him come before she activated the transporter? Should I let you find your pleasure, *Lady Captain*?"

Eight

Honora dragged in ragged breaths, trying to hold on to the conversation, knowing he was revealing something to her, knowing he wanted to punish her, but she was too close to the edge to really hear him.

"Don't stop." She gasped.

"I should stop. I should ring my cock and pull away now . . . just to punish you. But I won't because I can't. Your pleasure is mine." He slammed harder, slapping the skin of her bottom with his belly and groin.

Anyone in the barracks would hear them, but she was past caring. The sensations were too delicious, too powerful—like his strong, jarring strokes that crowded her channel to bursting.

"Dagr, gods, end it," she cried out, bunching the blanket in her fists.

"Finger yourself," he growled.

Her face sank into the bedding and her fingers rooted between her legs to circle on the hard little knot. The friction he built with his harsh thrusts and the coiling tension she drew with each frantic swirl had her arching, moaning, mindless while he hammered her pussy until at last she screamed.

When hot cum jetted inside her, she slumped beneath him, breathing hard, her nipples raw and itching from the blanket she'd writhed upon.

His breaths gusted against her neck, a jagged texture to them that she found faintly alarming. She wished for a kiss, a little softness after the harshness of this taking, so she was disappointed when Dagr pulled away, rising swiftly behind her.

"Dress."

"Strip, dress," she muttered with a wag of her head and pushed off the bed. She bent to grab her uniform from the floor and tugged it over her curves.

She went still when she noted the pallor of his face. His eyes glittered angrily as they swept the room. Bleakness that squeezed her heart entered his expression.

He'd lost his brother here. He'd wanted to punish one of those responsible, but she knew now he couldn't be completely ruthless. At least not with her.

The leader of the Wolfskins could have taken his pleasure and been done. Could have humiliated her in untold ways. He could have strangled her and no one would blame him.

Instead, he'd allowed her pleasure, holding back until she came. Not that she thought for a second she really knew what was inside him or what kind of man he truly was. But she was beginning to learn.

Tugging the slide upward to close her suit, she wondered how she would have treated him if the roles had been reversed, but couldn't imagine it. She had no family—only a father who had disgraced himself and whose memory she had sought to obliterate from the annals by being the best, the most loyal of officers.

In the end, her loyalty hadn't been prized, hadn't been respected. It had been turned on her. She'd been sacrificed, and for what?

"Are you ready?"

Lost for a moment, she glanced up, blinking, but firmed her mouth at his cold expression and nodded.

Back at the cavern entrance, Honora colored beneath Baraq's knowing glare. He didn't say a thing, just turned silently to follow Dagr into the cavern and bent to pick up the handle of the hand truck where it rested in the dirt.

At the time promised, the portal opened in the center of the cavern, growing from a small blue, two-dimensional circle and stretching outward. It lit up beside Dagr, the blue and white light so bright it blinded.

Honora squinted against it. Dagr waved her through. She glanced to Baraq, who gripped the handle of the hand truck with both hands behind him. He leaned forward, gritting his teeth, and dug his toes into the dirty, pulverized stone on the cave floor, pulling so hard muscles bulged across the tops of his shoulders, and his face reddened with the strain. But the dark scowl on his face said he wouldn't be defeated.

He dug deeper and took a step forward, then another.

Honora glanced at Frakki and caught him watching Baraq, a reluctant smile tugging at one corner of his mouth. He noticed her stare and shrugged. "He would make a good Icelander."

Honora shook her head. Men, no matter the race, were all the same. She stepped through the portal and onto the solid metal flooring in the hold of her ship.

A quick glance around told her all was well, all systems running along nicely. But her crewmen were still lined up in two rows to the side of the long cargo bay.

Baraq growled behind her, pulling the truck, his body bent

toward the floor, but he didn't stop until Dagr shouted, "You are clear." He let go of the handle and stood, his chest heaving, head hanging.

Dagr strode up beside him and clapped his shoulder. Then he glanced behind him at the Viking princess. "Birget, come with me."

Honora stiffened, an unwanted flash of jealousy causing a twinge inside her chest.

Baraq stared after the blond woman, still gasping for breath, then looked up at Honora. "Don't lose sight of who he is and what he seeks. If he makes use of you, don't let it confuse you into thinking you can earn his trust."

"You think I don't know it's just sex?"

"Do you? I saw your face when you came back from the barracks. You looked shattered. Not an expression you ever wore after I had you."

Frakki pushed at Baraq's shoulder. "Move along. We need the portal cleared."

Honora glanced back and saw that the men were being herded into the portal, blinking out as they passed. Her breath hitched in her chest. She couldn't stand idly by and watch her people disappear.

"Why so many?" she asked, rushing to Frakki who stood to the side of the portal and watched her men file through.

Frakki pushed her behind him.

Her people filed by, white-faced, their gazes straight ahead and not meeting hers. After the last man passed through, the portal closed.

"Why aren't Baraq and I going with them?" she asked Frakki.

Frakki didn't answer her. He gave a wave to Cyrus, who still stood in the window of the transporter room.

Baraq grasped her forearm and pulled her away, walking her toward the ladder. He leaned in to whisper, "Dagr knows we're smart enough to figure out that we don't really have anything left to fight him for at this point. And he needs us to help run this ship. Cyrus has likely told him how few of us are really needed to navigate and keep basic systems running. We, the ones left behind, will be doing the grunt work."

Honora inhaled. "The air stinks here. He was right to move the men off. Atmospherics couldn't wash the air fast enough to accommodate everyone."

Baraq grunted. "Their world. It's harsh. But you're right. It smelled good." He placed his hand at the small of her back, and gave her a look that dared her to reprimand him.

She'd never have allowed the familiarity in public before, but she wasn't the captain anymore, and she didn't know what role she could assume. Baraq and she were in the same boat, and it was nice to share the ride with a friend, with someone she could trust.

The next time Eirik awoke, clothes were tossed at him through the bars.

"Dress quickly," Fatin said, her words clipped.

The clothes would certainly help ward off the chill, but he didn't like the greedy way her gaze ate him up when he shoved back the blanket.

He also didn't like the way his cock stirred, less disgusted with her interest than big Eirik was. "So she is beautiful," he muttered, staring at his cock, "but she is also a psychotic bitch."

Fatin's laughter was low and dirty. "Hurry. And don't worry about your cock. He's just what I want."

A chill bit his spine, but he grabbed the clothes as he scanned the area. She was armed this time . . . She was going to open the door of his cage.

As though she read his mind, she smirked. "This weapon will drop you like a stone," she said, bracing an elbow at her hip to raise the nozzle of the weapon skyward. "And I do know how to use it. I'd just hate wasting prime procreational material," she said, gazing at his cock again.

He pulled the trousers she'd provided over his hips. They were gathered at the waist rather than buttoned or tied, for ease of removal, he guessed. He pulled the knit shirt over his head, and before he'd finished tugging it to his hips, the gate of his cage clicked and creaked open.

Fatin waved him out and gestured for him to walk toward the other end of the cargo bay.

His bare feet padded on cool metal flooring. He walked past other cages, catching glimpses of the men with whom he hadn't had a chance to speak and share intelligence because he'd been unconscious so long. They didn't meet his gaze, which worried him.

This cargo hold was smaller, dirtier than the one he'd originally woken inside. The air smelled like petroleum and sulfur. Had they been transporting crude explosives?

The nozzle of her stun rifle poked at his back. "Turn right at the end of the walkway."

Eirik studied his surroundings, committing them to memory. If he got the chance to stage a mutiny, he'd need to know everything he could about this ship.

He turned right into a brightly lit, sterile room. A middle-aged woman in a white apron and gloves waited there, her eyes widening as they slid over his frame. "You weren't kidding when you said he was a prize. Get him into the stocks."

Fatin poked at his back, but he dug in his heels. He saw the contraption the woman meant and understood its use. "I will not," he gritted out furiously.

Fatin walked around him. "You will, or Miriam there will stick you again."

He cast a glance at the other woman. She held a long stick with a syringe at the end, much like the sticks his own people used when they conducted studies of the animals in the subterranean forests. No doubt the syringe contained a sedative.

"Do you really want to lose more days?" Fatin said softly.

Eirik lifted his upper lip in a snarl, but dragged his feet on the ground as he headed toward the stocks. Scowling to let her know how much he hated this, he raised his hands while she closed the locks around his wrists.

Miriam leaned her stick against a counter. Fatin placed her weapon on a bench. Then she strode toward Eirik and grasped the waist of his pants and dragged them down.

Eirik ground his teeth, heat filling his cheeks at the indignity. He stood with his pants around his ankles and still his cock rose, eager for Fatin's attention.

Miriam approached with a vial in her hand. "Do you want me to milk him?"

Eirik gave Fatin a dark glare. She snorted, then shook her head. "I'll handle this. I know what he likes." She leaned close and dropped her voice. "Don't I, lover?"

"Why are you doing this?" he asked just as quietly.

Her smirk faded. "You have something the Consortium will pay top dollar for."

"My seed?"

"And your handsome body. They'll steal your seed, but they'll also enslave you for their pleasure."

"How can you do this to a man?"

"You never questioned how Fatin the sex-thrall came to be in the miner's camp. Did you care? Give it even a moment's thought?" Her lips curled in disgust.

Eirik went still, watching her expressions and realizing she had reasons other than money for what she did. Reasons he probably didn't want to discover, because he didn't want to feel guilty over killing her.

Fatin wrapped her fingers around his cock, and Eirik sucked in a sharp breath, wishing he could resist, but already his balls hardened.

She drew the bench closer and sat at its edge, then leaned in and lapped at the crown of his cock. "They will love your body," she murmured. "Maybe I will pay for its use when I visit Helios."

Her mouth clasped around him, suctioning, her tongue sliding over his cap, tucking into the sensitive slit. A small, warm hand wrapped around his scrotum and gently massaged and tugged his balls.

His thighs tightened; his buttocks tensed.

She grabbed his hips, centered herself, and bobbed forward, taking his cock deep into her mouth, past her tongue to the back of her throat. Then she swallowed, the action kissing his head, and she loosened inside, taking him deeper, taking all his length into her throat while she sucked harder. It felt as though she would suck the seed from his balls, so strong were her rhythmic pulls.

He tried to resist, tried to think of something other than the way she worked him. He thought of Dagr and wondered what he was doing, whether he'd figured out what had happened. His brother wouldn't rest until Eirik was found. How he wished he'd stayed with the men at the fire pit trading stories. How he wished he'd read the deception in Fatin's eyes and thrust her away before she'd pricked him.

In the end, he couldn't fight her. Especially not when her hand released his balls, and fingers tucked between his buttocks. He roared when she penetrated his ass and fondled the gland inside him that conquered his control.

He shot his seed into her mouth, his body bucking, rutting wildly until he'd given her everything she wanted of him.

Fatin rose, held out her hand for the vial and spat into it. "We have to know you're fertile."

Creamy liquid slipped down the side of the clear glass tube. His seed. "That's all I am," he gasped.

"A whore? Yes." She smiled, but it didn't reach her eyes. "You'll make me rich." She came closer and kissed his mouth.

Too wrung out to resist, he slanted his face and kissed her back, then rested his forehead against hers. "You do know you've kidnapped a noble," he said quietly, locking his gaze with hers. "You'll be hunted. This won't be kept quiet."

She licked his earlobe and whispered, "That's my hope, Eirik Wolfskin."

Dagr followed Birget as she stomped down the main artery corridor toward the bridge. Birget's backside swayed temptingly as she swaggered, but not tempting for the reason she might have hoped.

His hand itched to leave it reddened. The girl was spoiled. Her father hadn't done her any favors. When his brother returned, they'd have to have long talk about how best to deal with *Princess* Birget.

"You're not going to the bridge," he called after her. "You will only cause a distraction there."

She slowed and craned her head around, a brow rising. "Then where am I to be? Everyone else has their task."

"You were so eager to be aboard this ship, I'm assuming any purpose will serve. We have set the females of their crew to serve us in the canteen. You can supervise them."

"You want me to watch the women?" she asked, her voice rising. Her face suffused with brilliant color.

Dagr continued, speaking in a calm, even tone as though he hadn't a clue how furious she was. "My men and the remaining prisoners must be fed. Make sure food is taken to all of them at regular intervals. Is that too much responsibility to entrust you with?"

Her lethal glare had the corners of his lips twitching.

"Why not have your captain set to the task? She is also female and has caused even more trouble than I have."

Irritated now, Dagr curved his lips downward to let her see his displeasure. He wasn't accustomed to having his decisions questioned or to justifying his actions. "I need to keep her close. She knows how the ship operates and her presence ensures the good behavior of her remaining crew."

She planted her hands on her hips and let loose. "Just because you fuck together does not mean you should put her above me. I am a princess, not a scullery maid."

Dagr stepped so close she had to tilt back her head to meet his gaze. "You are a woman who disobeyed the man responsible for your care," he said, narrowing his eyes. "If you wish a different sort of punishment, I will oblige you."

The flame in her cheeks crept down her neck. Fury glittered in her eyes. However, she took a step back and straightened her shoulders. "I will see to the meals, but don't expect me to remain in the kitchen all the time."

"Make sure everyone is fed and I'll be satisfied."

She gave a curt nod. "Which way is the kitchen?"

He lifted a brow and pointed down a corridor. "Acquaint yourself with the ship." Then he turned on his heel, giving in to a grin because of the chagrin in her expression. Birget wasn't accustomed to being governed. And she hadn't liked being reminded of a first tenet of warfare—reconnoiter your surroundings.

Heading back to the command deck, he pondered another

problem. Birget hadn't hidden her jealousy of the pretty captain. And he hadn't missed Honora's expression when he'd left with Birget. Women's squabbles weren't something he wanted to be in the middle of. With two strong-minded women in close quarters, he wondered if he shouldn't take measures to ensure they were both kept busy.

Once through the door, he spotted the large Outlander he'd battled. The man turned to watch as Dagr entered the bridge, his back stiffening.

Honora kept her gaze on the viewing screen to the front of the deck, watching the stars and the spinning blue planet below them.

"It is beautiful," he said.

"It's not real," she said, still staring at the screen. "Not an actual view of space. It's a bioluminescent reflection. Microscopic creatures live inside that screen."

He grunted and moved away.

Although most of the chairs were empty, the room still felt too small, choking. He stirred restlessly, walking the aisle in a circle, eyeing Honora—eyeing Frakki, who sat in one of the vacated chairs, looking ridiculous in his paint and battle gear with an expression of puzzlement on his face at the chirping lights that sounded from the console.

"Don't hammer them off," Dagr said dryly.

Frakki snorted, then grinned at Dagr. "Damned annoying."

Dagr aimed a glance at Honora, who watched him from beneath the fringe of her dark lashes. "Would you help?"

Her back stiffened, but in the end she shrugged and walked toward his second-in-command, leaning over him and tapping keys to silence the alarms.

Dagr halted beside Cyrus. "Where is my cousin?"

"Grimvarr wouldn't sit still. His pacing made me nervous, so I set him to guarding the ore."

"The ore doesn't need guarding. Who among their crew can even open the containers?"

Cyrus smiled. "He doesn't know that. He has another with him to keep him from being too bored and getting into trouble."

Dagr grunted again. Bored wasn't what he felt. Itchy was a more apt description. "You look comfortable," he said wryly. It was likely Cyrus hadn't stirred except for the trip to the transporter room since they first took the ship.

Cyrus raked a hand through his hair and grimaced. "Forgot how much I missed this. I'll get up shortly and make rounds to check on all the systems."

"What about the crew? Can we make use of them?"

"If we keep the nerve centers guarded, they can't hack in to get a message out or to disable anything. And if they think you'll harm their captain, that should be enough to keep them in line." Cyrus's lips twisted in a half smile. "But, Dagr, you can't look at her the way you do and convince them you'll slit her throat."

Dagr grunted again, knowing the woman was reducing him to primal communication. Just looking at her made him feel savage.

"She intrigues you," Cyrus murmured.

"She is strong, not so much physically, but she is self-possessed. Sure of herself. I like that."

"She's also so attractive a dead man would sit up and take notice. More than a match in bed even for a Viking?"

Dagr grimaced. "Are you counseling me?"

"I wouldn't dare." Cyrus smiled.

"Concern noted."

"Take my seat," Cyrus said, pushing up from the captain's chair. "You won't be able to access the systems . . . unless you want to, that is. I can enter you in the database too."

"No, I have no desire to command the ship." He clapped Cyrus's shoulder. "It's why I have you."

Cyrus bowed his head. "I'll be back shortly."

"Take that one with you," Dagr said, indicating the large Outlander who couldn't keep his gaze off his captain.

"His name is Baraq Ata," Cyrus murmured. "By the way he fidgets every time you disappear with the lovely Honora, I believe he's been intimate with her."

Dagr breathed deeply, eyeing the man. "Give him to the princess. She wants to learn the ship. He can be her guide."

Cyrus laughed. "Do you think to make them bond over their hatred for you? That could be dangerous."

"Birget would never betray a Viking for an Outlander's cause, no matter how angry she is with me. Baraq will do nothing to expose Honora to harm. But their mutual distrust will keep them busy."

Cyrus shook his head, then laughed softly. Turning, he lifted a hand. "Baraq!"

Baraq's guarded gaze sliced toward Cyrus. Cyrus beckoned him, then strode off the deck, not waiting to see if Baraq would follow.

Baraq looked at Dagr, but Dagr didn't betray a thought with his expression, letting the man make up his own mind whether this was at his behest.

"Best not keep him waiting, Baraq," Honora said softly.

Baraq tightened but ducked his head in a reluctant nod.

Honora swung to Dagr, and raised a finely arched eyebrow. The woman was far too clever.

Remembering Cyrus's warning, Dagr dug his fingers into the chair's arms and hardened his expression.

Nine

Birget eyed the silent man striding in front of her. He was tall for an Outlander, certainly taller than she. Swarthy skin and black eyes lent him an edgy, masculine, and almost sinister beauty, which made her nipples tingle and her core soften. A wretched reaction to a man who was far, far beneath her notice. Still, the steadiness of his gaze when he'd been assigned her, and then the stubborn tilt of his jaw, spoke of an inner core of strength. Hel, even his close-cropped black hair appealed. She had the overwhelming urge to scrape her fingers through it and see if the texture was as silky as it looked.

"Shouldn't you be telling me what you're showing me?" she asked, wanting to break the silence. He'd barely spoken a word since Cyrus left them together.

"Do you really care what you're seeing?" he muttered, glancing back.

She shrugged, really not all that interested. But she did want him talking. His accent was lilting to her ears, his tone deep and naturally sensual. "I guess I should care. It seems as though we will be here a while. I could get lost," she said, her tone teasing, but he didn't smile. Which annoyed her. She was flirting for the first time in her life and he didn't seem to notice. Maybe she should have practiced more.

They strode down another gray metal corridor with oval doors on each side. She sighed, bored and getting angrier by the moment. Dagr was trying to keep her busy and away from the command deck where everything was happening. And the man he'd assigned to accompany her had no respect for her rank or interest in her as a woman. Perhaps she should challenge him to a fight. At least then she could lose a little of the tension that kept her mood brittle.

Baraq halted unexpectedly, and she nearly plowed into his back.

He turned and speared her with a dark scowl. "Why are you with them? You're the only woman among them. And it's obvious Dagr wanted to drop you on the planet. Why would you resist?"

Again, Birget shrugged. Truth be told, she'd defied Dagr because she enjoyed annoying the Wolfskin leader. "If he had left me behind, I'd have been under guard, every movement and word weighed and judged. I am not a Wolfskin, you see."

He rolled his eyes. "That's supposed to mean something to me?"

"I come from a kingdom at war with the Wolfskins. The Black Wolf is my sworn enemy."

"And yet you fought to accompany him."

"Why should he and his clan have all the glory?"

Baraq shook his head, his lips curling in disgust. "Since you are all probably going to die, I don't see the precious glory."

She halted and looked him up and down. "You seem like a warrior."

Baraq planted his hands on his lean hips. "And I can't be a warrior if I'm not willing to die for a lost cause?"

"It's not lost. We will prevail."

"Because you believe your Black Wolf is invincible?"

She snorted, straightening as tall as she could to make her gaze level with his. "No, we will prevail because you are weak."

His jaws ground together. "Really, Princess?"

Birget arched a brow. "Look at you. Did you see how easily we took you, with swords and fists against your modern stun guns?"

"You surprised us. That's all. But without one of our own, a traitor to us, you couldn't continue to hold this ship." His hand waved in dismissal. "You haven't the necessary skills or training."

"Are you saying we are stupid?" she bit out. "Too primitive to best you?"

"I'd be a fool to say that," he drawled, "seeing as how you're the one holding the weapon."

She stepped closer, so close her chest grazed his. "Do you want to go to the brig? There's plenty of room there now."

"Not particularly."

"Would you like to have sex with me?"

Baraq blinked. "I beg your pardon?"

Perhaps she'd been a little too militant. She lightened her expression and lowered her eyelids a fraction. "There's not much else to do aboard this ship."

"So why not choose one of your superior specimens of manhood?"

She canted her head and sniffed at his neck. "They don't smell as good. You smell sweet. You wear perfume like a woman."

His body stiffened. "I wear a man's scent."

She leaned back her head to see his expression. "To entice your pretty captain?"

His cheeks flushed, and his eyes glittered angrily. "Is there something else I can show you? The latrines? The waste disposal unit? I can demonstrate their use."

"You could show me this," she said, cupping his cock. "Your suits hug your loins immodestly. I've watched it grow. You want me."

Baraq wrapped his fingers around her wrist and dragged it slowly from his sex, so slowly her fingers traced his entire length through his trousers. The man was semi-aroused. So why did he fight her?

"Don't you understand the word *no*? I may be aroused, but I still have the choice of whether I act on a physical response to a woman."

She tugged her arm, trying to free herself, but he held her a moment longer before he opened his fingers.

Birget spun on her heels and headed back toward the hold.

"Woman, we've already been there," he called after her. "You have no sense of direction."

"I'm sure one of your crewmates will be more than willing to give me what I want."

She widened her stride, head held high, but she didn't get far before he caught the top of her shoulder and spun her. He pushed her against the corridor wall, knocking the breath out of her, which excited her beyond all good sense.

"Why is it that I think this has nothing to do with me, and everything to do with your leader?" Baraq said, crowding his lean, muscular body closer to hers. "Will he care if you fuck your way through the crew?"

She tightened her jaw and narrowed her eyes.

He shoved his knee between her legs and slid it upward until his hard thigh pressed against the juncture of hers. "Will he care?"

"What is it to you why I do this?"

"Because I'm only interested in fucking you if he will care."

Birget huffed out a breath, eyeing the rigid cast of his features. He was every bit as angry with the wolf as she was. Was it because of the woman?

Birget gave herself a mental shake. She didn't really care why. Only that she'd have him and make sure Dagr knew she didn't give a damn about keeping her virtue intact for her husband. She'd have preferred taking Dagr as a lover, just to make sure Eirik always knew he'd had her first. But this man would do.

Already her body heated to the harsh set of his jaw and the strength of the thigh tucked so close to her sex.

She bit her lip and rubbed her pussy on him, liking the way the rough wool of the trousers she'd borrowed scraped against her folds. Her sex was moistening, her clitoris swelling.

"You're called Baraq," she whispered, unwilling to fuck him without at least names being exchanged. Sex for revenge's sake needn't be a cold act.

"Baraq Ata." His eyes darkened, and he slid his curved forefinger underneath her chin and tilted her head toward his. "And you?"

Such a small, but tender action. And it caused her sex to flood with moisture. Was that why he did it? Because he wanted her fully aroused, or because he valued the gift she would give him? "I am Birget."

"Sounds harsh," he whispered. "And yet your skin is soft, your curves feminine."

"It means 'protector.' Our language always sounded harsh and primitive to your people. You tried to stamp it out. Made us adopt yours. But we kept our names, and some of the old ones preserve the language for the day we return to Midgard."

"Do you really want to talk history right now?" he said, his lips hovering just above hers.

"No." But she was a little nervous. His hands roamed her body, delving beneath the layers of fur and wool to glide over her back and sides, seeming to shape her curves with firm caresses that pulled her closer and made her gasp with the pleasure of the sensation.

"I want a bed beneath your back," he rumbled, dragging his lips along her cheek.

"Hurry."

He lowered his thigh from between her legs, grabbed her hand, then pulled her toward a corridor, up a circular ladder to another constrictive passageway. They arrived breathless and grinning in front of a door that he swept open and gestured for her to enter. The room was small, smaller than the room that housed her clothing at home. But there was a bed, the blanket pulled taut, the pillow fluffed, the casings free of any wrinkles. A soldier's neat and meticulous bed.

He closed the door behind them and strode toward the bed, pulling back the covers, then turning to her. His hands made quick work of the laces that held together the fur vest and the tunic beneath it. When he found the metal breastplate beneath her clothing, he raised an eyebrow, but didn't pause as he raised it over her head. Then he eyed the stretchy cloth she'd used to bind her breasts close to her chest and reached for the knife at her side.

She inhaled sharply, having forgotten about her weapons and the fact that she was alone with a warrior who might be able to take her, but his steady gaze challenged her not to move as he pulled the knot tied over the binding and cut it. Her hand clutched the fabric against her chest. Her harsh breaths shivered through her.

When he slowly slid her blade back into the sheath, she couldn't take her gaze from his eyes because they smoldered, the slow slide of the blade drenched in sensual tension so ripe, so compelling, that a curl of heat tightened around her core. She squeezed her thighs together and dragged shivering breaths between her pursed lips.

His hand covered the one she held against her chest, and he cupped the back of her head with the other and tilted it. He would kiss her now. She knew because his gaze fell to her lips. She wet them with her tongue, eager to feel the press and warmth.

But before he bent to take her mouth, he squeezed her hand and pulled gently. She released the cloth that whispered to the floor.

He inhaled and cupped one breast, his thumb sliding over the pink crest, causing the nipple to tighten. His gaze met hers. He bent slowly, his lips sliding over hers, then opening.

She opened to him as well, accepting the thrust of his tongue, then sucking to draw it deeper, because her body was beginning to rock against the erection bulging at the front of his uniform. She needed something of his inside her.

Baraq broke the kiss first and turned her toward the bed built into the wall. When she stood with her knees against the mattress, he pulled the rest of her clothing away, and then pushed her down to sit on the edge.

He stood back, toed off his boots, shoved down his trousers. The skin-suit revealed his sex, molding around the shaft that filled and rested against one thigh. He released the fastening at the top of his collar and slid it down the suit, peeling it open. His chest was broad, the hair covering it as dense as a Viking's but straighter, silkier-looking. She wanted to touch it to discover its texture for herself.

When he pushed the suit the rest of the way off and straightened, she couldn't look away from the stalk rising from his groin—thick, with bluish veins that ran up and across the length of him. The skin that stretched around his cock was satiny and brown, the crown swollen and purple. A bead of moisture glistened at his opening, and she leaned forward without thinking and swept it away with her tongue.

His hands sank into her hair, and he pulled back her head. "Not yet," he ground out. "I'd not last long." Baraq turned her again, arranging her lengthwise on the mattress. Then he came down on top of her, his knees enclosing hers, his cock pressing into her belly and causing her core to cramp with need.

Having never had a naked man lying against her body, she blinked at him, surprised at how pleasant and overwhelming it felt. Her nipples tightened, beading harder and scraping his chest every time he took a deep breath. His cock was steamy and hot, digging into her belly, and she knew it would come inside her, had watched men frigging with women in her own keep and knew how it was done, but she couldn't quite believe his would fit inside her. Still, she wished he'd hurry so they could try.

"You're beautiful," he whispered.

"You don't have to praise me," she said, her throat tightening. "I am here. I will do this with you. I won't change my mind."

He smiled even while a frown lowered his brows and once again gave him a sinister appearance. "Are you trying to rush me?"

"And if I were?"

"I'd say I have little power. You and your kind have taken my ship and my captain, but here, I have you trapped beneath me. I want to savor the moment. Any objections?"

The words reminded her how vulnerable she really was. Her mouth dried instantly. She shook her head. "Has anyone ever told you that you look like a demon or a vengeful god?"

He kissed her mouth, then slid his lips along her cheek to her ear. "Never," he whispered. "If I'm so frightening, why me?"

"I didn't say I was scared of you, just that . . . you're so dark. And the way your eyebrows arch like a bird's wing . . ."

She lost her train of thought when he sucked the spot just behind and below her ear. Her toes curled.

Baraq scooted down her body, his tongue flickering, his lips suctioning. When he latched on to a nipple, she nearly screamed because the electric tether stretched between her nipple and her womb tightened and sparked. She undulated beneath him, rolling her thighs against his cock, trying to tell him with her body that she was ready for him to take her.

But he moved farther down, parting her thighs and pushing his knees between them. The wet, succulent sound her pussy made as it opened had her blushing, but he didn't seem to mind and instead chuckled, low and husky, while he fingered her opening, tracing the edges of her folds down and up.

Lulled by the lazy caresses, her head rolled back and forth on the bed; her chest lifted and fell faster with her deepening breaths. He pushed against her inner thighs and she opened them, letting them fall to the mattress. The cooler air licking at her hot sex was enjoyable, but not nearly as much as his feather-soft touches.

When he slid the tip of a finger between her folds, she froze, in an agony of anticipation for him to slide inside her and ease the ache blooming in her pussy.

Birget reached above her for the pillow and shoved it beneath her head to elevate it so she could watch as he thrust his fingers inside.

However, his face moved toward her sex, and she snapped her knees up to halt him, catching his shoulders.

He raised his head, eyebrow arched. "I take it no man has ever taken you in his mouth?"

She shook her head. "I know it's done, but . . . it's embarrassing."

His lips twitched.

"Laugh at me and I swear I'll cut your throat."

His gaze softened. "I would never laugh, Birget. I'm honored to be the first to give you this pleasure."

She thought she should tell him he was her first in every pleasure, but didn't want him stopping, or, worse, mocking her later, after he'd gotten what he wanted from her. Perhaps he wouldn't even notice she was a virgin.

Fingers opened her and tugged her lips upward. He blew air at her sex and it touched her bared clitoris, causing her to jerk.

Wet fingers smoothed over it and again she jerked.

Looking up, he said, "Sensitive, are you?"

She nodded.

"This better?" He held her gaze and stuck out his tongue to lick softly at the round, red button.

Her belly and thighs quivered, but this was bearable and so pleasurable she felt close to bursting. His tongue swirled again, and she came off the mattress. "Baraq!" she cried out as darkness closed in and bright sparks exploded at the center of her vision.

When she stopped groaning and pulsing against his mouth, she realized his mouth suckled her, there between her legs. His tongue soothed her clitoris while his hands, one beneath her ass and the other petting her stomach, squeezed and caressed.

Birget raked her nails through his short hair and he glanced back up her body, lifting his mouth and grinning. "I had to brace you with my weight to keep you pinned to the bed. You're strong."

She met his smile with one of her own. "A Viking's peak isn't a gentle, rolling slope."

"I'll keep that in mind." He kissed her belly and crawled up her body, looking like a lynx stalking prey, and her breath shortened again. This time, she reached up and smoothed her hands over his hard, muscled chest, then spread her fingers to sink into his hair. "It's soft as silk."

"Nothing else is soft," he growled. He dug his cock into her belly to emphasize the point.

She swallowed hard and scraped her fingertips down his belly, enjoying the play of his muscles, rippling as she scratched by. Again her fingers spread and tugged at his hair. "Not so silky here," she said softly. Lord, she could already imagine how the wiry curls would feel against her pussy.

He growled and kissed her hard. He lifted his mouth an inch from hers and stared into her eyes. "Put me inside you."

Breathing hard, her thighs quivering around his hips, she centered the blunt knob of his cock at her entrance, then swirled it around, wetting it.

Air hissed between his teeth and he leaned his forehead against hers. "You're killing me."

"Make it quick," she whispered.

He made a sound between a groan and a laugh, but as soon as she pulled her hand away, he leaned up on arms, dug his knees into the mattress, and slammed inside.

Honora strolled around the bridge, resetting systems to kill the shrill chirping of the alarms.

When they all quieted, Frakki sighed his relief. "My thanks, lady," he said in his oddly growling voice.

She shrugged. "The sound was getting on my nerves too."

He sat at the communications console. How simple a thing it would be to flick the command feed switch and let some ensign on a listening post hear what was happening on her ship.

Cyrus wasn't here. No one would be the wiser. Her hand hovered for a moment, but Frakki lightly wrapped his fingers around her wrist, his gaze boring into hers.

"Think before you act," he said softly, turning his head in Dagr's direction.

She inhaled and nodded, then moved away. If she had flicked that switch, what would it matter? The ship would be surrounded by small, deadly war cruisers, and then the negotiations would begin.

If a reasonable ransom could be reached, her ship would be returned, another cadre of officers transported to assume command.

If the ransom were unreasonable, or if command thought an example should be made, the Vikings would be given a choice to surrender or to die. Her officers' and her crew's lives wouldn't enter into the decision of whether or not to destroy the ship in retaliation and set a more terrible example.

In the end, her life was over whatever the disposition of her ship. Humiliation wasn't the worst that would happen. Execution would be the punishment for her abject failure. She'd been duped into abetting the kidnapping of a prince.

She took a deep, shuddering breath.

"Honora."

Dagr's voice pulled her as though he tugged an invisible chain. The heat of his gaze warmed her. She read desire and connection in that glance.

That sense of connection was no more real than the reflected lights twinkling on the viewing screen. Her reaction made no sense. He wasn't her savior. Still, she walked close enough that he snagged her hand and pulled her onto his lap, tucking her against his body, and she gladly accepted his embrace.

Cyrus strode onto the deck and his eyebrows rose, but he didn't comment.

"Cyrus, tell us both what you found," Dagr said.

Cyrus eyed Honora again but took a deep breath. He stepped off the dais and strolled to the navigator's console, touching the screen to open files he'd stored in the corner. A manifest filled the screen.

"A ship called the *Orion* docked with the *Proteus* yesterday and took on unspecified cargo. The *Orion* is the only ship they've welcomed in weeks. The last resupply was a month ago. It has to be the one the bounty hunters left on."

Cyrus glanced up at Honora, and she nodded, seeing no point in denying it. "I didn't know the name of the ship. Never inquired." She cleared her throat. "Part of the cargo they took on, the 'specified' cargo, was equipment for salvage. They'll trade it at Karthagos, one of the feral colonies along the frontier—a no-man's-land so far as the order of law is concerned."

Cyrus nodded, his glance warming in approval of her cooperation. "I've calculated their speed, using the specs of the transport craft, and figure that we can reach the planet right on their asses. If we can catch them in the port, we can either pay ransom for the Icelanders' return or take the ship in a raid."

They both turned to Dagr, whose face betrayed nothing. His eyes, however, sparkled with excitement. "If you know all this, why aren't we already on our way?"

Cyrus grinned. "I wanted your approval because the moment I cloak the *Proteus*, every Consortium ship in the sector will be hunting for us."

Dagr's hand tightened around Honora's waist, and she felt his chest expand. "When do we reach Karthagos?"

"We'll be snaking through a wormhole later today, same one the civilian transport will have taken. Then we'll skirt the outer edge of the armada guarding the frontier. We should arrive at the planet tomorrow afternoon."

"You say that so casually," Honora said. "And yet I'd wager you've never been there."

Something flickered in Cyrus's eyes, but then he shrugged. "Neither have you."

"We aren't criminals . . . or weren't. Karthagos is a dangerous place. Filled with hybrids, some so far from human they aren't recognizable. If the bounty hunters have friends there, they'll have a huge advantage over us."

Dagr rubbed the back of her neck, soothing her. "They don't have wolves at their backs."

She shared a slow smile with Cyrus. Sometimes, Dagr sounded guileless, but she knew he was far from that. He had an unshakable confidence in himself and his people. Her earlier trick, removing the gravity, had shown her how adaptable they were.

Cyrus turned away. "Turk, set the cloak."

Turk's young face betrayed a moment's doubt. He darted a glance at Honora.

"Do it," she said, quietly. "We're already committed. We'll follow this through." She blinked when his expression cleared and a lopsided grin split his face. She snorted. "Just like a man to think going 'a-pirating' is a grand adventure."

The fall of the cloak was imperceptible, but once it was in place, Turk set a new course, and the planet revolving slowly below them grew smaller on the viewing screen.

Dagr tensed under her.

She leaned back to read his expression. "You've never been off your world before, have you?"

His jaw tightened, and he shook his head.

Honora reached up, cupped his cheek, and looked into his eyes. "It's as much in my own interest as yours to retrieve your brother and the other captives. I'll help you."

"No more tricks?" he asked, his voice sounding slightly strained.

"You have most of my crew on your planet. I wouldn't endanger them for the sake of my pride or my life."

Dagr's hand cradled hers and he brought it to his lips. His kiss was gentle. "Is there anything Cyrus will be needing us for until tomorrow?"

Her mouth curved. "Not a thing he shouldn't be able to handle by himself unless we run across a Consortium ship. But he will need relief."

"Do you need sleep now, Cyrus?" Dagr asked, his gaze never looking away.

Cyrus chuckled. "Maybe later, if one of the women in the kitchens is obliging— Oh, 'sleep' wasn't a euphemism?"

Dagr cut him with a glance that only deepened the other man's laughter, but didn't bother with a reply. He rose from the chair and pulled Honora after him as he strode out into the corridor.

She didn't have a chance to catch her breath. When the lift doors closed, he cupped her ass and brought her up his body, where she wrapped her legs around his waist. When the doors opened, he cupped her head and bent forward beneath the low ceiling, stalking steadily toward her door.

She appreciated having such a strong lover. Baraq had been the strongest until now, and thrilling in his own way, but he'd been too aware of the difference in their ranks. Dagr didn't give a damn that she was captain of her own vessel, that she commanded a crew, had bested countless other hopefuls to earn her station.

He carried her through her door and took the three steps to her narrow bed and set her on her feet. His hands made quick work of his clothing. "How did Baraq take you on such a small bed?"

Honora blinked, surprised he knew about her affair with her security officer. She dropped her own clothing on the floor. "His bed is no bigger than mine. Bent knees shorten the frame. And you can put the pillow against the wall and sit."

He snorted. "When we are done, I will take you on a real bed."

When we are done . . . He talked like they had a future. But they didn't. However, she didn't mind so much him pretending. "I would like to see this great big bed of yours," she said, stepping in front of him, close enough her nipples grazed his chest. His icy-cold gaze made her quiver, but there was heat in the hands that closed around her waist.

His hands smoothed up her back. One cupped the back of her head, the other a breast, which he molded against his palm.

"I like this. Being naked with you," she whispered.

"I like being inside you much better."

She smiled. "How much do you trust me?"

His eyelids dropped. "I am guessing enough to allow you close to my balls."

She snickered, then bit her bottom lip. "Give me the pillow?"

His chest rose sharply, and he bent to snag the pillow. She grabbed it, and stepped away, dropped the pillow in front of her, and knelt in the middle of it.

Dagr braced apart his legs and turned his hands on his hips as she settled and resettled her knees.

His dark brows drew together in a fierce scowl. "Do you make me wait on purpose?"

"Maybe . . ." She glanced at him from beneath the fringe of her eyelashes. "What will you do if I don't hurry?"

His mouth curved in a wicked smile. "Bestow a woman's proper punishment."

At the word "punishment," her nipples prickled. "I take it that's something most women avoid?"

"Most do."

She bit her lip and tilted back her head. "But you smile."

Dagr cupped her chin and rubbed his thumb over her lower lip. "I smile because I think you would do well with a little discipline . . . applied with care and precision."

Ten

Honora could only stare, her pussy clenching and fluid slipping down to wet her cleft. The shock and heat his statement had produced in her left her slightly shaken.

Dagr pinched her chin, forcing open her lips, grasped his cock just beneath the crown, and brought it to her open mouth. "I want your tongue greeting me."

Honora shivered at the brusque texture of his voice, but never once thought to deny him. Holding his steady gaze, she stuck out her tongue and swabbed the smooth head, breathing deep to inhale the scent of his musk. She tried to bob forward to take more of him inside her mouth, but he held her back, letting her swallow only the tip. She rounded her lips, gripping him below the glans, and sucked. Her tongue stroked the broad head inside her mouth and caught a single bead of ejaculate. The hint of his salty, musky essence made her groan.

She resettled on her knees again, wishing she could sit on her heels to relieve the ache building inside her. Doing so would put her out of reach of his cock, and her mouth watered for more.

He released her jaw but kept his fist around his cock, letting her come only so far down the slick shaft. His fingers combed through her hair, soothing her, and she realized she moaned greedily, that she sounded desperate. And, fucking gods, she was.

She scraped fingernails up his inner thigh, listened to him suck in a breath as she neared his balls. She cupped the hard stones and squeezed gently.

His feet shifted restlessly, landing farther apart. He let go of his cock and both hands cupped the sides of her head, but didn't force her, simply held her as she took him deeper in her mouth. She sank, letting his cockhead glide along her tongue until it hit the back of her throat, and then she swallowed, giving him a caress that had him pulling at her hair.

"*Elskling!* Sweet Frigga . . ."

She came off him, and ran her tongue down one side, then up the other and back down again. She tilted his cock up and licked his balls with long, flat-tongued strokes, wetting them, then swallowing them both, mouthing them greedily while she fisted his cock and pumped it.

Dagr's fingers bit into her scalp and pushed her back until he was free.

His eyes glittered dangerously, and she rose shakily to stand in front of him. The expression he wore—cheeks sharpening to blades, skin reddening with strain—caused her a twinge of unease, but the sexy kind—the kind where a woman knew a man was about to turn her inside out.

He shoved her and she lost her balance, landing in a sprawl sideways atop her mattress, her breath leaving in a whoosh. He moved between her legs, pushing them apart, and knelt on the floor.

Honora came up on her elbows, gasping as his fingers stroked over her folds, then sank deep. Her inner muscles clasped wetly around him, and she watched her belly quiver and jump as he bent to take her in his mouth.

Still on her elbows, she raised her thighs over his shoulders, and let her head fall back, savoring the tug of his lips and the girth of his thick fingers as they fucked inside her again and again.

His head rotated as he lavished her clit with swirls of tongue and nips of teeth. Her thighs shivered on his shoulders, legs tightening to pull at him every time he suckled her hard and brought her to the edge.

His fingers thrust deep; then he turned the pads upward, smoothing over the spot deep inside that made her go wild, bucking against his mouth, kicking her heels against his back.

When he pulled away, she was a quivering mess. "Please," she moaned. "Please, Dagr, fuck me."

"On your knees," he said, his voice grating and tense.

She didn't need to be told twice. She rolled swiftly to her knees and faced her cabin's back wall, reaching up to brace one hand there, because if he slammed into her the way she hoped he would, she didn't want her head hitting.

His hands cupped her bottom, smoothing over the globes, rotating them, parting them. She appreciated the massage, but wanted him to put something inside her where it ached. "Don't tease. Fuck me."

His mouth grazed her bottom, teeth nipped her skin, and she jumped.

"Dagr?"

He slapped her bottom, making her jump. "You are so impatient. Would you have me rush to do your bidding?"

Her cheek stinging, she glanced back, trying to read his

expression, but his features were set, his eyes shadowed. What was the answer he wanted? Fuck yes, she wanted him to rush, but she sensed he tested her. "I don't want to tell you what to do," she lied, then suppressed a sigh of frustration as he turned her body to face him. Was he arranging her and rearranging her on purpose? Or was he really that indecisive?

The thought flitted through her mind, but never took root. When he leaned over her, his mouth an inch from hers, she couldn't help the shiver that skittered up her spine. He wanted to keep her moving, uneasy, guessing at his intentions. The more he pushed her, the less resistance she could muster.

"Do you like it when I command you?" he asked, his voice and sweet breath caressing her ruffled nerves. "Do you want to be taken, Honora?"

"Yes . . ." She groaned against his mouth, her eyelids drifting down.

"Will you be my sex-thrall, *elskling*?"

He spoke so softly she wasn't sure she'd heard him right. But his gaze bored into hers, hot, hard, melting her from the inside out.

The idea of it shocked her, tantalized her. Was this a game? To be a sex-thrall was the lowest of occupations for a woman to take. And yet, to be in his thrall was exactly what she wanted. She licked her lips, delaying her answer.

"Will you obey me, whatever I ask of you?"

Perhaps she could negotiate. "Here, in this room," she whispered. "Yes."

He shook his head. "Not nearly good enough, thrall. If I want sex somewhere else, will you obey me?"

"Dagr . . ." She groaned again.

His mouth drew closer, skirted her lips, and sucked on an earlobe.

She tilted her head, enjoying the sensations of his hot breath gusting against her ear, stirring her hair, the glide of his tongue as he followed the rim of her ear. Then he bit her lobe, causing her to jerk, and pulled away.

His gaze held hers, boring into her, frightening her just a little. "If you want sex . . . with me . . . you must obey."

Blood pounding through her veins, Honora swallowed hard. "I will be yours," she said, her voice deepening with tension. "Wherever you want."

"*When*ever."

She screwed up her face, knowing he'd expect her to keep her promise—no matter what. Could she trust that he wouldn't push her past comfortable limits?

His steady gaze said he knew exactly what flitted through her mind. She drew in a deep breath, understanding that her answer was important, that their relationship, however long it would last, might set off in another direction. What did she ultimately want?

She trembled against him, imagining what surrender would be like. What being owned body and soul by a man like Dagr would mean. Again, her choice came down to trust.

And he hadn't earned it. He'd threatened to behead her the first time they'd met. Had threatened her crew. And yet, even when he'd had the chance, had her alone and at his mercy, he'd seen to her pleasure before his own.

His fingers rubbed her ears; nails scraped her scalp. "It is not such a complicated question."

But it was. And she knew she should take more time, but he wanted an answer, and she needed to give him one. Did he expect her to keep her promise? *Really?*

He wasn't asking for her to swear fealty to him. Wasn't asking her to support his cause. Only to surrender to him as a man.

Heat rolled off his skin, warming her, arousing her. Her pussy melted and throbbed. Already her body was conditioned to do his bidding. What did it matter if she gave him the words?

He nuzzled behind her ear, slicked his tongue along the curve, and sucked her earlobe into his mouth again.

She tilted her head, quivering as he teased her. "Dagr..." she said breathlessly.

"Be my slave, my thrall," he whispered. "Give me yourself, without reservation, without thinking."

Her nipples contracted, growing painfully hard. "I'm afraid."

"Does that excite you?"

She shuddered. "Yes..."

"Be mine..."

She turned her head and glided her mouth along his cheek. "Yes...yes..."

Dagr pulled away, leaving Honora blinking, her legs sprawled open, her chest and face hot and rosy with arousal.

"Please..." she said, her eyes filling, frustration tightening her face.

"Come with me," he said, holding out his hand.

She slid off the bed and looked around for her clothing.

"Leave them," he said, curling his fingers to beckon her.

"But we can't parade naked through the ship. Someone will see...and it's chilly."

"None of your crew will see you, and you won't be cold for long."

Her heart thudded dully in her chest, understanding this was her first test. "What about your men?"

"They will think nothing of your nudity. You will walk behind me and they will know you are enthralled."

Her eyebrows lowered as she reconsidered her promise.

"Do you defy me already?"

"I thought you'd have a little more care for me than to humiliate me."

"There is no embarrassment. My men, should we pass any of them, will admire you, but it is not my purpose to display your capitulation. I only seek more comfortable quarters. There is a larger bed in the spa room."

He'd scouted out the gym? The one truly warm place on the ship. And the one made for physical recreation—of all sorts. "The spa's on the first level at the other end of the ship . . ."

"Your point?"

She took a deep breath. "We'll be crawling down ladders and through hatches to get there."

He curled his fingers again.

A breathless laugh escaped her. "We can hurry, right? You won't make me walk purposely slow."

He grinned, grabbing her hand, and opened her cabin door. The corridor outside was deserted, but he darted out, pulling her behind him.

"You've only been on board a day and already you have me completely throwing away all discipline," she grumbled.

He laughed, and she smiled, bemused at the husky sound. Then he turned away and she had her first glimpse of his back. She sucked in a deep breath. Besides the muscles that bulged away from his spine and widened his upper back and shoulders, a large tattoo of a wolf, teeth bared and leaping upward, stretched from between his shoulders, down his back, the tail wrapping around his waist. The detail was amazing, every hair and muscle defined in black and shades of gray. A wolf to define the leader of the Wolfskins. Honora sucked in another breath and sped behind him down the corridor.

* * *

At the end of the hallway, Dagr looked back and gave her a wink, then climbed down the ladder to the lower level, waiting at the bottom with his hands holding the rings surrounding the ladder while she hesitated at the top. Beyond all good sense, he felt happy and free. Her disgruntlement amused him.

"I can't do this," she hissed.

"You do this every day," he chided.

"I'm not talking about the ladder."

He grinned up and gave her waggle of his eyebrows. "Would you deny me now? Before we've sought our pleasure?"

She wrinkled her nose. "I don't suppose you'd look away."

He didn't move, didn't change his expression, just waited for her to concede, knowing she would.

She descended quickly, and he watched her bottom quiver, her sex, still wet, glisten between her legs.

Her arousal fed his own and his cock rose painfully high, bobbing against his belly as they strode toward the open bay and the small gymnasium tucked at the far corner.

His cousin Grimvarr sat throwing runes in a game of chance with another man, as they guarded the containers. His head turned toward them, his eyes widened, and he climbed quickly to his feet. Both men straightened, their lips twitching as they scanned Dagr's body, then Honora's. He heard her groan behind him, and he winked at his men.

The gym was empty, but he hurried through it, to the room at the back where a low-lying bed that was only slightly thicker than a mat sat in the center of the floor.

"It's meant for massage," she said, coming up behind him.

He eyed a curved bench with two padded steps that stood at the end of the bed, then returned his gaze to Honora with an arch of his eyebrow.

She had the grace to blush, knowing well that her descriptions were only half correct. She cleared her throat. "It's to hold your clothing."

Only they both knew it was just the right height, just the right angle, for sexier forms of recreation.

"Your crew uses this room for sex, yes?"

"As you observed. There's more room here. They book it in advance."

"There aren't many women aboard," he said, his skin crawling at the implications.

"Most Helios aren't strictly heterosexual."

Dagr grunted. Most Vikings wouldn't be so quick to admit their homosexuality or act on it so publicly. "The mattress, it will be comfortable enough for you on your knees?"

She hesitated, one thigh turning toward the other. "Shouldn't we lock the door first? Or at least turn the window to frost."

The windows that opened to the cargo bay were clear, and Grimvarr and his friend still watched. "You can change the glass? Why are the windows ever clear?"

"Sometimes," she said, color flaring on her cheeks, "lovers like to be watched."

"Have you availed yourself of this room before?"

She nodded, her cheeks blazing hotter, but her jaw firmed.

"And have you wanted to be watched?"

She shook her head. "Never, and Baraq and I kept the door locked."

Dagr walked to the far wall and the open cupboard that held stacks of thin linen towels. He pulled out one thick white towel and began ripping it into long strips, keeping her in the corner of his eye, knowing that what he had to say would be easier for her to take if he wasn't looking directly at her.

"In my keep, I am lord. While I have concubines to see to my comfort, I am not exclusively theirs. I have availed myself from time to time of my right to mate whomever I wish. Wives, concubines, I may join my men to take my pleasure with their women. I have the right, and sometimes I exercise it."

He finished tearing the last strip and turned his gaze to Honora, whose eyes had widened. He held the strips gripped inside his fists. "In my culture, virility is prized. Necessary to our survival. I like to be watched. My people find comfort in knowing I am strong and robust in everything I do. There is no shame, no embarrassment." He paused, waiting for her expression to change as realization hit her. When it did, he nearly groaned.

Her body quivered head to foot, nipples shivering and ruched. Her eyes were wide, dark, and glistening in her pale face.

His cock pulsed against his belly, swelling painfully, so full and hard the skin felt ready to burst. "You know what I want," he said, his voice suddenly hoarse.

"You want the men in the hold to watch us?" she said, sounding hopeful.

"I want them to join us, Honora. They will serve us both."

She groaned and shook her head. A look of dismay and, for the first time, a hint of true fear slid across her face.

Dagr's heart softened. Yes, she might be a leader among her own people, but she was woefully unprepared for life outside her ship's thin shell. "Come to me." He stood perfectly still, waiting for her to decide whether she could accept his rule.

Honora looked away, drew deep, ragged breaths between pursed lips to pull strength around her. He knew when she steadied, because her gaze lifted to his and she slowly strode toward him.

When she stood directly in front of him, completely naked in her body and desire, she whispered, "What do you want me to do?"

Dagr leaned down. She tilted back her head. They kissed, only their lips touching for a moment. "I won't ask for more than you can give," he said quietly.

With doubt still shadowing her eyes, she nodded.

"Turn around and put your hands behind you."

Honora glanced down at the strips of fabric he held. "You're going to bind me?" She hadn't thought it possible for her heart to pound faster or harder than it did now and not explode from her chest.

"Do you object?"

She shook her head, feeling a little dazed, and turned, clutching her hands together at the small of her back while he tied them. When he finished she tugged, testing the knots. The binding wasn't too tight, but she'd have to pull at them a while to work herself free.

"Are you all right so far?" he said softly, his hands smoothing over her shoulders and down her arms.

He stood so close she felt the heat radiating from his skin. Her nipples tingled and lengthened, beading painfully hard. "What's next?"

His hands rose in front of her face, holding another strip of cloth.

She sucked in a deep breath. "I don't know if I'll like this," she said, wanting to duck beneath his hands and run, but also intensely curious about what he planned. "I don't know if I'll like not being able to see what you do . . . where your men are."

"You have to trust I will see to your pleasure and your comfort. Do you trust me, Honora?"

"No!" She laughed once. "You've stolen my ship. You hold my crew hostage for my good behavior. How do you expect trust to exist?"

His hands glided around her chest, cupped her breasts, and massaged them gently. "Do you trust me with your body, Honora? With your pleasure?"

Her body rocked, following the gentle roll of his caresses. "I shouldn't."

He kissed her temple, then tied the cloth around her eyes. When he stepped away, she felt abandoned. And immediately her heart quickened, partly from fear because she really shouldn't trust him, and partly because she didn't know what would come next and how he meant to employ his men in bringing her pleasure. She wasn't a prude, had participated in a threesome a couple of times at the academy, but she'd led a pretty circumspect life ever since.

Masculine voices and heavy footsteps entered the room. Once past the door, the men grew quiet, and she guessed that Dagr warned them into silence.

Clothing rustled. Weapons clanked and thudded as they were placed on cabinets.

And then true silence descended. Honora's pulse pounded against her temples as she waited in an agony of anticipation.

Heat approached her chest, the only warning she got before two mouths latched around her nipples and suckled. Honora's mouth dropped open while her sex clenched and her back arched to push her breasts deeper into their mouths.

Another man stepped behind her and rubbed her ass. Easy, nonthreatening, and not very sexual caresses. They soothed while the mouths sucking at her nipples clamped harder and nibbled the small, tortured buds.

She wondered which of them suckled and which stood behind her. From her quick glance when she and Dagr had passed them in the hold, she knew one of the men was his younger cousin, who had reddish brown hair and a beard that skirted his mouth and chin in a thin, sexy line. The other was like most of the Vikings—large, with a bushy blond beard and braided hair. The tickling abrasion from the bushy beard told her which man suckled her left breast, but she still was uncertain about the identity of the one laving her right. Her thighs and buttocks clenched; liquid spilled from inside her and dribbled down her inner thighs.

She imagined how she must look, her slight frame dwarfed by three large Vikings, and she grew so excited she gulped for air.

"Breathe or you'll faint," Dagr whispered into her ear.

So he was behind her, the one fondling her ass. Which meant the two towering giants from the hold were kneeling in front of her. Were they completely nude? Would she know the extent of their attributes or was Dagr only teasing her now?

And then warm hands grasped her shoulders and turned her. Something scraped slowly across the floor and she knew it was the bench. Gooseflesh prickled on her skin. The scraping stopped just in front of her and she was pushed down. Her knees met the upper padded step; her belly lowered to the smooth upholstery.

She was leaned the wrong way, she wanted to say, her head lower than her ass, but she guessed immediately that Dagr wanted her kept off balance, unable to help herself.

Large hands lifted and placed her knees farther apart, opening her sex, parting her ass. She almost blurted there were bindings for her ankles, but what would that reveal?

One palm caressed one cheek, then withdrew. Then a slap landed in the exact spot.

Honora gasped and tensed, wanting to complain, but the warm hand smoothed again, soothing the sharp ache while fingers trailed the length of her pussy.

Something cool and thick slithered over her hip. She couldn't help the shiver that racked her, couldn't help the little moan as it tapped her bottom, and she knew it was a leather belt. It lifted from her flesh, then stung her, the sound loud in the silence.

The belt landed again and again but she bit her lip to hold back her cries. She didn't want Dagr to stop, to think her weak or to know how excited she was becoming. Although how could he miss the fact that she loved it when her bottom rose to seek the next lash?

The stings were painful, but lit a fire beneath her skin that rippled up her spine and through her channel. Again liquid trickled between her legs, wetting her thighs.

A hand found it, rubbed it over her skin. A tongue followed the hand, lapping up the trail to her pussy but halting before touching her swollen folds. Then it swept away again.

She was left there, shivering on the bench, her pussy pulsing, making soft, succulent sounds as it clasped air.

When lips trailed down her back, she arched, trying to press closer, but her thighs quivered too hard, robbing her of the strength to move.

Fingers dug into her scalp, pulling up her head and forcing her mouth open. A musky scent—not Dagr's—assailed her nostrils. Then the blunt, round head of a cock pressed against her lips. She opened eagerly, swallowing the crown and swabbing it with her tongue, but it pulled away and she groaned.

Whose cock was it anyway? Had Dagr really let one of his men use her mouth?

Hands cupped her ass and rubbed oil over the sensitive globes. Her cheeks were parted and more oil drizzled over the crease separating them, and she vibrated on the bench.

"No, no, no . . ." She moaned, knowing what was coming.

The cock pressed against her mouth again, and she opened

obediently, sucking on the crown and nibbling the cushiony head gently, using her tongue to stroke the underside while she began to suction rhythmically, bobbing forward the little she could to consume more of the man's length.

Fingers swirled on her ass, stirring, stirring, making her bottom rise and fall to follow the pleasurable, teasing touches. Then the end of a thick finger pressed against her opening and she froze, moaning around the thick cock filling her mouth.

Fuck, were they all made this way? *And fuck, fuck, fuck . . .* the finger pushed into her ass.

She stiffened on the bench, her mouth tightening on the cock. "Easy, darkling," the man whose cock she sucked crooned, petting her hair and rubbing her cheeks. "Relax. Don't bite."

She grumbled around his cock, but eased her jaw, trying to ignore the digit thrusting deeper into her behind. The cock in her mouth crowded deeper, pushing over her tongue, tapping the back of her throat and withdrawing. "Swallow, Lady Captain. Give me a deep kiss," he whispered.

She'd never be able to look him in the eye again, which meant she'd blush every time she saw either of the younger Vikings. She took a deep breath and worked the back of her throat to swallow, the opening and closing her of throat caressing his cockhead. Then she eased open her jaws, breathed through her nose, and let him push deeper, concentrating on not gagging while he rained praises on her and caressed her cheeks and hair.

In and out he thrust, and she swallowed him whole, moaned around him while the man behind her worked another finger inside and eased the tension in her tight ring.

The man in front of her groaned, then pulled out, leaving her dragging in deep, shuddering breaths and missing the fullness.

Footsteps shuffled on the floor; fingers rimmed her mouth.

She stuck out her tongue and licked them, then wrapped her mouth around them to suck.

The fingers withdrew, but a thumb pried her mouth open wide and another cock butted against her lips.

She stroked it, recognizing its taste, and opened wider to let Dagr thrust deep into her throat. "You're so perfect. So loving and womanly," he crooned. "Such a hot mouth. Such a skilled tongue. I will let you suck my men until they come. Will you swallow?"

She nodded around him, groaning as he continued to sweep in and out.

The fingers in her ass retreated, her cheeks were parted, and a thick round knob pushed against her tiny opening. She groaned loudly, trying to complain around the cock gagging her mouth, but Dagr pulled her hair and rubbed her ear at the same time, confusing her with pleasure and pain.

The cock pushed against her asshole, then finally popped inside. She slumped over the bench, breathing loudly through her nose.

Dagr pulled his cock from her mouth but his hands stayed on her face and hair. Then his mouth rubbed hers and her lips trembled.

"Are you a little overwhelmed?" he whispered.

She nodded, trying to reach for his mouth again. But he moved away, leaving her weak and shivering, her ass burning around the invading cock.

Her pussy was drenched and throbbing, and fingers were playing inside it, languidly swirling.

Her sex was making lush, wet noises that would have embarrassed her any other time, but now seemed only to increase the ardor of the man who invaded her there. Two fingers were joined by another and she was fast approaching her climax. "So full..." She moaned.

Fingers and cock pulled away. She quivered on the bench,

waiting, but silence surrounded her. Were they just watching? What did they wait for?

Fingers pushed her hair from her sweaty face. "Would you like to be untied?" Dagr asked softly beside her ear.

"Please," she whimpered.

"Would you like to see us?"

She opened her mouth to repeat her plea, but realized she might not be able to give herself freely if she had to stare into two sets of strangers' eyes. She shook her head.

The binding around her wrists gave. Warm hands pulled her up, then lifted her from the bench and carried her. She was laid gently on the mattress, her arms and limbs arranged gently as though she were a doll. Then the mattress dipped to her sides and at her feet as the men joined her.

She lay on her back and one man lifted her torso and leaned her against his, so that she half reclined against a hard wall of warm muscle. His hands glided up her belly, and then gently clasped her breasts. Thumbs toggled her aching nipples.

She sighed and relaxed against him.

Another pushed apart her legs and settled between them. When a mouth glided along her folds, pausing to suck on her silken lips, she scooted her heels up the mattress and parted her thighs to give him unimpeded access.

The pace of his strokes and kisses was slow, soothing. While her breaths were still deep, her heart still thudding in her chest, she was able to gather her wits, recharge her strength.

She didn't think either the man who held her or the one lapping at her pussy was their leader. Their smell was as earthy as Dagr's but not flavored with his unique musk. "Dagr, are you with me?" she asked, because she had to know.

Fingers raised her chin. A thumb caressed her bottom lip. A

now-familiar caress that instantly reassured her. She sighed when his mouth settled over hers. He knelt beside her, she decided. "Does it bother you to watch another man pleasure me?"

"Do you mean does it make me jealous?"

"Yes."

"It makes me hard, ready to fight. But they only stoke the fire for us both. When I take you, you will know it is me."

"Because you'll ravage me?" she asked, giving a gasping laugh.

His mouth covered hers again. His tongue stroked into her mouth, and because she'd been conditioned to do it, she sucked on it, pulling in rhythm to the slow throb in her pussy.

He pulled away but pressed a kiss against her forehead. "You please me."

"I shouldn't care so much, but I want to please you."

He pressed his lips against hers, and then hovered there, breathing against her. With her breasts being massaged, her pussy teased, her arousal was never allowed to ebb away. She floated on a sea of sensation, feeling pampered and cherished.

Dagr kissed her lips again. His hands cupped her cheeks and tilted her face toward his.

"Honora," he whispered, "will you do anything I ask?"

Eleven

D o you think I'll try to weasel out of my promise?" she asked, noting her voice trembled.

"I would be sure. We will not go easy."

The breath Honora sucked in was thin. Her heart felt trapped, vibrating so fast inside her, she might have swooned, but Dagr cupped her head and tilted it back to open her airway.

The man behind her stroked her belly in soothing glides. The one kneeling between her spread thighs rubbed her folds between his fingers, tugging in an oddly comforting rhythm.

"Too much?" Dagr's voice was strained.

And she wished she wasn't blindfolded, if only to see how terribly aroused he really was. If he felt even a fraction as excited as she was, they would incinerate each other. "Please," she moaned.

His lips teased her with a swirling kiss. "Please, what? Touch you, lick you?" Again, he kissed her. "Suck you?"

She groaned, sounding like a wounded animal, and she stirred restlessly inside the embrace of the man behind her.

Dagr's lips kissed her harder. "Tell me."

"Fuck me!" she cried out, clamping her thighs around the Viking between her legs, eager for the men to take her and no longer caring whether Dagr asked something she might regret later. She ached, head to toe, for release.

Hands clasped her thighs, prying them wider, and then a mouth worked her pussy again, teasing her with nibbles and luscious laps that built the tension in her womb, but slowed every time she neared the precipice.

Hands slid up her ribs to cup her breasts, and the one behind her rolled them and thumbed her nipples.

Honora yearned for rougher treatment, to be pinched and bitten. Her body undulated. Her whimpers mewled, her moans becoming more insistent.

The men laughed softly around her.

The mattress dipped along one side, and she knew Dagr lay down. The mouth between her legs disappeared. The man behind her helped her to sit, then urged her to straddle Dagr's body.

His cock nudged between her legs, and she eagerly reached down to center him, stroking his shaft in her hand before feeding him slowly inside her. When she sank a few inches, she braced herself against his chest to slide down his length in short, pulsing glides, taking him deeper and deeper, sighing, her head lolling because the sensations were too wonderful, too much.

She was so wet, so swollen. His cock felt huge, like a post nearly splitting her in two, and she said so, sounding surly and petulant, and making the three men around her laugh.

Their soft, masculine chuckles made her shiver, made her nipples tingle and tighten harder. "I ache, Dagr. Gods, how I ache."

Hands cupped her breasts and massaged her gently. "Where? Your breasts?"

She slowed her downward thrusts and nodded, biting her lip.

His torso rose, his mouth rooted at her nipple, and she aimed it straight into his mouth, shuddering hard when he bit it. "Oh . . . Oh . . ." she said tightly.

His mouth caressed the tip he'd bitten then licked it to soothe. "Where else aches, *elskling*?"

"My cunt," she said, using the harsh word because she didn't want nice, didn't want soft.

"Cunt," he repeated, still using his lips to torture her nipple. "Your cunt, *elskling*, is so hot it burns my cock. What do you say to that?"

"It's hot for you. It aches, all the way inside. All the way to my womb."

"What about your ass? Does your ass ache?" he asked so innocently, softly . . . *craftily* . . . that she groaned.

Again the men laughed.

Hands smoothed over her back. Over her ass. Around her tummy. Fingers sank into the top of her folds and rubbed her clit.

Her inner muscles clamped hard around Dagr's cock, and this time he groaned. He kissed her nipple, then wound his arms around her back and brought her down. They kissed, mouths circling, tongues gliding.

Then her rear was molded by large, rough palms, her back made to arch, lifting her butt. Her cheeks were parted, and more hot oil trickled between them. When she felt the nudge of a blunt cockhead, she moaned into Dagr's mouth and pulled his hair.

The cock pushed past the tight ring, making it burn, then kept pushing relentlessly until it sank deep. The Viking behind her began to stroke; hard bone and muscle slapped her ass.

Her head was lifted, her mouth forced from Dagr's, and she was urged to brace herself on her arms. When a soft crown bumped against her lips she didn't hesitate, taking the musky, salty head into her mouth and swirling her tongue over the crown, down the sides, as she bobbed forward and back.

The men didn't allow her to move again after that. They held her still, bouncing against her ass, shafting her mouth, slamming upward to fuck her cunt.

Every orifice filled, Honora's body caught fire, shivering hard, the muscles of her belly and thighs jumping. She locked her elbows to stay up because her arms felt rubbery. The heat inside her cunt and ass built, friction burning like fire, her mouth stuffed so full she could tell them with only her moans how agonizing the building tension grew.

They showed no mercy. And after a time, she was fiercely glad for the blindfold because it soaked up the tears she shed. The cock gagging her mouth muffled the sobs.

When she came, her climax seared her veins. The rush of pleasure swept her whole body, washing over her skin in hot waves. Her orgasm unwound the curling tension, sprung in an instant and exploding outward, her cries muffled around the thick cock still working her mouth.

Then the cock in her ass thrust faster, harder, grunts growing louder until the Viking behind her shouted and pulled out, letting his cum paint her buttocks.

The cock in her mouth quickened its strokes, punching deep in short, fast thrusts, then pulling away at the last moment to spill his seed onto her face. She licked her mouth to catch what she could. Then he too was gone.

The blindfold was tugged from her face but she kept her eyes closed.

Thumbs swept over her closed lids, wiping away moisture. She turned her face to kiss the palm warming her cheek and sobbed, this time the sound clear and humiliating.

Arms encircled her, pulling her down. Dagr pressed her face into the corner of his shoulder. "Leave us," he said quietly.

Footsteps retreated.

"Did we cause you pain?" he asked, kissing her temple, his palm wiping semen from her cheek.

She shook her head. "I couldn't control myself. I didn't know myself. I was frightened."

"Did you find pleasure?"

"Too much," she said, taking another shuddering breath and nuzzling into the corner of his neck, reassured by his familiar scent.

"Too much pleasure. How is that possible?" His voice held a hint of a smile.

"I wanted it to be you. Only you."

He kissed her hair, then rolled slowly, taking her beneath him. He hovered, his body pinning her, chest to toes. "You please me, Honora." His blue eyes, always so sharp and blazing, appeared to thaw. "I try to fight this feeling. This need for you."

She placed her palm alongside his cheek. "Because I'm your enemy?"

"Because you're a woman, and I am a warrior."

Confused, she frowned at him. "But I too am a warrior."

One corner of his mouth curled upward. "And we battle every time we fuck."

She cringed at the word, wanting him to use the softer expression. Because she'd already started to think of what they did as more than just sex. With him, she was completely free, completely unable to resist his command. She rolled her eyes and gave him a shaky laugh. "How embarrassing it is to find out I'm just a woman."

"Don't be embarrassed," he said, cupping her face with his

fingers stretched alongside her cheek and his thumb beneath her chin. "I told you I am skilled."

His slow smile lit up his eyes, and Honora melted again, liquid spilling from deep inside her body to anoint his cock.

She lifted her legs and wrapped them tightly around his hips. "Then take me, pirate king," she said teasingly, but meaning it with all her being. "Ravish me until I'm breathless."

With his hair falling around her face like a curtain, he rose.

Honora took deep, cleansing breaths, knowing from his tightening expression that he was ready to unleash a storm on her.

She ran her hands over him. Gliding over his straining biceps, over the rock-hard muscles cloaking his upper chest. So much power rested there. He could snap her bones with just his long fingers, and yet he was careful with her.

She wasn't dainty, wasn't delicate, and yet he made her feel that way. Which should have pissed her off, but instead caused her chest to tighten, her eyes to fill.

In truth, she'd begun to wonder what it would be like to be cherished by a man like Dagr.

Dagr began to stroke into her, slowly sinking, tunneling inexorably deeper until each thrust rubbed her hot, silky walls over every inch of his shaft.

He fought the urge to pound into her, knowing she'd been sorely used and that the heat he felt caressing him was due to rawness. She would take it, never complaining. And likely she would find her pleasure in it too. But he didn't want to wait long to have her again.

There was something about Honora. Something that pulled him. Already he thought about the time after this mission was through. He'd keep her. Whether she wanted it or not. He'd make room for her, send Tora to Odvarr, give Astrid to Frakki. He'd have no need of another concubine with Honora warming his bed.

And she might fight him, might rail against giving up her place on this ship, even her world, but she'd adapt, and he'd never let her regret it.

He sank deeper, thrust harder, churning in the warm cream her body made to ease his way.

Honora's thighs shifted higher on his hips, hugging him tightly, tilting her pussy to take him deeper. She arched her back and rose to press kisses against his chin, his jaw, the side of his neck. Before falling back, gasping.

His body was tight, hard pressure building in his balls, and he knew he was close. He didn't like the distance between their bodies and lowered himself.

She sighed and sank her face into the corner of his neck, her tongue licked at his sweat, and then her teeth bit.

It wasn't a soft bite, would likely leave a bruise, but it was enough to send him straight over the edge. He roared and hammered hard, desperate to finish the race, to spend his seed inside her womb.

When release came, he felt it start as a tingling in his toes that swept up his legs, strained his thighs, cramped his balls, until they exploded.

He didn't slow until the liquid pulsing through the end of his cock waned. He swam in the moisture filling her deep, hot well, continuing to stroke into her because he didn't want to leave the haven of her warmth. Didn't want to pull away and be the warrior king who must insist on her surrender. For now, he wanted to hold the woman in his arms, caress her with his body, sleep inside her strong embrace.

Baraq sat on the side of the bed, his head bent, his hands braced on his knees. "Are you trying to get me killed?"

Birget remained on her back and closed her eyes. He'd noticed.

It would have been hard not to, given how loudly she'd screamed. "Of course not. Why are you so upset? Every girl has a first time. Even your precious captain."

"We're not talking about her. How old are you?" he said, aiming a worried look her way.

She snorted. "I'm not a child. Just particular."

"You're a princess. Were you supposed to keep your virginity for a noble?"

She shrugged, feeling only a pinprick of guilt for what she hadn't saved for Eirik. "What I do with my body is my business."

"Is Dagr going to come after my cock for taking you?"

Birget snickered. "Dagr gave you to me. I'd bet money he knew exactly what would happen. Besides, he's much too preoccupied with his own bit of pussy to care what I do." She wrinkled her nose. "I do have to say, though, that what came before was much more enjoyable than the actual fucking."

Baraq rolled his eyes. "If I'd known, I could have taken greater care."

"If you had known, you wouldn't have come near me. Am I right?"

Baraq sighed. "Did I hurt you badly?"

"Not once you tore through my maidenhead."

He grimaced. "Our women have it surgically removed."

"Is a woman's purity never prized? Even when they are newly breached? I mean, we are not a monogamous race by any stretch of the imagination, but a woman's first time is important."

"It's traumatic for the male too," he muttered.

She snickered, and then smoothed her hand over his strong back. "Why do you sit so far away?"

His muscles flexed beneath her palm. "I should dress, before someone finds us like this."

"Dagr will not take revenge for my decision. Lie with me."

Baraq's expression was troubled when he gazed down at her, but he let her pull him down beside her. His strong hands turned her when she would have cuddled her breasts against his chest. "You're much too tempting when your nipples are poking at me."

She grinned, liking the feel of his hard, muscular belly against her back, his groin cupping her buttocks. When his hands smoothed around her belly and up to gently mold her breasts, she thought she might understand the attraction of sex. Her skin tingled all over. "This part is nice," she whispered.

"Fuck," he growled. "This part is pure torture." His cock prodded her backside. He hadn't come before, having pulled out the moment he'd torn her hymen.

"I could help you with that," she drawled.

"You should get some rest. My condition is my penance."

They were silent, and she hoped he enjoyed holding her as much as she liked being held. "Are you in love with her? With your captain?"

Baraq pinched her nipple. "We came together because it was convenient. I was of an appropriate rank, and we never let our relations get closer than . . . recreational release."

She winced, not liking that he might think this was something so shallow, so worthless. " 'Recreational release' sounds rather cold."

"It's often how it is between men and women. Not every liaison is about affection or love."

"I don't need love," she said, infusing haughtiness into her tone to tweak him. "That emotion only interferes with a warrior's focus."

He grunted. "You are with Dagr. Since you aren't of his clan, are you destined to marry him?"

"Freya, no!" she said, her heart beating fast because she had suffered one moment, back in her father's keep, when she'd wondered what it might be like . . . "I am promised to his brother."

Baraq groaned and squeezed her breast again. "This can't happen again."

"You complain too much." She rubbed her bottom against his cock, enjoying the sound of his ragged breaths. "I think it's because you haven't taken your ease."

"Just be quiet and don't talk about it," he growled, a hand clamping on her buttock to hold her still.

"Your body is so hard, your muscles tight, you will never rest," she said softly, innocently.

"I am the master of my body."

"Truly?" She dragged his hands off her breast and hip and turned inside his embrace to face him. "Let me explore. I'll satisfy my curiosity, and you won't be left quite so grumpy."

He held still so long, she knew she had him, even after he thinned his lips and shook his head. Sweat beaded on his face and chest.

Birget placed her hand alongside his cheek and rubbed her thumb on that tightened lower lip. "I'd like a kiss before I sleep," she whispered.

His gaze narrowed. "I don't trust that look in your eyes."

She grinned, enjoying flirting, acting the woman for once. "Are you afraid of me?"

He shook his head, his lips curling in mild disgust. "Afraid for my life and my balls, and I'm not too sure which I prize more at the moment."

She slid her hand down his throat, past his chest, and scraped her fingers through the silky black hair arrowing down his lower abdomen. When she reached the erection thumping against his belly, she ran a fingertip slowly down his length. "How can you feel so soft and so hard at the same time?"

She wrapped her fingers around him like a gear stick on a snoweater and glided her thumb over the smooth, cushioned head. She glanced back up to find his dark gaze staring at her face. "I can do this quickly. Show me what pleases you."

His eyes fluttered closed and he groaned.

She smiled, letting him see it when he speared her again with his intense gaze.

"You're lethal, Princess."

"Not something I haven't been told before, but in an entirely different light."

A strangled laugh escaped him, and he cupped the back of her neck and brought her close. His kiss was quick, hard, and then he pushed on the top of her head, urging her down the mattress.

He didn't give her time to savor her victory or to lick the many places she wanted to taste along the way. He pushed her down until her face was even with his cock, but then she didn't care that he'd deprived her of the journey.

Birget ran her nose along his steamy shaft, smelling his musk and her own. Her tongue followed, licking tentatively, then lavishly once she decided she liked it.

"You're killing me," he moaned, lifting his buttocks and rubbing his shaft against her cheek.

She liked the way his hands cradled her head, the way his fingers dug into her hair and tugged. She sensed the violence he could unleash and decided then and there that she'd have that for herself. Just once. She was promised to Eirik, after all.

For now, she needed to enslave Baraq. Learn how to control a man with her womanly wiles.

Warming his cock in her hand, she scooted down and stroked his balls with her tongue. Something Ilse said could make a warrior tremble.

They'd joked that it was as much from worry about having teeth so close to a man's most precious jewels as it was from pleasure, and the wicked glint in Ilse's eyes had intrigued her.

As her tongue laved his balls, wetting them thoroughly, she had the urge to fill her mouth with them, and she opened her lips to suction, and then pulled them inside where her tongue continued to slide over them.

Baraq groaned loudly, the tension in his voice spurring her on. And now those fingers clutching her hair pulled her closer, telling her of the pleasure he was incapable of describing with words.

She suckled his balls, rubbing her tongue on them, and felt the subtle changes, the way they hardened, the way they drew up closer to his groin. Releasing them, she came back up his cock, and eagerly opened her mouth to clasp it around the tip, her tongue torturing the sensitive skin just beneath the ridge encircling it.

His fingers gently guided her down his shaft, and he stayed still while she sank and rose, taking a little more of him every time she dove.

Birget glanced up and found his dark, gleaming gaze staring intently as she took him. His cheeks were reddened, the bone beneath more pronounced by the tightening of his features, and sharpening by the second.

His breaths were ragged and coming faster, and she noted that her own weren't exactly even. Her pussy was quickening again, moisture trickling from inside and wetting her lips and thighs.

"Birget," he said softly. "Are you aroused?"

She nodded, his cock still trapped inside her mouth.

"Would you like to orgasm?"

She sucked harder on his cock.

His eyelids fluttered, and he shook his head. "Bring that pretty ass of yours around, darling. We can pleasure each other."

Without removing her mouth from him, she slowly crawled around, guided by his strong hands, until her thighs were spread over his face, her pussy hovering above his mouth.

At first, she couldn't move, struck still by the wicked flicks and strokes of his tongue. He climbed the length of her furrow, lapping with broad swipes of his tongue. Then he gently suckled her lips, teas-ing them with gentle bites that made her quiver. When his fingers rimmed her entrance, her pussy squeezed, trying to trap the digits.

He slipped one inside her. "Does this hurt?"

She came off his cock, gasping. "No."

"Do you want more?" His voice was as tight as the rigid body beneath her. How odd when her own body was becoming fluid, her pussy softening.

"Please."

He slipped another inside, and then pressed his lips against the top of her pussy. A gentle touch that soothed, until he started to suckle the spot, lips pulling. Blood rushed to that spot and her pleasure knot swelled, tortured by the flick of his tongue inside his mouth.

"Ahhh." She groaned, rubbing her face on his cock, undulating her hips in shallow motions until he cupped her ass and squeezed hard to hold her still.

Which maddened her. She opened her mouth and drove down his cock, sucking him as deep inside as she could, stopping only when his blunt head met the barrier of the back of her throat. Then she clasped him hard with her mouth and drew as strongly as she could, sucking relentlessly, her tongue lashing him furiously while he wagged his head between her legs and pulled her clitoris.

The explosion when it came surprised her so much her teeth bit down.

She caught herself before she did damage, but Baraq's whole body seized. When she wrapped her teeth with her lips and resumed sucking, he shouted and rolled his hips up and down, up higher, slamming into her mouth, then erupting, spurts of salty seed coat-ing her tongue. She swallowed it down, greedy and triumphant while her own body's release ebbed.

When his bucking quieted to gentle tremors, she came off his cock and licked it up and down, enjoying this phase of sex as she watched his shaft soften. "He is not nearly as impressive now."

He grunted. "Come here."

She crawled clumsily around, her knee slamming his nose, then bumping too close to his balls for him to hide a wince. When she lay pressed against his side, her head on his arm, she sighed.

His eyelids were drifting down. Then he darted a glance her way. "This can't happen again."

"I agree," she said, hiding a smile, knowing her words belied her intention.

"We'll rest a bit. But we can't disappear for long. Someone will come looking."

Birget snuggled closer, resting her cheek over his heart. The steady thrum was comforting and drugging her to sleep. She yawned and slid a hand across his belly.

He dragged it up to his chest. "No playing there. Sleep."

As Birget drifted off, she thought of Eirik, the man she hadn't met, but whose existence had spurred this journey. She wondered if he'd be as attentive to a woman's pleasure as Baraq.

Her last thought had her smiling. Why couldn't a princess have both a husband and her own concubine?

Twelve

The next afternoon, Dagr watched as tension tightened the features of the Heliopolites. He figured he'd better start worrying. The order had gone out minutes ago for everyone aboard the *Proteus* to grip hold of something solid. All life-support systems had been turned off. No sound other than the beating of his own heart registered.

Without the hum of machinery, every breath, every word sounded hollow. The air already grew stale and cold. No lights showed other than those glowing on the bioluminescent screen, which reflected glints of starlight bouncing off the ring of battleships and cruisers lined up at the perimeter of the frontier.

They'd cut engines after pointing the *Proteus* at a gap between those ships. Now they made a silent run through treacherous territory, hoping the armada wouldn't detect the cloaked transporter.

A loud groan of metal made Honora wince.

Dagr's attention sharpened.

"Just the hull creaking. Normal," she whispered. "And we don't have to worry about them detecting sounds in space, just our particle signature, which is why all systems are off."

"Then why are we whispering?" he groused, impatient with the silence and the waiting.

Her lips lifted in a small smile. "Nerves, I guess." She sat on the top step of the dais, her hands around a rail to keep from floating away.

Cyrus sat in the captain's chair, gripping the arms. Dagr had chosen to rest beside Honora, also clutching a rail. Glancing down, he smiled to see his fists clenched so tightly his knuckles were white.

The slide through the wormhole the previous afternoon had been anticlimactic. The ship's stabilizers made the journey undetectable for the passengers, although the pinpoints of starry light stretched and twisted as they flew through it. Rather like the bright flares of the Dragon's Fire Borealis in the night sky over Skuldelev.

Thousands of leagues beyond this perimeter, if they succeeded in passing through the armada's line without being blown to pieces, lay the feral colony where the bounty hunters' ship was scheduled to deliver the legal part of their cargo.

Dagr focused on the destination, because for now, he could do nothing. With slow strums of his fingers, he stroked the black stone strung around his neck, then dropped it in disgust when he realized what he was doing.

If Cyrus and Honora could remain calm, and they knew the dangers they all faced, then so could he. Inaction was his bane. His muscles were stiff from waiting. It left him feeling ineffectual, something a clan-lord should never experience.

They continued to drift through the armada's net, the silence stretching so long that at last Dagr's eyelids drifted downward.

"Restart the engines," Cyrus said, his command jarring in the stillness.

Head snapping up, Dagr blinked and glanced at Honora, who wore a wide grin.

"Did I wear you out last night?" she asked, her voice pitched low.

Dagr grunted, his blood heating instantly at her intimate tone. "Which of us was so spent she trembled?"

A blush suffused her golden cheeks, but her amber eyes sparkled.

"You were not afraid?" he asked, lifting his chin to the screen and the fading glints of armada ships.

Looking chagrined, she shook her head. "I have to admit I'm finding this whole adventure exciting."

"You missed your true calling, Lady Pirate," he drawled.

She wrinkled her nose, then turned away as lights flickered and weight dragged them firmly to the steps.

Her smile was slow to fade, but fade it did. Her glance swept the command deck and he knew she counted her days aboard the *Proteus*.

"Why did you do it?" she asked, turning her head to capture his gaze. Her cheeks reddened and she must have felt the telltale heat because she ducked her head.

"Do what?" he said beneath his breath, although he thought he knew.

"Why did you share me yesterday?" she whispered. "You don't seem the sort to share your toys."

"You are right." Dagr considered ending his response there, because he wasn't accustomed to having his motives questioned— about anything. But her expression, so vulnerable and open—not something she was likely aware of—moved him to answer. "I don't indulge often in group fare. But I wanted your complete surrender." The sudden heat in her glare seared him.

"You wanted to dominate me." Her chin jutted upward.

Her rapid change of mood amused him. "You make that sound like an evil thing. Do you not feel better now? More relaxed with me?"

Her back stiffened. "Now that I'm willing to let you lead, you mean?"

"I will treat you well, Honora," he said softly, preventing himself from reaching out a hand to soothe her. "You will have no regrets."

"Because you say so?" she said, her tone tart. "Do you think I won't miss everything I strived so hard to achieve?"

He didn't respond, holding himself still because to answer her now would only further spur her anger.

"You have no idea how hard a battle earning this berth was," she whispered harshly. "I had so much to overcome. A tarnished name, my sex. And it only took an hour for you to destroy it all."

Dagr cupped her cheek, running a callused thumb over her smooth skin. "Tell me what you battled to get here."

She shook her head, then took a deep breath before she again raised her gaze. "What happens if we never find your brother?"

His stomach clenched at the thought—a possibility he shoved aside. "You mean, to you?"

"And my crew and ship . . . to you and me."

He pulled his face into a stony mask, unwilling to argue over this. "I will not rest until I find him."

"Then you will likely die." She sighed and her shoulders slumped. "What happens then to your kingdom? To your people? You don't think your attack will go unanswered, do you?"

He ground his teeth. He'd thought of the consequences, but had refused to listen to the voice inside him that urged caution. Thor's thunder! He was a Viking. The Consortium had overstepped. If the Icelanders didn't meet them with violence, they might as well surrender again to the yoke of slavery.

Honora fell silent, her gaze dropping to the hands she held curled together in her lap. She had been an instrument in his brother's abduction, but he couldn't hold tight to the need for revenge that her actions justly earned.

He would show compassion. Enslave her in retribution for his brother's abduction. Her ship was forfeit as was the freedom of all her crew.

He wouldn't explain that to her yet. Already she'd ceded ground in their sexual war. Remembering how lovely, how embarrassed and aroused she'd been with his two men, he felt a deep satisfaction that eased the horrible tension that had ridden the back of his neck for days.

"Have you thought about how you will gain permission for us to dock at Karthagos?" she asked.

"I will tell them I'm a pirate and that I've captured a Consortium ship filled with pure light."

Her one-sided smile pleased him as so many things about her did. She wasn't one to dwell long on her problems.

"That should do it." Her eyelids drifted down and she peeked teasingly from beneath the thick fringe. "Pirates have colorful names. Have you thought of what yours should be?"

He smiled at her teasing manner. "What do you suggest?"

"Something you might actually answer to. The Black Wolf, perhaps?"

He grunted, knowing the rude, masculine sound of it aroused her. "You like my tattoo."

"I've always been a sucker for a man with skin art."

"It's not intended as art. The wolf is my totem." At the arch of her eyebrows, he shrugged. "One of my concubines is a believer in the old religion. Teiwaz is my totem." He lifted the stone amulet and pointed at the arrow. "By surrounding me with the symbol and infusing it with her prayers, she seeks to protect me."

"Your concubine?" she said slowly. In a heartbeat, her features tightened. Her breathing hitched.

Again, he held still, his gaze searching hers. Better for her to know now than to think he had misled her. "I am a king among my people. I am entitled to many wives and concubines. I have only two who serve me. A modest number."

She nodded—too quickly—and glanced away.

He considered telling her now that she'd have that same place of honor in his household, but something made him stop.

Too much, too soon. They barely knew each other, and there was still so much to be done.

Honora pushed up from the step. "We should have a plan," she said, her voice brisk. "For how we will approach Karthagos's secure airspace. They will see a Consortium ship, hear your very unlikely story that you captured it, and be suspicious this might be a trap. The Consortium has rumbled for decades about launching a new offensive to increase their territory. We should agree on a strategy now." She paused beside the captain's chair and gave Cyrus a pointed stare. "Cyrus, since you're so good at subterfuge, you should probably join us."

Cyrus's mouth tightened for a moment, then eased slowly into a smile. "I'll take that as a compliment, wench."

"Talking like a pirate already," she muttered.

When she'd passed him, Cyrus winked. "I need to pierce my ears."

"That's not what I'd pierce," Honora said, giving him a false smile over her shoulder.

Dagr laughed and clapped a hand on Cyrus's shoulder. "Find Frakki. We'll meet in the canteen."

* * *

Every Viking not needed to keep the ship secure ringed the table where Dagr, Honora, Frakki, and Cyrus sat.

With Turk guarded but at the controls, the rest met to devise a plan to capture the civilian transport ship at the dock in Karthagos. They'd hashed through the details of acquiring permission to dock, but now haggled over who would be part of the delegation to barter for the information they needed to find the ship.

"I should accompany you," Honora said, bracing for an explosion.

Dagr's glare was as sharp as his name. "You're a prisoner. You'll remain aboard this ship."

Honora blew hot. She leaned over the table and tapped it with her forefinger. "A prisoner who is the captain of the hostages." She leaned back, and took a deep breath. "They will expect you to keep me close and to flaunt my capture. And you'll need me there to prove up your claim."

"What do you mean?"

She knew she had him now. He might struggle with his desire to keep her, a woman, safe, but the mission came first. "They will suspect this is a Consortium trick. A Trojan horse."

The blank look he gave her said he hadn't a clue what she was talking about. The most famous battle in her people's history before their exodus into space, and the barbarians had never heard of it.

"In our legends, a wooden horse was left at the gates of a great city-state as tribute, left by the warriors the city-state defeated. The horse was enormous and the Trojans rolled it through the gates, where they let it sit as a symbol of their victory while they drank and feasted. But when the celebration fires died that night and everyone slept, the men hidden inside that great horse escaped. They opened the gates and let in the Greek army, who then sacked the city."

"They will think this ship is a Trojan horse," Dagr said quietly. "That Consortium soldiers will sneak into their midst."

"Yes. You can't let me remain aboard my own ship. You need me as a hostage while you meet with the men who hold the captives to prove your strength."

"Why can't Baraq pretend to be the captain?"

"Because there is likely already a bounty on this ship. And my name will be out there." She grimaced at the thought of the heads nodding, memories nudged to recall her father's shame. "They'll know you lie if you tell them Baraq is the captain."

He leaned forward, his pose challenging. "Why couldn't I tell them I killed you in the taking of the ship?"

She inhaled, thinking hard, but in the end shrugged. "Baraq is in charge of security. He doesn't know as much about the ship as I do. It wouldn't be believable that you killed me, but kept him alive. He's not essential to you." She held his stare, daring him to tell her she exaggerated to serve her own agenda.

He remained silent so long, she had to resist the urge to fidget beneath his fixed stare.

"Shouldn't I fear that you will tell them I'm not a pirate?" he asked softly, but with each word so distinct that no one doubted his anger. "That I seek vengeance against the hunters who stole my people?"

Honora raised her chin higher, unwilling to be cowed. She wasn't some soft, petted *concubine*. She hadn't earned her rank by showing weakness. "You will tell them the truth. Your brother is among the captives taken by the bounty hunters, and the Black Wolf will capture a dozen Consortium ships if he must to rescue him. You aren't a pirate because you are born to it, Dagr. You are defined by the actions you take. They believe in vengeance. They honor strength and ruthlessness."

"Will they not think me weak if they see you unharmed, walking beside me?"

She cleared her throat, wincing at the glee he might evince at her next suggestion. "You can't show me mercy or compassion in their presence."

His eyes glinted. "Have I ever? Truly?"

Honora felt the sting of his softly spoken barbs. He was angry because he didn't want her with him. He also didn't like that she was right and argued with him in front of his men. She gave him a fierce glare. "You will have to try harder to convince them."

Dagr grunted, and Cyrus chuckled.

She aimed a sharp glance at her old friend. "You're coming with us. The maps you've drawn tell me you've been here before."

Cyrus gave a sharp shake of his head. "Can't."

"He must stay aboard the ship," Dagr said, his tone brooking no argument.

Honora's back stiffened with stubbornness. "But that doesn't make sense. He knows the terrain."

"A bounty is posted for his return to this very planet."

She swung toward Cyrus. "Is this true?"

"First, you're pissing off Dagr by doubting his word—but that's not my problem." Cyrus leaned back in his chair and his expression turned sour. "After I was sentenced for disobeying that order, I was pressed into service aboard a private frigate. They bought my sentence. When they docked at Karthagos, I jumped ship."

He shook his head, disgust curling his upper lip. "Like an idiot, I got drunk and recaptured, but this time, I was enslaved by a woman pirate. When I escaped her clutches, I headed to the one place I knew even pirates feared going."

Dagr smiled his approval. "You see the courage he displayed— coming to New Iceland and facing barbarians, then leaving the safety of our world again to aid me. Do you see why I trust him?"

Honora released a pent-up breath. "He stays, then."

Dagr arched a brow. "You take charge naturally. But you do know it is only because I allow it."

Blood thumped through her body. "I would think you'd want the person most qualified to draw up this plan."

"Most qualified. And yet you also have never been here."

She didn't bother reminding him that at least she'd known what Karthagos was. When she saw his smile deepening, she felt heat creep across her cheeks. He was teasing her. In front of all of them—amused by someone so small and so *female* addressing tall, hairy barbarians like a field marshal.

She pressed her lips together to still her own smile and caught his slow wink.

"I will go." This flat statement came from Birget on the edge of the circle surrounding their table.

Humor fled Dagr's expression in an instant, and he slammed his fist on the table.

Honora jumped, but Birget merely smirked.

Dagr's nostrils flared. The sharp glance he shot the Viking princess would have cowed anyone else, but Birget stubbornly jutted her chin higher.

"Must you defy me again?"

The princess shrugged, completely unperturbed by his show of temper. "You know that I will only escape." Her eyes widened innocently. "Then I would be on my own and unprotected."

Dagr growled, his face turning an alarming shade of red. "Birget!" But he seemed at a loss to say more as he gnashed his teeth audibly.

Birget lost the mocking expression. "I would see this feral outpost. And I can lend my weapon. Is this place truly so treacherous that a Viking should fear it? Especially a *Valkyrja*?"

Eyebrows bunched, Dagr turned his gaze back to Honora.

His brooding expression told her that he blamed her for this insurrection. She fought a smile. She'd bet money he'd never been defied before, but here two "weak" women tested him at every turn.

Dagr's shrewd gaze landed on Baraq, who stood next to the Viking princess, his expression carefully neutral. "You will be her personal guard. If anything happens to her, I will flay the skin from your body."

Baraq caught Honora's gaze. She gave him a subtle nod, surprised he still sought her approval when she was as much a captive as he was.

"It's decided," Dagr said, looking around the circle. "Frakki will be in charge of defending the ship against any security breaches. Cyrus will monitor all traffic on the airwaves and oversee the unloading of the ore, if we manage to strike a deal. We four will disembark with an additional two of my own guard to watch our backs."

With plans laid, Honora slumped at the table, still not believing she'd won. She didn't watch the group as they left because she was weary from schooling her face into a hard mask.

When the last set of footsteps shuffled out, she sighed and pushed up from the table. Silence surrounded her. Silence and solitude. Something she needed now to gather her thoughts and prepare herself for what was ahead. So much had happened in the space of a couple of days.

She busied herself pouring a cup of kava from the large urn beside the entrance to the dining room, hoping for a few minutes of alone time. Her stomach gurgled and she laughed, remembering she hadn't eaten since rising that morning with Dagr. Their quick repast hadn't been nearly enough to satisfy. She'd burned substantial calories.

A broad hand slid over her hip.

She didn't jerk in surprise, because part of her had known he'd stayed behind. He hadn't let her out of his sight for more than a quick trip to the head since they'd first squared off against each other at the taking of her ship.

"You will pour me one," Dagr said, his body blanketing her back.

She didn't mind that he didn't really ask or say please when the heat of his large palm, as it smoothed around her waist, soaked right through her skin. She handed him her cup and reached for another.

"I regret that you are the captain of this ship."

Her glance snapped to his face. The sharp intelligence in his cold blue eyes softened the longer his gaze held hers. How had she ever thought him primitive? "Why do you regret it?"

"I don't want you in harm's way. I have put you there."

Her body melting at the low, rumbling tone, she forced herself to challenge him. "Because I'm a woman?"

His jaw tightened, and he gestured for her to take a seat, then sat beside her. He looked incongruous. A Viking in fur and tanned skins, holding a mug that looked small inside his large hand.

She took a sip from her own cup, which she held in both hands. "How do you suggest I show no mercy?"

So that was what bothered him. She suppressed a smile. "Same as you would with any other prisoner."

"I don't fuck other prisoners. And I can't beat you."

"But you can be physical. Put me on a leash, chain me. Jerk me occasionally. It's a feral colony; they will understand the implication."

"What exactly does 'feral' mean?"

"You've led a sheltered life, Viking." She waved a dismissive hand. "The streets of many frontier planets are mean, dangerous. A feral colony has the added risks associated with the outcasts of the feral experiments." At his deepening frown, she relented in her teasing. "They are hybrid humans. Mixed with animal DNA. Mostly from Earth—your Midgard."

"Midgard." He leaned forward. "It still exists?"

"I don't know," she said honestly. "The planet's so very far away, and the Consortium leaders who brought us don't permit travel to that part of the universe. But like your people, ours brought animals from there to populate Helios, to establish a familiar food supply, and to make Helios seem more like home. Those animals were used in the experiments."

"I hate admitting that I know little of the history of the Outlanders."

The way he spoke, as though realizing he'd made a mistake and was slightly stunned at the thought, made her smile.

His dark brows drew together. "I have never had an interest in learning because I spend so much of my time worrying about the present and the future of my people. Were your ancestors also enslaved when they were brought to the stars?"

Honora set her cup on the table and hunched toward it. "They were captured, plucked from sailing ships, but they were allowed their freedom after a time, after our captors were sure we'd embrace our relocation. Helios was a lush planet. Warm. Rich with natural resources. We adapted and thrived."

"Then why were we enslaved?"

With a shake of her head, Honora sighed. "The old guard of the Consortium wasn't responsible. Heliopolites, my people, insisted. I think it's the nature of humans. We're greedy. We like our comforts. And we wanted to control the price of the ore, to reap all the profits. We couldn't find cheap enough labor willing to work in the severe conditions of New Iceland. So my ancestors remembered stories of barbarians who lived in Earth's colder climates and convinced Consortium officials to let them send anthropologists to study your culture and figure out a way to get you to willingly come through the portal and do the work."

"You should have remembered that men will always strive for freedom. Whatever the cost."

Why did she feel guilty over her ancestors' decision? She hadn't been alive, had had nothing to do with enslaving the Vikings and forcing them to work on that inhospitable planet.

Then the image of the captive she'd seen rose in her mind, his stark blue eyes, so like the ones watching her now, looking up at her from where he lay naked on the floor of his cage. The man could have been Dagr's brother. Nausea twisted her stomach. "Those on Helios don't know the conditions you live in, don't understand anything but how much they have to pay for their comfortable lives. They won't rest until you're brought to heel."

Dagr's gaze rose from his nearly empty cup. "Is this the way you feel about us? That we are barbarians who should be grateful to work as slaves beneath the ice?"

"I have to admit," she said honestly, acknowledging what her answer said about her strength of character, "I never gave it much thought. I just followed orders."

He set aside the cup. The firm line of his mouth indicated he hadn't liked her admission. "We call you Outlanders," he said, his tone brusque, argumentative.

She wasn't going to take the bait—but only because she wanted to annoy him. "I know. It's quaint. But not too specific. There are an endless multitude of species that operate in the known universe. We're human like you, and our origin was also Earth."

He folded his arms over his chest. "Anyone, anything, not of our world is *Utlending*—Outlander."

"You say that like it's a curse."

"We mean it as one."

They squared off again. Both their faces set, their gazes warring but not relinquishing.

"We'd better find restraints for you to wear," Dagr growled, ending the contest.

Honora wrinkled her nose, inwardly groaning because the first wave of heat washed over her. "You're going to enjoy this, aren't you?"

"For however long we are on the planet," he said with a smile that didn't reach his eyes, "you will have to do everything I say without complaint, or I will punish you."

She sucked her lower lip between her teeth. "Why is it that I just creamed?" she whispered.

"It's because now you know that I will dare much to make you admit your need for discipline. I will find your limits and exploit them." His large body leaned closer.

Which caused a corresponding increase in her body's temperature. How did he do that? "Do we have time?"

He took her mug and set it aside, then lifted her to sit her on the table. When he pushed her to lie back, she didn't hesitate. "Someone might walk in," she said, turning her head to give him access to her neck where he bit the cords of her tendons and licked his way down to the top of her suit.

His hands slid under her outer layer of clothing and closed around the breast covered in the skin-suit. "Have I mentioned how much I hate this thing?" he said, plucking it and letting it snap back against her body.

The sting excited her. She inserted her hand between their bodies and cupped his sex, which twitched and hardened as she squeezed. "Maybe we should go back to my room."

"Cyrus is outside the door. No one will pass."

Her eyes widened. "How did he know to do that?"

"He had only to watch my gaze fall on you while my frowns deepened to know what you were doing to me."

She feigned a scowl. "I didn't do anything to you except talk sense."

Dagr kissed the tip of her nose, then bit it. "You defied me. Again. You know I don't want you anywhere near danger, and yet you continue to put yourself in its path."

Humor drained from her as she thought about what lay ahead for her. "I have little to live for as it is, Dagr. Would you deprive me of even this small adventure?"

"You have so little to live for? Because of me? Because I took your ship?"

"Yes. You don't think my command will let me return to it once you're through and spit us back, do you?"

His head cocked, glance homing in on her face. "How severe will be your punishment?"

"Execution." Her stomach cramped at the word. There was no other possibility. "They don't suffer failure on such a large scale. And I'll be up on charges for kidnapping your brother. They'll make an example to ensure that every Helio strives to do their best."

Dark brows scrunched over the bridge of his nose. "Even though they are the ones responsible?"

"Someone must take the blame."

He grunted, a hand moving around her back to support her weight, the other cupping her head. "Then it is a good thing I will do for you."

"What's that?" she asked while her body awakened inside his embrace. When his hips surged against her, the layers of clothing did little to mute the electric current that arced between them.

"I will give you a home," he whispered. "A place in my household."

Her eyes blinked, then widened. Irritation stiffened her body. "You will make me your slave?"

With a thumb running the rim of her ear, he shook his head. "My concubine. It is a place of honor for a woman."

Anger trumped irritation, and she shoved at his chest. "A place of honor? Where will I sleep—*wedged* between the women you already keep?"

"Thank you." His ice-shard blue eyes narrowed to slits. "I wondered where I would find the anger to treat you as I must." He pulled away his hands and straightened, and then stalked out of the room.

Honora jackknifed up, anger trembling through her.

Cyrus poked his head in the door. "He's furious. What did you say?"

She shrugged, and sat up as calmly as she could manage, given that her belly still quivered. "I refused his invitation to join his many women back home."

Cyrus's mouth dropped open. "I'm shocked he asked."

"Because I'm not Viking?" she bit out, and then clamped her jaw.

"No, because he rarely bothers thinking about women or their problems. He disallows catfights or discord. He considers them unimportant. The taking of another concubine is significant."

Climbing down, she straightened her clothing, not meeting his frowning gaze. "He considers women unimportant?"

"Not the women; the problems they bring. Women themselves aren't unimportant, Honora. A woman is the center of the Norse life. The mother. Women provide comfort and service. That is what a warrior needs and cares about."

Although irritated beyond anything, she appreciated the insight. "Do all Vikings feel that way? That women are to provide service?"

He shrugged. "Women understand the warriors. They mind

the home and children so that warriors can worry about defending their lands and carving up the planet to get at the ore."

Honora felt like steam was rolling from her ears, she was so furious. "And when he takes a concubine, is she 'mother' or 'whore'?"

Cyrus's frown deepened; so did his voice. "Concubines are cherished for their service. Cared and provided for. Not bought. I'm sure there's not a Viking on New Iceland who wouldn't offer you the same arrangement. It's a hard life and they're hard men. They'd be happy for a strong partner."

"You admire that in them, but you've lived in a more developed culture."

"More developed? I was raised with more amenities, perhaps, but I would never think of the Icelanders as primitive." His head shook and his mouth pressed into a thin line. "They value honor and courage. They enter battle prepared to die for each other."

"He wants me to service him like a sex worker."

"He's offering you a permanent place in his household. That's far above a whore. You insulted him."

Insulted him? Her jaw dropped. "I think you've spent too much time among them. You've inhaled their ice-cold air and let it freeze your brain." She swept past him, her chin high. "I'm captain of my own ship, of my own destiny."

Cyrus grabbed her arm and pulled her close, his gaze intent. "Your ship was forfeit the moment you allowed bounty hunters to kidnap men from their world."

Struggling to grasp a small bit of hope, she tugged her arm from his grasp. "This isn't over. I'll go to Karthagos and act the cowed captive, but when we're done and he gets what he needs to find his brother, that's it. That's the end of my cooperation. I'll retake this ship."

"I know you'll try," Cyrus said, his back stiff. "And I won't blame you. I would have fought to the death for the right to continue to captain my ship."

She fell silent, remembering his fall. "Why didn't you just say yes? Why didn't you follow orders? They were mutants."

"They were half-human and I couldn't in good conscience deliver them to their owners." His fist rocked against his thigh. "They were to be baited for entertainment, then released as game for pleasure hunters."

"Is it true you slept with one of them?" The sharp edges of his cheeks and jaw sharpened like blades and she knew she'd gone too far. "I'm sorry. I just don't understand."

"No, you wouldn't. You wouldn't question an order because you're too scared to end up like your father. Your father fell in love with a spy who led him to betray his oath. You're sleeping with your captor and loving it. What do you think they'll say?" He leaned close, his lip curled in a snarl. "The apple doesn't fall far from the tree, sweetheart."

He turned on his heel, and for the second time, the door to the canteen slapped closed, leaving her wishing she could restart the day. Her shoulders slumped. She didn't like feeling small. And she especially didn't like the feeling that she might have hurt Dagr, as improbable as that might seem.

He'd stolen her pride along with her ship. Why the bloody fuck should she feel guilty?

Thirteen

Dagr didn't find keeping Honora on a very short leash difficult or even particularly distasteful. In fact, the whole business of collars and lengths of braided leather made him hard.

Honora strode before him, her ass twitching as she angrily stomped ahead. He'd insisted that she strip to her skin-suit, seeing as how she was a captive and he didn't want anyone watching them to think he valued her modesty.

And he'd managed to say it without breaking into a grin. However, he was feeling a lot less smug the longer he followed in her wake.

The skin-suit hugged her bottom like his palms itched to do, defining the deep crease. The looks she received from those they passed made his teeth grit, because he knew how lovingly her attire molded her feminine folds and areolas. He'd taken the time to caress her nipples just before the dock's gate had opened and the gangway was extended to the ship. He'd done it purposely to make sure the little berries pressed impudently against the thin suit mainly because she'd groused a little too loudly and long about the indignity of wearing just her suit among the Karthagoans.

All the while he'd tweaked her nipples, he'd done his best to arouse her. Her eyes had glittered with anger, but she'd kept silent, her chin rising proudly even while he'd felt the tremors slide over her skin. Honora couldn't help but surrender her responses each and every time he demanded.

They hadn't spoken directly to each other since she'd thrown his offer to make her his concubine in his face. He hadn't told her he'd wanted to make her his *only* concubine. Especially not after she'd let him know just how little she valued the honor he extended.

She thought service to a king demeaning, but what other choices did she have? His muscles tensed. Would she really choose life as an outcast or death by execution over living with him?

He swung the end of the braided leash and snapped it at her buttocks. She shot him a deadly glare, but he smiled back, truly enjoying the game they played now.

As soon as they'd entered Karthagos airspace, contact had been made with the ground control. Dagr had transmitted the message, asking for permission to dock after confirming the rumors that had already reached the colony that Vikings had indeed pirated a Consortium ship.

Permission had been granted, their business stated—they had a shipment of ore to barter for goods and information.

Aware that Karthagoan spies trailed their steps, Dagr stayed alert, his gaze scanning for trouble, as did his Vikings and his future sister-in-law. And while Honora went nearly naked and weaponless into the streets, Birget had armed Baraq, giving Dagr a shrug when he'd leveled a glare. "We need all the warriors we have."

At the end of the gangway, he'd paid the port checker for

docking and for information regarding the bounty hunters' transport without giving away the nature of their inquiry.

The port authority had been unwilling to divulge privileged information, but had directed their party down a rat's warren of narrow streets to the transport's offices.

The sun that warmed the atmosphere of the planet enough to keep it habitable didn't produce an intense light, so shadows loomed around corners and under stoops. A hundred pairs of eyes watched from the shadows or from behind darkened windows, but Dagr didn't worry. He'd seen the size of the average Karthagoan and knew he and his warriors were intimidating enough to make them hesitate. As well, besides the crude weapons they carried, they still had the *Proteus* officers' stunners hidden in their furs.

The alley they followed opened onto a street less claustrophobic in dimension than those they'd traveled so far. Shadowed by the dusklike afternoon sun, he eyed the street up and down. "Vikings, stay alert."

"We see, Captain," Grimvarr said. His men had been cautioned not to call him "milord." To the people who might overhear them, he was Captain or the Black Wolf.

And what his men saw was a deserted avenue. Shades drawn over windows. Wind whistled between buildings, stirring dust and dried vegetation. The air smelled of burning fossil fuels.

Dagr stepped out of the alley and headed to the right, toward the hunters' office, jerking Honora's chain to keep her abreast of him. They walked along a planked sidewalk, passed a tavern with tinny music spilling over the tops of half doors, the only sound besides the whistling wind.

The hunters' office sign read CLOSED but Dagr tried the door handle anyway. It swung inward. Inside, the office furnishings were sparse and tattered, the floors dirty cement, the walls weathered wood. A counter halted their progress. The outer office was deserted but a clicking sound emanated from a room behind the counter.

Dagr nodded to Grimvarr. His cousin raised the counter ledge and quietly folded it open. He slipped beside the doorway, his stunner raised, then nodded to Dagr.

Dagr dropped Honora's leash, pressed a finger to his lips, and pushed her behind him, then straightened his shoulders and walked through the door.

Inside, the tapping continued, but the desk where it came from was empty. He heard a slight sound to his right, then felt the nozzle of a weapon press behind his ear.

"Easy now, barbarian," a woman drawled.

Two men, dressed in trousers, long jackets over lace-edged shirts, and tall leather boots rose from behind desks with weapons aimed at the doorway behind Dagr.

Dagr slowly raised his hands. "I've come to conduct business with the proprietor of this company."

"You're talking to her. How opportune for you since I'm rarely in port. But you did see the sign on the door. I'm closed at the moment. You should come back tomorrow."

However, her dry tone implied he'd have an even harder time to find her then. "Seems odd for you to be closed so early in the day."

"Word's out that Vikings landed," she said, humor in her voice. "And they have a Consortium ship. The very same one colleagues of mine were aboard just days ago. Funny coincidence, isn't it?"

"It's no coincidence, lady. I followed your colleagues here."

The nozzle pushed harder against his head. "State your business."

"May I lower my hands?"

"I don't think so. And no more of your crew can come through that door if they don't want to wear your brain matter," she said, nudging behind his ear again.

Dagr grimaced at the stab of pain. "I want to barter for the men the hunters aboard your ship took from New Iceland."

"That won't be possible. The cargo is already promised."

"I can double your asking price."

"You don't understand. I wouldn't stay in business long if I didn't keep my promises. I was paid well for that cargo. If you're interested in more Vikings, I can arrange another shipment."

Behind him, Honora's soft hand rubbed his back, a silent caution not to push too hard.

Irritated at yet another obstacle thrown in his path, Dagr ground out, "If we can't barter with you, can we approach those who purchased the men?"

"Why are you so interested in this cargo?"

"One of my men was captured. I don't take kindly to being raided."

The woman's laughter was soft and sexy. "You don't like being bested or caught by surprise, do you?"

"Do you?" he said, turning his head to get a look at the woman despite the weapon that scraped across his cheek.

Her hair was long and black, and fashioned into small, tight braids that fell past her breasts. She was dressed in a silk shirt with bell sleeves, her middle cinched by a corset. Her legs were encased in leather breeches and her feet stuffed into tall black boots. She was a beauty. Her lush mouth curved at his inspection. "Do you like what you see?" she asked, a dark brow arching.

A faint stirring roused his cock, purely male, but not terribly urgent. "Perhaps. But I don't like women pointing weapons at my head." With an economy of movements, he raised his arm, shoving up her weapon, which exploded beside his ear, the round showering them with plaster from the ceiling. But he was on her, the wrist holding the gun slammed against the wall. With one hand, he raised her by her neck until her feet dangled.

His men entered the room, Grimvarr rolling, then coming to a crouch with his weapon trained on the men who failed to protect the woman's back.

They raised their arms, their guns tilting from their fingers.

Dagr grunted, then returned his gaze to the woman.

Her dark brown eyes glittered with anger, but she didn't betray any fear. He lowered her slowly, moving in to trap her with his body, using his size to intimidate and letting her feel the press of his superior muscle against her slender frame. "I will know where the captives have been taken," he said, pitching his voice low.

She hesitated, then gave a small, tight nod, her lips crimping with displeasure. "I'm not the one you need to talk to. I didn't arrange the transfer of the cargo."

Dagr gave her a chilly glare, a silent warning that he wouldn't abide any tricks. "Honora," he said over his shoulder. "Check for weapons."

Honora snorted, then eased under his arm, coming between his body and the female pirate's—for the woman couldn't be anything else dressed as she was.

Dagr almost smiled at Honora's action. Was she jealous that he stood so close to the other woman?

Honora pried the weapon from the pirate's hand.

"Hand it behind you, *elskling*."

He couldn't help it; standing with Honora's body pressed against his front, knowing Honora's breasts were flattened against the lady pirate's, Dagr began to harden. He thanked the stars he didn't wear anything as revealing as a skin-suit because anyone seeing him now would know his thoughts were of sex.

As it was, his nostrils flared, dragging in the mixed feminine musks.

The lady pirate was tall enough she looked right over the top of Honora's head and smiled. "You made a thrall of a Consortium crew member?"

"She's the *Proteus*'s captain," he drawled. "I keep her close to assure her crew's good behavior."

The pirate arched a brow, admiration glinting in her dark eyes. "I'm Captain Roxana."

"I'm the Black Wolf," he said softly. Honora stiffened between them, but he couldn't worry about her jealousy now. He needed the other woman's cooperation.

Roxana's head leaned against the wall behind her, and she blew between pursed lips as Honora ran her hands down her body. "This is the most interesting pat-down I've ever had. Do you two tag-team your sex too?"

Honora popped up and pressed her body closer to Roxana, standing on her toes to meet her gaze directly. "Don't you wish," she growled. She raised a long, slender blade she'd pulled from somewhere on Roxana's body and placed the tip against the woman's jugular.

"Honora, love," Dagr said softly. "We need her to talk before you gut her."

"Are all your thralls this possessive?" Roxana said, the corners of her mouth twitching.

"Honora, was that all?" he said, lowering his voice in warning.

Honora took her time pulling away, making sure to rub her bottom against his groin—an unsubtle reminder of whose ass he should be thinking of.

Dagr let go of Roxana and stood back. "Who is it I need to talk to?"

"You'll need an introduction to the person who handled the money for the captives. Will you follow me?"

Dagr swept his hand to the side to indicate she should precede

him. She swept past, her spicy scent tickling his nose, her ass swaying enticingly. "Boys," she said over her shoulder, "lock up, then follow us."

Honora glared daggers at Dagr, but he shrugged. No other solution existed. He was dependent on the lady pirate's cooperation.
Still, Honora's jealousy amused and aroused him.

His contingent trailed them out of the office, weapons con-
cealed, but ready for trouble. Dagr placed his hand around the
pirate's hip and leaned close. "You do know that I will kill you if
you betray me."

"Do you think that lessens my attraction for you?"

He swatted her bottom and grinned, enjoying the verbal play.
Roxana was a strong, intelligent woman, qualities he admired,
but he wasn't truly interested in bedding her. However, Honora
didn't need to know that. Fury reddening his captive's cheeks and
the tight set of her features promised a fiery retribution later when
they were alone—something he intended to milk for the greatest
satisfaction.

They walked the planked sidewalk back the way they'd come,
halting in front of the half doors of the saloon. Music tinkled from
within. The scent of ale hung sour in the air.

Roxana pushed through the doors and every head turned their
way, gazes widening on the appearance of his warriors, then homing in on Roxana's proximity to Dagr. The music quieted; voices
trailed off.

She stepped backward, pressing against Dagr and lifting her
face to his, the pose intimate. "Your men will need to fan out and
take seats. Pretend not to be looking for a fight."

Dagr gave a subtle signal to his men. He didn't need to tell them
to keep their heads clear and their weapons handy. The atmosphere
inside the bar was so thick an ax could have cleaved it in two.

Roxana flung back her hair and walked straight for the bar.

Dagr followed on her heels, all the while watching the rest of the room out of the corners of his eyes. But his attention strayed almost immediately, snagging on the face of the barman.

The creature's skin was striped gray and black with fur as short as a mouse's. His lip was split like a cat's, his eyes gold, large, and unblinking as he stared back at Dagr. The cat-man grinned, the tips of his white fangs appearing beneath the upper lip. "First trip to Karthagos?"

The voice was human enough if one discounted the underlying purr. Dagr nodded, then aimed a glance at Roxana.

Her lush mouth curved into a delicious smile. "Billy isn't a pet."

The barman laughed. "What can I get you? Would you like dark mead?" he asked, eyeing Dagr's furs.

Dagr nodded, not trusting his voice because a growl was working its way up his throat.

Honora snickered beside him. "Billy's a hybrid. So are they," she said, pointing her chin toward two nearly naked barmaids, both brown-haired and pale-skinned. But they appeared human, their bodies free of hair. While their bodies were more deeply muscled than most females, their shapes were feminine, their breasts tipped with rosy nipples and their skin a smooth pearl white.

"Look at their eyes," Roxana whispered.

The women turned, and their eyes caught the lamplight, reflecting off flat, golden discs like a lynx's eyes in pure light.

"It's not natural," Dagr said.

"Of course it is. Now, anyway. They breed their own litters these days."

Roxana accepted a shot glass of an amber liquid and tossed it back with a jerk of her head. Then her gaze sliced around the room. "He's not here."

Dagr dragged his gaze from the hybrid women. "Who's not?"

"The one you need to talk to. Horace." She leaned an elbow on the bar. "He handled the transaction and gave us the stake to launch the mission. Fatin, the hunter in charge of the extraction team, hasn't returned yet either."

"Will Horace be here later?"

"Maybe, but you can't just park here and not raise suspicions that you're lying in wait."

Damn. Irritation tensed his jaw. The woman was right. It was becoming an epidemic. "What do you suggest?"

She lifted her chin to the rooms lining the upstairs balcony. "I suggest we entertain ourselves," she said, her voice dropping to a sultry rumble.

Honora's breath hissed between her teeth; her feet scuffed the floor.

Roxana smacked her lips at Honora. "She can come too."

While Dagr enjoyed Honora's fiery response, he didn't think putting two strongly opposed women in the same bed was a very good idea.

Honora's hands fisted, and she stepped around Dagr, who laced an arm around her middle to pull her back. "We will have to think of another way to pass the time."

Roxana pouted, but turned her back to the bar and leaned her elbows on it. "Who is truly enthralled?"

"You can choose one of my men."

She heaved a deep sigh, her gaze regretful as it raked his body, but she eyed the two Vikings who flanked him. "I'll take them both."

Dagr nodded and the men followed Roxana up the stairs.

"Do you trust her?" Honora bit out.

"You found all her weapons. My men aren't fools."

Her amber gaze nailed him. "Were you attracted?"

Dagr lifted the beaker the barman slid his way and drew on it. "The only thing that aroused me was the way you grew enflamed."

Honora's lips twisted into a snarl. "I was angry. Still am. But not over her. You're enjoying this too much."

He curved a hand behind her neck and pulled her close. "I don't mind you showing your claws."

"Careful. I'll be wanting to see her fur," the barman teased behind them.

Honora's eyes widened. "I'm not . . ."

The cat's lip split in a wide grin. "Do you think I'd care?"

Dagr growled and looped his arm around her waist, pulling her toward an empty table. He sat and pulled her onto his lap, laying her backward over his arm and giving her a hard kiss. With just a nibble, her tight lips relaxed and responded.

A throat cleared, and he glanced up. Birget turned a chair and straddled it backward, lifting a brow toward Honora. "You should get your own room, but then again, I don't think Roxana would mind you both joining her two studs."

Dagr's cock roused uncomfortably against Honora's hip.

Her eyelids drifted down, but she watched him from beneath her dark lashes, a small frown bisecting her brows.

"Admit you're jealous." He leaned close. "Just the mention of her name has your back stiffening."

Her lips pouted. "I'd never be jealous over you."

One of the hybrid barmaids sidled up beside Dagr and leaned close enough her ripe breast rubbed the fur cloaking his shoulders. Her exhalation rumbled. "What can I bring you, master?"

Dagr felt his loins tighten at the vibrations that shivered against him, at the catlike purr underlying the woman's voice.

Honora stiffened in his arms and he gazed down, expecting another jealous flush, but found her gaze curious.

The barmaid gave Dagr a look that begged permission. At his nod, she leaned over him to lower her face to Honora's.

Honora pulled back, her eyes widening, but the woman merely nuzzled her cheek. Honora's breath hitched. The curiosity burning in her amber gaze intensified.

The cat's eyebrows gave a wicked waggle. "Imagine what I might do for you, lady." She turned her head toward Dagr. "Do you have the ore to purchase my talents?"

Dagr cleared his throat. "We've time while we wait for an associate to arrive. We'll take a room. *Alone.*" He wasn't quite ready to share Honora yet, despite her curiosity.

The half-breed feline pursed her lips in disappointment, but swaggered away, her ass twitching. All that was missing from the picture was a long tail.

He pulled his gaze away and glanced down at Honora, whose expression brimmed with rueful amusement. One of her sleek brows arched. "You can deny all you want, but this," she said, grinding against his erection, "isn't all for me."

Unwilling to be drawn into conversation with a jealous woman, he grunted, then aimed a pointed glance at Birget, ignoring her disapproving glower from across the table. "You two keep an eye out for trouble. We'll be busy 'blending,'" he said, smiling.

Birget's face blushed a bright red while Baraq's shoulders shook.

Honora's was reddening too, but not from embarrassment; he could smell the strength of her arousal. He rose, jostling Honora in his arms and causing her to yelp and clutch his shoulders. His smile didn't wane all the way up the stairs.

An attendant on the floor above opened a door for him. He swept inside and set Honora on her feet. A sumptuous bed on a raised platform sat in the center of the room. A washbasin with a faucet above it was tucked into a corner. Other than that, the room was bare.

Honora wasted no time stripping off the skin-suit. His own clothes landed in a pile and he stalked her, walking her backward to a bed piled high with downy pillows. He unlatched the collar from her neck, and dropped it and the leash to the floor, planted his hand in the center of her chest and shoved. Then he climbed onto the bed to hover over her.

Honora watched him, her golden-brown eyes slitted. She lay still except for the thumb toggling her nipple. "Are you sure it's me you want in this bed, *Lord Dagr*?"

Her voice, mimicking the purr of the barmaid, slid over him like a sensual caress. Honora was learning to tease. "Don't you think that if I desired another bedmate, she'd be here? After all, you are my captive. You must do my bidding, even if it is to cool your heels below while I seek my pleasure with another."

He plucked her hand from her breast, latched it with the other and held them both high above her head as he lowered himself.

When he had her under him, he pressed his thickened cock against her mound. "Any doubts this is all for you now?"

Her lips twitched, and then she laughed. She wrapped her legs around his waist and squeezed.

Dagr centered himself at her entrance and stroked deep, closing his eyes for a moment to savor the pleasure of her wet heat.

When he glanced down, he found her staring up at him, studying his expression. "What do you see, *elskling*?"

She wrinkled her nose. "You're very beautiful."

He arched an eyebrow. "You say that as though that doesn't please you."

Honora arched, pulling her hands from his embrace. She trailed

her fingertips down his cheeks, rubbed his mouth with a thumb.
Her gaze, almost shy, rose to lock with his. "Every time I see you,
I find something new to admire. When you're fierce and hard, I
tremble, but you still take my breath away. When you're like this,
relaxed," she paused and swallowed, "you're a very handsome man.
I can see why Roxana was eager to have you. And I get why your
concubines would be willing to share you."

Dagr held himself still despite the pulsing of her inner walls
around his cock. "But you are not."

"It sounds selfish, especially after the pleasure you afforded me
with your men, but I'm greedy."

He smiled and leaned down to kiss her. "I like that you're possessive. In any other woman, that quality would annoy me. But I
find great satisfaction in your jealousy."

Her lips twisted. "I shouldn't tell you a thing. It will only make
your head swell."

"Too late," he growled, giving her a sexy dig of his cock. Then
thrusting his arms beneath her, he embraced her, cradling her body
against his. They stroked together, heat building inside her narrow
channel. The first flutters of arousal clamped around his shaft, and
he rolled, settling with her knees on either side of his hips.

She bent, kissing his mouth, his chin, burrowing into the corner
of his neck to suck at his skin. "Have I told you I love the way you
smell?"

He found himself smiling at the ceiling and clutched her hips
to force her to move on his cock. "Are you next going to praise my
breath?"

She giggled, a sound that was slightly strangled because he
flexed his hips to drive up as she sank down his shaft. "Do you want
me to? Should I praise the strength of your arms, the thickness of

your cock?" She groaned and crashed down against him again. "Because right now, all I can think of is how good this feels . . . "

Since she needed no more encouragement to move, he slid his hands from her rump and cupped her breasts, tweaking the nipples and enjoying her sounds—breathy moans, desperate murmurs. She thought him beautiful, but she was that and so much more.

Every day, every hour they spent together, she surprised him. Pleased him in ways he wasn't yet ready to define. More sure than ever before, he knew he'd never let her go.

Fourteen

Honora floated on a wave of pleasure. Although that was probably not the right description. The waves were growing choppy, violent even, and her thighs were quivering with the strain to keep up the pace.

She halted her movements. "Enough. Wait." She gasped, leaning on a hand planted against his chest while she tried to catch her breath. "I don't know how you do it. I'm out of breath."

Dagr's smirk, so full of masculine pride, stretched across his face. "You are the weaker sex."

She scowled.

His hands smoothed over her slick skin. "Would you like me to take over?"

She blew out a deep breath, studying him, making him wait. His body was tense, his cock thick and urgent inside her. Stars, she loved his stamina. "Would you mind—just until I catch my breath?"

He lifted her slowly off his shaft, then flipped her to her back—
so suddenly, she gave a startled shriek.

Leaning over her, his gaze trailed down her body and back up to
cling to her mouth.

She wet her lips. An invitation he couldn't miss.

"Do not ask unless you mean to follow through," he warned.

The low rumbling of his voice did things to her. Her belly tightened. Her womb cramped. She wrapped her hand around his shaft
and tugged.

He crawled up her body until his knees straddled her shoulders.
Then he cupped the back of her head to take the strain as she rose
to accept the thrust of his cock, all the way to the back of her throat.
He pumped slowly in and out, ripples of tension sliding across his
belly. She reveled in the power she wielded as she submitted to the
forceful strokes.

Honora moaned around Dagr's cock and sucked it hard, drawing on it deeply. Her tongue stroked his cap, and she suctioned
her mouth so hard Dagr cursed, then quickly pulled away, ringing
his cock as he gave her a narrowed glance that made her insides
quiver.

She didn't protest when he once more changed position, scooting down the bed to lie between her legs. His eagerness to have her
every way he could pleased her.

He tucked his face between her legs and lapped over her sex
with his wicked tongue. His large calloused hands cupped her buttocks, squeezing as he pleasured her. At first, he nibbled at her folds,
and then sucked them into his mouth to tug and torture her.

Squirming, she dug her fingernails into his scalp and pulled.
"That feels so good. Feels like more . . . "

His tongue stroked her clit. Then fingers pulled the top of her folds to draw up the hood cloaking it. He blew a stream of steamy air over the sensitive knot.

Honora lifted her knees and let them splay wide. "Don't tease."

A tap landed on her clit. "Would you tell me what to do?"

She groaned. "Are you always this touchy? It was just a little slip." He pinched her clit, making her jerk. She hissed between her teeth. "Not nice!"

"Will you continue to complain?"

Honora gave him a nearly cross-eyed glare but kept silent.

His mouth curved. His hands delivered a sexy caress. When he relented with his teasing and bent over her again, her breath left in a relieved rush because he went straight to the source of her delight.

His tongue flicked and feathered her clit until her abdomen vibrated from the pleasure. "I'm close, so close!"

"Then, come, *elskling*. Come!"

Honora didn't need any more encouragement. She soared over the peak, shocked still and shuddering. She moaned, unable to breathe for the beauty of the moment.

His hands slid from under her. Fingers stroked her sex, soothing her now. Kisses dotted her thighs and mound.

She felt limp, replete. Wonderfully boneless. She could happily drift into sleep, but knew her lusty lover wasn't nearly through with her. As soon as the thought flitted through her mind, Dagr stirred and knelt beside her. His fist slowly stroked his cock, drawing her attention. When he was assured of her interest, he raised his eyebrows.

Honora gifted him with tired smile and rose to lean on her elbows. "I'll have to add another quality to that list of things I admire. Your tongue's amazing, pirate."

*   *   *

Dagr's skin felt stretched tight. Every muscle in his body was tense, rigid. Lust held him in near agony, he was so aroused. The mission had been forgotten in the last half hour while Honora had writhed like a wanton, suspended beyond herself by the lush eroticism of their encounter. He'd felt the wild thrumming pulse too, and wondered if they'd been fed an aphrodisiac in their mead to increase their arousal to a fever pitch. Or maybe it was just the woman.

Even with her hair a wild, wet tangle, her skin rosy and slick, she was so beautiful, so desirable, he ached.

For the moment, he didn't care about the cause for his heightened lust. Blood thundered through his veins. His cock was swollen, his balls rock hard. He needed release.

Honora gave him a sultry look from beneath her dark eyelashes. "I suppose you want me to do something about your current state? Looks painful."

Dagr grunted. To say anything now would only be stating the obvious.

He liked it when Honora arched that brow, as she was doing now, daring him to take the reins again—which he inevitably did each and every time they came together. But he knew her ploy. She pushed, only because she wanted to be forced to surrender.

Holding out his hand, he waited while she took her sweet time sliding her palm across his. He closed his fingers and dragged her to her knees. Then he fisted his hand in her hair and pulled her face toward his groin before releasing her. Not a very subtle command, but he'd earned a little compensation.

Honora leaned forward, darting a glance toward his face.

Anticipation sizzled as he braced apart his legs. She pushed away the hand fisting his cock, replaced it with her own, and squeezed hard.

His thighs trembled, and that was before she stuck her hand between his legs and gently gripped his balls.

The sweet witch leaned lower to rub her cheeks against his inner thigh, then up his shaft, her tongue darting out now and then to wet him. His cock tapped his belly in soft pulses.

Honora smiled, a feline glint in her eyes, and pulled it down to her mouth—the wet, succulent, messy kisses she pressed against the shaft destroying his control.

He rocked his hips forward and back, seeking entry into her mouth, but she suckled his head, then trailed away. He reached down and threaded his fingers through her hair to force her down his cock, but she raked him with her teeth, the sparkle of humor in her eyes saying she knew exactly how close to the edge of violence he really was.

"Master," Honora whispered, then bit her swollen lip.

"I like the sound of that," he growled.

Her lips pursed, then stretched. "It's so strange, but my pussy's still wet. Would you lie on your back on the mattress? Notice, I asked."

So she would play at submission. "I thought you were too tired to ride."

"I've recovered. And I've thought of a better way to satisfy you."

Dagr wanted to push her to the mattress and fuck her hard, but excitement shimmered in her eyes. So, feigning reluctance, he lay on his back, stuffing a pillow under his head and fisting his cock, stroking it while she crawled toward him, her breasts pink and peaked and swaying beneath her.

Honora straddled his hips, grasping his cock and centering it between her nether lips. She pressed downward, her lush, wet heat surrounding him again. She pulsed twice before grinding down the last bit until she rested against him, his cock completely sheathed.

Faint ripples caressed his length. Dagr growled, wanting to wrest control, but still curious to see what she would do.

Honora leaned back, and one of her hands raked up his inner thigh to cup his balls.

Dagr ground his jaws together, trying to stifle the shout clawing its way up his throat. In the end, she wouldn't let him come quietly.

Honora leaned farther, slid a finger deeper between his legs and rubbed his asshole, causing his whole body to jerk, his belly to quiver. Then he dug his heels into the mattress and pumped up to meet her downward thrusts, shouting when his balls exploded and his seed jetted toward her womb.

When her contractions had wrung him dry, he lay back, covered in sweat and shuddering in the aftermath.

Honora eased off him, then moved down and took his softening, wet cock into her mouth.

He dug his fingers in her hair. "I'm done," he growled.

"I want the taste of you," she whispered, then swallowed him again, her mouth making moist noises that made him smile.

A light tap sounded on the door and it opened.

Dagr pushed Honora off him, and rolled to his side, ready to answer a threat, but the barmaid from below entered, smiling, her arms filled with towels.

"I thought you might need these," she said, kicking the door closed with a heel.

He looked toward the stand with the basin of water. Towels and washcloths were stacked beside it.

When he glanced back, narrowing his glance on her, she shrugged. "I have something else for you too." She came closer, one knee on the mattress as she bent to whisper in his ear. "Do you want to rise again?" She opened her palm to show him a paper wrapper.

He looked to Honora who shrugged a shoulder. "I have no reason to be jealous. We'll never see her again, and I'll be right here."

But she feigned indifference. Her eyes glittered with excitement. Seeing no objection, only curiosity, he turned back. "I suppose my interest depends on whether I will feel drugged with whatever it is that you hold."

Her lips twitched, the dent at the center stretching. "The powder will make you harden, and your next release will be difficult, but you could pleasure your lady again."

"And you too, I suppose?" he drawled.

Her gaze raked his body, then clung to his cock. She grinned. "I haven't had a cock like yours in ages. I'd like to repeat the experience."

Her covetous glance was mildly gratifying, but his natural distrust made him wary. "What happens when a woman swallows your powder?"

She gave a feminine shiver, then blinked her gold eyes. "She becomes mindless with desire."

"Put it on your tongue and share it with me."

Her body stiffened. "Do you think I want to poison you?"

"Shouldn't I be wary?"

She arched a brow and tipped back her head, sprinkling the powder onto her tongue. Then she bent and kissed him, sharing the powder with long swipes of her sandpaper tongue.

He drew back and stuck out his tongue. The cat-woman's eyes glinted as she gave him another sprinkle. He swept out an arm behind him, snagging Honora and pulling her close. They shared the powder between them in a long, steamy kiss.

Honora pulled away, breathing hard. Her glance went to the other woman. "Since this is your turf, I'll let you take the lead."

Surprised, Dagr glanced from one female to the other. The barmaid tossed back her head and pointed toward Dagr's cock. Honora smiled and resumed suckling.

At first, Dagr felt nothing, just the mild pleasure of another kiss and the warm comfort of Honora's mouth caressing him below. The kiss lengthened, deepening, while his tongue dueled with the cat, and Honora's hot mouth suckled him like a puppy. Soon, his breaths deepened as his loins filled with heat that stiffened him, crowding him into Honora's mouth. She reacted eagerly, backing off his cock as he hardened, allowing him to unfurl while she ran her open lips along the sides of his shaft.

He broke the kiss, gasping, then stuck his forearm beneath his head to lift it higher and watch as she devoured him. While she moaned around him, she cuddled one leg between hers and rocked against it, the moisture spilling from her pussy anointing his skin.

The barmaid's fingernails scraped his chest, tickling his nipples, which drew into tight little points. "Fuck her. Eat me," she whispered.

Dagr growled when she plucked his chest hair. But the suggestion held merit. Heart racing in his chest, he rose to his knees, shoved Honora off his cock, then forced her to her belly while she laughed at his haste. Not until he slid into her juicy cunt did the tension ease enough for him to remember they had another partner.

"Your name," he demanded, his voice rasping.

"You may call me Kit." Then Kit stood on the mattress and straddled Honora's back, inching forward until her pussy was just in front of his mouth.

He leaned into her, thrusting his nose between her lips, scraping his whiskered chin against her delicate folds, then thrusting out his tongue to delve deeper. Her soft, silky pelt soothed his nose and cheeks, but it was the hardening knot at the top that interested him most. While he hammered Honora with his cock, Kit raised the hood that cloaked her nubbin and he dove in, latching around it with his lips and sucking.

The drug searing his veins kept him hard and on the edge, pumping relentlessly into Honora until she sobbed and shouted and bucked. He suckled Kit, teething on the button, until her fingers clamped around his ears and her pussy crushed against him.

Both women came in a noisy rush, Honora screaming, Kit squalling like a cat. Still he couldn't come.

When Kit collapsed beside them, he flipped Honora and drove into her once more, urging her arms and her thighs around him while he plowed her, his heart bursting in his chest, his body desperate to erupt.

In the end, Kit had the cure. A single digit penetrated his ass and stroked over the small gland deep inside him until he showered Honora in ropey bursts of cum. He stroked Honora long after he'd pumped himself dry, unwilling to lose the hot friction burning his cock.

Finally, she pulled him down and kissed him, framing his face with her hands and diving between his lips to caress his tongue with long strokes of her own.

He rested on his elbows, cupped her cheeks between his palms, and kissed her more gently. Her eyes slowly opened, blinking up at him. The red blur of her lips, the pink tinting her bronze cheeks, and the sheen of sweat slicking her skin made her lovelier, sexier, than he deserved.

He turned to Kit. "How much to buy your freedom?"

"Was I that good?"

"I don't like to think of any of my sex partners enslaved."

She blinked, a wariness entering her expression as she sat up and ran her fingers through her hair. "Even if I were free, where would I go?"

"I have a castle full of warriors who would find your many differences enticing," he said, not fearing that he'd revealed too much about himself.

"You would free me from being a whore here to make me one for your Vikings?"

Dagr frowned. "You would have your choice of lovers and you may learn a craft, earn your own way."

"You have other half-breeds in your employ?"

"None. Ours has been a sheltered society."

"And I should welcome being the freak among you?" Kit shook her head. "No, thanks. I'll take my chances here."

Dagr sighed, seeing her point. "My thanks, Kit."

Kit drew a deep breath, thinned her lips, then met his glance again. "Roxana has you waiting for one called Horace. But he will only tell you that you seek Fatin. She was Roxana's partner, but she betrayed Roxana and robbed her of a valuable cargo. Delivery was to happen here, but Fatin heads straight to Helios. She thinks she can get a better price and that they'll actually let her penetrate their airspace because of what she carries."

"What is the name of her ship? What class?" Honora asked, shrugging at Dagr. "We have to know we're still talking about the same ship."

"A freighter class ship called the *Orion*. She has a day's lead on you."

Dagr bent and pressed a hard kiss against Kit's mouth. "My thanks again, lady. I'll arrange payment to be delivered. Enough to buy your freedom should you change your mind."

Kit nodded. "Roxana shouldn't be trusted. She's a pirate in her own right." Kit placed a hand on his arm. "If she thinks she can gain by serving you to the Consortium, she will."

Fifteen

Below in the tavern, Honora and Dagr found Birget with Baraq and Roxana's two flunkies knocking back shots of liquor and laughing uproariously.

The two henchmen were glassy-eyed, and it didn't take but a glance at the floor to figure out that both Birget and her guard were spilling their drinks on purpose.

Dagr grabbed a wooden chair and sat.

Honora, heat creeping into her cheeks at Baraq's pointed glare, slid into a seat across the table from him.

"Roxana's still above?" Dagr asked.

Birget nodded, the movement crisp. Alcohol hadn't dulled her edge.

"Roxana's a go-er," one of her men slurred.

Dagr lifted a shot glass and clinked it against the talkative pirate. "Roxana own more than the ship Fatin stole?"

The man stiffened and shot a heavy-lidded glance around the bar. "Shhh . . . No one's s'posed to know. 'Bout Fatin. Bad fer bizss-ness."

"No sign of Horace?"

The man snickered. "Horace is hiding. Roxana will cut out his innards if she finds out he knew anything about Fatin's plans."

Irritation simmered in Dagr's narrow gaze. "Then why are we here?"

The man next to the talker elbowed his friend.

The talker rubbed his belly and gave him a scowl. "I need 'nother drink."

"You've had enough," his companion growled. "Roxana's gonna cut off your balls."

Dagr nodded to Baraq. "I'm heading to the privy."

"The privy, he calls it," the merry pirate laughed. "It's a frigging pisser."

"Shut up, will ya?" his friend said, growing pale beneath Dagr's pointed glare.

"She's pretty, even if she makes me dick shrink," the man said, raising a glass to Birget. "Seein' as how ever-one else had some fun, what ya say?"

Birget snarled, stood, and clapped the man across the temple with the hilt of her dagger.

He slumped, his head thudding onto the table.

His friend swayed in his seat but nodded. "Thanks. He was annoying the piss out of me."

Honora tilted her head toward the man and eyed Birget, whose slight nod indicated she would follow her lead. Then Honora slipped into the seat on the other side of the pirate. She leaned in, unzipped her skin-suit, and let the sides peel open, exposing her cleavage. She waved a hand at her face. "I'm so hot. Must be the alcohol. Drank too much," she said, laying her head on his shoulder. She placed her hand on his thigh and squeezed.

His leg jumped, then both eased open. He pressed his hand over hers and moved it over his cock.

The smirk beneath his long-handled mustache made her skin crawl. "Oooh, and I thought the Viking had a big one," she said between clenched teeth.

"I'm Black Bart. Been a pirate all me life. Do what I want. Takes what I want."

Honora smiled and rubbed his chest. "Seems to me you're under Roxana's heel. She snaps her fingers and you obey."

His upper lip curled into a snarl. "The bitch holds me ship. Can't leave port without her say-so."

She widened her eyes. "You have your own ship?"

"I contracted for cargo, but she let the bitch Fatin take what was mine."

"So your ship's still here, docked, until Roxana snaps her fingers again and tells you to go?"

He aimed a deadly glare her way, and his fingers squeezed painfully over hers, holding her harder against his groin. "I think I want me some Consortium ass."

Honora leaned back as he bent forward to kiss her.

She hadn't known Birget moved, until a blade beneath his chin made the pirate freeze.

Birget leaned in and wrapped her elbow around the pirate's head. Anyone seeing them from the back would think they'd all kissed. "This ship of yours . . ." she said softly, scraping his chin with the point of her blade. "What's it called?"

"The *Daedalus*." The pirate glared. "But what do you care? You can't take it. Karthagos's docks are well guarded. It's part of why we do business here."

Birget leaned closer and licked the side of the pirate's face. "No reason, pretty boy. Just wondered where your berth was." The pirate lifted an eyebrow, his gaze sweeping over Birget's long frame. He let go of Honora's hand.

She wiped it on her skin-suit, making a face.

Birget leaned toward the pirate, her lips pursed, but then she clipped his jaw with a fist.

He slid down bonelessly in his chair.

"We leave them for a moment and already they've found trouble."

Honora glanced over her shoulder to find Dagr, Baraq, and his two Vikings leading a disgruntled Roxana.

The pirate eyed her unconscious men. For the first time, fear tightened her features.

Honora's gaze slid to Dagr and her heart skipped a beat. She didn't miss the narrow-eyed look he aimed her way.

L et's go," Dagr said, annoyed at lingering in this soulless place, and angry at yet another woman who'd managed to put a spoke in his progress. His small contingent walked out onto the street, heading back to the ship.

"You can leave me at my office," Roxana said breathlessly, tugging at her arm.

Dagr didn't release his hard grip. "I think not. We have need of a ship. You have a fleet."

"Not a fleet. Really," Roxana said, breathlessly as he pushed her along. "Only a few ships. Nothing in port at the moment."

"The *Daedalus* is docked and empty of cargo," Birget said. "That's what we got from the pirate at the table."

Dagr shook Roxana, wishing she were male because he really needed an enemy he could go a round with. "Lead us there."

Her head lolled forward, and then snapped back, her black braids swinging. A snarl curled her lips. "It's docked three berths from yours."

Dagr grunted and pulled her along beside him. "Why'd you waste my time, waiting on Horace?"

Her mouth tightened into a thin line.

"Have you already sent word to the Consortium of our whereabouts?"

Roxana lifted her brows. "How could I?" she drawled. "I've been with you ever since we met."

Dagr studied her expression, wondering if she was really as good a liar as she thought.

"Gods, I know that look," Honora muttered. She patted Roxana's shoulder with false sympathy.

Dagr turned his glare on her, and Honora raised both hands in surrender.

The trip back to the docks was made in silence, everyone in the party aware of the many gazes following their progress from behind curtained windows and from slanted rooftops.

"You know you won't get away with this," Roxana said, dragging her heels. "If they see you forcing me aboard your ship, you'll never get clearance to leave."

"Forcing you?" Dagr said. He pulled the woman against his side and draped his arm around her shoulder. "Smile or I'll strip you here in the alley and have you. It won't be rape, you know it, but it will certainly prove your willingness to be with us."

Roxana snorted, then smiled slowly—not a hint of humor reaching her hard eyes. "I think I hate you."

"No, you don't. Your heart leapt at the thought of being taken against a wall, everyone watching. Tell me another lie."

The gangway loomed. Roxana pulled back, digging in her heels. "I won't go aboard."

"What have you to fear? Once we are beyond the stratosphere, we'll transport you back."

Her body went rigid. "You're taking one of my ships!"

"Borrowing. And I'll pay for the use."

"You think you have enough money aboard your ship to pay for one of mine?"

"I have a king's ransom of pure light." He couldn't help biting out his words.

Roxana stared into his eyes. "You're telling me the truth."

"His brother, the one your Fatin kidnapped, is a prince of New Iceland," Birget said. "He's willing to pay you for the ship, and forgive you for your involvement in the crime. Take his offer."

Roxana's face drained of color. She stepped from beneath his arm and straightened her shoulders. "Why didn't you kill me?"

Dagr met her gaze, let her see his quiet fury.

She backed up a step, but he grabbed her arms again and pulled her close. "Killing you," he said, bending over her so closely their breaths intermixed, "though satisfying, would not help me find my brother. I want your ship. Something that won't attract attention for its . . . particle waves."

Roxana nodded her understanding. "Very well. I'll give the checker a nod. You needn't hold me. I come willingly."

Dagr gave her a cold smile and turned to Baraq. "Tell Cyrus he will remove himself and one container of ore from the *Proteus*."

Roxana gasped. "Cyrus . . ."

Dagr's sharp gaze lanced her. "Onto the ship, Roxana."

She shook her head. "This Cyrus . . ."

"A man in my employ. Get on the ship. You've already promised your cooperation."

Her jaw sawed shut, but she strode up the gangway. Inside, Roxana hung back, her gaze sweeping the Vikings who were busy using a crane to lift one container of ore onto a cart for delivery to the other ship.

Honora lingered, watching Roxana's strange behavior. When Cyrus shouted to Dagr and slid down the ladder, both feet bracketing the rungs as he glided down, she saw the woman's face blanch.

Cyrus gave the party arriving a quick glance, then swung back to Roxana. He stepped closer, his expression hardening, daggers in his eyes.

Roxana swallowed hard. "Hello, Cyrus."

"You two know each other?" Dagr asked, his glance cutting between the two.

"She's the one who owns my papers."

"The woman who kept you as her slave?"

"Her thrall," Cyrus ground out.

Roxana's chin rose. "You were a well-compensated thrall. I paid you portions of my takes. You were earning your freedom. I wasn't the one who enslaved you to begin with."

"That didn't stop you from using me for your pleasure."

She raised a dark brow. "I don't remember you minding all that much."

Honora watched, transfixed by the roiling emotions that caused Cyrus's expression to harden and the lady pirate's to pale.

"What's she doing here?" Cyrus asked, his gaze never leaving hers, a muscle in his jaw jumping.

"She's here to ensure our departure," Dagr drawled. "We're purchasing one of her transport ships too. We'll need it to get to Helios."

"What about her?"

"I told her she'd be transported back to the surface once we were clear."

Furious red blossomed in the centers of his cheeks. "She's mine, Dagr."

"I don't go back on my word," Dagr said quietly.

"I'll sell you his papers," Roxana said, directing her words to Dagr. "Along with the ship. He'll be free and clear to travel anywhere in the known universe, a free man. Right now, he has a bounty on his head."

Dagr turned to Cyrus. "What do you want to do?"

"I want to enslave her," Cyrus said between clenched teeth. "Make her bow to me the way she forced me to endure a hundred indignities."

Dagr shrugged. "You've earned the right to her."

"B-but we have a bargain," Roxana sputtered.

Cyrus smiled, but the gesture didn't reach his eyes. "If I didn't owe Dagr a debt, I'd keep you. But we have need of only your ship. Sell it and my papers to Dagr. Then we're through . . . for now. One day, I'll return and we'll settle our personal debt."

Roxana drew herself up. Her chin tilted high.

If Honora hadn't had tons of recent experience, she wouldn't have recognized the look on the other woman's face. There was longing there . . . and arousal.

Cyrus and the dread pirate Roxana . . . Honora snorted.

Cyrus swung his head toward her, his eyes narrowing into a bitter glare.

She lifted her brows in innocence. "Did I say anything?"

He stomped off.

Honora cleared her throat to get Dagr's attention. "So who will pilot the *Proteus*?"

Dagr's face, while still hard and unyielding, softened, so slightly only she recognized it. "We have mutual interest in recovering the hunters' ship. But we both can't follow it. Roxana's transport is our best solution. The *Daedalus* will still need a distraction, something to lead Consortium ships down another trail."

Honora's stomach dove toward her toes. "You're talking about letting them get a whiff of the *Proteus*. You would sacrifice it?"

"Where is the sacrifice? We will only run so far."

"You want me to captain the ship, lead it away from my higher command. You would trust me to do that? To openly defy them?"

"I would trust you with more, but you won't have to prove yourself. I will remain aboard your ship, along with several of my men. Enough to sustain the plausibility that we were responsible for the capture by ourselves."

Honora felt light-headed and drew a deep breath. "But they'll imprison you. No matter that you're a king."

"For a time, perhaps. But I have a plan."

"This is foolhardy. Insane. Go with Cyrus. I'll stay here long enough that the other ship can be well away before I meet up with the armada." Her breath hitched around the lump in her throat. "You don't have to sacrifice yourself."

"And I promise that is not my intent. I have two purposes, Honora. First, I must recover the captives. But I must also strike at the heart of the Consortium or they will never leave my world alone."

"But you can't win."

"Because they have ships and superior weaponry?"

She took a deep breath to reassure him, but let it out. "Well, yes."

"They don't protect their homes, their families. They don't have as much at stake." He clenched his jaws. "They underestimate us if they think that my demise, or my wolves' demise, will end the conflict."

Fists tight at her side, she stared into his eyes. "You talk about dying as though it doesn't matter."

"Every life matters. But how you spend it, what you stand

against, defines you. I will not surrender. I will not allow any Outlander to dictate how I live or die."

Honora felt a burning at the backs of her eyes and swung away from Dagr.

When his hand closed around the top of her shoulder, she tried to jerk away, but his arm encircled her waist and pulled her against his belly. He nuzzled the side of her cheek. "I promise I don't intend to commit suicide."

She turned inside his arms and stared up at him. "Will you tell me what you plan?"

"No, because I have to know you're safe. That you won't be part of this."

The gruff texture of his voice had her melting. Did he truly care? "I'm already part of this." She pressed closer, inhaling his musk.

"But they will not know that."

She rubbed her cheek on his chest. "How soon?"

"We still have ore to deliver, to Kit and to Roxana. Then we will divide the men. The *Daedalus* will leave first; then we will make our way back, through the armada. When we pass through their ranks, we will lead them on a chase."

"So we still have some time left?"

Dagr's mouth stretched with a soft smile. "How do you want to pass the time?"

Threading her arms beneath his and rubbing her palms up his back, she leaned closer. "I would remember the taste of you. The smell. The heat."

Dagr's jaw flexed. He cupped her face between his palms and bent to kiss her. "This will not be the last time we are together."

"How can you promise me that?" Her gaze savored the lips just inches from her own. "You don't have a clue how powerful they are. How far they can spread their tentacles."

Dagr trailed his lips along her cheek. "I have never felt this way for a woman, Honora. The gods can't be so cruel to give us a taste of what life would be like for us, then separate us forever."

She clung to him, burrowing her face into his chest, sinking into his warmth because she felt suddenly cold, suddenly frightened. Something she wasn't accustomed to, but she realized she'd never cared for anything or anyone as much as she did this man whom she hadn't known even a week ago.

"We still have some time," he whispered. "Be with me."

Although that was exactly what her heart wished, she struggled to be practical. "We have preparations to make."

Turk cleared his throat. "Honora . . . Captain," he said, grimacing. "I have the controls. I'll use the intercom if I need you."

Dagr led her away, his hand clutching hers.

Honora felt slightly nauseous. Her eyes were scratchy. Gods, she was going to cry. She sniffed.

Dagr's hand tightened, but he didn't turn. "No tears, *elskling*. If you cry, I fear I won't have the strength to do what must be done. This is why warriors don't love."

She smiled at that. "That's ridiculous."

He grunted, a sound that suspiciously resembled a laugh.

She rounded on him and smacked his arm.

His one-sided smirk said he'd done it on purpose, pissed her off to keep her strong. The fact he knew her so well already warmed her from the inside.

She'd trust him. Trust that he wasn't just hoping, wasn't really planning to commit suicide to save his brother and the other captives.

With hurried steps, they made their way to the gym. This time she locked the door as soon as they entered, flipped the switch to frost the windows, and then began to remove her clothes with shaking hands.

He was already stripping, skimming down his trousers before she'd even removed her boots. She stalled because she wanted to imprint this picture of him, so tall and thick and proud, in her mind and heart. Because there was no way he could persevere. No way he would walk away the victor.

And she didn't care now whether or not she lost her command, was stripped of her rank, or even prosecuted. She might as well be dead. Without him, without the love that filled her to bursting this very moment, she had no reason to live.

He strode for her, his expression stern, but now she saw the pulse pounding at his temple, the tension rippling along his jaw, not from anger, not because he wanted sex—at least, not just that. He needed her.

He might not be capable of feeling as deeply as she did now, and she thought it was probably a good thing, because she understood why a Viking warrior eschewed the emotion. It crippled. It froze. It weakened.

Her legs trembled, and she sank to her knees on the floor.

Dagr plucked her up and sat her on the bench. He pulled the slide at the top of her skin-suit and peeled it down. His hands slipped inside, warming her breasts because she was shivering despite the balmy temperature of the room.

He removed the suit, kneeling to take off her boots and slide the trousers and insulated skin past her toes. When he stood, he picked her up again and headed toward the door at the far end.

She snuggled against his chest, smiling softly. Dagr knew every feature of her ship. She wasn't surprised he knew about the bath with the jets, large enough to accommodate three Helios, but just big enough for Dagr and her alone.

He set her at the edge of the sunken tub and softly ordered the settings he wanted. While the water rose and the jets began to swirl, he gathered cloths, towels, and scented soaps. When it was full, he descended into the small pool and reached for her.

Honora wound her arms around his neck, her legs around his waist, and clung, resting her cheek over her strong heart, while the warm water swirled in the strong jets and bubbles burst against her skin and her sex.

Dagr kissed her hair. "You will like our hot springs."

Again, he talked about a future they most likely would never share. She closed her eyes and swallowed the lump lodged at the back of her throat. "Tell me about them."

Holding her close, Dagr sat on a submerged bench.

Honora spread her knees on either side of his hips and eased down, riding the long ridge of his cock between her folds. She rubbed slowly back and forth, teasing him by stroking him but never taking him inside. "Tell me about your hot springs. I didn't know there was any warmth to be found on your world."

His face was split by a boyish grin. "We pride ourselves for our stealth and secrecy. Your people abandoned us to work in deep mines. But they never explored the world beyond the deposits of ore beneath the permafrost."

She rubbed her cheek against his, enjoying the rough scrape of whiskers that had sprouted on his face. She liked that he didn't wear a full beard like so many of his men, and enjoyed this hint of masculine bristle. "Tell me."

His hands settled on her hips, thumbs caressing her abdomen. "Soon after the Norsemen arrived on New Iceland, the animals they brought escaped from their cages. The people thought they were all dead. Frozen. Then one day, a man saw a crow flying. He followed it into a cave, and discovered another world beneath the cold surface of the planet—a place scoured out by water heated by pure light and streaming through the rock in wide rivers. The melted water formed large caves, which are lit by the ore. Rock and dirt deposited by the rivers on their banks grew lush forests. Our animals had found the caves."

She stopped her shallow movements to listen. "Why don't you live there?"

"Some do, growing crops, hunting for meat for our tables. But most of us work to support our only industry. Mining."

"It must seem like a wonderland. This underground forest."

"It is. And the springs I mentioned, some are as hot as this bath. With restorative powers."

She tilted her head. "You're telling me this. Aren't you afraid I'll tell my own people and they'll have even more reason to conquer your world?"

Dagr bracketed her face with his wet hands and kissed her mouth. "I trust you, Honora, to not betray my people. It's my desire that you return with me. Our world can be harsh, but I will see you kept in comfort. I will spend some of my wealth to provide you the things you need to be happy."

"I don't need things, Dagr. I need a purpose. I need to be part of something bigger." She dipped her head to rub the tip of her nose against his. "But I also need you."

"I am yours."

The moment was very nearly perfect. Or so she'd thought until he began to caress her. His fingers spread and raked slowly down her back, then slid under her ass and massaged her buttocks.

She gave a little breathless murmur and rolled her hips in another teasing glide that swept her cleft forward and back along his shaft.

His fingers tightened. Dagr lifted her and his cock tracked down her buttocks, then traced a path toward her labia. At her entrance, Dagr held her still, his gaze locked with hers.

"Yes, please," she whispered.

He brought her slowly down his cock, all the way until her pussy met his groin. Then he ground her forward and back, her clit rubbing against his pubis.

Her pussy clenched him hard, a cramping need curled around her womb. "I'm going to come," she moaned.

"Yes, please," he mimicked.

Only he sounded anything but submissive and pleading. She smiled, then let her head fall back and allowed him do all the work . . . lifting, lowering, grinding . . . until her body caught fire, and she fisted her hands in his hair and rubbed her breasts on his chest, her pussy against the hard bone of his groin. She blew into a million little pieces, riding a tide of wet, hot bliss. She shuddered against him, panting hard.

Dagr pulled her hair, which reminded her that her fingers were still tangled in his.

She unwound her fingers and gave him a small, apologetic smile. "You have a gift. I forget myself every time."

Dagr's long-fingered hands rubbed over her shoulders; his fingers trailed down, over her breasts. Then he turned his palms to cup her. "You inspire me." His thumbs scraped her nipples.

She groaned at the tingling he started there again.

His touch left her chest, and he reached for one of the folded cloths. He worked soap into the cloth, then began to bathe her while she remained on his cock. "Raise your arms."

She did so, then giggled when he washed her armpits.

Dagr slid the cloth there again, and she wrinkled her nose, trying to hold back a laugh. With her arms raised like a child and him tickling her, she shouldn't have been quite so aroused, but everywhere he looked, her skin flushed. When he circled over her breasts, her tips extended, growing rock hard.

He cupped water in his hands and rinsed her skin, then lifted her and latched on to a nipple, sucking it into his mouth, then widening his lips and pulling the whole breast inside.

She felt the ungentle tug all the way to her toes and undulated, crying out when the sensation became too much.

When he came off it, he did so slowly, suctioning all the way until all that he held between his lips was the tiny, hardened point.

"You're killing me," she said, tugging a long, wet strand of his hair.

He released her breast, his mouth making a popping sound. Then he lifted her the rest of the way off his cock and stood her in front of him.

Rising, he pulled her hand and they both left the water. He tossed a towel at her, and she grinned when it slapped her chest. Feminine power rippled through her, building her excitement. He was in a hurry now, impatient and aching, if the size and redness of his erection were any indication.

She dried haphazardly, turned on her heel, and strode into the other room. She crawled onto the mattress, wagging her ass, because she could hear his footsteps pad on the tiles behind her.

Hands clamped on her buttocks. Fingers crushed her, holding her hips in place.

His mouth licked and kissed her bottom. Then teeth bit.

She screeched, but the sound was cut off by the quickness of his next move, which flipped her to her back. She opened her legs without hesitation, and he aimed his cock at her entrance, nudged it once, then sank himself to the hilt in her silky, creamy depths.

Sixteen

Dagr came down over Honora, needing to touch her everywhere as he began to pump inside her. Her thighs scissored restlessly around his hips; her head thrashed on the soft pillows. The amber of her eyes melted beneath a golden, glossy sheen.

He framed her face and kissed her. "You cannot cry."

"Really? You think you can mandate what I feel now?" Her words were tart, but the hoarseness of her voice said how much she fought for control.

He pulled out of her and rolled to his back.

"I take it you want 'service'?"

Positioning his hands behind his head, he growled. "Use that word again, and I will spank you."

A muffled giggle sounded, but she rose beside him, settling on her knees as her gaze slowly roamed his body. He knew what she was doing, and he wished she wouldn't. He'd already committed her body, her sweet face, to memory.

She traced the outline of the wolf's tail that curled around his hip. "Will you turn over? I'd like to take a closer look."

Her eyes had at last dried and sparkled with mischief. He gave her a one-sided smirk and rolled to his belly, resting his forehead on the backs of his hands.

She shoved off the mattress, and her footsteps padded toward the line of cabinets across the room.

He didn't look around, content to let her surprise him. When warm oil drizzled over his back, he smiled.

Her small hands rubbed and squeezed his muscles with surprising strength, an elbow digging into some particularly tense muscles lining his spine. "You are skilled," he murmured.

"I'm inspired," she quipped. "I haven't felt this much muscle on a man, up close and personal, before."

"It's a wonder you Heliopolites ever breed."

"We breed just fine, but I'm thinking there'd be a spike in pregnancy rates if you guys ever landed on our planet."

Dagr grunted, pulled back to his brother's fate. Anger mixed with disappointment made his voice harsh. "That's what I suspect this is all about. That your people want to breed with ours. Did you know?"

Her hands slowed their movements for a moment, then pressed harder. "I didn't give it any thought."

"You think that ignorance excuses you?"

"No, it damns me. I know that."

Dagr swallowed to ease the tightness of his throat. "You will make this right," he said gruffly.

She sighed. "I will help you, yes. But there's no making this right. Not if we can't find your brother and the others the hunters captured."

He raised his head, but didn't look back. "Did you see them?"

"Yes."

"How were they kept?" He braced himself for the answer.

"In cages," she whispered. "Like animals. I was appalled and demanded they leave my ship immediately. I threatened to send them all to the surface if they weren't gone soon."

His shoulders bunching anew, he bit out, "If you'd done that, I never would have needed to leave my land or my people." *And I never would have met you.* Confused, because now he couldn't imagine having to choose between two different fates, he let go of the anger and let her hands soothe the tension in his body.

W e never would have met," Honora said, straddling his buttocks. She didn't want to talk about her mistakes. Didn't want to dwell on what was coming. Instead she concentrated on the wicked bounty beneath her.

She bent over him, pressing kisses against his oiled and scented skin, rubbing her softened lips across him. Then she stuck out her tongue and followed the deep indentation of his spine, licking in a lazy zigzag down his back.

When she'd curled herself as far inward as she could, she straightened again and traced the leaping wolf. The picture was so detailed, every tuft of fur was outlined. "It's beautiful, this beast on your back. It's a wolf, isn't it?"

"You don't have them on Helios?" he asked, his voice sounding rusty.

"None living. Only in stories and paintings. They died long ago from overhunting."

"They roam our underground forests. Not many. We keep track of the packs. Trap them from time to time to see how healthy they are."

"Are they dangerous?"

"Not to humans, unless backed into a corner. They shy away from man. Do you really want to talk about the wildlife on my planet?"

She lay over him, pressing her breasts against his back, snuggling her cheek against his shoulder. "Not really, but you must admit you haven't given me much of a chance to learn this particular view of your body."

"I would turn over."

"I'm not done exploring."

He grunted, the sound lifting his back. "Why am I starting to tremble?"

"Are you afraid, Viking?"

"For my manhood."

Chuckling, she scooted down his body until she knelt over the backs of his calves. She poured more warm oil over his buttocks. The muscles here were beyond firm, and he clenched tighter when her fingernails raked over them.

She braced her hands on the mattress and slid one knee between his thighs to ease them open.

His reluctance was palpable, and a low growl rattled through his chest.

Honora laughed again, softly, her own body tensing with arousal. How far would he let her go before putting a halt to her exploration? Or would she be the first to fold?

Putting her weight behind her, she massaged his ass, rubbing his skin, working her fingers into the muscle until his thighs quivered.

"Woman," he groaned.

She bent closer and traced two fingers down the crevice, then followed them with her tongue, delving in between, coming to his small furled hole and hesitating, because she knew how good it felt, but she'd never dared this before. She circled it with a fingertip.

His breath hissed between his teeth. "Careful . . ."

"Was Kit the first to take you here?" she teased.

"Would you rather have been my first? Do you even dare?"

"What do I risk?"

"A woman's punishment."

She knew exactly what he meant, and the thought only made her cream. She nuzzled his firm backside with her nose, slid her lips over him, and sucked at his skin, leaving a love mark here and there, but finally stopped teasing, coming again to the divide and sinking her tongue into it, touching his anus, sliding her tongue over it, then darting back.

Dagr's back muscles bulged with tension; his hands clutched great fistfuls of bedding. Every part of his body was hard, quivering, and she licked him again, moistening the skin, and then tucked an oil-slicked finger inside him.

She knew her physiology. Knew where the little gland rested. Stuffing another finger inside despite his muttered curses, she rolled the tips of her fingers over his prostate, swirling on it until his buttocks lifted off the bed and he dug his cock into the mattress.

"Witch! Stop!"

She laughed and bit his buttocks and pulled out, scrambling away but not quickly enough.

He shot up and grabbed her head and pulled it toward his cock, his fingers sliding to either side of her ears as he directed her over him to suck him while he slammed his hips forward and back.

He didn't last longer than a single deep-throated lunge. Spurts of salty cum coated her tongue. She swallowed it down, groaning around him, her bottom in the air and her pussy clasping.

When his fingers unclenched from her hair, he pushed her away. She backed up on all fours, eyeing him with trepidation, because his eyes were dark, narrow slits, his cheeks starkly defined by the tension riding his features. He looked every inch the primitive warrior.

"You know what comes now."

She lifted an eyebrow. "A woman's punishment? Do you think I'll just bend over and present my ass like a good little thrall?"

His mouth stretched into a thin smile.

Her heart rate kicked up, and she darted off the bed, running for the door.

He caught her before she pulled the latch down, and then she was swinging high, her body folding over his shoulder. He turned and walked over to the bench, which she knew wasn't just for holding clothes.

"Surely the fantastic blow job mitigates the punishment," she gasped when he bound her hands to the bench.

His response was to push her thighs apart and latch her ankles to the padded step.

Honora couldn't help it; her pussy spilled fluid, wetting her labia and seeping onto the bench beneath her.

He walked away, and she strained to watch him over her shoulder. He found the flogger amid the implements in the cabinet and stroked his fingers over the flanged ends before looking her way.

The jut of his jaw and the heat of his dark gaze kept her breaths shallow and rasping.

"Gods, I ache already, Dagr. I didn't intend to trample on your dignity . . . much." She wrinkled her nose. "I'm guessing by how excited you got that you aren't accustomed to having that done to you. And yet, you let Kit do it and didn't threaten her with punishment. Don't you think I deserve that pleasure too? I mean, really, before us, no one's ever played with your ass before?"

He gave a sharp shake of his head. "Never."

"Helio men often take male lovers. Don't Vikings?"

"Some do," he said, fisted hands resting on his hips, "but I have never felt even a stirring of desire for another man. I have never allowed anything to penetrate me."

"Until Kit." Her neck was getting a kink in it, staring over her shoulder like she was. "Then why didn't you stop her?"

"The drug robbed me of inhibition."

"Then why are you punishing me? If you didn't want it, why not stop me?"

"I gave you fair warning. I assumed you wanted punishment. That teasing me beyond control gave you pleasure."

"You let me do it, even though you found it disturbing, because you wanted me to enjoy myself?" Pleasure teased more sweet cream down her thigh. "How sweet."

"Not sweet, *elskling* . . . Strategic."

She gave a strangled laugh. "Because now you have me where you wanted me all along, and I have to be compliant because you set the terms?"

"Exactly," he said, nodding. "Now, do you submit to your punishment?"

Honora hung her head and closed her eyes. Truth be told, she was exactly where she wanted to be, burning for the stinging strokes because she'd carry the marks a little longer on her skin. "I deserve punishment, Viking. Do I get any last wishes?"

"Do you think you will die from pleasure?"

"Maybe."

"Ask, *elskling*," he said softly.

"I want your hand to deliver the punishment. I want your fingers emblazoned on my skin. Make it last past today. I want the fire to burn me far past the day we part."

His hands dug into her hair, and he raised her head. His gaze sharpened at the moisture welling in her eyes. His jaw flexed. From emotion? She hoped so, but knew it was likely just arousal stirring inside him again.

Warriors didn't love. Didn't regret partings.

She licked her lips, then bit into the bottom one, a slow, deliberate provocation. He cupped her chin, rubbed his thumb over her bottom lip, soothing it, then stuck it into her mouth and pulled down her jaw.

When he stepped closer, aiming his slackened cock at her mouth, she had to cant her head to scoop all of him inside. She tasted herself and his cum, chased with a hint of salt. Her mouth watered, and she sucked and pulled on him, waiting as he slowly filled again, licking every bulge and vein as he tightened and his girth consumed the space inside her mouth and throat.

Fully aroused, he withdrew, stroking himself slowly in front of her, while her own body tightened and more fluid slicked her thighs.

Her gaze made a languorous climb up his taut abdomen and massive chest. She sighed like a wanton, feeling her lips go slack, her breaths pant. "Please, Dagr."

"Do you want your punishment, or do you want a fucking?"

"You will give me both."

A single brow arched.

She might be tied like a roasted goose, but she knew who really held the power here. He'd give her everything she wanted—here, inside this room. Dagr might not know how to voice his emotions, might not feel as deeply as she did, but he wanted to leave her happy, sated. She gave him a one-sided smile. "You will give me both, please."

He bent and mashed his lips against hers, then circled her. Hands trailed down her back, stroking her skin, the rough calluses scraping like fine sandpaper, lifting gooseflesh everywhere they traveled.

When he cupped her bottom, she lifted into his palms, her head dropping low as she closed her eyes and savored his gentle roughness. Strokes, squeezes, so soothing and arousing. She imagined how his large hands looked against the soft flesh of her bottom and wondered again how she compared with his pale-skinned concubines.

His mouth sucked at her skin, gliding to kiss her ass, suctioning to raise his own little marks. She loved that he wanted to mark her like she had done to him. With his breath gusting against her skin, his fingers grazing her sex, but never settling or penetrating, she began to move restlessly.

He'd promised punishment and he was working up to it, but she was dying here.

"The women of my clan are bold and speak their minds, but at the bottom of it, they submit to their protector, consider his needs above theirs." His words teased her neck. "You are more delicately made than they are, and generally measure your words more carefully than they do, but you are stronger, more independent, at your core. I find myself relieved that this is so, because you can love a man, and not be consumed by him."

"You think you know me so well?"

"I know you love me."

Her eyes filled immediately, and she was grateful he couldn't see her face. "You think that makes me weak?"

"In the moment, when you are needful of my touch, you are weak. However, I know when we part, you will do what you must to survive. That keeps my will strong, my heart free."

"So that you can walk away?" she said, anguish trembling through her. "You think that's something I want to hear? Now?"

"You misunderstand. I have never felt for another woman what I feel for you. I think that if we had more time, I would open my heart to you, Honora. I trust that you would carry on after I am gone. That is what makes me strong, knowing that you will survive, that you live. It is as close as I have ever been to love, *elskling*."

"I'll take it," she whispered, tears spilling from her eyes and her throat tightening. She wouldn't tell him how crippling the fear of leaving him was. He thought her strong. She knew she'd want to cling and cry against him, but she'd have to remember to raise her chin and give him a smile. "Words are nice, Dagr. But my body burns for you."

His tongue stroked between her labia. "Your body melts. But I will make your skin burn." He kissed her again, and then a stinging slap landed on her right cheek.

She gasped and jerked against her bindings. Her heart fluttered in panic, then surged again as heat redoubled inside her body. Giving a sexy moan, she undulated, arching her back as far as possible given the restraints.

Another slap to the opposite side was followed by a firm rub of his palm. "I can see my fingers on your skin."

"Give me more. Make them distinct. When I look at my ass, I want to remember how strong and large your hands are."

His fingers spread over the mark he'd already made, then lifted, tagging the same spot.

Her bottom felt on fire, and she knew welts would rise, perfectly aligned. But thoughts of the future, of poignant physical reminders that she would carry with her for a short while, faded as the burn built beneath her skin, making her quiver and shake.

She panted noisily, unable to catch her breath as he struck her, over and over. She tossed her head, groaning, felt the slide of liquid excitement trickling from her pussy, moistening her lips, dampening her belly as it spread across the padded bench.

He slapped her again, and then rubbed his face against her, his fingers gripping her thighs hard. His movements stopped.

Her breath caught, and she tightened her thighs on the step, waiting because she could hear his harsh pants and wished she could turn and wrap her arms around him. But she suspected he wanted it this way, didn't want for her to see him lose even a little of the shield he kept around his heart.

"I need you," she said, her voice tight.

The bindings around her ankles gave. He blanketed her back and reached for the cuffs at her wrists and released them.

Then he was rising, lifting her from the bench and carrying her to bed where he laid her in the center and followed her down.

His ice blue eyes, always so chilly, were wild and wide. His skin was a hectic red. She embraced his face and pulled him down, slanting her mouth to kiss his, strumming his lips with the tip of her tongue, then stroking inward. The kiss was soft, exploring, as she tried to calm him with her mouth while her hands petted his face, stroked his hair and his shoulders.

When at last she encircled his large body with her arms and held him, he sighed and sank onto her. Her breath caught as she took his weight.

His eyes darkened. He deepened the kiss, his tongue tangling with hers while he groaned and his body ground into hers.

Honora opened her legs, bending her knees so her thighs cradled his narrow hips. His body drew back, his cock pressed against her center, and the blunt head drove between her folds and plunged deeply.

Her body sensed a difference in his actions. She arched beneath him, her breath leaving in rush. As he drove relentlessly into her, his breaths shuddering, his face still wild, his expression desperate, she knew he'd broken.

Rather than let him know that she knew, she pulled him closer and snuggled her face into his neck, kissing him, licking him, biting at the end when his whole body quaked and his cock grew more rigid. Warmth flooded her channel.

Honora squeezed her eyes shut, fighting tears. Her breath tightened in her throat. She'd won his love; she knew it. But she also believed he might never voice it.

In the end, it really didn't matter. She'd never wanted love in her life, never expected it. But love in the form of a tall, proud Viking had found her. The knowledge of that love was something she'd hold close like an unspent treasure.

Seventeen

When Dagr's explosive release ebbed, he froze atop Honora, wondering what had happened, not understanding—or wanting—the emotions rolling over him. Queasiness grabbed his stomach. He felt as though a sea serpent had butted his skiff from beneath him, tilting him crazily toward thin ice.

His body tensed, growing rigid, and he planted his hands on the bed on either side of Honora's shoulders and lifted his chest from hers. His gaze remained firmly on her hair, because he couldn't meet her eyes. Not yet.

Something had happened. And he knew exactly when—between the moment he'd decided to give her everything she wanted and when he couldn't bear to strike her one more time.

His hand had lain against her skin, which he'd watched redden, turning a deep, bruised pink, and he'd rebelled. Even knowing this was something she'd begged for. His chest had tightened; his heart thudded dully against his breastbone and he'd bent to rub his face on her, shutting his eyes tightly, his stomach knotting in revolt.

Even now, Dagr had the overwhelming urge to draw her close, bury his head between her breasts, and never let her go.

Instead, he withdrew, clamping his jaw as his cock slid from the warm haven of her pussy. He rolled to his back and hid his face in the curve of his arm.

Honora lay beside him, her breaths every bit as ragged as his. She quivered, her shaking continuing unabated for several long seconds.

He uncovered his eyes, stared at the ceiling, and willed himself not to care. Instead, he extended his arm, inviting her to roll close, and then cupped her against his side. "We should sleep," he said, his voice gruff.

As she nodded, her cheek rubbed against his chest.

He kissed the top of her head and let out a deep breath. "I will find you. When this is over, I will search for you. Wait for me."

"Wait, like a woman should?" Her body tensed. "Wouldn't it be easier for me to stay with you?"

"There will be a battle. I want you away from the fighting."

After a long, pregnant silence, she said, "If we part, I'm afraid we'll never find each other again." Her fingers slid over his stomach. "Or that you'll . . . get busy. You do have a kingdom to run."

He grunted. She didn't know her worth. He wouldn't tell her how important she really was to him. If he failed in his quest, ignorance might be a blessing.

Birget eyed Cyrus and Roxana, amused by the female pirate's wariness. The woman had lost her bravado. Her skin was pale beneath the dusky pigment. For his part, Cyrus's whole body betrayed tension. A snarl twisted his mouth, and he bit out orders like a dog barking as it circled its prey. The transfer of the containerized ore was complete. A smaller portion had been delivered to the saloon for the purchase of the cat-woman's papers, should she choose to use it for that purpose. Something Birget had shaken her head over. She couldn't imagine a fuck being worth that much.

Then again, eyeing Baraq's lean, muscular frame, she couldn't deny that physical attraction was a very strong motivator. Baraq hadn't sought her out again, which seemed to increase her awareness of him, and she wished for another chance to take him inside her body and prove that she was made like any other female and capable of climaxing while riding his cock. Tension swirled in her belly. He was beautifully made. Wondrously strong—even for an Outlander.

Baraq's gaze sliced her way, and his brows lowered in warning. He stood beside the gangway, eyeing activity on the dock. As long as they remained on the planet, they were vulnerable.

Birget gave up trying to keep her distance. The pull of her attraction fueled her moves as she strode reluctantly his way, wishing he seemed a little happy with her company.

His gaze scanned her impersonally, then returned to the gangway. "What are you doing here?"

She pouted, angry that he wasn't as eager to see her as she was him. "You're my companion, remember? Dagr gave you to me."

"I'm not yours," he ground out, a muscle in his jaw jumping.

Birget couldn't resist the urge. She leaned against his chest and traced the length of his nose with a fingertip, drawing his hard, dark gaze. "You could be," she whispered.

Baraq snorted, and closed his fist around her hand, squeezing, warning her to behave, and then dropped it. "How? Do you think Dagr would enslave me to you? Wouldn't he worry about his brother's claim?"

She shrugged a shoulder, pretending unconcern. The same worry had been spinning in her head ever since they'd had sex. "You're not a Norseman. He has nothing to fear. You're far inferior to our men."

Baraq rolled his eyes, but a smile tugged the corners of his lips. "Then why bother yanking my leash, Princess?"

"I should have collared you, just as Dagr did your captain. Speaking of which . . ." She said the last bit under her breath.

Dagr approached with Honora beside him. She didn't miss the way the Wolfskin king cupped his captive's elbow. The man was always touching her, pulling her close for an embrace, or simply following her with his sharp blue gaze.

His obsession with the woman met with amusement among his men, most notably Grimvarr, whose expression seemed to hold a hint of pride whenever he beheld them, which had her wondering why.

Birget sniffed. Their relationship would soon be at an end. Did Honora believe this was anything but an interlude, a tryst to stave off boredom?

Frakki ran up the gangway, his face alight with excitement. "Captain Dagr," he called out loudly.

Dagr waited for him. "The *Daedalus* is supplied?"

"Yes, and the ore is safely in the hold. We're ready to transfer crew."

Dagr looked around at the men gathered in the cargo bay. They'd been told the crew would be divided up—one half moved to the civilian transport, the rest remaining aboard the *Proteus*. Dagr hadn't informed them of the assignments yet. Whoever remained on the *Proteus* would suffer capture by the Consortium.

Birget wasn't eager to be imprisoned, but she would accept whatever assignment Dagr gave her. She'd insisted on accompanying the wolves, had fought alongside them. Her own people were among the captives whose freedom they sought.

Still, she was as tense as the men gathering around to hear Dagr's final decision.

Dagr's glance swept the Vikings. He was the only one relaxed among them. His features were set, his frame still. "You know this vessel can't follow the *Orion* without attracting the attention of every Consortium ship in the sector."

Heads nodded. Square jaws firmed. Birget felt a burst of pride to be standing among such fearless warriors. Their story would be heralded for ages. She hoped she'd be around awhile to brag.

"The transport we've purchased is unencumbered and, as a private vessel, can approach Helios's solar system without drawing attention. That doesn't mean that those who crew the ship won't face mortal dangers.

"If you're able to catch the *Orion*, you will have to take it by force. If it arrives at Helios before you catch up, then you will have to slip into port by stealth to rescue the men."

Dagr's expression grew grimmer; a muscle flexed at the edge of his strong jaw. "Those who remain on the *Proteus* face an uncertain future. We will draw away the armada so the transport can slip through it without anyone making the connection between the two ships. The *Proteus* will flee, possibly drawing fire. If we survive the race, we will be captured. I do have a plan for escape, which I will discuss with the men who stay with me only after we've left Karthagos."

"You will need crew capable of piloting the other ship," Birget broke in.

Dagr gave her a tight smile. "Yes, and Cyrus will be its captain."

In an instant, Cyrus stepped into the circle, his hands curling at his sides. "I'm not leaving you, Dagr."

Dagr gripped his upper arms. "Friend, if the Consortium finds you aboard the ship, you will be dead."

"As will you."

"Perhaps, but like I said, I do have a plan. I need you on that other ship." His hands dropped away from Cyrus, and his steady gaze cut toward her. "Birget . . ."

She jerked, and then stiffened, wondering what menial responsibility he would give her. "Yes, Dagr."

"You will accompany him."

Her breath caught for just a second. She didn't know whether to be relieved or not. "Of course. Whatever your wish," she said, surprising him and herself with her quick agreement.

One corner of his mouth lifted. "As the captain of the *Valkyrja*, you are accustomed to leadership. You will be in charge of the mission to rescue my brother, your future husband, and the other captives."

Her jaw sagged just a fraction before she strengthened it and straightened her shoulders. Pride warmed her heart. "I'm confused. You've resisted allowing me any place on this ship. From the moment we met, you've belittled my skills."

"You're strong, resourceful, and brave—as you've proven every time you defied me. And you are a noble, born to lead." He nodded to Baraq. "You will act as her next in command and her personal guard. If anything happens to her, it will be your head."

Baraq gave him a curt nod.

Birget held still to keep her excitement at that assignment a secret. Baraq didn't look her way, and she didn't dare glance at him.

"They'll have only a skeleton crew," Honora said, once Dagr confirmed that the rest of the *Proteus*'s crew would remain aboard the ship.

"But enough to point the ship where needed. Cyrus will be

stretched, but he has assured me that whoever captains the ship has everyone he needs so long as my men follow his directions."

Worry bled from Honora's face. "You kept my crew away so they wouldn't hear the instructions."

"The less they know, the better. I am assuming they'll be interrogated."

"Are you going to tell me your plan?"

He shook his head.

"Let me guess," she said, a smile that wasn't a happy sight curving her mouth. "The less I know, the better."

He pulled her against his side, and she rested her head against his chest.

Birget gave a soft snort.

"So she takes comfort from him," Baraq said under his breath. "That doesn't make her weak."

She turned to study his taut features. "Are you envious of what they share?"

One dark eyebrow rose. "I'm envious that her burden will be so much lighter than mine," he drawled.

"Grimvarr."

As Dagr's attention moved on, Birget at last shared a charged glance with Baraq. Tension had eased from his face. Was he happy to remain with her?

A hand touched the small of her back and she breathed deeply.

Grimvarr stepped closer to Dagr, his hand on the hilt of his sword. "Cousin?"

"I would have you travel with them. My brother's fate is uncertain. I risk imprisonment or death. You are our heir. It's best we travel separately."

Grimvarr's upper lip lifted in a fierce snarl. "I belong with you. Who better to watch your back?"

"Don't argue." Dagr sighed. "*Please*, cousin. Birget may be in charge, but you are the highest ranking among the wolves after me. She will have need of you to ensure the loyalty of the men. She will rely on your counsel."

Frakki stepped forward. "You will not leave me behind," he said, his deep voice growling.

Birget grinned at the bearded man's intense scowl. She had no doubt Frakki would battle Dagr himself if his king tried to leave him behind.

Dagr smiled and reached out to clasp Frakki's forearm. "We will face this together. I trust you with my back, friend." He divided the rest of the wolves, sending to the transport only one of the Outlanders, besides Cyrus—a crew member with navigational experience.

Birget hesitated before breaking away to join the men heading down the gangway to the other ship. "If you need to grab your belongings, say your good-byes . . ."

Baraq shook his head, aimed a glance at Honora, who gave him a teary smile, and then turned on his heel to follow the rest of the men down the gangway.

Which left Birget hovering, waiting for Dagr to spare a moment for her to speak with him.

When he'd finished with his men and those staying on the *Proteus* broke up to head to their assigned stations, his head turned her way. "Still here?"

Birget frowned, grateful he'd said something to piss her off because she felt the strange urge to cry. "Thank you."

Dagr's expression showed no softness, just his usual hard, stoic face. "Birget, if you don't want this responsibility, the only other option I can offer you in good conscience is to leave you with enough ore to buy your passage back to New Iceland."

Be excluded? No. She squared her shoulders. "Dagr, I know I've defied you and have given you no reason to trust my motives or my good sense."

"You wanted to be seen as your own person. Not a woman who would be a pawn. I understand."

"You're more magnanimous than I would have been."

A brawny shoulder lifted. "I was stubborn. I should have given you respect and appropriate responsibility. But I am sending Grimvarr and Baraq along with you because they are both experienced fighters. Grim is young, but he trained under me. He thinks before he acts. And I've tested Baraq's mettle. He's strong and intelligent." A finger jabbed the air. "If they advise you, listen."

She nodded. The moment to leave was upon her, but she didn't know how to say good-bye. Should she say her farewell to her brother or her king?

"Still here?" he repeated, more softly this time.

A dark brow arched, but she didn't miss the deep inhalation. Maybe she'd gotten to him as well. Taking a risk, she stepped closer and slid her arms around his waist.

He was slow to return the embrace, but his hug was hard, breath-stealing, and he lifted her off her feet for a moment, before letting her back down.

Birget sank against his chest and accepted his embrace, taking strength from him.

Dagr pressed a kiss against her forehead and released her. Then he slipped the black amulet he wore around his neck over his head and dropped it over hers, pulling her braid through it and touching the stone where it lay against her chest. "From this day, you are my sister. And a Wolfskin. Have pride in both your families."

Birget blinked at the moisture welling in her eyes, and grasped the amulet, still warm from his skin, inside her fist.

He tucked a finger under chin to raise her face. "Be careful, little sister," he said softly.

Tears continued to fill her eyes, and her nose burned, but she didn't feel shame. She nodded, turned to Honora and gave her a little bow, then executed a sharp about-face. As she marched away, her heart soared. She, Birget of the Bearshirt clan, had earned the approval of the Black Wolf.

Baraq waited in front of the transport ship.

The sight of him gave her comfort and strength. She wasn't sure she liked the fact she wanted to lean on a man. Her chin shot up. "Tell me why I shouldn't just leave you on the dock?"

"You don't trust me, Princess?"

"Don't mock me, not now. I would know that you come willingly and without an ulterior purpose."

"My reasons for falling in with the Black Wolf's plans have nothing to do with you, even as attractive as I find you. I'm not a man whose principles will be swayed by a pretty face."

Birget frowned as heat blossomed on her cheeks. She was setting out on a mission that, if successful, would be added to the sagas that chronicled her people's history. However, a backhanded compliment from an Outlander warmed her, melting her insides.

A feeling that could prove disastrous. For the first time, she worried about whether she had done the right thing seducing him. "Then why?"

"Because I am obligated to find those men—to save my captain and myself, and to do the right thing." Baraq turned on his heel and walked up the gangplank.

But he walked slowly, speeding up only when she stomped on the gangplank behind him. Birget smiled, her chest filled with happiness for the respect she'd earned, and for the man who would share the adventure.

*   *   *

Dagr watched her leave, giving a silent prayer to the gods he didn't really believe in to protect Birget and aid her in finding his brother.

"Do you regret leaving it to her to find him?" Honora said, slipping her hand inside his.

He squeezed her hand, then dropped it. "She is a Viking. She will do everything in her power to succeed. Whether or not she's happy with her future husband." He glanced down. "Don't we have a chase to lead?"

Honora closed her eyes for a brief moment, and then took a deep breath. "I wish we had more time."

"We'll have a lifetime, Lady Captain." He would make it so.

Eighteen

*E*irik braced his hands against the bars of his cage as the spacecraft shuddered and rattled around them.

"What is happening?" one of the Vikings farther down the row of cages cried out.

"My guess is that we're entering a planet's atmosphere," Eirik shouted, holding tight to the bars of his own small prison.

Up and down the line, the men shared worried glances as the spacecraft continued to shimmy. Then it jerked, sending them banging against the bars before the glide path of the craft evened out. The sensation of a swift descent unsettled Eirik's belly.

Without windows into the world they entered, Eirik could only guess at what happened, until the descent abruptly halted and the ship groaned and thudded, settling at last. The hum of the engines died away, leaving a silence that was as frightening as the moment he'd woken naked on the cage floor.

"We have no weapons, but we cannot let them take us from this ship," said Hakon, the Berserkir in the adjacent cage.

Eirik eyed the tension in his fellow captive's face and knew he must look every bit as stern. They hid their trepidation, tamping it down while they schooled their heartbeats into steady rhythms. Panic and fear wouldn't serve them now. They needed an opportunity. Just one.

"Keep an eye out," Eirik said softly. "If they give us the break we need, I will signal you."

Despite the fact most of the men here were Bearshirts or from southern clans, they had listened to him from the start, respect for his family's name and reputation giving him an edge. Someone needed to be in charge.

"And if we don't get that break?" Hakon said, his brown eyes flashing from beneath blond eyebrows. Hakon had become Eirik's de facto second.

"If we don't get an opportunity now, then we wait. We may be warriors and prone to act first, but we are also Icelanders. We have thrived on a planet where weaker men would have perished."

Hakon's lips lifted in a fierce snarl. "These Utlending bastards will not stand a chance against our might."

"When the time comes," Eirik cautioned.

Hakon's jaws ground together, but he ducked his head, the closest to a nod of agreement he would give Eirik. Of a similar size and strength, Hakon wasn't swayed by Eirik's rank or reputation. Which was what made Eirik trust him all the more.

Footsteps stomping closer on the metal grate flooring drew all the Vikings' gazes.

Fatin and the white-coated bitch, Miriam, strode at the head of a long column of soldiers, wearing helmets and armed with laser guns and stun batons.

Eirik shot a glance down the line of cages and gave a subtle shake of his head. Not yet. Maybe not at all this day.

Fatin stopped in front of his cage. Excitement glittered in her black eyes. "You really shouldn't worry all that much."

Eirik grunted and gave her a sharp, deadly glare.

"Posturing still, I see."

She came closer, close enough he could have reached through the bars and broken her neck, but the glint of humor in her eyes said she knew he wouldn't risk the consequences. Not yet, *he repeated to himself.*

"Don't get so worked up, Eirik Wolfskin. Your life won't be so bad. You could have a very comfortable one, filled with privilege, if you cooperate."

"You have said I will be a whore to the women of your world. How can I accept such a fate?"

"By making the best of the opportunities you will have. As long as you live, Viking, you have a chance to earn your freedom."

Why she said such things to him while her expression brought to mind of one of the soulless creatures from Hel's cold realm confused him. As did his reaction to her presence. The thin fabric of his pull-on pants couldn't hide his automatic response to the spicy scent of her skin or the sight of her slender curves.

Her lips curved into a lush smile. "Such a shame we have no time . . ." *Then she laughed while a low, warning growl rumbled from his chest.* "They will love you. Give them raw. Let them think they tame you into tenderness." *She turned.*

Eirik watched as she waited for a door to be opened at the side of the ship. When it swung open, she grasped both sides of the doorframe and leaned out, her chest rising as she inhaled. A trill of laughter erupted, and she flung back her head.

Eirik continued to stare. Wondering. The woman seemed triumphant. Was it only the successful delivery of her cargo? He didn't think so. So many things didn't seem to align—not her coldness or her quiet concern. Not the cool demeanor when she stood a distance from him and the other men or the heat that rolled off her skin and darkened her eyes when she stepped closer.

He'd take heed of her warning. Play the game she suggested. By rights he shouldn't trust a word she said, but he'd watch and wait.

Fatin flung him a dark, enigmatic glance, then stepped into the sunlight that gleamed through the open doorway.

Honora sat once again in her captain's chair, fidgeting, adjusting her seat up and down, making the cushion plump, then deflate. For some reason, her chair didn't feel as comfortable as it once did. Worse, her authority didn't feel natural. Just days had passed since she'd acted as the rightful captain of the *Proteus*, but her entire life had changed, even her way of thinking.

All due to the man who stood behind her and whose large, warm hands cupped her shoulders, calming her as they crashed through the armada's front line at light speed. "Rear view," she said quietly, waiting as the microscopic creatures in the viewing screen realigned to give those on the command deck a visual as Consortium ships peeled away one by one to join the chase.

"Turk, how long until we make the wormhole?"

He didn't reply immediately, the set of his shoulders—hunched toward his console—indicative enough of his worry that she didn't ask him again.

"Forward view." Gods, she felt the need to vacillate endlessly between the two views, but decided to keep her focus on their destination—as far as they could get from the other transport making its way now through the gaps they'd widened in the armada's coverage. Cyrus would have to worry about his own ass now.

She pressed her forefinger into the long indent beneath her finger to call the computer. "Can we tap into the chatter on the command freqs?" she asked.

"We are being jammed, Captain Turgay."

Dagr's thumbs pressed into the back of her neck, just beneath her hair.

Honora groaned and let her head fall back. "You shouldn't do that," she breathed, watching him watch her. "I need to concentrate."

"There is nothing you can do. I would ease your tension."

Searching his face, she wrinkled her nose. "Your touch doesn't soothe."

A smile stretched across his features.

Gods, he was a handsome man. His fingers sank into her hair and pulled back her head even farther. Then he bent and kissed her, still upside down. Softly. Just lips rubbing against hers, his nose pressed against her chin.

Her mouth stretched now, and when he pulled away, she realized she did feel less tense. "Thanks."

"Captain!"

She jerked upright.

"A ship is bearing down from straight ahead," Turk said, excitement raising his voice. "They're pinging our calling freq."

Honora pressed her forefinger indent. "Go ahead and open the channel," she said, and then turned to Dagr. "All you have to do is speak."

"This is Dagr, the Black Wolf."

"I am Commander Arikan," came a terse response. "You have violated Consortium laws. Surrender now, or we will be forced to destroy the ship and kill everyone aboard."

Honora lifted her finger to break the connection. "How far to the entrance of the wormhole, Turk?"

"Three minutes. They must know that's where we intend to go. They're trying to cut us off."

"They won't give us three minutes. They'll have us surrounded sooner than that." She glanced over her shoulder. "Dagr, what do you want to do?"

"Let me speak."

She hesitated, her gaze taking in the determined set of his face.

"Trust me, Honora."

She opened the circuit again.

"Commander Arikan," Dagr said, his voice taking on a sly tone. "I am considering my options. I am a businessman and would strike a deal with you for the return of your valuable ship and crew."

"We don't deal with pirates."

"I take offense to that term. And I understand you must set standards or the riffraff of the universe would think your ships fair game. However, I seek no ransom. Nothing is damaged, no one killed. So far."

"You captured our ship. That brands you. Surrender first; then we will talk."

"How foolish would I be? I would lose any advantage I currently hold."

Honora's stomach tightened until she thought she might vomit. Arikan's voice was hard, merciless.

"From where I sit, wolf, you have no advantage. The *Proteus* has only limited defenses. My vessel is a warship and fully armed. If I give the order, you will be obliterated."

Dagr grunted. "Then you will not only lose this ship and her crew, but something else even more valuable."

"I haven't time for you to be vague."

"Then I won't waste words. I'm a businessman. I traded *Proteus* crew members for a king's ransom in pure light."

"Are you trying to bribe me?" Arikan said slowly.

"Never," Dagr said, arching a brow at Honora, who shook her head at his audacity. "I'm only proving that I have a working relationship with the leadership of the strongest kingdom on New Iceland. I and my men will surrender to you, and you will give me your word to hear me out before you decide our disposition. I have a proposition which I will not discuss where anyone else might be listening."

Honora stiffened. The thing he'd alluded to before. The plan he hadn't wanted to share in front of anyone else so that if questioned, they wouldn't be able to divulge any of it. She hoped like Hades he knew what he was doing.

A long silence ensued. Then the viewing screen changed, without Honora having done a thing. The Commander's face appeared, so large every wrinkle and even the hook of his aging nose were amplified.

"They've taken over the controls," she said calmly, assuming a neutral expression now that Arikan was watching them.

"Silence!" Dagr bellowed, his hands clamping harder on her shoulders.

She understood. The deception had begun. She was back to being the captive. At least while in sight of others. Honora didn't have to pretend to feel trapped and defeated. From here on out, she was flotsam, drifting on the whim of the higher-ups. Her life was bound to change, possibly to end.

"My men and I are prepared to gather for transport to your vessel," Dagr said.

"That's not acceptable. We will send a boarding party to the *Proteus*."

"And my men will capture them or die trying. You will do this our way. The *Proteus* was only a stepping-stone in my plan. I needed your attention. Now that I have it, I would speak with you directly."

Honora wondered what he could possibly say that would stave off death or imprisonment. And why be stubborn over the location of the surrender? Did he think she would be better off if her ship wasn't invaded by her own people? That might be true.

Arikan's eyes narrowed to tiny slits. Fury glazed his leathery cheeks. "Captain Turgay."

She straightened her shoulders, ignoring the press of Dagr's hands. "Yes, sir."

"You will resume command of your ship once the pirates are transferred. When I give the order, you will proceed directly to the Heraklion port on Helios."

She nodded her acceptance of the command, even knowing he was telling her she delivered herself into custody. Heraklion wasn't the military port. Any military ship forced to dock there would be overrun by law enforcement.

Arikan thought she wouldn't balk at the order. And the old Honora would not have thought twice, regardless of the personal price.

"Black Wolf, make your way to the cargo bay. We will transport your entire party aboard at the same time. Captain Turgay, you will verify the ship is free of infestation."

The viewing screen darkened.

Dagr grabbed her arm and forced her from the chair, bending her arm painfully behind her, making her grimace. But once he'd walked her into the corridor, he pulled her into his arms. Vikings walked past them, having heard the instructions, their faces grim.

She wrapped her arms around his shoulders and hugged him hard, sinking her face into the corner of his neck to hide her tears.

"I will find you," he said, his voice roughening.

"You'll be dead." She sniffed. "Fuck, we'll both be dead."

His hand clutched the back of her hair and pulled until she

met his gaze. "I have something your commander will not be able to resist."

Tightness clogged her throat and she swallowed hard. "You don't know them. He will follow protocols. He has no flexibility to act."

"He has pride and ambition. He will hear me out. Do not do as he commands, Honora. Do not head to Helios."

"I must. They will track the ship. I can't deviate from the path without drawing fire. And to cloak again . . ." She shook her head.

"Find a way to escape. Make your way to Karthagos." His gaze was intent, searching. "I will find you there."

Honora nodded, knowing she'd do no such thing.

Dagr glared, his hands tightening on her upper arms like he wanted to shake her.

She gave him a small, trembling smile and cupped his cheek. "We will both do what we must to survive. That's the best I can promise."

He nodded, then grabbed her hand and headed down the corridor to the ladder leading into the cargo hold. A portal had already been opened; his men stood to the side of it, waiting.

Honora didn't dare cling, because she feared she'd fall apart. When he dropped her hand, she hung back, watching as he approached his men, giving each a steady stare. When his gaze fell on Frakki, the other Viking came to attention, his hand on the pommel of his sword.

Dagr slid his own sword from its scabbard and raised it above his head. "For Thor! For New Iceland!" The Viking's shouts reverberated around the hold, echoing off the metal hull.

Their shouts were accompanied by ferocious smiles. Swords were resheathed, and Frakki led the men through the portal until at last only Dagr remained. Alone with him in the hold, Honora curled her fingers into her palms. "You shouldn't keep them waiting."

Dagr curved his fingers around her face.

She leaned into them, storing his scent, the scrape of his callused palm in her memory.

His head tilted; his lips hovered just above hers. His ice blue eyes, always so cold and hard, melted with his heated stare. "I have always believed that warriors should guard their hearts against the softer emotions. That they would be weakened. It was a lie, told father to son. I suspected it to be a lie when my brother was taken and I knew I couldn't rest until he'd been returned.

"I thought it might be a lie when my rage set me on a path to punish those responsible for the abductions—because only great love for my world, my people, could have made me so very furious.

"But I wasn't certain until this moment that I do love. For I love you, Honora. Believe me when I say—*I will find you*. Live, so that I can find you." He pressed his mouth against hers, gave her one last dark, penetrating glance, then turned on his heel.

Honora couldn't have given him the words if she'd wanted to. Her jaw was slack, her throat tight and burning. Her gaze clung to his tall, imposing form as he stepped through the portal, blinking out in an instant.

At the sight, her shoulders slumped, but she firmed her jaw and turned away. Then she heard the stomp of booted feet and turned back. Soldiers, five of them, entered the hold. So the commander hadn't trusted her after all to return to dock.

"Captain Turgay," one of the new arrivals said, his hard gaze sliding down her body in a quick, dismissive gesture. "We are your escort."

Thinking quickly, she said, "Are you crew for the ship or strictly security? We're shorthanded . . ."

"Security. When we infiltrated your systems, we ascertained you had sufficient crew to pilot the ship. The women can continue to service the canteen. We are here only to ensure another incident doesn't occur."

"You think you're equal to a Viking invasion?" she snorted, but decided not to continue the argument.

His head shook. "A larger contingent couldn't be spared. Not with command planning an invasion."

A chill of horror crept slowly down her spine. "An invasion?"

The man's lips twisted into a nasty smile. "A lesson the Consortium has approved. They're heading to New Iceland. Since it's apparent the pirates have knowledge of the *Ulfhednar* mines and keep, they will provide the intel needed to launch an attack."

"Too bad you're sitting this one out." Without betraying a flicker of emotion, Honora made an excuse to head back to the command deck. Somehow, she had to find a way to warn Dagr's people. Having seen how effective the Vikings were in hand-to-hand combat, she knew they wouldn't be vanquished easily. The thought of the pain Dagr would suffer if he lost even one of the people he loved had her mind racing to devise a plan. She had only herself and Turk to carry it out.

Her stomach roiled at the thought of what Dagr must be facing aboard the warship this very moment and hoped her warrior had one heck of a plan, or he'd have front-row seats while he watched the destruction of his kingdom.

Nineteen

Dagr gritted his teeth and narrowed his eyes to fierce, angry slits, but otherwise didn't flinch. Fiery flicks from a laser whip had laid open a dozen bloody stripes on his chest and back. He stood with his wrists locked in stocks, his ankles shackled. His torso was naked and gleaming with sweat and blood.

No sooner had he and his men stepped through the portal than they'd been placed under arrest—his men whisked away to the brig while he was marched to the bowels of the great ship.

The master interrogator set aside his whip and smiled a toothy grin that raised every hair on the back of Dagr's neck. Given the large assortment of tools he'd laid out on display on a metal tray at the start of the torture, the old man was only warming up.

The scrawny, wizened man made a great show of selecting just the right instrument, his hand hovering over a delicate picklike tool.

Dagr wondered what kind of damage such a tiny implement

could do, until he saw the man hold it up to the guard who stood just inside the closed hatch door, nearing the man's eyes. The guard flinched, but the old man merely turned the pick to catch the flickering light.

Dagr glanced away, unwilling to give him the satisfaction of knowing he was concerned about his intentions, knowing that any resistance, even holding back his screams, would make the coming tortures all the worse.

Pride held him still and quiet. His captors didn't know it, but they were torturing a Viking king.

He held on to the belief the Consortium commander was only trying to soften him up before questioning him. That this gruesome indignity was meant only to intimidate. As state-of-the-art as the rest of the ship had been, the interrogation room was pure theater. Dark and shadowed. Flickering lights. The cloying, sickly sweet smell of blood. So warm that everyone inside the room sweated.

So warm, Dagr's own sweat burned the many angry cuts crisscrossing his skin. He'd expected pain, had emptied his mind so that the throbbing wouldn't get to him, but he was impatient and stirred in his bonds. The interrogator likely took that as fear, and Dagr really didn't care. If they thought him fearful, at least they wouldn't think him selfless.

He needed them to believe he was anything but that. "I made a deal," Dagr bellowed. "I have information to trade. Valuable information."

"You can spill your guts to me. And you will . . . eventually." The old man eyed his belly and trailed his fingertips along each ridge of muscle.

When the bastard's fingers reached the waist of his trousers, Dagr tightened in revulsion, reading the arousal that dilated the other man's rheumy eyes. "Tell the commander," he ground out between clenched teeth, "that I have the key to entering the strongest kingdom on New Iceland. The key to the Vikings' wealth."

"Why should he believe you could give him that?" the old man said, a hand hovering over another of his barbarous tools. "You're a pirate. You're only trying to delay the inevitable."

Dagr jutted his chin. "I am a distant cousin of the *Ulfhednar* king. An heir. If you take his kingdom and put me in his place, I am willing to share the profits from the mines."

The old man's head swiveled toward Dagr, his long nose quivering as though smelling something foul. "Why should we be willing to share anything with you?"

"You need me to keep the cost of warring against the *Ulfhednar* to a minimum. I am Viking, and I know who is discontent with the present ruler. I can help you to defeat them, and then help you move against the other kingdoms."

"We don't need your help."

"Truly?" Dagr gave him a hard smile. "Then why steal men? I think you intend to breed a stronger warrior to defeat them. Why wait? My men will lead you inside their walls and lend their weapons and skills to defeat them."

The interrogator looked to the side as though listening intently, and Dagr supposed he might be—if he wore some sort of auricular implant.

However, in the end it didn't matter. The thin old man shuffled to the tray and selected something that looked like a cage small enough to trap a fat mouse—a honeycomb wire contraption that tightened with screws.

The old man's gaze dropped to Dagr's groin, and the Viking clan-lord decided he'd had enough. He tensed his muscles, readying himself. The interrogator wasn't going to get anywhere near his balls with a castration clamp.

When the old man drew near enough, Dagr jerked his knees toward his chest, snapping the wires that bound his legs to the links driven into the floor. Then he swung out and wrapped his thighs tightly around the interrogator's waist, squeezing hard enough he heard a rib or two pop.

The man inside his grasp screamed until he'd let out all his air. The guard inside the door rushed toward them and tried to pry Dagr's thighs from around the old man, who continued to cry like a scalded cat. The hatch door flew open and two more guards ran into the room, carrying spears they used to tap Dagr on his back, his buttocks, stunning him, but not lessening his will.

"Kill me now," he roared, as he fought his restraints, "but I've had enough of this. I will speak to your commander or I'll take the information I have to my grave."

"That will be all," came a calm voice at the doorway. Commander Arikan stepped inside the room.

The guards straightened so suddenly it was as though the stun guns had been applied to their own spines. At Arikan's wave, they faded against the wall.

Dagr tossed back his hair and blinked sweat from his eyes, watching the tall, lean warrior approach.

Arikan dressed like his soldiers in an unembellished black skin-suit that peeked from the open lapels of his black officer's coat, lavishly braided golden epaulets no doubt designating his rank, and trousers that hugged his long legs to his shiny black boots. His short black hair and long thin nose gave him a pinched appearance, and the impression that little escaped his notice.

The old man laughed breathlessly, but groaned when Dagr tightened his thighs and dug those popped ribs deeper.

"You can let him go," Arikan said, meeting Dagr's gaze over the top of the old man's head. "You have your wish. I am here."

"To die or to bargain? I had expressed the desire for both."

"One at a time, then," the other man said, anger glinting in his tight face. "First, I would hear what you know that will change my mind concerning your worth."

Dagr unwound his legs and dropped the old man, who crawled to a corner, moaning. "The stocks?"

"Should I trust you won't attack me?"

"I don't care how many men you surround yourself with while we talk. You have my weapons. I handed them over willingly." His voice hardened. "I did not bargain to come aboard this ship and be tortured. I bargained for an audience, knowing full well the risks. I can help you."

"And what will I get that I cannot on my own—without the burden of having to deal with you?"

Dagr bowed his head, pretending obeisance, pretending willingness to subjugate himself to Arikan. "If you grant me my heart's desire, my gratitude will make you a very wealthy and powerful man."

Arikan gave a soft snort. "I already possess wealth."

"The wealth of kings?" Dagr said softly, glancing from the corners of his eyes.

A dark brown brow lifted. Arikan's gaze sharpened. "You're speaking of ore. We have tried for the last three centuries to wrest back control of the mines from you barbarians."

"We are physically powerful. Stubborn beyond your ken. You possess fine weapons, but those weapons will not stand you well in a ground attack." He shook his head and lifted it an inch, but kept his gaze deferential. "Not with the added complication of a hostile environment. And not without an advantage or two."

"What are you proposing?"

"My men will lead you through a secret entrance into the king's keep." Dagr straightened. "If you cut off the head, you control the beast. I am a distant cousin to the ruling family. I have a claim to the throne, but no loyalty to the Wolfskins. Help me take the kingdom, and I will assure a steady production of ore at a price attractive enough that you won't wish for the headache of conquering the barbaric bastards."

"You call them barbarians and yet you dress in skin and fur."

Dagr pressed his lips into a feral smile. "To strike fear. And it worked well aboard the *Proteus*. War paint, a little gnashing of teeth and shouts loud enough to rattle a man's brains . . . We met only token resistance."

Arikan stayed silent and unsmiling, his expression calculating. "Show me this entrance that will give me the element of surprise, and we will talk about your reward."

"Do you think I should trust you not to let your scrawny torture-master resume his work on my scrotum?" He shook his head. "Remember, getting through that breach in the keep's security is one thing. Fighting them hand to hand is another. Let me lead the charge. You might not have to share a thing with me if I am the first slain."

Arikan's lips twisted, and then eased flat. "We will talk. After your wounds have been tended." He turned toward the door, signaling the guards to follow.

"My men?" Dagr called after him.

"Are safe inside the brig. They will remain there for now. I can't have them frightening the women aboard the ship." Arikan glanced over his shoulder. "You will take dinner with me in my cabin. After you've described your plan, my officers will discuss whether they believe you, and whether your plan holds promise. I will send along a healer to see to your wounds and to let you savor the functioning of your scrotum—for one more night at least."

Dagr rubbed his wrists and followed the commander out the door of the chamber, glad to quit the dark, cruel atmosphere. As they strode through long corridors, his curiosity kept him aware of his surroundings.

The corridors aboard this ship weren't as cramped as *Proteus*'s. Two men could walk abreast and open their arms. Dagr was escorted by a double column of warriors, dressed in deep-space gear and composite armor and helmets. They led him to a large room, a more richly appointed spa than Honora's ship had boasted.

Inside, cubbies lined the walls and he stripped off his bloody clothing and hung the items inside one, then padded barefoot, heedless of the guards flanking him, toward the another door. A large sunken tub sat in the center of the floor. An attendant rose from a bench and approached.

The attendant was female, and Dagr sighed at the knowledge he couldn't beg off using the woman due to his injuries because he would appear weak. Although attractive, he didn't want her.

Slightly darker-skinned than Honora, her coal black hair hung to her hips. She wore only a short skirt, wrapped around her waist and knotted at one hip. Her body was smooth, sleek, long-limbed— and her expression was avid, heating quickly.

She knelt on the floor, her head bent. He knew she only pretended respect, because she gazed up, flirting from beneath her eyelashes.

"I would bathe," he muttered, cursing the stirring of his cock. Concentrating on the sting of the bloody scores striping his skin, he breathed easier when his shaft didn't fill.

"I will help you. I exist to serve." The gold bracelet around one wrist affirmed her claim. She rose slowly, her chest only inches from his, her dusky nipples blossoming. "I have disinfectant salves that I can apply before you bathe that will keep the cuts from bleeding into the water and will mute the stinging."

"Fine," he said, nodding, and then glared behind him at the two guards who'd accompanied him inside.

They smirked, but didn't back away. They'd report whatever happened to his keepers.

Dagr sighed and fisted his hands on his hips, giving the girl a look that had her hesitating just a second.

She smoothed her expression and approached, carrying a bottle and strips of clean linen. "If you'll sit on the edge of the bath, I'll attend your wounds."

Dagr climbed down a couple of steps into the tub, then sat, hot water swirling on his calves. The girl dipped clean linen in the pool, then daubed away the blood and sweat on his back. When she applied the salve, it instantly numbed and sealed the wounds. Dagr felt relief immediately and sighed.

Then she came around him, dropped her short skirt on the floor beside the tub, and, completely nude, entered the water to kneel on the step between his legs.

She worked diligently, dabbing salve on his stomach, her lips pressing into a straight line and a frown marring her lovely, finely arched brows. "So many marks," she murmured. "Was it very painful?"

He didn't answer, staring beyond her shoulder as she worked.

"They say you are from the cold planet." She shivered delicately. "I cannot fathom surviving there. Your race must be very hardy."

Dagr cleared his throat. "We are acclimated."

She finished slathering salve into the bloody welts and set aside the bottle. Her gaze met his, directly. Her expression not so much dismayed as curious. "You don't find me attractive, do you?" she whispered, softly enough the guards could not hear.

He looked her fully in the eyes this time. "You are lovely but I have much on my mind."

"If you do not take me . . ." Her glance fell away, worry knitting her brow.

"Will you be harmed if I do not?"

"Not exactly, but they will wonder if I tried hard enough. I might be demoted to servicing crew." A sigh escaped. "There are so many."

Dagr felt a moment's compassion for the beauty who was as much a captive as he was. He tipped up her chin and bent toward her, stopping when his mouth was an inch from hers. "Can we pretend?" he whispered.

Her expression smoothed, free of any worry, and a smile tugged at the corners of her mouth, growing radiant when he grinned. "We can." She wrapped her arms around his shoulders, but was careful to maintain space between their chests. "Come into the pool. They won't know exactly what we do beneath the water, and you do need to bathe," she said, wrinkling her nose.

Dagr laughed loud enough to satisfy the guards, and whoever else might be watching, and lifted the girl into his arms. No promises had been spoken between him and Honora, and his people would think nothing of his taking this woman to assuage his passions, but it seemed the stubborn ship's captain had stolen all his ardor. While their futures were uncertain, he didn't want the distraction . . . and didn't want to mar the memory of what they'd shared.

Honora leaned over Turk's shoulder, pretending to look at the readings on his console. "The viewing screens are set to malfunction?" she asked as quietly as she could. Guards strolled along the aisles, watching her every movement.

"They will reflect our current location, then flicker off and on," Turk whispered. "The image will be frozen so they won't guess at our headings due to any familiar constellations." Turk's one-sided smile and the gleeful expression he wore, only for her, reassured her that he was content to follow her plan.

No one else aboard the *Proteus* knew that she was going to commandeer the ship for a second time.

"Coordinates are set?"

"New Iceland is locked in. Autopilot is set to get us there, then keep the ship in orbit. Once we're in range, the transporter will open a portal on the bridge."

"Only problem is our gear," Honora muttered. They needed cold-weather clothing. "Let me handle it." Her mind raced with the possibilities.

"Is everything all right?" The officer who had spoken to her when the security contingent arrived strode up beside them, suspicion burning in his eyes.

"Just double-checking the coordinates. We don't want to take a longer route than necessary to get home."

His gaze darted from her carefully controlled expression to Turk's guileless stare, then huffed and marched away.

Honora didn't linger. "Here we go." With swift moves, she left the dais, heading toward the corridor at the rear of the bridge.

The security officer stepped in her way. "You do realize now that you can't go anywhere unaccompanied."

"I do now," she said, fighting to keep her tone even, "but I would like to go to my quarters to use my own latrine and freshen up. Will you have to come inside to watch?"

His cheeks reddened. "I'll remain outside your door."

"For my protection? How kind of you," she drawled, then began to step around him.

His eyes narrowed, but he backed away. He fell in behind her when she swept past.

Once inside her cabin, Honora quickly ran water to mask her sounds, and then toggled the comm switch on the wall. "Computer, set ship's temperature ten degrees higher than cold storage."

She flushed the toilet, satisfied when the air turned chilly almost immediately. Honora stuck her head out the cabin door. "Do you feel that?" she said, widening her eyes.

The guard cocked his head. "It's getting cold. What did you do?"

She raised her eyebrows and jammed a hand on her hip. "You think I want to freeze my ass off? I don't know what's wrong, but we need to get everyone into cold-weather gear quickly."

Ducking back inside her own cabin, she pulled out her hooded cloak and gloves. Then she made her way down the line of cabins to retrieve Turk's gear.

Back on deck, she almost grinned at the sight of everyone bundled up. The air had gotten so cold she could see her own breath.

After suiting up, Turk revolved in his chair and gave her the signal, a subtle tip of his head. They were almost there, just a few moments more.

Sitting in the captain's chair, she depressed the comm to the computer, and then waited . . . Her breath caught in her throat.

When the first little glimmer of light brightened the center of the dais, she said, "Restore temperatures to previous setting." Then she dove through the widening circle, Turk on her heels.

They landed in a drift of snow.

Honora scrambled to her knees and glanced back. The portal had closed, and no one had been near enough to follow. Pulling her hood forward to cut the biting cold, she shouted above the wind, "You're sure they can't follow?"

"The computer was set to erase our coordinates, then obey preset coordinates back to Helios. The viewing screens will do a restore in about an hour so they'll get an inkling where they are and don't panic. By the way, why do we care?"

Accomplishment zinged along her nerves and Honora grinned. They'd done it. She headed up the hill toward the gray door, feet sinking deep into the snow.

"We just gonna knock?" Turk asked, nerves causing his voice to rise.

"Hope someone's there to hear or we'll freeze to death." Honora raised both hands and pounded on the heavy metal door.

When no one responded, Turk stepped beside her and pounded with her. With the cold seeping through her clothing, she refused to stop, her fists aching from the effort.

The door slammed open, and she and Turk fell forward, landing in a heap at the feet of the red-haired giant.

The Viking scowled down at them, then glanced quickly over their shoulders. "Are you alone?"

"We are," Honora said, her teeth chattering.

"Get inside," he said, his voice surly.

When the door closed, she turned to face him and realized he hadn't come by himself. Several others stood behind him, their faces filled with suspicion, gazes hard—hands gripping short swords and knives.

"You're the woman, the one he brought with him," he said, his voice low and ominous. "Where's our lord?"

Honora blew a breath through pursed lips, and straightened her spine. There was no easy way to break the news. "I need you to listen. You're all in danger. Consortium ships are on their way here. They plan an invasion. I came to give you warning and to help."

"Help? How?" His gaze narrowed. "And how do I know you aren't part of a plan to trick us all?"

"You don't know me. And you don't have to trust me. You just have to get me to Dagr's keep so I can talk to Odvarr."

The red-haired man eyed her, then Turk, his lips curling in disgust. "Neither of you would be worth the clout." He turned away and spoke to the men nearest him. "We'll close the minehead. Send everyone here to guard the ore." As his men hurried away, he set his fists on his hips and lowered his shaggy eyebrows in a fearsome scowl. "I'll take you to the keep, and you'll tell your story to Odvarr. But you'll both make the trip bound."

Honora gave him a short nod, grateful he hadn't killed her on the spot, and that she'd have a chance to get word quickly to the rest of Dagr's people. Still, she dreaded telling them that their clanlord was now the captive.

Twenty

The great ship's cargo hold was completely unlike anything Dagr had seen before. The space wasn't intended for cargo. The wide, open expanse was a staging area for a military force. The number of warriors lined up in three companies, four rows deep, sent a chill through him. Their armaments were another concern—laser spears, mortar guns, composite armor and shields. Beneath the warriors' accoutrements, they were also dressed for the climate in the latest, thinnest cold-weather garments designed to allow them a full range of movement.

Beside him, Frakki growled. "This is your plan? To bring an army into our midst?"

Frakki wasn't really questioning him. Dagr understood. His friend and second-in-command wanted a last reassurance, a final farewell before facing a battle that might mean the end for them all.

Dagr turned away from the long, precise rows of well-armed, well-trained warriors and eyed his own ragtag crew. He and his own men were dressed in furs. Their arms had been returned to them, but seemed pitiful in comparison. They didn't stand in rows, but managed to look more menacing than an entire battalion of perfectly identical Consortium soldiers.

He hadn't had a chance to speak to his men alone. Just before marching here, he'd had to brief them in the brig, with guards present to report back every word, while he'd laid out his "plan" to take the keep at Skuldelev and wrest the throne from their present king.

His pride in his men, who hadn't betrayed any surprise or any emotion whatsoever, gave him hope that they would pull this off. When he'd detailed where exactly they would transport to, he'd seen the light dawning in their eyes. Not a one had betrayed fear at his bold plan.

Commander Arikan strode toward him. "Are you and your men ready?" he asked, eyeing their clothing, a slight smirk curving his mouth.

"We'll lead you to the postern gate. Are your men prepared to step out on ice?"

"They wear cleated boots."

"Good," Dagr said, smiling inside.

"Leave the rest to us." Arikan jutted his chin toward the soldiers. "We are better armed. Better trained than any barbarian clansman."

Dagr hoped his gaze didn't reflect an ounce of his anger. Each of his men was worth a dozen of the little men lined up like toy soldiers.

The commander raised his hand. Up and down the lines, calls to attention were shouted out, ringing against the metal walls of the staging area.

A bright, narrow beam of fiery light burst in the center of the room, quickly expanding, exploding outward, the boundaries of the circle spinning.

Dagr stared and swore he could see the frozen blue sea and the dark shadow of the Keel Mountains in the distance. A driving snow was falling. Would Arikan hesitate if he saw how far from the keep they would be?

"Go now!" Arikan said, lowering his arm, his back to the portal.

Dagr tucked his head toward his chest and raised his sword, not looking back, and stepped through the portal and onto the frozen waters of Hymir's Sea.

They've come! They've come!" came the whispers up and down the wallwalk.

Honora ran to a guard who leaned over the parapet, his hand pointing.

Vikings scrambled from below, climbing the stairs and ladders to get to the top.

"Are they daft?" Odvarr exclaimed loudly.

And next to her ear. Honora shook her head to clear the ringing and aimed a glare his way. "Shhh! The wind will only carry away so much of our sounds."

"Why bother being quiet? They've already proven themselves fools."

"That is a whole battalion of Consortium ground warriors," she said, whispering furiously. "Men trained well in hand-to-hand combat, and armed to the teeth. Shouldn't you be sending your own barbarians out to meet them before they reach the walls? They carry small cannons!"

"We needn't bother. Do you hear them?"

Sure, she heard the rhythmic, snow-muffled stomping of hundreds of feet. So why did he look so gratified? Her gaze ran over Odvarr's craggy face. She'd never understand any of them. They seemed to thrive on conflict.

She and Turk had arrived at the keep the previous afternoon, bound like roasted geese and greeted with suspicious stares and muffled laughter. Honora bore the indignity, filling in Dagr's man in charge, the surly giant Odvarr, on what had transpired since Dagr's last stop for ore.

Odvarr's shaggy eyebrows had risen, but he'd stayed silent throughout the retelling. Of course, she'd left out the more intimate details.

Not that that had saved her from scrutiny by his two concubines. Astrid had looked down her nose from her great height, her glance skimming her body, then sniffing as though Honora were of no consequence. However, Tora had chided Odvarr for leaving her and Turk bound.

Under her insistence, the giant had reluctantly freed them. "Do not think I won't split the two of you from gut to gullet if you threaten anyone here."

Tora's eyes twinkled. "Do not worry about him. He's still smarting over the trick the last guest we held here played on him."

"Do you hold all your guests prisoner?"

Tora had folded her hands over her belly, and her friendly gaze had narrowed. "Well, you aren't really guests, are you? Dagr never gave you leave to come here." She'd sighed and her stern expression softened. "However, the great risk you took coming to warn us says a lot about you."

Then she'd fussed over them, waving a team of servants through the great hall to feed them, asking endless questions about Honora's home, her ship, the people she knew.

And especially how Dagr had been when they'd parted. "Did he seem grim?" she'd asked.

Honora shrugged. "Not any more than usual."

Astrid's eyebrows shot up. "You spent a lot of time in his company, then?"

Honora's cheeks had warmed beneath Tora and Astrid's fascinated stares. "He . . . demanded that I remain close . . . to ensure the good behavior of my crew." She had been just as curious about the two women. Knowing he had his choice of Viking women, she'd been surprised that he hadn't chosen the most beautiful or even younger women.

"It can't be. She's a tiny thing," Astrid said under her breath to Tora. "He'd break her like a twig."

Tora patted her hand. "My friend, you've known this day would come."

"But she's . . . not Viking. Her skin is dirty."

Honora had had enough of them speaking as though she wasn't even there. She cleared her throat. "My skin's bronze."

Astrid's hard-eyed gaze bored into her. "Her hair's mud-colored."

Pride inching her chin higher, Honora replied, "It's actually a deep russet."

Astrid snorted and aimed a confused glance at her sister concubine. "She knows nothing about our history."

"And yet she's human too," Tora said softly. "We all have a common history, a common origin. Perhaps he sees a way to breach the divide between our peoples."

A political arrangement? Honora shook her head. "You place too much importance on me. I'm a disgraced ship's captain, not someone a noble would consort with for a political alliance."

"And yet, you've slept with him," Tora said, studying her.

Honora's cheeks burned hotter, but she nodded.

"More than once. I'd hazard a guess that he didn't wait long past the taking of the ship to claim you."

Honora's mouth dropped open.

Tora smiled. "It's all right, dear. You're among friends."

"Friends!" Odvarr and Astrid exclaimed in unison.

"Friends," Tora said firmly. "Our Dagr has made his choice."

"But he didn't even want her here."

"Likely for her own protection. Am I right?"

Honora saw no reason to argue, since the woman had somehow guessed right about everything else. "That's what he said, but he might have been sparing my feelings."

The three Vikings sitting opposite her froze, their mouths half-open, then erupted in peals of laughter.

"He wanted to spare your feelings?" Astrid said, holding her sides.

"He's a sensitive man. More so than I originally thought," Honora said, feeling foolish for having mentioned it at all.

"Tell me," Tora said, wiping her eyes. "Was he wearing a stone talisman when last you saw him?"

Honora shrugged, not understanding, and then remembered the amulet Dagr had given Birget. "He passed it on to Birget before she boarded the transport ship to follow Dagr's brother."

For the first time, Tora's soft mouth pinched into a tight line. "He is stubborn beyond belief. The man needs to learn to pray."

Honora had had enough of small talk and turned to Odvarr. "You have to believe me. Consortium ships are headed this way. They intend to attack this keep and seize the mines."

Odvarr didn't respond with a gesture or an expression.

"Are you going to do nothing?" Honora said, jumping to her feet, anxiety fueling her muscles.

"It's already done," Tora said, her voice soothing. "As soon as you were brought into the keep. Odvarr set guards on the wallwalk and scouts along every access road to the keep. We will know if anyone comes."

"And if they teleport directly inside the keep?"

"They will be like fish in a barrel," Odvarr said, crossing his burly arms over his chest. "There isn't a wolf inside the keep that isn't standing ready and armed."

Honora sighed. "I can't be idle. Please, may I keep watch too?"

"And do what?" he said, eyeing her as though she were an annoying insect.

"I can shout. *I* can pray."

"Do you have a god you have a relationship with?" Tora asked.

"Not really. I haven't believed for a very long time."

"Then let me introduce you to our Dagr's god. The one who blessed his sword and whose symbol he wore around his neck—until he decided to gift his well-being to that arrogant bear."

Honora liked Tora from the instant they'd met. But as the evening had worn on, she'd warmed to the woman's natural warmth and good humor, melting just a little beneath her coddling when she'd fed her, then insisted on bathing her and tucking her into bed.

In all her life, Honora had never been treated like that. The servants in her father's house who'd seen to her instruction until she was old enough to enter the academy had otherwise left her to herself.

She wondered if Dagr knew how different his world was, how wonderful it was to someone who'd never felt she belonged. She'd fallen asleep admitting to herself that she wanted to belong here. Wanted to belong to Dagr.

The fierce cold wind stung her cheeks, centering her thoughts. Her eyes watered and she blinked rapidly as she stared through the snowfall to see the shadowy figures spread out on the ice, marching toward them now.

They approached as quietly as a battalion of men could, likely hoping the whistling wind and the scurry of snow on the frozen surface of the sea would leave them undetected until the last moment.

Had they chosen this route or had Dagr? Arikan, the arrogant bastard, might have thought that seeing his men spread out would have the Vikings shaking in their boots.

If Dagr were alive, he might have bleated out this route during torture to ensure his people had warning. Dagr could already be dead; likely was.

Sorrow trembled through her, but she firmed her shoulders. She could still do one last thing for him. She could witness his enemy's defeat.

She stared at the dark figures blurred by the snow, until they neared and clearer outlines formed. Her gaze narrowed on one with a familiar proud gait. Heart racing, she leaned over the parapet, gripping the edge hard.

A hand closed around the neck of her cloak and pulled her back. "Are you trying to kill yourself? Or me?" Odvarr muttered. "Dagr will have my innards for dinner if you fall."

She shook her head and pointed. "Look!" she hissed. "At the front of the formation. It's him!"

Odvarr squinted, then leaned over the wall. "'Tis him, all right," he said, nodding as though he'd never had any doubt about his survival. "I hope he plans to start running soon."

"If he runs, they'll know he's betraying them and they'll kill him."

"If he doesn't, the serpents will eat him."

"Serpents?"

She swung back to look at hundreds of figures, no longer shrouded because of diminishing snowfall. From her perch on a wallwalk, at the top of a rugged cliff, she could see the frozen ocean all the way to the horizon.

Another glance below and she sucked in startled breath. Long streaks of vibrant color skimmed below the ice. "Does he know?"

"Of course he does. 'Twas his plan," he said, giving her a harsh smile filled with pride. He turned and bent over the railing. "Men! To the skiffs. Your king has turned dragons to our cause!"

Cheering arose, cries that didn't diminish as the men below raised their swords and shook their fists. Their fervor filled her with exhilaration as though this were her own battle too.

Honora followed on Odvarr's heels, racing down the steps. "Should everyone abandon the keep? What if the Consortium transports some inside?"

"The house guard will handle them," he bellowed over his shoulder.

Voices shouted from below, and the great iron gate that guarded the entrance to the keep was cranked up. Honora joined the press of men spilling out the gate, and followed them down a steep cliff-side path to the beach below.

Along the edge of the water, a dozen or so skiffs stretched along a stone-and-timber dock with a steeply peaked roof.

Explosions sounded, and Honora stilled before looking out toward the advancing battalion, expecting the fire to be directed their way. However, confusion reigned on the ice.

The serpents' presence had been noted.

Soldiers fired lasers at the ice beneath them.

Ice cracked and flew upward as large-headed beasts crashed through the thick layers. Men slid down the sides of the ice floes, tumbling into frozen water and the gaping mouths of the large beasts, gnashed and chopped by rows of long teeth.

Frozen in horror, she didn't move until a Viking sped past her, knocking her to the side.

She caught the back of his cloak. "Take me with you."

He scowled, but didn't pause.

She took it as assent and ran after him to the end of the dock and the last skiff.

"I'll steer," he said. "You cling to the bow. When we fly past them, offer your hand." With his sword, he cut the ropes cradling the boat. It fell onto gritty powder, and he dug his heels in and pushed with all his might to slide it out onto the ice.

Honora followed closely, unwilling to let him leave her behind, and managed to jump onto the bow when the skiff glided free. She clung to handholds as he dropped the sails, and the craft lurched and skimmed crazily across the ice until he steered with the ropes wrapped around his back and flowing through his hands.

Honora's hood blew back in the wind, but she didn't care. She didn't want her sight obscured. "There," she cried triumphantly, and pointed as she spied Dagr and his contingent skimming on their feet across the ice just ahead of the men running for their lives on loud cleats behind them.

"The sound attracts them!" she called out to her fellow sailor, and he flashed a smile. "Won't our noise attract them as well?"

He laughed and jerked a chin toward the crowd. "They are far louder."

Honora watched the horror unfold. Sea beasts lifting the ice, crashing down over men, large mouths opening to clasp around their waists and carry them under the blue water.

Consortium soldiers ran until they were isolated on broken floes, then lay pressed against the ice, some with hands over their heads to shut out the screams, some sitting and firing over the edges at the beasts circling below them.

The Vikings stayed ahead of the front rank of ground fighters. Before long, some of them realized the trick that had been played and raised their weapons to fire at Dagr and his men.

Faster boats skimmed across her skiff's path; spears sailed, slicing through the air, arrows winging in delicate arches to thud into soft necks and eyes left vulnerable when the men threw down their shields in their helter-skelter run.

Once she saw a skiff closing in on Dagr, she shouted to the man behind her. "Get me closer to the front line! This has to end."

When he drew near enough to be heard, she stood, one hand on the mast of the small skiff. "Put down your weapons! You can't save yourselves without our help! Put down your weapons!"

Skiffs had already carried their own back to shore, but turned back to pick up soldiers who threw down their weapons.

In the rear of the scattered formation stood Arikan, his back straight but unmoving. He'd figured out what attracted the beasts. Had he bothered to tell his own men or had he let them draw away the beasts' interest to save himself?

Her companion skimmed along the edge of the unbroken ice, careful not to slow their pace because dragons streaked beneath them, their brightly hued bodies curling and then shooting toward another hapless victim.

Open water separated her skiff from the rear of the battalion and the commander's own guard.

His eyes blazed, promising retribution. Then a portal opened behind him. He and those closest to him hurled themselves toward it, barely beating one giant serpent whose head followed them through only to be cut off when the light blinked out. Its body slipped slowly into the water.

She had only a moment to wonder at the uproar the beast's head would cause aboard the ship. A blast of light streaked toward her, too fast to avoid. The mast splintered beneath her hand, and with a shout, she was tossed overboard onto the ice, skimming facedown on the slick surface and watching a blur of orange swim beneath her.

Twenty-one

Just as his skiff crunched against the rough edge of the beach, Dagr jumped to the ground, then spun to see how the battle fared. What there was left of a battle, anyway. The action was mostly a retreat—an ignominious run for safety. He counted heads quickly, assuring himself that every one of the men who had accompanied him had made it.

Frakki ran to his side. "Shall we save the bastards?" he said, disgust flavoring his tone. He nodded toward the Consortium soldiers doomed to die if the Vikings didn't mount a concerted rescue.

Odvarr loped toward him, his chest heaving, his face creased with worry. "Dagr, your woman!" he shouted, pointing toward the open waters.

A woman was on the ice! Dagr turned in time to see a slender figure pitch over the side of a skiff and slide on her belly perilously close to the edge. He didn't bother asking what Honora was doing there, or, more precisely, what she was doing on the frozen water.

He broke into a run, heading for the closest boat, Frakki on his heels.

They both swung up, Frakki taking the steering ropes, and Dagr balanced on his feet at the raised nose of the small craft. He cupped his hands around his mouth. "Stay still, Honora," he shouted, although the wind, the hollow roars of the beasts, and the screams from the remaining soldiers drowned out his voice.

He ignored the slashes of laser light that pounded the ice around him, dared the soldiers sure to die a gruesome death to kill him because he wasn't turning back. If the goddess Hel herself reached up from her frozen kingdom to drag him down, he'd fight her.

"Dagr . . ." Frakki said quietly, dread in his voice.

"I know."

Beneath them a dozen sea serpents, blue, green, and orange, swam, tracking them like prey, spiraling, shooting away for a few feet, then circling in closer.

One tapped beneath the hull of their small craft, and the ice groaned and crackled.

Behind them came the scraping sound of more skiffs joining them on the ice. His men were skilled with the boats, often skimming just offshore. Just far enough to drill into the ice to fish, but close enough to the keep that the guard on the wallwalk could give them fair warning. None of his men was as skilled as he at escaping the beasts because none dared travel the open seas.

Still they followed him, shouting and hitting the ice with the points of their pikes to draw the beasts away.

In the distance, Arikan's men continued to fire, shredding the solid surface beneath their feet in their panic, drawing the creatures who banged their heads from below to crack the ice, then shoot upward, mouths agape to catch the men before diving deep to devour them.

Dagr could worry about only one Consortium officer, who now lay on her belly on the ice, her face turned toward him, her eyes beseeching. That she was terrified was evident by the paleness of her skin and the roundness of her eyes. And by her silence. Honora was rarely silent.

When their skiff drew near, Frakki slowed only a fraction, just enough for Dagr to jump off the boat. He rolled, leapt to his feet, and ran for his woman, brandishing his sword and hoping that another of the boats was close enough to retrieve them once he had her before the dragons burst through the ice.

He prayed as never before—to Thor, who'd blessed his fathers' sword. Prayed that, just like Thor who'd felled the giant Hrungnir with his mighty hammer, that his sword and his will would be enough to save the only person who'd ever made him feel complete, the woman who held the other half of his heart.

Honora lay flat on the ice, her head raised, watching Dagr draw near. As her muscles contracted with cold, relief and abject fear for him warred inside her.

He threw down his cloak, his furs, never slowing, running full out, his dark hair whipping behind him, his expression so fierce it took her breath away.

A loud thud sounded beneath her.

Honora couldn't hold back a scream as the ice cracked and lifted, splintering into large pieces like a jagged puzzle. She scrambled for a handhold, sliding gloved fingers over one raw edge.

A serpent pushed up, its dark orange head lifting the shardlike section of ice she held tight to, pushing on one edge with the end of its nose and tilting her toward the water. With her arms stretched, her body swinging, she cast a glance toward Dagr, sure he would be the last thing she saw in this life.

Dagr was close, and not slowing, although the ice broke beneath his feet. He took one last step and leapt onto the serpent's head, landing hard, and gripped his knees on either side of its wide skull.

Their gazes met for a moment, Dagr's filled with love and regret. Then the beast pulled down its head, dislodging the icy shard she clung to and sending it sliding across the ice, away from it and Dagr.

"No!" Honora screamed, watching in horror as the beast shook its head, trying to dislodge Dagr, but he held tight, the hand not holding his sword gripping horny spikes atop the beast's sawtooth brow.

The creature flung back its head one last time, and then tucked its head down, preparing to dive.

With a roar, Dagr let go of the spikes, turned his blade upside down, gripped the pommel in both hands, and plunged it downward, piercing the beast's translucent blue eye.

The creature let out a loud, hollow squall, then crashed down its head, slamming the ice and breaking it. Water closed over it, submerging the beast and taking Dagr down with it.

Desolation clawed at her chest and Honora screamed again, shoving up to her feet and running to the edge of the ice to peer deep into the water, uncaring whether another beast burst from the water. Her heart was already lost in the cold, cold depths.

Cold water closed around Dagr, shocking him for a moment, causing him to gasp and lose the little air he held inside his lungs. He had only a moment to save himself. The beast he rode thrashed in the water, heaving up and down. When its head tucked down again, Dagr knew it would dive and he'd be dead. With a surge of desperation, he got his knees beneath him, pushed against the beast's head, tugged his sword free, then swam upward toward the gleaming opening in the ice.

When he burst through the surface, he dug his blade into the edge of the ice and dragged himself from the water. He pulled deep breaths of air into his lungs, fighting the enervating cold seeping through all the layers of his clothing. He pushed to his feet and forced his legs to move, running toward Honora, who gave a cry and started toward him.

"Hurry!" he croaked. Where one dragon bled, dozens more would follow.

"Dagr! Gods, Dagr!" Honora cried out, running, then falling to her knees and sliding across the ice toward him.

Glancing back to gauge the nearest boat's speed, he ran past her, grabbing her arm and swinging her behind him. "On my back. Hold tight."

For a second, he relished the weight of her body against his; then he was running, awkwardly now, weighed down with Honora's arms crossed in front of his neck. The boat skimmed closer, and Dagr saw Odvarr on the bow, twirling a rope in the air.

When the boat cut in front of them and turned, Odvarr sailed the rope toward him.

"Don't let go!" Dagr shouted to Honora, grabbing the rope and winding it around his arm a second before the slack was taken up and he was pulled off his feet. He landed on his belly, both hands holding tightly now to the rope.

Every sharp edge and bump in the ice beneath his body cut and bruised him, but the shoreline was in sight.

His men ran up and down the beach, cheering and shouting

encouragement. Until at last Odvarr swung them toward the edge and men rushed onto the ice to surround them, throwing cloaks around their shoulders and grabbing them up to carry them.

Odvarr came running up, Frakki on his heels. "He slay the beast! Dagr slay the serpent!"

All turned to gaze out to the water lapping at the edges of the broken ice. The long, ridged back of a large sea serpent bobbed listlessly in the opening.

Dagr turned to look, but couldn't really care. Fists thumped chests; his Vikings roared. The sound encouraged him, but Honora's teetering smile was what warmed him through and through.

Honora glanced around her at the stragglers, the remnants of the Consortium's mighty army, scattered in the snow rimming the beach. They stared at the wild barbarians, awe and fear causing their faces to pale.

If her cheeks weren't frozen, she'd have laughed. Instead, when Dagr held open his arms, she moaned and fell against him, rubbing her cheek against his chest. His familiar scent calmed her racing heart.

Odvarr clapped his shoulders, a huge smile splitting his face. "I'm going to fashion a tale, milord. A new chronicle. *Dagr and the Serpent.*"

Dagr grunted and his gaze lowered to Honora. "I have a finer tale, one fraught with many dangers, and a woman . . ."

Odvarr barked a laugh while Honora ducked her face to hide her blush. Seemed she did a lot of that these days.

His dark eyes flashing, Dagr reached inside her cloak, gripped Honora's waist, then bent to kiss her. The biting cold, the dozen little bruises on her back and belly, even the loud roar of his men faded in the splendor of his perfect kiss.

When another round of toasts began and Dagr's back was turned, Honora slipped quietly from the table in the crowded hall.

The prisoners had been secured in the dungeon beneath the keep. Men were dispatched to King Sigmund's keep to relay the Wolfskins' demands for ransom to Commander Arikan. Dagr's brother and the other missing men were part of the terms.

Whether the Consortium dragged out the negotiations for months or not, Dagr felt at least hopeful that this tack might work. He worried over Cyrus and Birget's mission, and what Sigmund would say about his daughter leading an expedition to Helios.

Honora watched and listened while all the arrangements were made, feeling useless and abandoned, knowing she'd lost her place, her purpose. But what had she expected? She'd served her purpose and was done. The clan-lord had more important matters to attend to.

Still, Tora and Astrid had quietly moved down Dagr's table to give her room beside him. She honestly didn't know how she felt about their tacit acknowledgment that she'd supplanted them or she might have told them they needn't bother. She was numb. Frozen through and through.

So much had happened in such a short span of time. Her life turned upside down, violently so. Even now, she felt as though she still gripped the edge of the ice, dangling, trying to hold on for dear life.

Outside the hall, she plucked a thick, furry cloak from among the many hanging from hooks along the wall and wrapped it around her before heading outside.

With leaden steps, she trudged through gritty fallen snow toward the stairs leading up to the wallwalk, ignoring the guards she passed. She didn't stop until she reached the spot she'd stood earlier that day when the advancing army had been spotted. Moonlight gleamed on the mended ice and reflected off the snow-covered beach and cliffs. There was a rugged beauty to this world, one she hadn't noticed the first time she'd been here. But now, she finally had a moment to really see, and the view was breathtaking. Cold and unforgiving, yes. However, the moon overhead shone like a smooth-faced, pale sun. Moonlight refracted on crystallized snow clinging to the edge of the wall like a rainbow. And other than the scurrying of frozen snow and the thin wail of the wind over the ocean, it was quiet. Peaceful.

Which only increased her sense of loneliness and impending doom.

Tonight, the Vikings might celebrate, but she knew the war was far from won. Helios would never concede the mines. Although why her people wouldn't find another solution, one that didn't require them invading this frozen, inhospitable planet, she'd never understand. A different breed of people were needed to thrive here. She wasn't sure she was cut out for the harsh life, and she had one really big incentive to try to make it work.

If the Wolfskins' ruler truly wanted her.

A cloud crossed the face of the moon, darkening the night. The thick, furry cloak wasn't enough to keep the cold air from seeping through to her skin. She shivered and turned away from the view to return to the hall, but stopped in her tracks.

A tall, dark figure blocked her way. When the cloud drifted, moonlight shone. Dagr's closed expression, eyes glittering darkly, square jaw tightening, forced her to remember who and what he was. A Viking—a barbarian with a dangerous reputation. If he'd played her, used her to get what he could, and was now done with her, there was nothing to stop him from tossing her over the wall to the beach below. She swallowed hard.

As his gaze narrowed on her face, his head canted. "Are you afraid of me?"

Honora cleared her throat. "I disobeyed you. My people, with the lone exceptions of myself and Turk, are prisoners in your dungeon. I suddenly wondered if that wasn't where you thought I belonged too."

His expression hardened like the water freezing, one feature at a time.

A sudden wariness crept over her, and she backed up a step.

"Do you intend to jump?" he said, his voice tight and dangerous.

"Should I save you the bother?" she quipped, then glanced behind her to see how close she was to the edge.

When she swung back, he had her, his hands closing around her forearms. She tugged to free herself, but his fingers tightened like steel manacles. "You're hurting me."

"You confuse me," he whispered furiously.

She froze, confused herself by the heat simmering now in his angry gaze.

His grip eased, and a thumb soothed the skin he'd nearly bruised. "Odvarr tells me you thought my people would need warning. He thinks it's amusing, but you've won a champion in him. He wouldn't be happy if you pitched over the edge."

But what did Dagr think? Would he be happy if she was out of the way? She raised her chin. "So I'm a funny little thing to you all now." One side of Dagr's mouth quirked, but she couldn't tell if it was the start of a smile or a snarl.

"He thinks you're small, but have a heart worthy of a wolf. He thinks you should be bred." The lines at the sides of his eyes wrinkled. "He offered."

Her breath caught in her throat and her eyes bulged. "What did you tell him?"

"That the only wolf you'd breed with would be me."

In that instant, Honora acknowledged that her body didn't have an ounce of pride left. Her bones melted like honey, and her blood thrummed in her veins.

The answering flare of his nostrils said he knew she was aroused and that once again, she was pliant, ready to let him wrest control.

His hands tugged her closer.

She stumbled against him, her palms pressing against his chest. Glancing up, she didn't bother hiding what she felt—every shred of trepidation and hope. "Are you angry I came here?"

He bent toward her, his mouth inches from hers. "I promised you I'd find you. I didn't have as far to look as I expected."

"So now I'm convenient?" His masculine grunt caused her belly to clench.

"Hardly so. You nearly brought us both to our deaths on the ice." His thigh slid between hers, pressing high until she rode it.

She bit her lip to still a moan. "I was trying to rescue you."

Dagr rubbed the end of her nose with his, and then drew back, his face freezing again. "I am the Viking. I know the creatures and the ice. You were reckless. I should punish you."

When he pulled her closer, she shivered. Although this time, not just from the chilly air. His cold, cold eyes pierced her, opening a deep wound she thought might never heal. He regretted her interference and didn't respect her strengths.

"I'm cold," she said, tired of waiting for an indication of what he wanted. Tired of wanting to hear something he'd never say again.

"You will take better care of yourself," he said, his tone gruff.

Honora pushed at his chest, trying to free herself. "Why do you care? I'm one of those responsible for your brother's kidnapping. Why aren't I in the dungeon?" *Say something, Dagr. Tell me why I'm here.*

Disappointment deepened the longer he stared. Then, abruptly, he released her and turned away, his jaw working as he stared out over the icy sea.

Honora drank in the sight of him, her body and soul captive to her Viking warrior. Knowing she was at the end of her pride. "I accept your offer," she said softly.

His head swiveled toward her, brows drawn together. "Which offer was that?"

"The one to become your concubine."

"Huh," he grunted, and his jaw tightened. If he'd looked angry before, now he was furious.

"That is if you still . . . want me. Dammit, I'm a fool." She backed away and turned, heading toward the stairs. When a scuff sounded behind her, she ran.

Hard hands landed on her shoulders and spun her around. Dagr pushed her back against the cold rock wall. "If you cry, your tears will freeze, and if you sicken and die, I will beat you."

"Again, why do you care? You have everything I could give you." The backs of her eyes burned but she refused to allow tears. Not where he could see them. "There's nothing more to take."

"I have everything?" Dagr cupped her cheeks, preventing her from glancing away. "Do I still have your heart, *elskling*?"

Her lips trembled, and she couldn't stop the sob that rocked her body. He wanted everything, every ounce of love and pride she had left. And yet, he'd offered nothing of himself in return. "I love you," she blurted, then blanched at the baldness of her admission.

"I shouldn't. I know I'll only have a small place in your life, but I'll take it if it means I can be with you now and then."

"You'd accept so little?" His gaze honed. "Would you truly lie wedged between my other two concubines?"

She ducked her head. "You don't have to mock me."

"I promise I am not." His callused thumb slipped under her chin and lifted it. A slight smile curved his hard mouth. "It's odd. But hearing myself say that made me angry. For you."

Honora didn't understand, but stood silent while he studied her face. She studied his. The hood of his cloak rested on his shoulders, and she wondered if he cared that he'd lose his ears or nose to the bite of the bracing wind. But the wind wouldn't dare, would it? He'd plunged beneath frozen water, riding a dragon—to save her.

Why did she doubt him? Was she really that insecure? "I'm sorry, Dagr. I owe you my life. I haven't any right to make demands."

"You would never have been in danger if I hadn't invaded your ship." His ungloved fingers ran lightly along her neck. "But why are we talking? We find ways to twist our tongues and our meanings every time we do."

The silence stretched between them, and Honora felt the knot of her insecurity loosen. The Black Wolf wouldn't be freezing his bollocks off on a wallwalk if she didn't mean something to him. He could have his choice of any woman in his kingdom. And yet he stood here, pressed against her, his body rigid, his expression waiting...

"I don't really want to talk," she whispered, then stroked her lower lip with her tongue.

His expression heated, his eyelids lowering.

Since she hadn't much practice looking like a stone, she knew he had to read every little thing she felt. "I love you," she said again, knowing her need and love for him was naked on her face. "I can't help it. I wish I didn't, not so much anyway, but I do."

His mouth stopped her from talking, landing on her opened lips, his tongue thrusting deep. Stopping before he could give her back the words. If he ever would again. Had he only said he loved her to make her strong?

Honora clung to his arms as her knees gave way. She moaned into his mouth, mewling as emotions swept through her, so alien, so welcome. For the first time in her life, she felt tethered to a place, to a man. She belonged.

Twenty-two

Dagr's sigh was so deep, so long, he had the whimsical thought that the sound had come all the way from his toes.

He lay on a bed of soft grass beside a pond, pure light blazing from a wide vein in the ceiling of the tall cavern. Honora's shivers from the walk to the cave's entrance had finally abated. Sweat oiled her skin, which aided the rhythmic glides she made, forward and back, as she rode his cock.

She paused midstroke, certain of his attention, or so the one-sided smile said. "Answer me one question?"

"Anything," he growled, reaching for the notches of her hips to push her into motion again.

Her eyes slid shut, and she bit her bottom lip, the sexy dent between her eyes deepening as he slid his thumb between her folds and rasped the callused pad over her clitoris. She shook her head, her sleepy-eyed stare making him smile. "Um . . . I have a question."

"So you said."

With a quick move, she reached between her legs and pulled back his thumb. "How did you board my ship? I don't know why I didn't think to ask before, but now the curiosity is killing me."

"As is the anticipation," he muttered.

Honora's grin was impish and adorable. Adjectives he hadn't thought were in his vocabulary, but his lady captain was expanding his horizons by the minute.

"Such a grumpy wolf," she purred. "You'd think the number of times you came last night would have taken off the edge."

"How can my interest wane when your climaxes are so loud they rob me of concentration? My needs are more refined than a simple spasm. I want—"

"To explode like a cannon?" Her eyebrows waggled. "If you hurry and tell me, I'll oblige you."

Dagr didn't worry that she'd betray him. But he did like surprising her. Surprises always led to rewards for his thoughtfulness. And he was imagining how her excitement over the revelation of the artifact would transfer to his cock. He imagined a dozen different ways she'd take him, hopefully with her mouth sucking his essence from his balls and her tongue stroking him with wild abandon. He couldn't help the matching grin that stretched his mouth.

She bent back his thumb more. "Dagr! Pay attention!"

The intent look on her face aroused him further. "Have you no sense of decorum?"

"Decorum? You're a Viking."

"And you're not. I'd expect a little more fear and awe from a puny thing like yourself."

"Just because your . . . proportions . . . are nearly large enough to make me come like a rocket the moment you push inside me, it doesn't mean you can rest on your laurels, milord."

"I like the way you say that."

"What? Come like a rocket?"

"*Milord,*" he growled.

"I'll only say it when you're very, very good."

Dagr pulled her down, his arms encircling her and squeezing. With her breasts flattened against his chest and his cock pulsing inside her, they couldn't be any closer, physically, than they were at this moment.

He freed a hand and pushed back the hair sticking to her cheek, then reached up to plant a kiss on her soft mouth. Her tongue charged forward, pushing against his, daring him to take.

Dagr rolled, bringing her beneath him. When she'd wound her legs around his buttocks and her arms around his back, he leaned up on his elbows. "You're happy here, aren't you?"

"Are you wondering if I'll be satisfied here, earthbound as I am?"

He nodded, not liking that her mind had caught his meaning so quickly. Was it because her loss was foremost in her mind?

"Dagr," she said, her fingers twining around a strand of his hair, "I've come to realize that my ambition was a reflection of my need to regain pride in myself. My father's fall from grace changed my world, stole the ground beneath me. For the longest time, people would stare after me and whisper about my father, our family. His foolishness allowed a spy to infiltrate his command. He wasn't the only one who was punished. He died in prison, but I had to fight for respect. I followed in his footsteps, gained my own berth, to bury the hurt he caused me."

"Has that hurt gone? I robbed you of your victory."

Her hand cupped his cheek, and her wet gaze locked with his. "I was enslaved to an idea, and I didn't know it. I don't need to be a starship captain to be fulfilled. But I must have a place in your keep, and a purpose other than fulfilling your sexual needs."

His brow lowered. "I cannot let you war."

Honora gave him a small smile. "I will still train. Just in case. But I won't insist on fighting dragons or Consortium soldiers, hand to hand."

Dagr grunted, surprised she'd conceded so readily. "You have a place."

She rolled her eyes. "Wedged between your concubines. I know. But even Tora and Astrid have important duties of their own."

"Have you seen either of them in my chambers?"

Honora shook her head slowly. The hope that beamed from her amber eyes made him feel mean for not having explained it to her before. "Astrid has agreed to go to Frakki. And Tora has accepted Odvarr's offer of marriage."

"So they're no longer your concubines?"

"Nor will I take another."

Honora's eyes filled, warring with her happy smile. "I made no demand."

"And I served my own needs," he drawled. "I want no other woman in my bed, save you. However, I don't want you as my concubine."

Her smile faded, her lips thinning with annoyance. "Are we back to me being your thrall?"

He quirked a brow. "Why would you think that?"

"Because it's the only other position you've offered me."

"Huh." Dagr grunted, then laughed. Trapped with his cock buried deep inside her body, crushed beneath his weight every chance he got, no wonder she'd assumed he wanted her as his sex slave.

Eyes flashing, Honora smacked his shoulder. "Laugh at me, and you can forget about me ever obliging you again."

Dagr wrapped his hand around hers, and then grabbed the other when she smacked his arm, and stretched both high above her head.

Her scowl was dark, but about as intimidating as a grumpy kitten's. He couldn't help the next bark of laughter or the one that followed when she began to squirm and buck furiously beneath him. Did she know the more she fought, the harder her pussy clenched his cock? He thought better of mentioning it.

At last she fell back, panting beneath him, her scowl softening into a look of feminine puzzlement.

He relented, dipping to kiss her mouth, then the tip of her nose. "I don't want you as a sex-thrall, although the thought of having you play that role for me in private is worth exploring. Honora, *elskling*, I want you for my wife."

She lay silent a long time, and then drew a shaky breath. "Why?"

Not the response he'd expected. He knew she loved him. He'd thought she'd screech happily and press kisses about his face.

Instead, she gave him her stubborn face, her chin jutting, a militant gleam entering her eyes. "I haven't held back a thing, Dagr," she said slowly. "Not about what I feel for you."

"Do you think me lacking in courage?" he said, softening his voice too, because he knew where she was leading him.

"Never. You're the strongest, bravest man I've ever met. But I would know how deeply it is possible for you to feel."

"I'm a warrior."

Her features tightened, as though she girded herself for injury. "Yeah, yeah, and warriors don't love. *Ever*, right?"

"Is that what you want from me? Love?"

"Not if I have to force you to say it. And definitely not if the words aren't the truth."

"I didn't tell you a story before simply to give you strength and make it easier for you to say good-bye." Dagr bracketed her bronze cheeks with his palms, cupping them tenderly. "I believed what my father taught me. That love weakens a man, makes him vulnerable.

And yet, I fought a dragon for you. He was wrong." Tears leaked from her eyes, and he swept them away with his fingers. "I want you for my queen. I will cleave to you alone, take no others to my bed. Because I do love, Honora. I love you."

Her arms surrounded him, her hands clutching him hard. Her face scrunched up, mouth trembling, eyes drowning, and yet she'd never been as beautiful as she was at that moment. Arousal stirred, awakening a new energy, a fresh desire to mark her as his. Only when she grew full with his child would the primal hunger inside him abate.

As he entered her, his strokes fierce and raw, he let go of his disappointment that he hadn't solved the problem of his brother's return, let go of the rage against her kind that had driven him. Instead, he'd trust in the powers that be, the ones who had delivered his enemy to his bed, who'd shown him how much stronger a force love could be than hate, or even honor.

As Honora's tears dried, her skin blossoming with ruddy excitement, her golden eyes sparkling with happiness, he couldn't help but believe that a higher purpose had been served. He'd trust in it, and in Cyrus's cleverness and Birget's stubborn pride, to save Eirik.

With the spiraling explosion sharpening his thrusts at the end, he wrapped his arms around Honora, pressed his lips against his lover's mouth, and sailed over the shimmering bridge.

Eirik tried not to breathe too deeply. The rotten, sour smells of his dark, dank prison already made his skin stink. He didn't want the awful stench inside his lungs or belly.

He hadn't seen the other prisoners, not after they'd been herded like cattle through a chute once the hatch had been opened at the side of the ship and his keepers applied their prods to their backsides to move them out in single file.

With only brief impressions of his new home, of searing heat and blinding, harsh sunlight, he'd shielded his arm over his eyes and stumbled down the gangway, through the iron-barred alley that disallowed any thoughts of escape.

He'd been led to this cell, deep inside an enormous stone building. A brief glimpse of an open arena, and then he'd been shoved down two flights of narrow stone steps.

Once they'd slammed the solid door and slid the eye-level window closed, he'd been left alone, no sounds penetrating his prison other than the hum of the light above him, and the sounds his own body made.

His thoughts drowned it all out, screaming inside him. He'd wanted to beat his fists against the door, rail at his captors, but he didn't know if anyone watched him, and wouldn't give them the satisfaction of knowing how close to abject despair he was coming.

Hel, he'd even suffer Fatin's derision, her cold, calculating touch, just to feel or hear another human being.

He didn't know how long he'd been here, there being no window, and no way for him to know how the natural passage of time was counted on this planet, but he knew it was long enough he'd stopped believing that anyone would come to his rescue.

They must think me dead, *he thought.* Like Father, lost on the ice. One day waving as he skimmed away across the frozen blue water, never to return. Only Eirik wasn't lost. He wasn't dead.

A key grated in the lock at his door, pulling his glance. The heavy door swung open, and two sweet-smelling women strode inside, dressed in short, white skirts. Their breasts were bare. Leather sandals with straps that laced up to their ankles. Both dark-haired and ombré-skinned. Like the witch, Fatin. They carried an urn of water and linens.

He pressed a hand against the wall of his cell and pushed up from the floor.

"There's a guard outside the door," the one nearest him said. Her dark, sloe eyes glittered as they raked his body. "We're here to bathe and dress you."

Pushing past them would earn him nothing. He clenched his fists at his sides and held himself still as they brought their clean, sweetly fragrant bodies close enough to strip away his clothing and bathe him like a mother might a child. Only their hands lingered over his sex, and although he might have wished otherwise, his cock unfurled, coaxed by their hands and then their lips to deliver his body's nectar. Or so they called it.

Dressed now, and more relaxed, he allowed another woman just outside his cell to lead him through a winding warren of corridors until they climbed a final set of steps and she pushed open the door, letting sunlight drench them.

Eirik closed his eyes, lifting his face to the light. But he wasn't allowed to savor the sensation. A prod behind him reminded him not to dally. He stepped out onto a platform in the center of the arena. A stage surrounded by thousands of men and women dressed in long robes and jewels.

A blended roar of voices greeted him. Women's excited chatter, men's laughter. He emptied his mind of the indignity, of standing in the center of the stage, hands rising, voices shouting. Then one voice separated from the throng, for it was nearer and familiar. His head swiveled toward the sound, caught the triumph glittering in Fatin's eyes as she met his gaze for a moment, then turned back to the crowd, accepting rapidly escalating bids.

A woman near the front of the stage shouted something that sent the crowd into gales of laughter.

Fatin turned toward him, warning him to behave with her cold, black gaze. When she was within arm's reach, she pulled at the tie on his hip and unlaced it, letting the short, skirtlike garment the women had dressed him in fall away.

　He stood nude, his body exposed to the air and the rapacious gazes of the crowd. His head cleared of the numbing despair, all focus homing on Fatin's slender frame. No matter the outcome of today's shameful events, he vowed to have his revenge. One day, Fatin would be the slave; one day she would know the shame he felt.

　Something of what he thought must have transmitted. Fatin's look of triumph faded, and her eyes became dark mirrors of doubt.

　Slowly, his body warmed; his cock expanded. The things he would do to her, the many ways he would take her, filled his mind. No woman would ever know the depths of depravity he would visit on her body.

　Frozen, her gaze locked with his. Eirik let the smile tugging at his mouth expand.

Be frightened, sweet Fatin. Be waiting for me.

About the Author

DELILAH DEVLIN is an award-winning author of erotic romance with a rapidly expanding reputation for writing deliciously edgy stories with complex characters. Whether creating dark, erotically charged paranormal and futuristic worlds or richly descriptive Westerns that ring with authenticity, Delilah Devlin "pens in uncharted territory that will leave readers breathless and hungering for more" (*ParaNormal Romance*). Ms. Devlin has published more than sixty erotic romances in multiple subgenres and lengths. To learn more about Delilah, visit www.DelilahDevlin.com.